About the Author

Roland Moore is the award-winning series creator and script-writer of the BBC1 period drama Land Girls. He's delighted to be able to expand on that world in a new series of novels for HarperCollins.

His lovely wife is a great source of support and his son often comes up with helpful suggestions – even if they mostly involve laser beams and robots.

You can find out more about Roland on Twitter @RolandMooreTV or at www.rolandmoore.tv

LAND GIRLS

The Homecoming

ROLAND MOORE

A division of HarperCollins*Publishers*
www.harpercollins.co.uk

Harper*Impulse* an imprint of
HarperCollins*Publishers*
1 London Bridge Street
London SE1 9GF

www.harpercollins.co.uk

A Paperback Original 2017
2
First published in Great Britain in
ebook format by Harper*Impulse* 2017

A catalogue record for this book
is available from the British Library

ISBN: 9780008204433

Set in Birka by Palimpsest Book Production Limited,
Falkirk, Stirlingshire

Printed and bound by CPI Group (UK) Ltd, Croydon, CR0 4YY

To Wanda, with all my love.

Chapter 1

Extract from the diary of Connie Carter:

"It's all gone wrong. I don't know what to do. There was me with my stupid, perfect happy ending and it's all crumbled to dust. Maybe I should have realised that I just wasn't 'good enough'.

But I never thought your whole life could just sort of fall apart like that. And fall apart so easily, either. Each bit of happiness falling like it's in a row of dominoes or something. If she knew what happened, Mrs Gulliver would be pulling one of her sour old looks and saying something like "I knew she was rubbish, that Connie Carter". She'll be pointing fingers with the rest of the I-told-you-so-brigade when they all find out. Maybe she'd be right. There's too many things that have happened to him, all because of me. He doesn't deserve that.

The worst thing is that I don't know where he is. If he'd said where he was going, even if it involved never wanting to see me again, at least I'd have known, wouldn't I? I could cope with that, eventually. But I don't even know if he's still alive. No, can't think like that. He is alive and I just hope he comes back. And it's not like there's anyone I can talk to about it, is there? No one I can ask. No one I can pour my heart out to.

Got to keep it a secret.

That's why I started to write this diary. Never kept one before. And probably won't keep this one going for long. See, where I come from, you don't tend to write down your thoughts and feelings and stuff, in case someone finds it and uses it against you. I'd never have written things down in the children's home. Last thing you want is someone mocking you and seeing that you're not as tough as you're making out. I can take care of myself. Always have done. But a lot of my mouth is just a front. It's obvious really, I guess. But no point telling everyone, is there?

So this might be the only time I write this stuff down.

I feel on edge the whole time. I can't settle. Certainly can't sleep or eat more than the barest amount. Esther, the warden at the farm, has been understanding. She's been nice. Not that she knows the truth. She thinks I'm ill. That's because that's the lie I told her. I couldn't tell her the truth. Whole can of worms that would be, wouldn't it?

That's why the I-told-you-so-brigade don't know nothing yet.

Best to keep it that way.

Best to keep the big old secret. Isn't it?

But the trouble is, I can't just stay indoors pretending that I'm ill. I'm sure some of the other Land Girls have spotted me in Helmstead, walking aimlessly around. Or in the fields, where it looks like I'm enjoying a summer walk, lost in my thoughts. I just keep moping around, searching in vain for some clue. Keep thinking I'll see him in the High Street or walking along a path somewhere. How can I search properly, though, when I'm sneaking around trying not to be seen?

This isn't helping. I'm wasting time in here writing this, and it's not helping.

Yeah, I've got to tell Esther what's happened, at least. Tell her how I've blown it. Then I won't have to pretend to be ill any longer. Yes, that's what I'll do. She might be able to help me. The Land Girls might be able to help me.

Time to let the dreadful cat out of the bag.

Chapter 2

A sparrow searched for an early-evening supper, hopping over train tracks on a remote stretch of countryside railway that cut through a valley. In this place there were no houses and the fields were overgrown with long grass. The grass was shorter only where twin slivers of darkened silver snaked across the landscape. As the bird pecked for a worm between sleepers, some scant twelve feet away from it, two men were busy working on the line. The bird was the only one that saw them. It didn't care what they were doing as long as they didn't come too close. To the casual observer, it looked as if the men were engaged in routine track maintenance. Perhaps tightening some bolts on a wooden sleeper or filing down roughness on the long, thin metal track itself. But if you looked more closely, you might realise that these men weren't employees of the train company: you'd realise they were dressed in black; wearing balaclavas to obscure their faces. Not train-company uniforms.

The men were moving fast, jittery nervous movements almost parodying those of the bird, as they worked on the track. They glanced around at regular intervals to see if anyone was coming, checking the line for oncoming trains, the fields for any passing walkers. Somewhere in the sky – some distance away – there was the bumble-bee buzz of a Spitfire's engine. Even this far-off sound made the taller man nervous. He craned his neck and started scanning the clouds. Would they be seen?

"Quick, hurry up –", he urged.

"Don't keep on!" The shorter man didn't need telling. He knew they had to be quick. They both knew that the consequences of being caught would be severe. They couldn't let that happen. But this bad-tempered exchange mirrored much of the conversation that they'd had since they'd set off in the early hours on this mission. Ever since the taller man had packed the red sticks into his holdall, along with the timing wire and detonator and they'd walked across the fields, feeling butterflies thumping around his belly.

The short man worked on the track while the taller one kept watch. The short man's stubby fingers were trying to finish something that he'd been shown only once the night before. He hooked a pair of red wires around the metal bolts that fixed the device to the sleeper, trying to remember how the contraption should work. Was that right? It had looked a lot easier when he had been shown this in the woods around the camp fire, the convivial laughter of his friends spurring him on to think that this would be a great victory for their cause. He felt the pressure to get this right, but pressure was something he didn't respond well to.

The tall man sank to his knees, craning his ear near to the track.

"I don't know if I can hear a train."

"Don't be stupid. It's not due yet. Shut up, I'm doing it as fast as I can." The shorter man increased the pace, stripping the ends of a wire with a pair of pliers. There shouldn't be a train for forty minutes. They'd planned this well so that they would have time to plant the device and get away before it came.

The short man finished his work and indicated he was ready. The taller man delved into the canvas holdall. Carefully he produced the explosives: a bundle that looked like red seaside rock bound with thick, black tape. The shorter man was sweating now in the evening sun as he laid the sticks on the track. He turned them upwards so he could easily stick the wires into the detonator charge that was already in place, his hand shaking from nerves. The back of his neck hurt, a tension headache on its way. He wished he'd paid better attention around the camp fire, when this had looked so easy and straightforward.

"Careful." The tall man was good at making redundant and obvious statements. "Don't blow your hand off."

The short man scowled at him through his balaclava. "The clock. Give me the clock."

The tall man pulled the alarm clock out from the holdall and handed it over.

The short man fumbled it and it fell onto the tracks – the chimes clanging, the first seconds of an early-morning alarm call. He retrieved it, checked it wasn't damaged and put it into place. Finally the short man pressed the exposed wire into the putty around the connection.

"Thirty-eight minutes?" he asked.

"Thirty-eight minutes. Yeah. The train will be here then," the tall man confirmed, checking his own watch. The Brinford to Helmstead line was run with regimented efficiency, but even if the train was late, it wouldn't matter. The track would still be wrecked and the train would derail. It's just that, if possible, their masters wanted the train to be caught in the explosion as well. The two men hadn't asked any questions as to why but they assumed it was to garner maximum exposure in news stories. Maximum disruption and casualties.

Soon they had finished their grim task and were scampering off the tracks and across the fields to the seclusion of a copse of conifer trees. The tall man and the short man barely exchanged a goodbye as they went their separate ways. Once on his own, the short man stopped to breathe properly for the first time, the tension in his neck causing his temples to erupt in pain. But it didn't matter. He'd done it and he'd got out in time. He hoped no one had seen.

Back on the tracks, the bird hopped near to the explosive charges, searching the earth that had been disturbed by the men's boots. After a moment, it flew off to find dinner elsewhere. It had no idea what would happen in thirty-seven minutes time.

Connie Carter's legs were attracting attention.

Of course, most of the time she was used to this, because men would give her a top-to-toe appraisal whether she wanted it or not; their eyes darting quickly, sometimes almost imperceptibly, especially if they were married men, from her long black hair, past her high cheekbones and soulful brown eyes all the way across her ample bosom and down to her toes. Connie knew that most of the time this perusal was motivated by lust or at least an appreciation of the female form. But today, Connie's legs were attracting attention for another reason. It was because her feet were leaving a trail of thick mud on the train platform. The railway guard – a red-faced jowly old codger with a whistle hanging from his lips like a forgotten Woodbine – scowled at the clods of dirt falling from Connie's boots.

"I've been workin' in the fields, ain't I?" Connie answered his unspoken question, her incongruous East-End voice cutting through the countryside air with the shrillness of an air-raid siren.

The guard shook his head and walked down the platform.

"Someone's got to sweep it up," he muttered. "That'll be me, won't it?"

Connie didn't have the energy to argue. Her back was sore and her feet were throbbing from digging all day at Brinford Farm, where she and some of her fellow Land Girls had been seconded. She'd been at it since six in the morning and now it felt that even her blisters had blisters. Connie just wanted to get back to Helmstead: the picturesque village on the edge of the Cotswolds, where she was usually billeted as a Land Girl. The twin delights of a hot bath and her husband would be waiting. Helmstead had been home for the last year – a place where she was finally part of a family, of sorts. A place where she'd married Henry Jameson one month ago.

Connie and Henry were an odd match in a lot of ways. She

was a worldly young woman from Stepney in the East End; he was a naive vicar from the countryside, a man who had never even been to London. Some likened it to a wild cat marrying a tortoise. She'd try to shrug off the disapproving looks from the older members of the village; those who thought she wasn't good enough to be a vicar's wife. But the sour expressions and the comments hurt Connie deeper than she'd ever let on. Sometimes she'd close the bathroom door and confused thoughts would race through her head. What if they were right? Why couldn't they just accept her? She was trying her best. All she wanted to do was fit in. There was a nagging feeling that she didn't belong here and that one day she'd have to accept that fact and move on. It was difficult to put down real roots when you felt they were going to be ripped up soon.

But when she could shut those thoughts out of her mind and focus on herself and Henry, she liked the stability he brought into her life. She thought that perhaps he liked the spark that she brought into his. Perhaps her lust for life inspired Henry. Certainly his sensible ways tempered her from getting into too much trouble. Certainly, in a lot of ways, they would infuriate each other and Connie was mindful never to push him too far. If he didn't want to do something spontaneously, Connie would back down. She knew she wasn't an easy fit for the world of village cricket and afternoon teas at the vicarage and she didn't want to risk losing that. So she'd keep her thoughts to herself while secretly thanking her lucky stars that such a warm, decent man had taken her to his heart. It was too good to be true and she had to pinch herself for the chocolate-box turn that her life seemed to have taken.

Since meeting Henry, Connie rarely thought of those times before she joined the Women's Land Army; shutting out those dark bedsit days and endless nights. It had been a different time. A life that she hoped she'd never have to go back to.

Connie's thoughts were broken as a rough, wooden broom ran over her boots.

"Oi, do you mind?" Connie spluttered.

The old guard was sweeping the platform with an irritated staccato motion, sending clods over the side onto the track, where they would be someone else's problem.

"Disgraceful," the guard replied, without dignifying Connie with eye contact. "Brinford won silver in Best Rural Station last year. I don't need this clutter on me concourse."

"There is a war on," Connie muttered, not giving a damn for his concourse. What was a concourse anyway? The guard continued along the platform, the wide broom head scything a path through the waiting passengers.

Suddenly Connie felt a tap on her back. She turned around, her mouth ready to unleash some angry words on any do-gooder. So what if her boots were muddy? She probably had dirt in her hair and was enveloped in the unmistakable perfume of cow dung too. But it was a friendly face that greeted her. Joyce Fisher was smiling at her. Mid-twenties, a little older than Connie, Joyce was stoic and sensible, with a sunny surface. She was a woman committed to patriotism and doing her bit to win the war. After all, that was all Joyce had to cling onto, wasn't it? She'd lost so much and all the time the war was raging it stopped her dwelling on the thoughts of loss in her own head. The family gone forever in

Coventry. If the war ever ended, then Connie suspected that Joyce would find the silence hard to deal with.

"I thought I was going to miss the train," Joyce said, her soft eyes and sensible permed hair a welcome and reassuring sight.

"There's no sign of it yet," Connie replied. "Still, doubt it'll be late."

Joyce sighed in relief, unflappable as always. She handed Connie a small greaseproof-paper packet. "Cheese and an apple," Joyce said, by way of explanation. She'd waited behind at Brinford Farm as the farmer's wife had offered some food for their journey back to Helmstead. Joyce was worried that, despite the woman's kindness, she would take so long to wrap it all up that Joyce would miss the train. Not to mention the next one. "But I didn't want to be rude and just walk off."

Connie thanked Joyce and they opened their wrappers. Connie bit into her apple, wrapping the cheese back up for later. She knew Henry might like a bit of that.

The guard stopped his sweeping and eyed them suspiciously. "Hope you're not making any more mess," he muttered, moving with surprising speed back towards them. How could he have heard them unwrap a package at that distance?

"I've a good mind to give him what for," Connie said under her breath. She'd always fought her own battles and would never back down from a scrap. But this time Joyce touched her arm, holding her back. Joyce believed it was better to pick your battles, not engage in every skirmish at once.

"I leave you for ten minutes and all sorts happen. What's going on here?" Joyce asked.

11

Connie shook her head. It was nothing.

"That's what you said when you smashed the pub window." Joyce smiled.

Connie smiled at that memory too, a little embarrassed and amazed that she'd had the brass neck to do that. But the landlord had diddled them out of change one too many times. And he was a lecherous old sod, who made them all feel uncomfortable with his roving eyes. Henry had been annoyed about that, drifting into a sullen sulk for several days until Connie blurted out an apology. He'd given her a lecture about turning the other cheek. Connie had found herself drifting off as the words washed over her; annoyed that Henry was patronising her as if she was still a little girl at the children's home.

In the early evening sun, the two weary friends stretched their aching backs and Connie ate her apple. Behind them, a poster warned housewives not to take the trains after four o'clock so that factory workers could use them. Another showed two women chatting, not realising that a sinister man in a hat and coat was ear-wigging. Careless talk costs lives. Some more RAF pilots from Brinford Air Base decamped on the platform, their bodies laden with kit bags and great-coats. Connie scanned all the faces on the platform. She and Joyce were the only two Land Girls heading back. But there was an assortment of other travellers – service men, factory workers, a policeman and a middle-aged woman, who was clutching the hand of a nine-year-old girl. The little girl, her blonde hair in ringlets in a style that had been popular ten years ago, had been crying. Connie noticed the snaking lines of old tears on her chubby face and the way she was sniffing as she tried to control the flow. Before Connie could look any more, a portly man obscured her view – his shirt stretched tight over his large belly like the tarred cloth around Finch's haystack. The man's eyes darted to the distance in search of the train. He wore a trilby hat and a camera dangled around his neck, resting on the cushion of his stomach.

Suddenly the guard blew his whistle and everyone perked up as the plume of smoke from the steam train was glimpsed from behind a hill. Slowly the train chugged into view and Connie forgot the other passengers on the platform. Now it was all about getting a seat in one of the carriages. She needed to sit down. And from the weary look on Joyce's face, she did too. The two friends walked to the edge of the platform, trying to predict the position where the carriage doors would be. This was a routine that they had perfected since their second-ment to Brinford. Each evening they would wait for the train. Each evening they would try their best to secure a seat in one of the crowded carriages. The train came to a halt, the smell of soot thick in the air. The passengers already on-board flowed out of the carriage doors like water from a colander. And, with the train vacated there was the relatively good-natured but nonetheless urgent rush of the new passengers to find a seat. Some soldiers held back, allowing Connie and Joyce to get on first. Connie smiled charmingly back – thank you, kind sirs – and then suddenly darted, with little hint of any ladylike grace, along the carriage corridor to find an empty compartment.

They ducked under an RAF flyer's arms as he hoisted his kit bag up into the baggage rack and found themselves in an empty six-seat compartment. Mission accomplished! Connie and Joyce sat nearest the windows – until Joyce quickly changed her mind and sat next to Connie.

"Forgot, I don't like going backwards."

As the carriages filled up and the guard's whistle became more impatient, Joyce asked Connie whether Henry would be at the vicarage when she got home. Connie didn't know. Often Henry would cycle around the village in the evenings, administering succour and support to his parishioners.

"I told him, he wants to kick those needy old biddies into touch, he's a married man now," Connie said, partly to make Joyce laugh and partly to shock the middle-aged businessman who had entered their compartment. The businessman sat down and defensively rustled his newspaper open, a makeshift shield of the *Times* crossword to block out such coarseness for the duration of the journey.

The compartment filled up. The young girl who had been crying and her stern-looking mother entered. And then a fresh-faced young soldier arrived to make up the six. He sat down and studiously attempted to roll a cigarette for the first ten minutes of the journey. He obviously hadn't been smoking long and was all fingers and thumbs, with more tobacco ending up in his lap than in the cigarette paper. Connie was itching to snatch it from him and do it herself, but figured that wouldn't be the sort of thing a lady would do.

Joyce and Connie settled down for the journey as the train wheezed its way out of Brinford, the station guard diminishing to the size of a speck on the platform. He could be alone with his concourse now.

"Why are you still calling yourself Carter?" Joyce asked, breaking Connie's idle thoughts. "Heard you introduce yourself twice today."

"Had that name all me life. Not got used to being a Jameson yet, I suppose." Connie shrugged. "Connie Carter's got a ring to it."

"She's got a ring on her finger," Joyce retorted.

Why hadn't Connie been using Henry's name? It was an odd thing for her to do. Married women happily took their husbands' surnames. Secretly she knew that her explanation to Joyce was a lie. She didn't use the name of Jameson because she didn't believe it would last. Nothing ever did in her life. Part of her thought that her happy marriage would be a blip. Best not to get too comfortable with the luxury of Henry's surname. Another part of her hated herself for hedging her bets and not fully committing. She should dive in rather than just dangling her feet in the pool. But that's what came when you were buffeted from a lifetime of disappointment and rejection.

Connie shut out the thoughts and concentrated on the stern-looking woman and her tearful daughter. Connie offered a consoling smile to the girl, but the girl didn't acknowledge it. Was she too upset to notice? Or was it fear making her reluctant to smile back?

"My John's supposed to be on this train," Joyce said, interrupting Connie's thoughts. "But I didn't see him on the platform."

Roland Moore

"Difficult to see anyone in that scrum, wasn't it?" Connie offered.

John Fisher – an RAF flier – had been to the airbase in Brinford today and Joyce had been hoping to see her husband before they got back to Helmstead. He was Joyce's rock – her childhood sweetheart and the only part of her family that she hadn't lost in the brutal bombing of Coventry at the start of the war. It had been a lucky accident, which had meant they were in Birmingham on the night the bombs dropped. A sliver of serendipity that further cemented their relationship and their belief in their shared destiny together.

"Do you want to go down the carriages and find him?" Connie asked. "I'll keep your seat."

Joyce looked at the corridor outside their compartment. It was crammed with soldiers, pilots and factory workers. It would be nearly impossible to move down the train. Joyce decided to stay where she was. "I'm sure I won't forget what he looks like if I don't see him until Helmstead."

The young soldier dutifully finished his roll-up with an audible gasp of satisfaction. But the victory was short-lived as he raised it to his lips and lit it; it promptly unrolled, dropping tobacco onto his trousers. He cursed and hastily patted his crotch to put out the burning embers before they scorched his uniform. Connie couldn't resist letting out a small laugh. The boy looked back and smiled. He scooped up the tobacco and started to try again.

"Want me to do it?" she offered. Sod it if it wasn't the sort of thing a lady did.

"Can you roll them?" the soldier said in surprise, a glimmer of hope in his eyes.

"No. But I can't be worse than you, can I?"

Joyce nudged Connie to stop messing with the poor lad. "What? I'm just being friendly," Connie said, under her breath. The middle-aged woman with the tear-streaked daughter shot her a disapproving look.

The soldier sucked in his cheeks and doggedly resumed his rolling.

The businessman already had a pipe in his mouth – unlit at the moment and being sucked on like a baby's dummy as he contemplated the crossword.

The train snaked across the countryside. Fields of cows and fields of corn moved past the windows like frames at the flicks. The evening sun glinted low through the carriage windows, dappling the occupants with patchworks of light.

Connie entertained fragmented thoughts: Henry waiting with a cup of tea; Joyce joking in the fields with her; the snotty guard at Brinford station. The images washed over her in a hazy, comforting blur as the motion of the train and the evening sunlight flickered over her face. Sleep was a moment away.

The fields trundled by in a blur.

Connie tried to keep her eyes open. She didn't want to sleep now. She sat up, breathed deep and thought about Henry waiting at the vicarage with his warm smile and trusting eyes. He was a decent man, a man who loved her despite her faults. He loved her despite her troubled past. It was too good to be true, really, but she had to accept it and hope it wouldn't turn out to be some massive joke.

She glanced at Joyce – who was biting her lip. Connie didn't have to be a mind reader to know what Joyce was thinking about. She was thinking about her man too.

Joyce was worried about John. He'd been to the base to finalise his leaving the RAF. It would be a big moment for both of them. Suddenly, John would be close to the home of Pasture Farm, where Joyce was billeted; he'd be finally safe from harm; but would it mean he'd lose his sense of purpose? Both Joyce and John held on to their roles in the war – as it made sense of the carnage and loss they had experienced in Coventry. Connie often wondered what Joyce would do when the war was over – if it ever finished. Would she feel lost without it?

But Connie was too tired to ask about such things tonight. A bath. A cuppa. And Henry. Those simple things were keeping her going.

So instead, Connie offered a less emotionally taxing conversation.

"I won't miss this journey," Connie said.

True, it was pleasant enough if you got a seat away from the scrum, but it still added a long journey to an already-long day in the fields.

"Me neither," Joyce said, munching the cheese from her parcel. "Only good thing was not having to work with Dolores."

"Don't be 'orrible. Just 'cos she never says nothing." Connie thought about the near-monosyllabic Dolores, who had joined them recently. But the thought drifted out of her head, sleep threatening to cover her.

"I wish Finch would pick us up sometimes," Joyce said.

Connie wished he would to, as she bit her lip, trying to stay awake. Freddie Finch was the tenant farmer who lived in Pasture Farm. A ruddy-faced man with keen, smart eyes, he'd loaned out some of his Land Girls for the work on Brinford Farm. But despite having a tractor with a trailer that could easily give the girls a lift home, Finch wouldn't stretch his meagre petrol ration to pick them up unless he had to. It was fair enough, but it didn't stop Connie and Joyce from wishing.

Connie looked at the young girl again.

The whites of her mother's knuckles were showing as she gripped the girl's hand. Why was she holding on so tightly? That must hurt.

Connie offered a sympathetic smile to the girl. Nothing. She flashed one to the mother.

This time, she got a reaction. The stern-faced woman shot her a look that said stop staring and mind your own business.

This was like red rag to a bull. Connie didn't avert her gaze.

The girl was looking at the floor.

"Is she all right?" Connie asked, poking her nose in even further.

Joyce looked around – this was the first she'd registered the young girl and her mother. She played catch-up quickly and registered Connie's concern.

The mother frowned and shook her head – containing her fury at this interference.

"Of course she is."

The soldier looked up from his rolling. The business man buried himself deeper in *The Times*.

"Yeah?" Connie asked the girl directly.

The girl raised her sad face, her eyes vulnerable and moist.

"What business is it of yours?" the mother asked Connie.

"Connie ..." Joyce warned, about to tell her friend to pipe down.

But Connie wouldn't let this lie. Maybe it was hard to let go when she saw something of herself in the haunted eyes of this youngster.

"It's just that she seems—" Connie was about to say "sad", but she would never finished the sentence.

BANNGGGGGGG!

There was a deafening bang from the front of the train, accompanied by the ear-splitting wrenching of metal. Everyone was jolted off their seats, the world folding in on itself. The businessman's newspaper flew into Connie's face as she fell forwards. And then there was a loud crunching noise from behind and the sound of twisting metal. Slowly, the compartment shook and rolled, tossing over and over. Bodies bounced around the carriage as the floor became the ceiling and back again. Connie felt herself sliding across the floor. Joyce's elbow hit Connie hard in the neck as Joyce rolled on top of her. Connie could hear muffled screams. All the sounds were somehow distant, as if they had been muffled by cotton wool.

Connie thrust out a hand and grabbed the metal frame that secured the seats to the floor. With the other hand, she grabbed onto Joyce to try to stop them being tossed around the tumbling carriage.

The windows of the compartment shattered and there was a squeal of brakes. The outer door flung open and the young soldier was thrown into the air, rolling on the ceiling and then the floor, over Connie and Joyce, and finally spewing out of the opening to the outside world.

The businessman flew across the floor and hit the open door frame with a thud. Arms and legs and bodies intertwined as screams filled the air and the carriage tumbled.

Crunch. Crunch. Crunch.

Finally the nightmare seemed to end and the carriage came to juddering rest. It was almost the right way up again. The sounds suddenly became clearer. Screams. Connie slowly let go of the seat support and slid to the new floor. The first thing she focused on was the businessman's pipe. It was inches from her nose, resting in a sea of diamond-like fragments of broken glass. The businessman himself was behind Connie, sitting in a heap of Saville Row tailoring and blood; shocked and confused, but probably all right.

The little girl was crying, her leg wedged under the seat. A seat that had been mangled almost flat in the crash. Her mother was face down on the floor, knocked unconscious.

Connie could hear her own heart thumping in her chest.

The taste of blood was in her mouth.

"What—?" She struggled to talk, but her words didn't seem to come together; drunken sounds in her head.

Dust settled. Joyce looked up, her face bruised and slightly cut; her tight-permed-hair messed in all directions.

"Are you all right?" Connie finally managed to ask.

Joyce stared at her, as if she wasn't hearing the words. She'd gone into shock.

"What happened?" Connie asked. "Joyce?"

Again, Joyce had no answers. Or even acknowledgement that her friend was talking to her.

Connie knew she wouldn't get anything from her. She glanced towards the exterior door. Outside was grass. They had rolled down a bank and come to rest at the bottom of the incline. Connie got shakily to her feet, her balance slightly wobbly. She rubbed her neck and glanced quickly to check that Joyce wasn't badly injured. She guided her shocked friend towards the exit, their boots crunching on the broken glass as if they were walking on fresh snow. With Connie's help, Joyce jumped down onto the grass. It was a long drop without a platform. For some inexplicable reason, Connie saw an image of the guard back at Brinford station sweeping the platform. Or concourse, or whatever he called it.

"Flaming vandals," he muttered in Connie's head.

Joyce staggered a few feet across the grass, before falling softly onto her bottom. A soldier came over from another carriage to check she was okay and they sat together.

Still inside the carriage, Connie poked her head out and looked along the length of the carriage. Many passengers were dropping from their compartments onto the grass, where they struggled to come to terms with what had happened. Three-quarters of the train had been derailed and had tumbled down the bank, a wrecked and hissing snake in the long grass.

Connie put her head back into her compartment and turned her attention to the injured. The businessman was groggily coming round. He'd bitten through his lip in the crash. Connie reassured him that his injury wasn't as bad as it looked. He might need a new shirt, though.

She helped him to the door and he jumped down onto the grass.

Next Connie found the mother. She was unconscious. Connie got close and listened to the woman. She was breathing. She was alive.

"Help me!" the little girl said, her leg trapped under the twisted seat.

"I'll just get your mother first," Connie replied, as she flung the woman's arm around her shoulders and edged her towards the door. The dead weight was difficult to shift and Connie found herself buckling under the woman. Finally she managed to wedge her into the door opening and cry for help.

"I need some help! Someone come and help!"

Suddenly, behind her, a strange rustling noise attracted Connie's attention.

She turned to the source of the noise. It sounded oddly familiar.

"Fire!" the little girl shouted. "Help me! It's on fire!"

The whole corridor of the carriage outside their compartment was ablaze; thick black smoke billowing behind the glass. It wouldn't be long before it broke through the door and engulfed the compartment itself.

The girl was struggling to free her leg from the metal of the seat. But it wouldn't budge.

Connie tried to move the unconscious woman, who was wedged in the door. She realised she didn't have time for any more niceties.

"Sorry, love."

She put her boot behind the mother's bottom and gave her a hefty shove through the door. The woman fell out of the door, landing unceremoniously on the grass with a dull thud.

Connie raced back over to the girl and pulled at the frame. It started to bend and yield, but still the leg was trapped.

Knowing that it wouldn't help things if the girl panicked, Connie looked the girl in the eye.

"You've gotta move it as I try and pull the seat. Got it?"

The girl realised it was the only way. Connie smiled encouragingly.

The fire in the corridor behind Connie's shoulder was getting more intense. She could feel the heat as the flames danced hungrily behind the glass partition.

"One, two, three," Connie counted, and with all her strength she pulled at the metal frame at the same time the girl wiggled her ankle. With a jolt, the leg came free. Connie hauled the little girl to her feet. The leg seemed unable to support her weight. It may have been broken or just bruised – Connie didn't have time to check but ran with the girl's arm around her towards the salvation of the open door.

The corridor door behind them suddenly exploded as the fire broke the glass.

Invigorated by the fresh air of the compartment, smoke and flames exploded into the space. Connie didn't have time to hang around. She pushed the girl through the opening to the outside.

And a moment later, framed by an inferno, cloaked in thick black smoke, Connie stood in the opening herself.

The little girl looked up at the woman who'd saved her. She called for her to jump. But the smoke, billowing from the carriage suddenly covered Connie, obscuring her from view. The flames were raging in the carriage, pumping out more and more dark smoke. The little girl squinted.

She couldn't see if Connie Carter had made it.

Chapter 3

A tractor with a hay trailer stood in the country lane. The casualties from the train disaster: the walking wounded and those too shocked to speak, were hauling their aching and battered bodies up onto the trailer. Freddie Finch, a large, avuncular man in his late forties, was helping them. Although "helping" was a generous term for just telling them to mind they didn't snag anything on the lip of the trailer as they crawled up. Finch wouldn't stretch himself to help anyone physically, on account of his bad back; a condition that had oddly resisted any medical diagnosis and which seemed to move to different areas of his spine according to his memory.

"Mind your step. That's it," he said with a nervous chuckle as a young soldier climbed up. Finch glanced back at the surreal sight of the train and its carriages sprawled across a large area of grassland. The fire fighters had arrived and were trying to extinguish a blaze in the middle section. Some distance away, a large group of passengers were huddled together, being treated by a few village doctors and nurses. Some soldiers were building a pile of luggage as they recovered what they could from the wrecked train.

"I was just saying I wished you'd pick us up. And here you are."

Finch looked round to the sound of the voice. It was Joyce Fisher, bruised and suffering some small lacerations to her face, but otherwise all right. She'd recovered from the shock of what had happened and found her voice. She had a hair pin in her mouth and was busy tidying her hair as she walked towards the trailer.

"I'm like the genie of the lamp." Finch giggled.

"Mind you, didn't think I'd have to go through all this to get a lift."

Finch beamed a large grin. "Thank heavens you're all right. That's the main thing, eh?"

He plucked her from the ground and spun her round – chuckling with relief.

Joyce winced. Finch put her down awkwardly.

"Bruises." Joyce grimaced.

"Sorry, got carried away!" Finch chuckled. Realising that he was being watched by rows of blank eyes on the trailer, he placed his thick fingers on his lower back as it twinged with pain. "Overdone it."

Frederick Finch gave bed and board to Joyce – as well to Esther Reeves, the Land Girls' warden, her teenage son and three other Land Girls. Within the boundaries of the Hoxley estate, Pasture Farm sported a homely and quaint little cottage in its vast expanse of fields and outbuildings. Before the war, it had just been home to Finch and his young son Billy, but now Billy had gone away to fight and the house was rammed full of new people, the vibrant chatter and noise making it once more not just a house but a home. Finch enjoyed having the house feel so alive, full of strangers who became friends. It reminded him of before. It reminded him of when his wife was there, the fire roaring as she laid on feasts for their friends, a house full of laughter.

As Finch watched Joyce get up onto the hay trailer, he poked a stubby finger in the air and counted how many people he had on board. Joyce hid her amusement that Finch's mouth moved while he counted.

Reaching a tally in his head, Finch frowned. Someone was missing.

"Where's Connie?"

Nearer the wreckage, the young nine-year-old girl with blonde curls was wrapped in a blanket as the village doctor, Dr Wally Morgan, checked her leg for injury. He was a well-meaning but often drunken man in his fifties; a man unused to having to use his limited medical knowledge on such a scale.

"How's that?" Wally asked, manipulating her ankle.

The girl winced. He'd got his answer.

"Point your toes to the ground. Can you do that, dear?"

The girl tried her best. Her foot was moving fairly well. "Hurts a bit, I think."

"I don't think it's broken," Wally said, tapping her shoulder by way of closure as he got to his feet. He plucked up his medical bag, ready to move to the next patient. "Probably just a bad bruise. It'll go a pretty old purple over the next day or so, I'll wager."

Wally Morgan scanned the huddles of patients and helpers, deciding where to go next. This was a lot more activity than he was used to as a village doctor. He was already feeling that he'd reward himself with a drink or two tonight. This felt like proper war work, a step above looking at Mrs Gulliver's bunions. Wanting an easy win, he managed to ignore a man with a twisted leg and set off to see a young man who had a bleeding temple.

As she'd stood in the wrecked doorway, smoke billowing out around her, Connie Carter had felt the searing heat of the fire on her back. It felt as though it was already burning though her Land Army sweater; angry orange tendrils trying to fry her skin. The heat could overcome her at any time and topple her, unconscious, back into the burning carriage. That would be the end of it. As she stood there, it only took a fraction of a second, but for Connie the moment stretched out forever. She gripped the sides of the doorway, her boots crossing the threshold. A clump of mud fell from one boot. Dimly she thought of the station master at Brinford with his broom and his short temper.

"Mind you don't mess up my burning train."

A bloom of black smoke belched from the back of the carriage and engulfed Connie, pulled past her into the fresh air. There wasn't enough air to breathe. Connie felt herself totter, woozy, losing focus. She steadied herself, blinking to try to clear her head. More smoke rushed past her. It was getting harder to breathe, the air dry and somehow thin. She tried to focus and force herself forward. But her fuzzy brain suddenly couldn't work out which way was forward. Even though the opening was inches in front of her, she was disorientated and looking around for the way. But the black smoke was rushing past her, like a biblical plague of suited commuters. She couldn't see anything, even though logic should have told her to follow the direction the smoke was heading in. Towards the air. But logic wasn't working.

Connie swooned, almost fell. There was nothing left in her lungs. She couldn't see and all she could hear was the rush of smoke and the crackle of burning wood somewhere in the distance.

A gust of wind saved her life.

Outside the carriage, the wind poked a brief hole in the billowing blackness that was exiting the door. For a moment, Connie could see a soldier sitting on the grass in the distance, a man in shock being treated by a nurse.

She knew she had to head in that direction.

The flames staged one last attempt to grasp her, but Connie launched herself from the doorway, following the brief glimpse of light she'd seen. Her lungs were gasping as she fell in a heap on the ground. Looking behind, she saw tall flames consuming the carriage, dancing, blowing the glass out from the windows. One second longer and she would have been overcome with smoke and she would have collapsed into that inferno.

It had been a narrow miss.

Connie sobbed in relief and took hungry mouthfuls of air. Each breath made her hack up the acrid smoke that had tried to take over her lungs. It took several minutes before she could speak, and even as she got her voice back, the coughing would be there to remind her of her lucky escape.

Now Connie Carter sat on the grass drinking tea from a mug. Some villagers had lit a fire and were boiling a kettle to provide hot drinks for the wounded. The tea was weak and milky but it hit the spot. Connie noticed the young girl from the carriage and moved over towards her.

"How you feeling?" Connie asked.

"All right. Your face is all black."

Connie laughed. She hadn't seen herself, but she supposed that it would be. Certainly a thin smear of greasy soot covered her arms and hands. It probably caked some of her face too. She offered the mug. "Want some tea? It's weaker than a kitten, but it hits the spot."

The girl shook her head. "Not allowed tea. But thank you."

"What's your name?"

"Margaret Sawyer," the girl replied.

"I'm Connie Carter. Well, Connie Jameson. Keep forgetting. Married." Connie reached into her pocket and pulled out the parchment parcel. She opened it up, considered eating it, but then offered the piece of cheese to the girl. "Do you good to eat something, you know."

The girl looked uncertain. Connie wondered whether she had been told not to take things from strangers.

"It's all right. Your mum's over there. And I'm a vicar's wife."

Margaret overcame her reticence and took it. She gobbled

it down, taking another chunk before the first one was swallowed. Connie was surprised at how ravenous she seemed. "Blimey, doesn't your mum feed you?"

"She's not really my mum," Margaret said.

But before Connie could enquire further, they were interrupted. It was the portly man with the trilby hat and the camera that Connie had seen at Brinford station.

"Hello, ladies," he wheezed. "I'm Roger Curran from *The Helmstead Herald*."

"About time someone told us what was going on," Connie replied. "Why did the train come off the tracks like that, then?"

Roger was slightly wrong-footed. "No, I was hoping to ask you some questions."

"Well I don't know nothing," Connie said.

Margaret, with a mouthful of cheese, stifled a giggle at their exchange.

"They think there was an explosive on the line," Roger said in a hushed voice, hoping that the explanation might enable him to get on with his line of questioning.

"What, the Germans?"

Roger didn't know. The bomb could have been planted by Nazi sympathisers or communists or any group allied with the German cause. There had been several instances of terrorism in Helmstead and the surrounding areas in the last few months. The air base at Brinford had been bombed mercilessly in a raid by German bombers, and while that action wasn't terrorism, most locals thought someone had tipped off the secret location of the base to the enemy. And a sympathiser had even been shot dead at Hoxley Manor when Lady Ellen Hoxley had discovered him transmitting secret messages from the stables. The enemy was closer than anyone wanted...

Roger Curran explained that an explosive had been detonated as the train engine went across the track. The bomb must have been on a timer. It would have been common knowledge that, due to its proximity to the air base, the evening Brinford train would have had a large number of military personnel on board.

Connie hid her shock. Part of her had hoped the crash had been the result of a random accident. A rock on the line or something. It was terrifying to think that someone, or some group, was behind it. Terrifying that it was an act of war.

"Anyway, tell me what happened to you," Roger said, pulling out a small notebook. He licked the end of his pencil and poised it over the page to write. Connie didn't understand why people licked pencils. What was the point of that?

Connie wasn't sure she wanted to tell the story, playing down any suggestion that she had been heroic. But, despite her efforts at modesty, Margaret piped up:

"She saved my life. She saved the lives of everyone in our compartment. She was brilliant."

Connie blushed. She tried to downplay it, but was reluctantly forced to reveal that this was more or less the truth. She related the tale of what happened and Roger took a few pages of notes, his smiles of encouragement becoming more frequent. He sensed this was a good story for his paper. It might even give him his first front page since the Land Girls' Tractor Race. He ended by asking Connie where she lived.

Proudly Connie told him that she lived at the vicarage with her husband.

"This will be a lovely piece for the paper. 'Vicar's Wife Saves Lives'," Roger said. Then he turned to the young girl. "And where do you live?"

"I don't know if I should say," Margaret replied, offering a worried glance in the direction of where the middle-aged woman was.

"It's all right," Connie encouraged.

"Jessop's Cottage," Margaret admitted, hesitantly.

As Roger tried to place it, Margaret informed him that it was in the middle of a valley, miles from anywhere. The nearest landmark was Panmere Lake and Helmstead was the nearest town. Roger couldn't place it.

"Don't worry. Nobody knows it. Nobody comes there."

"Not even your friends?" Connie asked.

Margaret shook her head quickly, keen to close down all these intrusive questions.

As Connie mulled this over, Roger unhooked his camera from around his neck and started to frame a shot of Connie and Margaret.

"Perhaps, if you don't mind getting closer ...?" Roger said, wafting his hand for them to scrunch together.

Connie and Margaret shuffled closer over the grass – Margaret still wrapped in her blanket. They smiled weary smiles for the camera.

Roger clicked the trigger. "Cheese!"

He let the camera bounce back onto his ample stomach. "Thank you, ladies."

And then he tipped his hat and moved to another group. Even though he knew their story would take some topping. "Excuse me, I'm Roger Curran from *The Helmstead Herald*."

Connie turned to Margaret. "How you feeling?"

Margaret looked subdued and thoughtful. Connie tried to cheer her up. "Here, I let him take my photograph and I was covered in soot."

"It's all right. So was I." Margaret laughed. A nurse came over and helped Margaret to her feet.

"Your mum is being taken to the hospital. She'll be fine. But we need you to come as well," the nurse said.

Margaret looked back at Connie. The unhappy look had returned to the young girl's face. Connie felt concerned. What was she going back to? Why did no one ever go to the little girl's house?

"Thanks again," Margaret said.

"Take care." Connie watched the young girl as she was marshalled away. And then she was aware of Finch waving at her to get a move on. He wanted to leave now. Tipping the last remnants of her tea away, Connie picked herself up and scurried up the bank towards the waiting tractor.

When she reached it, the trailer was nearly full and people were shivering as dusk turned to night. As she hauled herself up, Connie was surprised to see John Fisher sitting next to Joyce. It turned out he had been on the train after all, squeezed into a carriage further down, just as Joyce had predicted. John had become a navigator for the RAF until he was shot down in France. The experience had been traumatic and he had left active duty soon after his recovery. Now he worked at Brinford Air Base as a clerk, his flying days over (to Joyce's immense relief).

"I saw Finch before I saw Joyce," he admitted.

"Flaming cheek," Joyce joked.

"He probably blocked her out. Like one of them eclipse things," Connie said.

Finch, at the front of the tractor with a starting handle, popped his head up. "'Ere! You can walk if there's any more of that."

Connie sat with Joyce and John as Finch cranked up the tractor.

It spluttered to life.

"Right, anyone not got a ticket? It's tuppence each for the ride." He chuckled, knowing full well that he was going to get a barracking for his cheek. But you couldn't blame a man for trying.

"With your driving, you should be paying us!" Connie replied.

"One more insult and you're out, Connie Carter!"

Everyone laughed, enjoying the catharsis of letting it out after the trauma they had faced. This was the Blitz spirit. You could bomb these people, derail their trains, take their homes, but they would still end up laughing, somehow.

The tractor set off on its bumpy and languorous journey back to Helmstead. And while others were looking back at the wreckage of the train as it faded into the distance, Connie was thinking about the young girl she had saved and hoping that she would be all right.

Connie strode through the village square as starlings swooped like Spitfires in the darkening sky. Her feet had gone numb from her heavy boots, but she dreaded taking them off in case she couldn't put them on again. She had visions of her feet swelling up like barrage balloons as soon as she unstrapped them from their straining prisons.

There was light and laughter coming from the Bottle and Glass pub as she passed it. Two GIs were hanging around outside, smoking and drinking in the late-evening air. One of them gave Connie an approving glance, but Connie wasn't in the mood for any harmless flirty chit-chat. Not tonight. After what she'd been through, she just wanted to get home.

The church stood on the horizon at the end of the village. And next to it was the small white cottage that she called home. Getting used to married life hadn't been as easy as she'd hoped. Their courtship had been a whirlwind of fun and romance; Connie enjoying how Henry would get tongue-tied and embarrassed at her antics. But those playful differences that seemed attractively engaging during the carefree stages of their relationship, now were weighed down by the serious-ness of her wedding vows. Couldn't she be more responsible? Couldn't he just loosen up a little? And one month in, they were still finding their roles in that marriage; both desperate to make it work, but both feeling out of their depth. Connie had no idea how a marriage was supposed to work. She was fumbling for the answers as she went along, while trying to fit into the new order. The regimentation of living with someone, respecting their routine. It was all new. Well, it was all new in that it mattered this time. She'd lived with a man before, but that was different. It was something she didn't want to think about. It felt like sullying what she had with Henry to even think about that.

Added to this difficult process of discovery was the hardship of wartime. It was tough having to wake up and go to work before her new husband was even awake. Most days Connie would get out of bed at five, kiss her slumbering, groggy husband goodbye and then tip toe across the cold floorboards into the bathroom to change into her WLA uniform. She'd put on her shirt, strap her braces over her shoulders as she hauled her heavy britches up – all the while hoping she wouldn't wake Henry. Then she'd grab something to eat and go out into the crisp dewy air, staring at the new day's clouds and walk to Pasture Farm – the place she had lived with the other Land Girls before she got married.

But that would be tomorrow morning. For now, Connie had reached the front door of the cottage. The place she called home.

She pushed it open.

Henry Jameson was standing in the corridor. A young man with a flicked fringe, dog collar and a permanent air of endearing bewilderment. Henry looked surprised to see her. But he didn't have any time for questions as Connie pressed him to the wall, sending a small engraving of Our Lord clattering off its hook to the floor in the process, and planted a smacker right on his lips.

"Gawd, I've missed you, 'Enry," she said. "Thought I'd never see you again."

She was about to kiss him again when she noticed that

three old women were also standing in the corridor. In their neat floral dresses, they looked shocked at the sight they were witnessing. All three clutched their handbags like protective talismans.

"I was just showing the ladies from the WI out," Henry stammered.

Connie mustered up a smile that would befit her status as a vicar's wife. "I ain't seen him all day," she muttered by way of explanation.

Henry opened the front door for Mrs Arbuthnott, Mrs Fisk and Mrs Hewson to make their way out. They left in constrained silence. Connie and Henry waved a cheery goodbye wave and when it was socially acceptable, Henry quickly closed the door.

And then Connie burst out laughing. The sound caught in her throat when she realised that she was laughing alone. Henry frowned and walked into the living room.

In a stilted atmosphere, Connie related the events of the train disaster as she chased the last remnants of sausage and cabbage from her plate. Henry ate his dinner and replied that he'd heard nothing about the crash, but then he had been trapped most of the evening with Mrs Arbuthnott, Mrs Fisk and Mrs Hewson discussing the morality of rationing. The two of them ate by candlelight, as they always did, the meal complimented by conversation about their days. But tonight, she felt like a scolded child.

For Connie, the evening meal was usually the highlight of her day: a chance to talk about their working days and share a laugh together, before going upstairs for a bath and bed. Neither of them had the energy to stay up late so normally they'd be wrapped in each other's arms by nine or ten at the latest. But tonight, it was already half-ten because of the extraordinary events of the train crash.

And there was an awkwardness, a sombre reflective air in the room.

Connie couldn't take any more. Feeling contrite for showing up Henry in the eyes in of his parishioners, she was also annoyed she was being put through this.

"I thought you'd be more pleased I wasn't dead," she said bluntly.

"Of course I am. Don't even joke about that."

"Well, why does it feel like I'm doing thirteen Hail Marys instead of enjoying my food?"

"There are ways of behaving," Henry said through tight lips. He didn't like confrontation. He just wished that his brash wife knew how to behave sometimes. "Couldn't you be more cautious when you come in?"

"Perhaps you'd like me to make an appointment before-hand." Connie got up, clanking her cutlery onto the plate.

Henry grabbed her wrist. She'd been grabbed by other men, forced back into her seat. But this was different. He wasn't holding her tightly, just enough to stop her in her tracks. He looked up at her with imploring eyes.

"Sorry," he said quietly. "Sometimes I don't focus on what's important. You're alive and I should be thanking God for that."

Connie sat back down and cleared her throat.

Despite their differences, she was grateful that this was her reward: a caring, handsome man who adored her – for the most part. It was her reward for all the cold, lonely nights she'd spent growing up in the orphanage, wondering where her mother was. Not that she would have recognised her because Connie never knew her mother, having been abandoned in the porch of a Stepney church at the age of three months. Being brought up in the orphanage wasn't unpleasant, but its rigid discipline and work ethic made Connie yearn to break the rules and express herself. Mr and Mrs Palmer, who ran the place for the Borough of Tower Hamlets, never beat any of the children. Instead extra chores were given by way of punishment. It wasn't a bad place, but with thirty-two children in one large house, Connie missed the warmth of a family's love. Now she was the sole focus of Henry's attention and didn't have to compete with anyone.

"Good sausages," Henry commented, finishing his dinner.

Connie couldn't help but laugh. The relief of something trivial and light after a day of turmoil. She told him that Farmer Finch had given them to her. In fact, they got most of their meat and eggs from the farm, with Freddie Finch ensuring that all his girls were well-fed and watered, "top ups" to their government-approved rations.

"I wonder if we should be making such liberal use of the farm, though," Henry finished.

Connie would have suspected that Henry's discussion about the morality of rationing with the three old witches might have prompted this, but the truth was she had heard rumbles of this argument before. Should they be given special treatment in the form of extra food when the majority of people adhered to strict rationing? Henry was a fair-minded man who believed in equal treatment during times of war and this preferential treatment clearly made him feel uncomfortable. Especially when some of his sermons were rallying cries to abandon the black market and make do with what you were given.

"Perk of working on a farm, innit?" Connie said, eager to close the conversation down. She was too tired to have this debate tonight. Too tired for any more friction. The last thing she wanted was to be talking about sausages after what she'd been through.

"I know, but—" Henry squirmed slightly. "And don't think I'm not grateful, but I just think that any extra we get, we should perhaps get by our own means."

Connie asked what he meant by that. "What, hunt for sausages ourselves? You do know they don't roam around like that in the wild."

Henry laughed, despite himself.

"I just meant that if we, say, caught a rabbit ourselves then it's an extra bounty from the Lord. I wouldn't feel guilty about that."

"I ain't got time to catch any rabbits, what with digging ditches all day," Connie said, clearing the plates. "And you wouldn't have the first idea what to do."

"You don't think I could catch one?" Henry asked.

Connie regretted saying it. It had slipped out before she could stop it. The perils of having an easy mouth and a tired brain. And now, he was glaring at her again. Well done, Connie.

First she'd shown him up in the community and now she was emasculating him. Just when things had quietened down again. "Sorry, I didn't mean—"

"You jolly well did. But I could indeed."

Henry simmered. He could catch a rabbit! He knew he could. Couldn't he? He wondered if Connie really thought he was clueless in the ways of hunting and fishing. Didn't she think he could do proper manly pursuits? He stared with sudden loathing at his neatly ironed cuffs and the genteel surroundings of doilies and oil paintings. And Henry Jameson made a silent vow to himself. He'd prove that Connie was wrong. He'd show her.

Margaret Sawyer had received an even rockier homecoming. Instead of showing relief that Vera and Margaret were all right after their ordeal, Michael Sawyer vented fury and frustration at how stupid they had been to take the train. Vera usually got a bus from Brinford to near Jessop's Cottage. How could they put themselves at risk by getting on a train packed with servicemen? Margaret had often seen Michael angry, but this tirade was a new benchmark in furious indignation. Even Vera had been taken aback. Margaret assumed that Michael didn't know how to show he cared, so he shouted to let out his feelings. She wished he didn't shout all the time.

Now, after Vera had gone for a lie-down, Margaret was the sole focus for his still considerable anger.

She was being scolded by him for taking the cheese from the woman at the train crash. Michael was grey-haired and tall, with gaunt features and a stick-like appearance. A bitter and shrill man, Michael Sawyer liked things done a certain way. His dinner had to be ready at a certain time every day. Bath days would be Tuesday and Friday. Margaret knew that something was wrong with him, some illness of the mind, although she didn't know what. It meant that he rarely strayed far from the house, making his wife responsible for running errands and going to the town. He also seemed very suspicious of outsiders, always talking of people being "out to get him". Margaret knew the word "recluse" and knew that that was what Michael Sawyer was, but she didn't know the full extent of his mental problems. Michael would spend his days in his shed or working their plot of land for vegetables. He didn't seem to have any friends or outside interests.

As he raged, Margaret knew from bitter experience that it was quicker and easier not to argue; just let him pour it all out and burn himself out.

His face was close to Margaret's and she could smell his bad breath as he spat his anger at her. He'd stopped talking about taking cheese from a stranger and was focusing his anger on the brazen woman who had given it to her. According to the reports from his wife, Connie was some sort of trollop.

"You don't take extra. You don't know where it came from. Your mother said she had lipstick like a tart."

"She was just being nice," Margaret stammered.

"Your mother said she poked her nose in!"

"She saved our lives."

"Your mother would have looked after you!"

Margaret couldn't take any more. She desperately wanted to snap and shout: 'Stop calling her my mother. She's not my mother and you're not my father!' But she knew she'd regret such a spectacular outburst and it would just prolong the punishment that was inevitably coming. Far better to just get it over with, go through the motions.

Let him burn himself out.

"Go to the place!" he fumed, brandishing his hand as if he was about to strike her. Margaret knew that it wasn't the right time to make a stand, so she obediently scurried to the 'place'. This was what they called the cupboard under the stairs. And it was somewhere where Margaret spent a lot of time. She'd be locked in there, in the dark, to 'think about what she'd done' sometimes for hours at a time. She'd eaten meals in the cupboard, tried to read a book by candle-light in there. The screws on the woodwork of the door had become as familiar as the things in her bedroom.

Margaret went into the cupboard. Michael closed the door behind her and he slipped the bolt across. "Stay there and think about it," he thundered through the door as he stomped away back to the dining table to finish his meal.

Margaret sat in the dark, cramped and lonely. She stared at the door, the missing section of skirting board on the floor, the collection of coats hanging from the hooks. It was usually a time of resigned sadness and usually it would overwhelm Margaret Sawyer with tears. But this time she didn't cry.

Because this time she was thinking about Connie Carter.

Chapter 4

"Ah, doesn't she look like Betty Grable?" Finch giggled as he looked at the picture of Connie in *The Helmstead Herald*. Connie winced in embarrassment. The photograph showed her with the girl Margaret Sawyer, Connie's soot-smeared smile a mix of bemusement and shock at the events that had just occurred. A streak of dirt ran down the side of Connie's face. Margaret was looking sullenly at the camera, wrapped in her blanket, clearly not quite registering what was happening.

"I think I'll pin this up in the kitchen to inspire the rest of you lot," Finch announced to the room. Connie and Joyce were drinking tea, waiting for lunch, along with their fellow Land Girls young Iris Dawson and new arrival Dolores O'Malley. The kind-hearted warden, Esther Reeves, was standing at the stove stirring a huge pan of parsnip soup.

"No, you blinking won't," Esther stormed.

"Why not? It's my kitchen," Finch replied.

"'Cos it's me what spends most time in here. No offence, Connie, love. It's just I don't want to be reminded about that awful crash all the time."

Connie couldn't blame her. The train crash had resulted in four casualties – including the young soldier who'd been trying to roll a cigarette. And over twenty other people had ended up in hospital with various injuries. Connie didn't want to be reminded of it either.

"I'll put it away, then," Finch grumbled. "Still who'd have thought? She might get the George Cross for this, you know."

"You're making me cross," Esther said, throwing him a look. Finch knew when it was best to let things drop. He pulled himself out of his chair at the head of the farmhouse table, took the newspaper and left the room.

"Also he's brought seven copies of the thing," Esther whispered to the girls. "He's more proud of what you've done, Connie, than anything his own son ever did. Tragic, really."

Connie felt awkward. She broke the tension by asking when the soup would be ready. Esther checked the taste one final time, indicated her approval and asked for Joyce to pass her the bowls. She ladled out the hot soup and handed it around. Dolores gave everyone a chunk of potato bread for dipping and everyone sat eating in hungry and appreciative silence. It would fill their bellies for the afternoon of digging ahead.

Connie had had enough of the photograph and the article to last her a lifetime. The newspaper had only come out yesterday but already Henry had talked about getting it framed and putting it on the wall somewhere in the vicarage. He was trying to patch things up after their recent arguments and she was touched by his efforts. Especially as she'd seen the way he'd grimaced when he'd read that she'd used her maiden name in the article.

"I just said it out of habit," she offered weakly. It was some relief that Henry didn't want to talk about it. With tight lips, he said it didn't matter, when it obviously did. Connie wanted to explain. But what could she say? She used her maiden name out of habit? Because it felt more comfortable? Because she was subconsciously wondering if one day she'd go back to it?

Instead he'd busied himself with celebrating his wife's heroism. But then he'd let slip something that perhaps made everything worse again –

"This will convince people you're not just out for yourself," he'd idly said.

Connie shot him a look as he instantly regretted his choice of words; wishing he could somehow suck them back in.

"Who's saying I'm out for myself?" Connie had stormed.

"Well ..."

Henry was forced to sheepishly admit that some of his older parishioners weren't very charitable in their views of his wife. They were suspicious of Connie's motives in marrying the young vicar. They spoke disapprovingly about her past, even though they knew nothing about it and were making most of the supposed "facts" up. Connie immediately knew the people he was talking about.

"It's those three old biddies from the WI, isn't it?" she thundered.

Henry sheepishly agreed. But before she went off on one and wrecked both their evenings, Henry stated that he always stuck up for Connie against any slight they threw.

"What slights? There are other slights? Oh, this gets worse," Connie said.

"You know how they are," Henry stammered. "All set in their ways."

"The way they carry on, you'd think I turned up to evensong in me knickers," Connie said. Despite her tough exterior, she was hurt by what people thought of her. She was especially hurt by what Henry thought of her. It was as if the naysayers didn't think she'd stick at her marriage were convinced she'd break Henry's heart. She was sure that some of them were keeping a tally of how many days they'd been married, waiting in anticipation for the break-up. And she knew he'd secretly like her to get on with it and behave as he thought a vicar's wife should.

The fact was that small-minded people would always judge her.

"If you turn up to evensong in your knickers, even I'd find that hard to defend." He smiled. "But I'd appreciate the view." He was making an effort again, even though he'd run a million miles if she actually did it.

Connie looked at the newspaper article on the table.

She thought of the finger-pointers reading it and judging – and she decided that she didn't want to see it anymore. Henry agreed to keep it out of sight but he'd put it in a scrapbook. He was proud of his wife. He knew they'd look back on it with pride in their later years. This comment gave Connie heart. He saw this as a long-term commitment. He was willing to work at it.

In Finch's kitchen, Connie mopped up the last of her soup with her bread. Joyce eyed Finch, who was draining the dregs of his bowl directly into his mouth. "Are you helping us this afternoon?"

Finch looked sheepish. He wiped his mouth with the back of his sleeve.

"Tea towel," Esther snapped.

But Finch ignored her. He shook his head at Joyce's question, tapped his nose and chuckled. "No, I've got a more pressing appointment, heh."

Joyce looked at Esther for an explanation. But Esther shrugged.

"Search me. I don't keep his diary. And I know it's best not to ask."

Connie glanced at the clock and mentally started to count down the hours until she could return to her home and her husband. Even though there was a war on, and even though she and Henry had frequent arguments, Connie felt the happiest she had ever felt.

As soon as the school bell rang, Margaret Sawyer burst out of school with an unusual keenness to get home. She barely had time to shout goodbyes to her friends as she legged it over the playground and out of the gate. Running past the village square, Margaret dodged a couple of GIs, who were making their way along the street. She ran past Mr Jeffries' sweet shop, a place where she usually liked to dawdle looking at the tasty confections in the window and imagining her perfect selection, and down the hill past a row of terraced houses. Then she was off over a field of long grass and down a ravine by a small stream, after several miles coming to a small thatched cottage amid a cluster of fields like a single flower sewn onto an eiderdown. This was home. Jessop's

Cottage, although Margaret wished she was back at her proper home in the East End of London. But she knew she couldn't go back. Her real mum was dead.

The cottage was a place remote enough from the village that no one came here. And that was how Michael and Vera Sawyer liked it. He would often rail against the conspiracies that he saw in every shadow; the untrustworthiness of human behaviour. Margaret let these rants pass over her head, failing to understand how he could get so riled over things that were probably the inventions of his mind. No one was out to get them. No one wanted to take their lives here away from them. And while Michael stayed in the cottage or worked the garden, Vera would make necessary trips to Helmstead but try not to get drawn into conversations with anybody. They lived like ghosts and Margaret supposed that was just the way they liked things: the three of them, insular and alone.

She flung open the door and heard Vera's voice call out.

"Margaret? Is that you?" She was clearly surprised that the girl was back so soon. Margaret said hello and put her school bag and coat neatly on a hook in the cupboard under the stairs. The place. She glimpsed the small wooden step that she would sit on for hours on end. Luckily, on this occasion, she closed the door on that sad and lonely part of her world. Maybe she'd be sent there later, but not yet.

The stern-looking woman from the train crash came through to the living room, wiping her hands on her apron. Vera looked the young girl up and down, suspicion in her eyes. Why had she rushed back?

"They let us out early," Margaret lied, trying to control her panting from the exertion of running all the way.

Vera seemed to accept this statement.

"Wash your hands, then there's some darning to do." Vera returned to the kitchen. With her out the way, Margaret had a scant few minutes to do what she intended to do when she'd left school so quickly. She looked at the small collection of letters on the sideboard. Underneath was a copy of *The Helmstead Herald*, unread and still folded neatly. Margaret tucked it under her jumper and ran to her room. Once inside, she quietly closed the door, hoping Vera wouldn't hear her latch and realise where she was. She pulled the newspaper from under her jumper and opened it out. Skimming through to page five, she found the thing she was looking for. Connie Carter in the photograph. Margaret pulled out the sheet of newspaper. She knew not to tear it as it would leave a single page on the other side of the middle of the newspaper, so she removed all four pages. She closed up the edited edition; worried that it felt thin in her hands. She had no choice but to trust that Michael wouldn't notice that four pages were missing when he read it. She tucked it back under her jumper and quickly folded up the excised pages and put them safely under her bed. But as Margaret turned to go back down to the living room, she realised Vera Sawyer was standing in the doorway.

"What are you up to?" Vera could read the guilt on the young girl's face.

"I just wanted to change," Margaret stammered.

Vera shook her head. "I'm not doing more washing. You wear your uniform for now. Come on." She pulled Margaret by the hand, downstairs to the living room. All the while, Margaret hoped that *The Helmstead Herald* wouldn't fall from her jumper. Luckily she made it to the dining table, where seven pairs of holed socks were waiting for her. Vera scowled and went to the kitchen demanding that the darning was finished by teatime. Margaret turned silently in her chair, placed the newspaper back where she had found it, and went to work on the socks. Phew, she'd done it.

Later, after tea, Margaret washed up the plates with one eye on the living room, where Michael sat reading the paper. He was dressed in his shirt and tie – an outfit in which he would inexplicably work in the garden. Standards had to be maintained, as he often said. Margaret hadn't thought much about it, but occasionally she would wonder how Michael made any money. She knew he sold, or rather Vera sold, vegetables grown on his large plot. It didn't seem to make much money, but enough for the family to get by. For now, Margaret was more concerned with *The Helmstead Herald*. Would Michael feel it was thin and realise a spread was missing? Or would he give the paper a cursory glance and then go back to his shed?

Finally, he closed the newspaper.

"Not much in it," he sighed, reaching for his tobacco.

"Nothing much happens around here." Vera shrugged as she knitted a brown scarf by the fire. "We should be grateful really."

"Surprising they didn't report on the train crash," Michael commented.

"They did," Vera said.

Margaret's blood ran cold. Had Vera already read the paper? Surely not – as she'd have kicked up a storm if she'd seen the picture.

"They did a front page on it last week. There was a picture of the train wreck and everything." She wanted to move on to another subject, wary that Michael would blow up again about them taking the train and risking their lives.

Michael knew about the front-page story, but just wondered why they hadn't done more on it, that's all. Like most people, he knew that they usually follow things up with a report centring on the human-interest stories around the main event. It was a good opportunity for the local rag to fill its pages with stories that might actually interest people for once.

"Maybe they will when they find out who did it," Vera said, missing a stitch.

"Who knows if they can ever catch these people." Michael rose from his chair.

Margaret dried the last of the plates and brought them through to the Welsh dresser. Carefully she opened the door and placed the china inside, aware that Vera would always watch her like a hawk to check she didn't chip anything. Relieved that all the plates were in place, undamaged, she asked if they needed anything else doing.

Vera shook her head. Margaret could go to her room and read her books if she liked. The young girl went off. She liked it when she was in her room with her own thoughts. Upstairs, Margaret opened her copy of *Black Beauty* by Anna Sewell and read a few pages. She listened as Michael moved to the front door and went outside to the shed.

With Michael gone, Margaret knew that Vera would come up to check on her soon, so she ensured that she was reading studiously when she entered. Vera asked if she wanted a glass of milk. Margaret declined politely. Vera left and as Margaret heard her footfalls retreating, she pulled out the pages of *The Helmstead Herald* from under her bed. She opened them up. A chance to study them at last. Margaret had heard from an excitable school friend that her picture was in the newspaper and now she could see it for herself.

There was the picture of Connie Carter with Margaret. The story was a report on what had happened and what Connie had said to the reporter. Nothing that Margaret had said was in the piece. Nothing about where she lived. Margaret was relieved. She'd had a horror that in a daze of shock she might have said that Vera wasn't her mother or something. But she still knew that if Vera even saw the photograph she would go mad. Any publicity would be hated by this private couple.

Margaret knew that she had to put it away. But she was mesmerised. She looked at the beautiful face of Connie Carter and thought about her kindness. The shared cheese, the offer of tea, the repeated enquiries about how she was. Connie had tried to find out if she was okay, even before the train crash. Connie Carter was even willing to stand up to Vera to ask that awkward question. Margaret's heart swelled with warmth and pride at the heroine on the page. She liked Connie Carter. She wished she was her mum.

Frederick Finch couldn't resist a good-natured chuckle at the sight before him. Henry Jameson dressed in a large pair of

Wellington boots that were far too big for him, looking like deep-sea diving shoes. He was also wearing an oversized gilet, which sat on top of his clergy uniform: dog collar still visible for added comic effect. And on his head was a tweed flat cap.

"Do you not have a mirror in your house, Reverend?" Finch joked. This was Finch's pressing appointment, the reason he couldn't help the girls in the fields. He was teaching Henry the fine art of hunting.

"If we could just get on, Mr Finch," Henry replied. "I've got a christening in an hour and a half." He didn't see what was so funny in his appearance and he felt that Finch's laughter was further emasculating him after Connie's mockery. He just wanted to catch a rabbit and prove Connie wrong. That would show her once and for all.

"Now, where are the guns?" Henry asked, keen to move things along.

"Guns? You don't need a gun to catch a rabbit."

"Don't you?"

"Well, you could, but it wouldn't leave much of it for your pot," Finch explained. "No, we use traps for those little fellas. Here's your weapon."

And Finch delved into the pocket of his ample cardigan and produced a ball of twine. He placed it in the soft hands of Henry Jameson.

"String?" Henry asked in confusion.

Finch tapped his nose in a you'll-see kind of way. Then he rubbed the back of his neck – mild concern filtering into his chubby features.

"You might have to delay that christening," he said. "Can't

see how we're going to do all this in an hour and a half. I bet it'll take that long for you to learn the knot."

"This is the first lesson. That's all," Henry said, regaining his enthusiasm. "As long as I can catch my own rabbit, eventually, and prove Connie wrong, I don't care how long it takes."

Finch exhaled. "All right. First thing is to tie a slip knot on the end of that twine."

"A slip knot?" Henry hesitated.

"Let me show you," Finch said, taking the ball of twine. This was going to take a long time.

A big blue bottle flitted annoyingly around Connie's nose. She batted it away with a muddy hand. Connie and Joyce were digging manure. It was one of their least-favourite jobs – but at least they were back on Pasture Farm. Their secondment had come to an abrupt end after the train crash. The track needed repairs and it would take over a week to fix them. And without the track, there was no way to get to Brinford Farm, other than in Finch's tractor and trailer. But he didn't have sufficient petrol rations to take the girls every day and bring them back. So the arrangement was curtailed. The girls were back on the farm they loved. It was just a shame that a tragedy had had to occur for that to happen.

Connie eyed Dolores O'Malley with annoyance. The older woman was resting on the handle of her shovel. Her third break in ten minutes. If she stopped any more often she'd start to develop roots.

"Come on, Lore, pull your weight," Connie said.

"I'm finding it's hurting my back," Dolores admitted.

"You need to get your shoulder behind it," Joyce offered. "Then it won't hurt your back. Lift from the knees."

"Really? How do you know all that?"

"Painful experience," Connie replied. "We've shovelled more sh—"

"She's right," Joyce chipped in.

Dolores reluctantly put her shovel back into use, cutting through the rich manure and transferring a load to the cart nearby. She was a prickly woman, hard to engage in conversation and quite shut off from opening herself and her feelings up. It wasn't that she judged the other women, just that she had no real desire to interact with them. This seemed odd. A strange way in which to make the time fly by at Pasture Farm. Joyce thought that this would make her war a lonely experience, so she and Connie had taken bets about who could get Dolores to open up the most. They'd both repeatedly tried different gambits, from Connie trying to find out her favourite dessert to Joyce talking about her husband in the hope that Dolores would share something of her private life. As it was they didn't know what her favourite dessert was ("I don't mind really") and they didn't know whether she was married or not ("It's nice that your John has left the RAF and is out of danger"). She was a very private person. The facts they did know were scant: Dolores had arrived on Pasture Farm a month ago from Reigate in Surrey (although she was from Dublin originally). Before being conscripted as a Land Girl she'd been working at the American airbase at Redhill as a nurse. And it was her experience as a nurse that was why she ended up at Helmstead as the Land Girls often had to take shifts at the military hospital at Hoxley Manor on the estate. Dolores's experience meant that she was given the position of ward sister when she did a shift there. It also meant that Connie and Joyce would have to take orders from her at Hoxley Manor: something that Connie, in particular, resented as Dolores would become very judgemental. She knew best when it came to nursing and she wasn't afraid to show it.

As they dug the manure, Connie winked at Joyce. To pass the time, she was going to try another gambit to find out more about Dolores.

"What's your favourite colour, Joyce?" Connie asked.

Joyce saw where this was going and replied, "Yellow is nice."

"Dolores?" Connie asked. Surely this couldn't fail? Something as innocuous as a colour. But it wasn't to be.

"I don't know really. They're all nice."

"But you must have a favourite."

"Not really. I haven't thought about it."

"Well what colour's your bedroom back home, then?"

Joyce could hardly contain her smile at how Connie had managed to get the conversation onto something quite personal from such unpromising beginnings. But maybe Dolores noticed the smile, because she clammed up even more than usual, portcullis defences coming down.

"What a strange question," Dolores muttered, continuing with her digging. "Why are there so many roots down here?"

Connie looked at Joyce and the two women shared a small shrug. Good try, Connie, but that one didn't work either.

"That's another penny you owe me," Joyce whispered, returning to work.

"I'm going to be broke at this rate," Connie grumbled.

Henry checked his watch. He had fifteen minutes before he was due in church for the christening. He calculated he could stay here for another five minutes before he had to rush back to the vicarage to prepare everything. It was annoying that Connie wasn't at the vicarage to put things in order. But he knew she had her duties as a Land Girl. However, there was a nagging feeling that even if that work didn't exist, would she be there helping him? He put the thought out of his head and stared at the trap.

He had just five more minutes to catch a rabbit. It had taken him ages to tie the knot. As fumbled attempt built on fumbled attempt, Finch had waited with glee for the vicar to let loose with a swear word. But like Connie and Joyce waiting for Dolores to say something personal, he'd been disappointed. Henry had kept his cool and eventually managed to tie it.

Now, he was lying in some heather in a wooded area of the farm. Finch was beside him. Henry was holding one end of the twine; the other was fashioned into a loop twenty feet away near a tree. Henry was waiting for a rabbit to hop over and put its foot in the loop. Then he'd pull his end, closing the loop and trapping the rabbit.

"Isn't there an easier way?" Henry whispered.

"All good things take time," Finch offered, sagely.

"You didn't think that when you made that carrot whisky. It was horrible," Henry retorted.

"I had overwhelming supply demands so I had to rush that. This is different. Nature has its own pace."

"But we haven't seen a single rabbit."

"Maybe it's because you keep talking, Reverend."

"I don't keep talking."

"Well, what are you doing now, then, eh?" Finch chuckled.

Henry shook his head. He was cold and the front of his body felt decidedly damp from lying in the heather for so long. He knew he wasn't going to catch a rabbit today.

That evening, Connie walked back to the vicarage. As usual, her muscles were aching and she had blisters on her hands. She was looking forward to supper with Henry and an early night. And hoping that they could just have a nice time. But then she remembered that Henry would be late back. He was visiting an elderly French man who lived in a cottage on the edges of the Gorley Woods. Dr Beauchamp was dying and liked Henry to visit him to give him strength and comfort during his final days. And the conscientious young vicar felt obliged, even happy, to do his duty. Connie knew that Dr Beauchamp liked to talk, at as much length as his breathing problems would allow, about how his country was now occupied by the Germans and about how proud he was of his own son, who was fighting for the resistance there. So Henry wouldn't be back until late.

Connie resigned herself to the mixed emotions of facing an evening alone. There would be no more disagreements or friction, but she'd miss him. As she approached the porch, she was surprised to find a visitor waiting on the doorstep of the vicarage. It was Roger Curran, the reporter from *The Helmstead Herald*. He tipped the small trilby on his head at her. Connie wasn't sure if it really was a small hat or that it just looked small on his large head. He smiled warmly at her.

"Mrs Jameson! I have the most splendid news."

"Oh yeah? What's that, then?"

"Do you know? I've often heard that vicar's wives make the very best tea."

"I wouldn't bank on it," Connie said under her breath. But with nothing more pressing to do, she invited the journalist inside, slopped water into the kettle and put it on the stove.

The two of them were soon sitting around the dining table and Roger Curran's podgy fingers were taking a second biscuit from the plate Connie had provided. He sipped at his tea and winced slightly. Connie knew it wasn't one of her best efforts, but she found making tea really unaccountably tricky. She had made Roger Curran a 'milky horror' (as she liked to call it), with too much milk and too little tea. She guessed that he might revise his patter about vicar's wives making the best tea from now on as he sipped it with a grimace.

"I'll come straight to the point, Mrs Jameson," he said, wiping a crumb from his lips. "It seems my little story has been picked up by one of the national newspapers."

Connie looked surprised. She wasn't sure whether she felt happy about that. "Well, can't you stop them?"

Roger smiled. "Oh no, it's a good thing. It means I get credit for a story that many more people will read. And that means a lot more people will know about your heroism. And I hope I'm not talking out of turn when I say that although the story is just the sort of inspiring thing that Blitz-torn London needs to read, its success is also due to how fine you look in the photograph, Mrs Jameson."

Connie felt uneasy at the attention. Henry wouldn't be happy about her being seen as some sort of poster girl for plucky Britain. The wolf-whistles outside the pub were enough to get Henry's back up, without any added spotlight. She put it out of her mind and asked about the explosion. Had the police found out who was responsible yet?

Roger shook his head, spraying crumbs like a Labrador shaking itself from a bath. "They're not sure. But the remains of the device were the same as one used to blow up a post-office truck a month ago. And the station guard at Brinford recalled a tall man taking the train, the same one you got, every day for the seven days before the crash. He wasn't on it on that fateful day, but people are saying that his other journeys were for reconnaissance. Check the timings and that."

It chilled Connie that a seemingly ordinary commuter, a man who would go unnoticed in the daily bustle, could have been there timing the journey to the precise second.

After another biscuit, Roger Curran tipped his small hat a second time and left the vicarage (his tea largely untouched). The story would be in a national newspaper! Connie shrugged. She hoped it would still be tomorrow's fish-and-chip paper and then it would all be forgotten about. But she would be wrong. It was a story that would change her life.

Margaret Sawyer froze in fear as she approached her house. Roger Curran, the reporter from *The Helmstead Herald* was standing outside the front door. He'd come to the house. No one ever came to the house!

He rapped on the knocker, brushed the biscuit crumbs from his tank top and cleared his throat. He glanced nonchalantly at the neat front garden, decorative rows of small box bushes trimmed into squares alternating with rhododendron bushes that were showing their last flowering for the season. The whole design was so regimented that Roger Curran assumed a soldier must live here.

Margaret ducked down behind a wall, peering over the top to see if Vera or Michael would answer. She prayed that neither of them were inside the house. Vera might be out selling vegetables and Michael was probably in one of the outbuildings, tending to his seedlings. And even if Michael was at home, he rarely answered the door, so she thought she might be safe on that score.

After what seemed like an age, Roger Curran turned on his heel. He glanced up at the house one last time and made his way down the path. He passed the low wall where Margaret was hiding, but didn't see her. She was relieved. So much for eagle-eyed journalists!

As she watched the rotund figure amble away down the lane, Margaret hoped with all her heart that he wouldn't return and that would be an end to it.

Chapter 5

Two days earlier.

The rain lashed down, turning the London pavements into glistening onyx walkways in the dying light of early evening. Vince Halliday shivered against the cold and pulled the collar up on his great coat. The coat used to belong to a GI, but Vince had won it in a game of poker. Or, to be strictly accurate a rigged game of poker. Still, who was complaining? Vince had a new coat out of it and the GI had learnt a lesson in not being gullible.

Vince was a powerfully built man in his early thirties with icy-blue eyes, slicked-back hair and an air of menace about him. Braces held his trousers high on a frame that had little definition. Vince's body was wide and he didn't taper at any point. He just went straight up and down, like a wide, imposing fence post. He enjoyed playing on his intimidating presence, liking the discomfort that other people could feel when near him. Vince's keen eyes darted from side to side as he crossed the Fulham Road, weaving around a pony and trap and then a car to make it to the other side. He made his way across to an alleyway, which was illuminated by the light of a single window from a block of flats. Vince squinted as his eyes adjusted to the gloom, wary of being jumped. Fulham was a rough area.

At the end of the alley, in a small, rain-lashed courtyard, was a butcher's van. As Vince approached, two heavy-looking men, pin-stripe suits and trilby hats denoting their status as wide boys, quickly appeared from the van. The one with the pencil moustache indicated for Vince to follow them. Vince's fingers gripped the cosh in his pocket. He might need it. As was always the case in Vince's life, when he met someone, he'd weigh them up for their potential threat value. Could he win against them in a fight? Vince decided that he could take these two apart if he had to. But he hoped it wouldn't come to that.

"You got it?" Moustache Man said as they swept under an awning and walked into a warehouse.

"Does it look like I've got it?" Vince replied, with contempt.

Moustache Man threw a look at his partner, a man with a large hooked nose and heavy eye brows. An ex-boxer, thought Vince. He thought he could still take him apart in a fight. Moustache Man was also assessing the situation. Was he losing face by being talked to in this way? Should he do something? But before he could decide on a course of action, an older voice bellowed from the recesses of the damp warehouse.

"Vince! I see you brought the crappy weather with you!"

A rotund man in a light-grey pinstripe suit appeared from the gloom and shook Vince warmly by the hand. Vince clocked that he was wearing a signet ring on each finger. It was his trademark: jewellery that could double as a knuckle duster. This was Amos Ackley – a comical-looking figure with a shiny bald head. But Vince didn't underestimate the appearance of this man and was somewhat relieved when he got his hand back in one piece from the crushing hand shake. A handshake that was designed to intimidate. Amos Ackley was an amusingly named, but vicious, gangster and black market trader, a man who had run most of Kensington, Fulham and Putney since 1937. As the authorities concentrated their efforts on the immediate effects of the war, the air raids, the destruction, the looting, Amos had seen his shady little empire expand, filling the darkness left by lawlessness. Now he liked to think of himself as Mr Black Market, a man who could get you anything you needed even without a ration book. He had the police in his pocket on the understanding that Amos wouldn't commit too many open atrocities on the streets of South London. But that was fine, the only people who usually felt his wrath were gangsters further down the food chain or those civilians, as he called them, who dared to resist his attempts at extortion and blackmail.

"Bit of rain is good for you," Vince said, smiling.

Moustache Man and Eyebrows circled round to stand either side of Amos Ackley. Vince noticed that both the heavies had a hand in their pockets. It didn't matter if they didn't actually have weapons in there because, like the crushing handshake before it, he knew this was being done to intimidate him. To show him who was boss.

"Now then, I'm looking forward to my Sunday lunch, Vince," Amos smiled.

"The sirloin is out of this world," Vince replied. "Succulent."

Amos laughed. "Hark at you, the flaming expert."

"I've had too much bad meat in my time to not know the difference, Mr Ackerly," Vince smiled.

"And you've lifted a lorry full of this stuff?"

Vince knew he didn't have to go into specifics about where it had come from. Amos wasn't interested in provenance. "It was supposed to be filling a load of yank stomachs, but their supply chain got broken, didn't it? I just need the three hundred and it's yours, van included." He knew three hundred pounds was a lot of money, but then he was selling a huge amount of premier quality sirloin steak. And in a country where meat was rationed, the sales potential of that meat was phenomenal.

Amos cracked his knuckles. A dark smile flickered over his face. Vince felt uneasy. Had he misremembered how much they'd agreed on? Or was Amos going to try to short-change him?

Or, the worst scenario of all, did Amos know what Vince was up to?

That morning, Vince Halliday had opened his eyes without getting a wink of sleep. He'd been too nervous. This was the big one. It would be a day filled with danger but, if it went well, it would end in incredible rewards. Three hundred pounds would set him up. It would allow him to get out of the rat hole where he lived and start again somewhere else. He stared at the yellowing ceiling paint and the plaster rose around the light. All being well, this would be the last time he woke up in this run-down tenement.

There was a soft tap on the door. Vince swung his thick legs off the bed and pulled up his trousers, hooking the braces over his shoulders. He opened the door a fraction, saw the friendly face of a wide-eyed girl with a battered cloche hat, and let her in.

It was Glory. Her real name was Gloria Wayland, but Vince liked calling her Glory. Although she always wore her desperately unfashionable cloche hat, Vince had never bothered to ask why. He guessed it had some sentimental value; but delving into that area had little interest for him. She was seventeen, tall and thin. Gangly from being undernourished from all her years in a children's home in Bow. When she left at the age of sixteen, she joined the Women's Auxiliary Army and learnt to drive an ambulance. But one night, a road near Shockley Aerodrome had been bombed and Glory crashed her ambulance into a ravine. With trauma from the accident, Glory's army career was cut short and she found herself on Civvy Street. It was a harsh place to be, and soon Glory was penniless and living on the road. That's when Vince had befriended her. There was no romance or sex involved, just the simple and unedifying business arrangement which Vince had found had worked with girls so well in the past. He would befriend a woman who needed help and then turn her to a life of crime. Many of Vince's scams would require a female face: someone to lure and distract his targets. This was particularly true of the wedding-ring scam. In this caper, Vince would encourage the girl to flirt with a rich married man (the target) in a bar or restaurant. Then the girl would take the man to a rented room, with the prospect of having sex.

But once there, Vince would threaten the man with violence unless the man handed over his wedding ring. Then with the wedding ring in his possession, Vince could extort money by blackmail from the rich man, threatening to give the ring to the man's wife and to explain how he'd come by it.

Glory was fairly good at the wedding-ring scam and they'd worked it successfully four times together. But just as often, she failed, due to her awkwardness and lack of confidence, to lure the man to the room. She knew that Vince had her on borrowed time. She had to prove her worth to him soon or she'd be replaced and out on her ear.

"Is it too early?" Glory asked.

Vince shook his head. "Haven't slept a wink anyway."

"Me neither," Glory said nervously.

Vince pulled a suit jacket over his shirt. The fabric was shiny and old. He turned up the collar around his neck.

"I was thinking," Glory said as she sat on the end of the bed. Vince looked at her sad and fragile face. "I was thinking that maybe we should just tick along as we are."

Vince went to interject, but Glory wasn't finished.

"I mean we're making money each month from the wedding rings and everything." She knew she was on thin ice; knowing that Vince wasn't happy with her success rate.

"Not enough, though." Vince bent down so his face was level with the young girl's.

"Trouble is, it's a lot of work keeping them in line," he said. "Each time I go to collect a payment, I think that this will be the time they jump me or they'll have a mob of mates waiting or the police."

"But this is too dangerous…" Glory pleaded.

"By tonight, we'll be out of here. Three hundred pounds, Glory." He let the words sink in. "Think what we could do with that money."

Glory had thought about it. A lot. With her share, she wanted to move to the country and put some money down on a cottage somewhere. She'd have ducks in the garden and then she'd find a husband and they'd live in the lovely cottage together. That was her plan. Each time she said it, Vince found it ridiculous, but he kept the thought to himself.

Vince planned to move up north and start a club. It'd be a club with roulette wheels and dancing girls. He'd make a fortune from the GIs and the business men up there. That was his plan.

Glory still looked scared and uncertain.

In truth, Vince Halliday was just as scared and uncertain. This wasn't a business deal. Vince wasn't really selling meat for money. That's because he didn't have the meat. Well, he had some, but not three hundred pounds worth. This was a scam. And if this scam, the big one, went wrong then he probably wouldn't live to tell the tale. But if it went right, then all his Christmases would come at once.

He had to brave-face it for the young girl's sake. Had to gee her up and get her on side.

"After tonight, we don't have to grub around no more," Vince said. "After tonight, we can relax and live all our dreams, yeah?"

Glory looked at him, searching for the truth in his eyes. Did he believe what he was saying? Wasn't he scared? After a long moment, she decided he was being honest and that he really believed it. She didn't realise he was lying.

"Right, that's the spirit, girl," Vince said, slipping on his brogues. "Let's go and get a cup of tea ..."

In the warehouse, a long, tense moment passed. Vince was certain that his heart was beating so loudly that everyone could hear it – like a klaxon warning of his guilt. Amos cracked a smile at last and revealed his hand.

"I ain't paying the full three hundred," he said, letting the words sink in without following them up. Vince gave a that's-your-prerogative kind of smile, but inside he was fuming and he wanted answers and explanations. Who did this jumped-up idiot think he was, welching on the deal?

"Really?" Vince said, as neutrally as he could manage.

Moustache Man sneered at him. Vince turned away from the underling with contempt.

"I'll pay two hundred."

"But Mr Ackley—"

"Don't Mr Ackley me, son. Three hundred's a heck of a lot of money to find. Come to think of it, two hundred is too. It'll wipe me out until I can sell on the meat," Amos Ackley explained. "But the way I see it, you've got a van full of prime steak that's going off by the second. So it's a buyer's market."

Vince looked the rotund figure in the eye. The moment hung in the air. Finally, he agreed. Okay, then.

Amos grinned and laughed. His signet-ring-adorned hand came thrusting out and crushed Vince's hand in a shake to seal the deal.

"Deliver it here in an hour," Amos said.

Vince's throat felt dry. Here was the moment of truth. The moment at which he had to pull the con.

"It's being driven to the common, at Barnes," Vince said.

"But I want it here," Amos spat.

"It's too risky bringing it here. The old bill know about this place, don't they?" Vince said. "The common is neutral. We've never used it before."

Amos Ackley looked at his colleagues. Moustache Man shrugged. It didn't seem to make much difference, did it? It wasn't that far to go.

"Who's driving it?" Amos asked.

"Glory," Vince replied. "That girl I work the rings with."

Amos thought she was a good kid. He liked her. He started to walk away. "My men will meet you there in an hour and they'll transfer the meat into this van. And then I'll give you the money."

"No," Vince said, the word coming out a little too abruptly. Amos Ackley stopped in his tracks at this unexpected and potentially confrontational utterance.

"What?"

"I need a deposit." Vince smiled.

"How much?"

"Half," Vince said, eyeing Amos without breaking his gaze. A shark-like grin spread on Amos' face.

"Get lost."

"Come on, you're already stiffing me on this deal. I need something," Vince replied. His throat was hoarse and his chest felt like it would explode with his pumping heart.

He knew that Amos was greedy. He knew that the gangster could make five hundred pounds selling all that sirloin. Slowly Amos's hand went to his pocket. He pulled out a wad of bank notes. He counted out one hundred pounds and held it out in his jewel-encrusted paw.

"You'd better be there, otherwise I'll turn London upside down," Amos growled.

Vince reassured Amos that he would be: he wanted the rest of the money, after all. He tucked the notes into the inside pocket of his cheap jacket and said thanks, before turning on his heels and walking away. It was the longest walk of Vince's life: with each step he was fearful that Amos would change his mind or he'd rumble the con and Moustache Man would whack him on the back of the head.

But Vince made it out of the warehouse and found himself in the cool rain of the alley. He glanced up as he walked so the water could cool his hot, tired eyes. And then he strode away as quickly as he could. He had half the money. Now to con the rest.

One hour later, Glory was waiting in an ambulance on Barnes Common. She'd killed the lights and was listening for any sound in the semi-darkness. The moon provided some illumination but she couldn't see much. Shadows were all around and soon Glory imagined danger in every one of them. Any sound startled her, from the cawing of a crow somewhere in the trees to the whistle of a man seeking his dog. Her hands were clammy so she rubbed them dry on her dress. Swallowing hard, she started to hum a tune – 'Yankee Doodle Dandy'

– to pass the time and to distract herself from the horror stories playing out in her mind.

She was wearing her best jacket and her white blouse. As always, the cloche hat sat incongruously on her head.

Suddenly, there was a tap on the window. Glory jumped out of her skin. But it was only Vince. He opened the door and whispered to her in an urgent voice, worried that someone might be in the dark listening.

He told her that he'd got one hundred pounds in his pocket and that Amos was on his way to complete the deal. Glory was nervous. She pleaded that they should quit while they were ahead. Take the hundred and scarper. It was a lot of money and they could get a long way away with it.

"Gotta keep your nerve," Vince said. "In twenty minutes, we can double it. And then we'll be gone. Promise."

Glory looked unsure, scared. At this moment, the already young-looking seventeen-year-old looked about twelve – a nervous and petrified child with a ridiculous hat. Vince patted the back of her hand where her fingers were clenched tightly to the steering wheel.

"Think of your cottage," Vince pleaded, playing her. "Hold your nerve, yeah?"

Glory hoped he was right. She wished she could be anywhere else. It was so easy how this had happened – so easy how trouble could find you if you made the wrong decision; took a path of least resistance because that's what the charming man in your life told you was best.

Vince went to the back of the ambulance and unlatched the back doors. The inside had been modified and instead of a bed and hospital supplies, the back was full of wooden crates. Vince moved the topmost crate nearer and opened the wooden lid. Inside were twenty greaseproof packages nestled in straw. Vince opened a greaseproof pack and looked at the succulent red steak within. Glistening in the moonlight, it looked wet with blood. Satisfied, he wrapped it up and put it back in the box.

The scam would work because of the fifty or so wooden crates; this was the only one that contained any steak. The other identical boxes were weighted with straw and wood to make them feel as if they contained steak as well. When Amos got here, it was crucial that he opened and inspected this one box. If he picked any other, then he would immediately realise that Vince was trying to con him. And the consequences would be severe. It wouldn't only be the steak that was covered in blood.

Glory had asked him, when she was pacing around his bedsit, wearing a furrow in the already threadbare carpet, how he would ensure that Amos Ackley opened the right box. How could he do that when there was only a one in fifty chance? Vince had smiled a reassuring grin. "Magic," he'd said. And with that he produced – with a magician-like flourish – a hair grip from behind his hand. As if on cue, a strand of Glory's hair fell down over her face. She was impressed with the trick, but it didn't relieve her of the knot of cold fear in her stomach. It was all very well making your friend laugh in the comfort of your own room, but a different matter when you so much relied on getting it right, in the middle of a common in the dead of night.

So how would Vince ensure that Amos would open the box?

With ten minutes to go, Vince wished Glory luck. He told her that if anything went wrong she should run for it and save herself. There would be no point in them both being killed. Glory hoped it wouldn't come to that. She shook Vince's hand. He looked at her young and innocent face and smiled. Did he feel a pang of guilt for involving her in this crazy scam? "See you, Glory."

"See you, Vince," she said.

Vince kissed her on the cheek.

And then Glory walked off into the night.

Now Vince had been right. The plan would involve magic, or rather the magician's trick of misdirecting an audience. You want a person to pick a certain card? You misdirect them. You want a person to lift a particular cup where you haven't hidden the bean? You misdirect them. Vince knew that Amos would want to see the back of the ambulance. Naturally, he would want to inspect the merchandise he was buying. The thing was, instead of a van full of meat, Vince had one box which contained meat. When Amos came to inspect the merchandise, he wouldn't be very impressed if Vince chose the box, opened it and showed him the contents. He'd smell a rat. No, so the trick would be to make Amos think he had free rein in his choice of box and then to switch the chosen box for the only one that contained any meat. But how?

Misdirection.

That's where the fact that all the boxes looked identical

came into play. Vince would ask Amos if he wanted to see the stock. Amos would pick a box at random. Vince would get the selected box from the van. On the outside it would look like the box that actually contained the meat and it would even weigh the same, thanks to the weight of wood inside it. But before they could open it, a carefully timed distraction would occur.

Misdirection.

Identical boxes.

Glory, hiding in the dark, would provide this distraction by blowing a policeman's whistle. She had to do it at the perfect time – when Vince had removed the box selected by Amos from the ambulance, but before Amos opened it. During this distraction, Vince would switch the boxes, for the one underneath the ambulance. The one that contained the meat. And then Amos would open the staged box, see the meat and be satisfied. Then he'd hand over the other one hundred pounds.

That was the plan.

Simple.

Glory's house in the country and Vince's life as a club owner depended on it.

At five minutes ahead of schedule, Amos Ackley appeared behind the van. Moustache Man, Eyebrows and two other men were with him. The men were jittery, moving their feet around in nervous agitation. In the distance, Vince could see the lights of the butcher's van parked up, engine running, the exhaust pushing out white smoke in soft clouds over the dewy grass. Vince couldn't be certain if more men were in the van. Could there be more thugs inside? It was a risk. There might be more people watching who might not take their eyes off him when the police whistle went off. Misdirection was all well and good, but you had to control where people were looking. Vince suddenly felt like running away.

"In here, is it?" Amos had an air of suspicion; the brusqueness of a man who wanted to get this over with. Vince had to tell himself that men like Amos always had an air of suspicion. It didn't mean they actually suspected anything was wrong, just that they were open to the idea that it might be. That's how they operated. Suspicion at all times. Trust no one.

"Yeah. It's all there," Vince said, indicating with as much nonchalance as he could muster, for Amos to take a look.

Amos stepped back and Moustache Man opened the doors of the ambulance.

Row upon row of wooden boxes stood in front of them. Each crate was marked with a stencil saying "Property of US Military".

Amos smiled. "Looks good. Let's see inside."

"Yeah. Choose whichever one you like," Vince said, knowing that the only box he wanted them to look inside was the one hidden underneath the tail gate of the ambulance.

"One?" Amos laughed. "For two hundred quid, I might open them all."

The others laughed. Vince felt his throat closing up. He knew he had to laugh as well and somehow he heard a small nervous giggle emerge from his lips. He hadn't thought about this possibility. Why hadn't he?

"Eeny meeny miney mo – that one," Amos said, pointing a stubby, ringed finger to a crate two down from the top.

Moustache Man obediently started to remove the crates above it. Vince watched as they were placed on the ground. He still needed to get to the full crate and he was hoping, with all his soul, that Moustache Man wouldn't block his access with the stack he was building.

Vince felt the plan slipping away from him.

Finally, Moustache Man reached the chosen crate and put it on the ground.

With no fanfare, Amos indicated for him to open it.

Moustache Man removed a small crowbar from his pocket and pushed the end under the wooden lid. But as he reached down, Vince leaned against the door of the van. It was the signal for Glory to cause the distraction.

Moustache Man started to prise the wooden lid off the crate, his black two-tone shoe pressed on top to get some leverage with his jemmy. In the deathless quiet, Vince heard the creak of the leather in his shoe as he strained.

Vince started to bite his lip. Come on, Glory.

The plan was falling apart.

Suddenly, a police whistle sounded in the night. Peep!

"Bloody hell," Amos snapped. "Sort that out." One of his men ran forward to the sound of the noise – while Amos and Eyebrows peered out into the gloom to see if they could spot how many coppers were out there. They didn't seem overly alarmed.

They didn't seem overly – misdirected.

Peep! Peep! Peep!

But to Vince's horror, Moustache Man stood still and didn't move. Moustache Man waited, with his foot still on the partially opened crate.

There was no way that Vince could do the switch!

The plan wasn't going to work!

He glanced into the distance, where the dispatched gangster was running to the trees. He was yelling, "Hey, you there!" He was going to catch Glory – the girl to whom Vince had promised everything would be all right. The girl he'd promised could get her dream cottage.

Vince knew that the situation was going badly wrong. There was only one thing for it. There had to be a plan B. Vince had to go on the attack. He had to pull the focus back from Glory and onto himself, if either of them had a hope in hell of escaping.

Out of the corner of his eye, he could see Glory being dragged out of the trees by the gangster. She stumbled into the grass and was roughly yanked back up on her feet. Amos was shouting that he couldn't understand why a girl was blowing a police whistle. And then he recognised her and everything fell into place.

"Gloria," he said, anger rising in his voice.

Vince had to act fast. He grabbed the crowbar out of Moustache Man's hand and brought it up hard under the man's chin. The gangster slumped unconscious across the box. Vince turned menacingly to Amos, waving the crowbar at him.

"Give me the money. And you let us go," Vince shouted.

The other gangster slowed, taking in the developments as

he returned, dragging Glory from the trees. He waited for his boss to tell him what to do. On the ground, a disorientated Moustache Man was nursing a broken jaw.

"I've got your girl," Amos growled.

Glory looked more wide-eyed than ever. Her cloche hat was askew on her head. Vince felt a pang of guilt. She shouldn't be mixed up in all this. But it was her who apologised. "Sorry, Vince," she said in a small, wavering voice. That nearly tipped Vince over the edge. He'd failed her and now they were both going to die.

"They were going wrong anyway," Vince said, offering a small smile, before turning his attention back to Amos Ackley.

"The money and you let us go."

"What if I get my man to kill Glory?"

"Then I'll kill you," Vince said softly, his eyes had narrowed and he was strangely calm, as if he'd entered some sort of meditative state.

Amos smiled, as if he thrived on this sort of adrenaline rush. He loved a good stand-off, whether it was in a game of poker or standing in the dark on Barnes Common. Who would blink first? The stakes were high – life and death. Amos knew that either way someone would die in the next few minutes. He loved that. His heart was pumping and he felt more alive than he had in weeks. He relished the challenge.

Vince seemed to be relishing it too. Even if it was mostly bravado. A need to save Glory.

But then Amos changed everything. He gave a signal to the thug holding Glory.

The man sprang open a long flick knife from out of his

82

left hand. Where did that come from? Now that's a magic trick, thought Vince grimly. Glory was trying to pull away, but the thug pushed her onto the ground.

"Let her go."

Amos shook his head, coal-black eyes boring into Vince.

Glory looked scared. The thug was gripping her arm above the elbow. A tight grip from a meaty fist. She glanced at Vince for guidance. What did he want her to do? Would it help if she screamed to cause a distraction or something? Or if she struggled?

Vince gripped the crowbar. He glanced from her and then back to Amos, staring intently – both men determined to break the other's nerve.

It was a stalemate.

But it wouldn't stay that way for long.

Chapter 6

As dawn added a purple tinge to the retreating night sky, the ambulance slowed to a juddering halt. The petrol tank finally empty with even the fumes that had sustained the last few miles gone. As the engine clattered to a bone-dry, choking standstill, the driver managed to use the last of the vehicle's momentum to tuck it onto a long-grassed verge. At the wheel, Vince winced as he wrapped the makeshift bandage tighter around his injured right hand. It had been bleeding badly, and it was only now that he noticed that the steering wheel was slick with redness. But it was a small price to pay for his escape. He staggered out from the cab, a gun butt sticking out from the belt of his trousers, and found his legs as he scanned his surroundings. It seemed to be the edge of a village: a fork in the road by some picture-postcard idyll of sleepiness. The place was called Thatchford Green, but the name meant nothing to Vince. He was simply relieved to be as far away from London as possible.

Walking along the road as the darkness finally lost its cyclical battle with day, Vince found himself in the village. He glanced up the main street and saw a pub. It was four in the morning, but maybe they would have a room for him to sleep things off.

He straightened his jacket, buttoning it to hide the gun and made his way towards the pub, bracing himself as he rapped on the door. After a moment, a bedroom light switched on above his head.

As Vince waited for a response, he noticed a newspaper vending stall next to the pub. The headline behind the mesh caught his eye.

"Courageous Connie Carter Saves Day".

Vince was surprised. He knew that name.

It couldn't be the same girl, could it? Vince plucked a newspaper from the pile behind the stall and leafed through it in disbelief. He was so engrossed, he didn't hear the angry voice of the pub landlord behind him. He didn't see the man standing in his vest and pyjama bottoms.

There was a photograph of Connie Carter and Margaret Sawyer on page three. He stared at the face of Connie Carter: her familiar smile. Her full lips. Bleeding hell, it was the same girl! He couldn't believe it. As he tried to make sense of it, Vince picked out a jumble of salient words as he scanned the page: train crash, vicar's wife, Helmstead.

Vicar's wife? What the hell? Was this some sort of joke?

"'Ere, I'm talking to you."

Vince finally realised that the landlord had appeared and was giving him daggers. Vince flashed his best approximation of a charismatic smile. It wasn't something that came naturally.

"Got any rooms?"

"Not for your sort," the landlord growled, spotting Vince's

makeshift bandage and bleeding hand. This along with his sharp suit and dark demeanour, meant he had trouble written on him as clearly as words through a stick of rock.

Vince smiled.

"Just one question, then, and I'll be on my way, yeah?"

The landlord pulled a face. He wasn't about to serve alcohol at this time in the morning. Not to this fellow. But the question wasn't about getting a crafty whisky or a breakfast pint.

"How far am I from Helmstead?" asked Vince.

A wailing scream came from elsewhere in the large house.

Connie ignored it. Hard as it was to listen to, she was used to the unpleasant background noise. One of the downsides of working in a hospital. Instead she got on with her work and pulled the white sheet taut. The tucked end came loose from the other side of the bed. Just as she got one end sorted, the other would always do this. Connie thought it was some sort of secret test to see how long it would take her to swear. But since Hoxley Manor's East Wing had been turned into a makeshift ward for the sick and injured, this was a regular part of her work when she wasn't toiling in the fields. Digging ditches and trying to get sheets to stay on beds. That made up her whole life, it seemed sometimes.

Joyce came over and pulled the other side of the sheet taut. Connie tucked it in and smiled thanks.

"Dr Channing said we can finish when we've made the beds," Joyce said.

This made Connie smile even more. With three more beds to make, and with Joyce helping her, she might be able to leave in about twenty minutes if she got a wriggle on. Then she might be able to see Henry before he went off on his evening visit to see the ailing old Frenchman, Dr Beauchamp. Perhaps she could cook him dinner and make him see that she could do all that sort of thing as well.

With new purpose, Connie unfolded a fresh sheet and moved to the neighbouring bed.

When she finished, Connie scampered home. Dusk was beginning to fall as she ran through the village, past the pub and down the hill to the vicarage. In the distance, far away, she could see a figure riding away on a push bike. Oh blast! It was Henry. Connie stopped in her tracks, annoyed to have missed him by such a narrow margin. One less bed and she'd have made it! But again, this disappointment was tinged with a slight relief. There would be no arguments tonight. Was that the way she should be viewing her marriage after only a month? It felt wrong, but she couldn't hide her feelings from herself.

The wind knocked from her sails, she trudged towards the front door; her legs suddenly feeling very heavy and tired. She entered the hallway. No old biddies there tonight. No Henry. The house was still and quiet without Henry inside it. A house, not a home. Connie closed the door and entered the parlour, where her spirits lifted in pleasant surprise. There was a note on the table next to a china plate covered by another plate. Connie read the note:

"I caught you some supper! Love Henry"

Connie's hand reached towards the plate and lifted the cover. What would it be? What could Henry have caught for her? Not a rabbit, surely –

Under the cover was a cheese sandwich. Connie grinned, warmed by his playfulness. He was trying his best. She would try hers too and have things spick and span for when he came home. She slipped off her boots and sat in front of the fire in the big armchair. Henry had left the embers burning, with a fire guard on the hearth. Connie placed some new wood onto the embers and watched the fire slowly catch hold as she sat there and ate her sandwich. The spoils of the wild.

After Connie had eaten she looked at the clock above the fireplace. It was half-eight. Henry should be back soon. Putting on her apron (Connie felt like a proper vicar's wife when she did this), she decided to busy herself with some chores until then. She unbolted the back door and went into the small vicarage garden to collect the eggs from the chickens. There were two deck chairs that she had put at the far end of the plot. The chairs faced away from the house, and Henry and Connie sometimes sat there in the evening, chatting over a cup of tea. On one side of the garden was a narrow chicken run that stretched the length of the grass. Part of the wooden frame had been broken and, as it awaited a proper repair, a large amount of mesh had been used to ensure the occupants didn't escape. Inside were two chickens, whom Connie had nicknamed Esther and Gladys (after warden Esther Reeves and local busybody Gladys Gulliver). Esther had laid an egg and Connie picked it up and shook it free of the hay that had stuck to it. Carefully she placed it in her apron pocket and looked around to see if Gladys had produced anything. Suddenly something caught her eye. Cigarette smoke was rising from one of the deck chairs.

Connie looked closer. Although the chair was turned away from her, she could see the definite indentation of a weight on the canvas. And on closer inspection: two silhouetted legs going to the ground.

"Who's there?" Connie said, in as commanding a voice as she could muster.

It wouldn't be Henry, would it? Playing a joke? No, he wouldn't smoke a cigarette, even for a lark. No reply came from the chair, although Connie could sense that the occupant had heard her and was now motionless, on edge and waiting.

"It's not funny," Connie said, looking for some weapon. But Henry was such a stickler for putting the few garden tools they owned into the shed that there was nothing to hand. She spotted a small earthenware flowerpot and picked it up. Anything would do.

No head was visible, which meant the occupant was either slouched down in the seat or was very short. Her heart was pounding as she neared the side of the chair.

"You've had your fun." Her mouth was dry and it was hard to swallow.

She reached the edge of the chair. Finally she could see the occupant. A big man, slouched down. The angular good looks of his face, his slicked hair, the cheap, dark suit. Eyes glinting in the night air. This wasn't right. It couldn't be right. Jesus, no...

And yet, Vince Halliday was sitting, as bold as brass, in her garden smoking a cigarette.

"Looks like you've had your fun too," Vince said, fixing her with his deep-blue eyes. "Nice set-up, Con. Vicar's wife, eh? Who'd have thought? I laughed when I saw that."

At first she couldn't believe it. How was this possible? How had he found her? She couldn't even really hear his words as her head swam with a seasick-like queasiness, half-hoping that this was some hallucination caused by too much sun in the fields.

"So what's the angle with you being a vicar's wife?"

"No angle," she stammered. Connie steadied herself. She felt as if she wanted to throw up. This situation was so wrong. A sickening juxtaposition of two things that shouldn't ever meet. This grubby bull wasn't part of her world of jam-making, tea-drinking and church fund-raising. Wearing her apron, Connie suddenly felt like a fraud, a silly girl playing at being a vicar's wife. It added to her own deepest fears that this was all some silly role-play. Who was she kidding thinking she could be a genteel lady? Who was she kidding thinking that she could escape?

As her mind focused and she snapped back to the moment, she knew one thing. She didn't want this. She didn't even want to ask what he wanted here, what he was doing. She just wanted him to go so she could pretend he'd never been here. Pretend he'd never soured the milk of her supposedly perfect life. But she found herself asking nonetheless.

"What do you want?" she managed, her voice shaky and small.

"Cup of tea would be a start." He smiled, blowing smoke up into her face, adding to her feelings of nausea.

"My husband is here. He won't take kindly to—" As she

said it, she knew how empty and impotent her threat was.

"He's not here, is he?" Vince still smiled, staying in his seat. Henry's seat. Vince must have been watching the house, waiting for Henry to leave. How long had he been keeping tabs on them? "The vicar's out, isn't he?"

"Well he'll be back soon," Connie said, turning to the house and half-hoping that if she turned back the whole thing would have been a dream and Vince would have vanished into the night air like bad cigar smoke. But in a lightning-fast move, Vince grabbed her wrist, his grip strong and powerful. It wasn't like the way Henry had grasped her the other night. This was visceral, animal-like, painful. She tried to pull her hand back, but to no avail. She wasn't going anywhere. He looked at the small flowerpot in her other hand and grinned at her.

"Go on, give it a go." He knew that she wouldn't use it as a weapon. And even if she did, Connie knew that it might only make things worse. Connie let the small pot slip from her hand onto the grass. Thunk.

"Please. He will be back."

"Good. Time I said hello, eh?" Vince let Connie go, her arm whiplashing back to her body. She nursed her wrist and was aware of something wet spreading on her stomach. Had she somehow been stabbed? In the woozy unreality of this moment, had Vince stabbed her? What had happened? And then she realised with some relief that during the struggle Esther's egg had shattered in her apron pocket. The yolk was swilling around the fabric, but the white was seeping through the lining onto her dress.

Reluctantly and with deep foreboding, Connie led Vince to the house.

A brown stain splashed onto the white linen tablecloth. Connie cursed herself as she found it difficult to stop her hand shaking as she poured tea from the pot. Vince sat at the table, the place where she and Henry had their meals, a malignant force in their genteel home. Amused that most of the tea was residing in the saucer, Vince tipped it back into the cup as he scooped it up in his big hands.

"Relax, Connie. Anyone would think you wasn't pleased to see me."

"You drink that and you go," Connie said with as much conviction as she could muster. Maybe if he drank it quickly he could be on his way before Henry got back from Dr Beauchamp's house and then she wouldn't ever have to mention the matter. It could be tucked away with all the other old secrets from her life: the degrading acts, the humiliation, the illegal scams.

"I'll go when I'm ready," Vince said, his gaze firm and cold.

As he raised the cup to his lips and slurped it, Connie noticed for the first time that his hand was bandaged. A piece of cloth, perhaps a shirt sleeve, had been wound tightly round and pinned in place. But it was dirty and soaked with blooms of old blood. It was probably an old wound. A couple of days old at least.

"What happened to you?" Connie asked, surprised that she cared even that much.

Vince nodded as he contemplated the question. What would

he tell her? Would it be the truth? Vince knew that truth didn't always play as well as a good lie that could get you a bit of sympathy and a bed for the night.

"Some people are after me," he offered flatly.

Connie's eyes flickered with something approaching concern. Vince smiled warmly at her. She snapped out of it, defences up. Would it delay him leaving in any way? When could she get him to go?

Deciding that taking charge and blocking out all her conflicting feelings was the best way to move things along, Connie revealed that she worked at Hoxley Manor some evenings in the temporary military hospital as a helper on the wards. As she was used to dressing wounds and treating people, perhaps she could look at Vince's hand before he left? The underlying message was that this favour would be all he would be getting from her.

Vince considered this and slurped his tea again. He winced suddenly. Connie knew that her tea-making was pretty poor but this seemed more than a reaction to that. Vince's hand was playing him up. Feeling her legs shaking, she went to get the bandages from the bathroom.

Vince stretched out his arm, keeping it still on the table cloth, as Connie carefully unwrapped the makeshift bandage. It was stuck to the wound, so she had to gently tease it away, little by little, checking his reaction at each stage. Vince told her not to worry about the pain. He could take it.

"Remember that time I got me head cut?" He lowered his head and lifted up his fringe to show an old scar. Connie knew full well what it was. The result of a bar-room fight with two loan sharks that had seen Vince come off worse, for once. Connie had spent much of that night patching up Vince by candle-light in his one-room flat.

"Yeah." Connie offered a tight smile, uneasy about being driven down memory lane.

He'd winced as she'd tried to clean that wound, so she'd stroked his hand as she'd done it. But tonight, a world away, she kept her mind on the job and her other hand on the table. He knew this too and regarded her with a wistful look. Perhaps he wished that he could turn back time.

Eventually she managed to remove the old dressing, wrapping it up on the table mat like a discarded snake's skin. Now she turned her attention to his hand. The wound itself wasn't pretty. A deep gash on the back of his hand, the skin around it flaming pink with infection. This looked serious. Was it a knife wound, she wondered? Connie tried not to let her face betray her.

"How did this happen?"

"Told you. People are after me."

"Looks like they caught you, don't it?"

Vince couldn't help but smile at her humour. They glanced at each other and for a split second an old, and dangerous, chemistry was back. "Connie—" he started, but Connie shook her head, unwilling to hear the rest of what he wanted to say. Whatever it was, it would make her feel uneasy, awkward, and perhaps in some small way, regretful. Regretful? Really? Where had that come from? The saying was true, some things were better left unsaid.

Connie focused back on the wound. But she could feel Vince's eyes burning into her.

"Does it need stitching?" he asked.

"No," Connie lied, keen to get him out of her life; a clean break seeming more attractive than any other complication.

But Vince knew what she was doing. He saw the moment of doubt. He spotted the hesitation in her eyes as she spoke.

"Can you stitch it?" he persisted.

"Told you, it doesn't need—"

Vince flashed a look of anger. "Don't lie to me, Connie." And suddenly Connie was plunged back into that fear she used to feel. The fear of his unpredictable nature and his sudden, violent mood swings. Suddenly she was two years younger, back in the East End. A lifetime ago. Her heart was pumping, an uneasy mix of fear and excitement. Adrenaline was coursing in her veins, and despite her misgivings, Connie felt energised and alive. It was wrong, but also worryingly familiar; the glimpse of an old life from behind the curtain of a new one. How could he make her feel so insecure, unsure of herself, in just one moment? This was dangerous. She couldn't trust her feelings. She couldn't think straight. But at a primal level, she knew that she had to get rid of him.

"Joyce, my friend Joyce, she's done stitching before. I could take you to her."

"You think I'm stupid?" Vince snorted. "You take me out of here and turn me over to the old Bill, is that it? After all we've been through."

Connie went to protest.

"Didn't stop you running out on me before, did it?" he muttered. She had no answer for that.

He shook his head and insisted that Connie do it. Despite her protests, he said that she'd better learn fast, hadn't she? Hastily, he wrapped the new bandage around his hand and told Connie to pin it. He would keep that on for now, until she got back with the things she needed from Hoxley Manor. Connie was worried about leaving Vince alone in her house. What if Henry came back? He'd be shocked to find a strange man in his home and there was no guarantee that Vince wouldn't attack him. And perhaps even worse – what would Vince say to Henry? What would he tell him? The past was a box best left closed. But what choice did Connie have?

Suddenly she had an idea. Hesitantly, Connie got to her feet and fumbled for her coat in the hallway. Vince came out and warned her that she'd better not go for help.

Again it was as if he was reading her mind. She'd already thought that she could head to the village hall rather than Hoxley Manor and ask the Home Guard officers there for help. Helmstead didn't have a regular police force any more, with its two full-time bobbies conscripted and sent overseas, but the Home Guard managed to instill some sort of order into the town. They'd be able to help. Yes, that was a plan.

Vince opened his jacket a little to reveal the handle of a revolver sticking out of his waist band.

"Don't do anything stupid," he warned.

Connie's plan shrivelled and died.

"I'm not stupid," she reassured him.

Her head swimming and feeling nauseous, Connie went

outside, closing the front door behind her. She gulped in the fresh air, hoping it would give her the strength to walk away from the house; the strength to make her jelly-like legs work. She took a few steps and nearly stumbled. She waited for her head to clear and walked as confidently as she could to the gate at the end of the front garden, aware that Vince's eyes would be on her the whole time. The man with the gun.

Connie moved off down the road. As she turned the corner she found herself on steadier legs. Mrs Gulliver was coming the other way with a prayer book in her hand. She scowled at Connie, but managed a strained smile and a good evening. Connie couldn't reply. She walked straight on. Mrs Gulliver mumbled and grumbled about flighty women – and went on her way. She wasn't a fan of Connie and this rudeness did nothing to change that view. But Connie had barely seen her. Suddenly Mrs Gulliver's disapproval was small potatoes.

And then a strange salvation seemed to find her in the village square as Connie was nearly knocked over by a man on a push bike. It took her a moment to realise it was Henry. He looked at her quizzically, baffled that she barely seemed to recognise him. Connie started to babble about how she needed him to stay away, how she could handle this. Just give her a little time. As he tried to play catch-up, he recognised that it was the instinct that had kept her going on the streets of the East End and in the orphanage; a default survival mode. Finally, he held her by the shoulders and asked her what was going on.

"What's happening now?"

The words stung. It was the implication that this was merely the latest unpleasant occurrence in a long line of misdemeanours. What had she messed up? What fresh hell was this? His troubled, long-suffering expression stung just as much. It seemed to say what a disappointment you are, Connie Carter. She felt like a child who had been misbehaving.

In a wavering voice, Connie admitted that Vince was back. Henry didn't know the name. Was this the guy who tried to ruin their wedding? Connie shook her head. Danny Sparks, another unwelcome blast from the past, had turned up days before their wedding with a plan to rob a petrol tanker from the US military. It didn't go well. Connie felt queasy about the whole episode. She'd hoped that their marriage had been a clean slate and that Henry wouldn't ever think back to what happened. Danny had threatened Connie and demanded that she leave Helmstead with him. He was going to hurt Finch. In order to save the people she cared for, she'd had no choice but to agree. Henry had saved her, displaying a rare moment of macho bravado that resulted in him knocking Danny out. At the time, it had felt like a euphoric display of his affection for Connie, but since then it had chipped away at Connie's confidence. She didn't feel worthy of this great and decent man; a man who had been forced to play the adult in their relationship; a man who seemed burdened by having to sort out the problems of her life. She never spoke about Danny to Henry, believing that the memory might fade away and become, at most, a small footnote to their happy lives together. But here she was, unearthing another slab of her gruesome past for him to sort out. Connie felt wretched.

As her breathing slowed, calmed by Henry's gentle presence,

he guided her over to the pub. To anyone looking, it appeared to be an idyllic situation – a young couple in love sharing a drink together on a sunny evening. Connie gulped down the cider that Henry had bought her and felt her head spin with a new kind of wooziness. Now, calmed by his presence and alcohol, Connie was able to slowly tell Henry what had happened. Despite hating herself for every word, she told him about Vince Halliday.

The young woman was dressed in a grimy frock. But her hair was clean and still wet from a hurried wash in the bathroom of a Lyons' Corner House. She stood on the street corner, a small hat by her feet, and sang 'A Nightingale Sang in Berkeley Square' to passing men and women. With her lovely voice, people stopped to listen and sometimes even contributed a coin to her collection. Connie had been forced to make money this way since things ended with Danny Sparks and she'd found herself out on her ear. But on this Sunday morning, Connie finished the chorus and noticed a burly man smiling awkwardly at her. He offered to buy her some food, intending to visit the same Lyons' Corner House from where she'd had to make a hurried exit earlier after being caught washing her hair. Connie suggested they go to a pub instead. And that's how she'd met Vince Halliday. A man who seemed like a benevolent spirit, or at least as benevolent as any men were capable of being.

Soon Connie was living with Vince, an uneasy marriage of business and occasional pleasure.

"So you slept together?" Henry found the words hard to say.

Connie nodded, feeling another mark against her. Yes, she'd slept with Vince. Just as she'd slept with Danny Sparks. And although she didn't really regret it, she hated seeing the hurt on Henry's face. He'd been a virgin when they married and Connie had intentionally not mentioned anything sexual from her past. As far as Henry was concerned, she kidded herself that he may even think she might be innocent.

In her more naive moments with Vince, Connie wondered if they were courting. But realistically there was nothing romantic about their life together. Vince bought Connie a beautiful dress. It was her uniform for the scams they would operate together. Connie would be the bait, to lure men in, and then Vince would extort money from them. It was the same scam that he'd later do with Gloria Wayland, to lesser effect. Few men could resist Connie and soon Vince was extorting money from a large number of married men in the East End.

Connie blushed with shame as she told Henry this. Was he judging her? His face maintained a neutral stance, but he showed encouragement for her to finish the story. Connie thought she might as well tell him everything. In for a penny...

One night the scam went wrong.

Working at one of the smart hotels in central London, Connie had swanned into a whisky bar and quickly aroused interest in one of the lone drinkers. The man was bald, stocky and had signet rings on every finger of his hands. Connie had misgivings immediately, wary of the signals her brain was trying to give her. Stay away from this man. But it was too late. She was already talking to him. He was already buying a drink for her. But something else was wrong. Vince wasn't there. Usually, he'd sit at the other end of the bar or restaurant, watching Connie luring in a gullible married man, and then he'd surreptitiously follow them to the hotel. But where was he?

As Connie led the man to the hotel, she hoped that Vince would be there soon. She needed him to jump the man when they got inside the room. Connie and the bald man walked up the stairs to the hotel room. He'd tried to kiss her on the way up, but she'd told him to wait. Plenty of time for all that.

Henry's face fell. Connie hated the effect this was having on him. But she had to tell him before Vince told him. Who knew what embellishments he'd add to stick the knife in? She soldiered on.

When they got to the room, the bald man went to lock the door. Connie told him to leave it unlocked and he became suspicious. First she didn't want to kiss him, now she wanted the door unlocked. What was going on? Connie couldn't come up with anything convincing, her usual quick-witted brain failing her spectacularly. On a short fuse, the man grabbed her by the throat and demanded to know what she was playing at. She felt his thumbs pressing at her windpipe. There was a strange wheezing sound, which Connie realised was coming from her. She tried to bat him away, claw at his arms, anything. As Connie struggled, the door flew open and a panting Vince Halliday burst into the room. He punched the man hard in the face, sending him crashing unconscious against the wall. Vince yanked Connie's arm and told her to get out. There had been a dreadful mistake.

"Ain't we going to blackmail him?" Connie asked, being shunted out the door. Vince didn't answer, too scared to even speak unless the man recognised his voice.

They ran as fast as they could back to Vince's flat. Once there, Vince explained that the man was Amos Ackerly, a vicious gangster. Vince was worried that he'd be a marked man now. Had Amos seen him? Connie was appalled that Vince was only worrying about himself. He'd seen her for sure, even knew her name! After a sleepless night, waiting for their door to be kicked in, Connie made a decision. She had to get away.

And that's why Connie Carter joined the Women's Land Army.

Henry exhaled loudly, his mind grappling with this previously hidden chapter of his wife's life. Disappointment and concern were jockeying for control of his face. "What do you think he wants?" Henry eventually asked.

"Not me, if that's what you're thinking," Connie said. "He's injured and on the run. If we can patch him up and get him on his way ..."

Henry nodded. It seemed a sensible plan. And yet, his eyes wandered over the square to where the Home Guard was just finishing its meeting at the village hall. Elderly men in uniform were chatting and laughing as they dispersed homeward bound for the evening. But Connie preempted what Henry was thinking.

"I thought the same thing," she said. "But he's got a gun and I'll bet he's quicker than any of those old boys."

Henry's face fell even further. A gun? Suddenly he looked a good ten years older.

She didn't want to endanger any of the men's lives. He knew each and every one of them – old campaigners from the first war, doing their bit, feeling useful again.

While Connie thought about the Home Guard, Henry saw himself lying on the ground waiting for a rabbit. He stood, taking decisive action. "You go to Hoxley Manor and get the first-aid things. I'll go and tell him that this is all we're doing – and then he'd better be on his jolly way."

Connie felt warmed by the slightly built, bookish man in front of her. He seemed to be rallying to her cause. Of course, the deserved rejection might come later, Connie thought. She didn't want to trouble him any more or put him in danger. "No," she said softly. "You stay here and have a drink. I'll go to the manor and then get rid of him."

"But—" Henry went to protest.

Connie shook her head. No buts. She wanted to sort this out herself. And that's what she was going to do. She left the pub, not knowing whether Henry Jameson would still want her after tonight.

Chapter 7

By the time Connie Carter got to Hoxley Manor it was nearly dark. Iris Dawson was surprised to see her returning to the hospital. It wasn't her day to be on standby. Surely she didn't love the place that much? Connie tried to wave away her friend's concerns. She just needed a couple of things, that's all. Iris wondered if she could help in any way. Ever-helpful Iris.

"Keep your eyes peeled for Dr Channing. That'll be a big help," Connie said, moving fast away down the corridor. Before Iris could enquire further, Connie had gone into the shadows of the stately home. What was she doing?

Iris looked nervously around. This sounded risky. All the women felt nervous around Dr Channing, for a variety of reasons. But being the youngest Land Girl, Iris felt particularly awkward around him. It was his air of seriousness and authority which made Iris feel as if she'd always done something wrong. A stern father figure whose sharp intellect made her feel inadequate about herself, especially about her inability to read or write. Whereas some of the others cooed about "dashing Dr Channing", Iris just felt intimidated.

But she did what Connie asked and stayed in the corridor, keeping watch; a nervous sentry.

Connie darted past the main ward on the East Wing. Some nurses were working with Land Girls, trying to get the patients comfortable for the night. An airman with only one arm was mumbling loudly. Another was shouting for water. Connie spotted Dr Richard Channing as he tended the mumbling man's bedside. Good, that'll keep him occupied for a little while, thought Connie. She opened the door to the supply cupboard – unsure of exactly what she needed. Joyce would know. But Joyce wasn't here. And despite seeing nurses stitch wounds on the wards, Connie had never really paid that much attention. She would look the other way or whistle a song to distract her while the gory stuff was happening. But here she was "Nurse Connie": in at the deep end. She hoped that some of what she'd seen, or more accurately hadn't seen, might just have somehow rubbed off on her. Connie filled her coat pockets with some dressings, and some thread and needles. Turning to go, she suddenly remembered the iodine tincture for sterilising the wound. She grabbed a small bottle and some cotton wool for luck and hastily made her way back into the corridor with her spoils.

Dr Channing was turning the corner! With reflexes like an alley cat, Connie threw herself back into the store room and waited for him to pass. When she could hear the sound of his brogues diminishing on the parquet flooring, Connie emerged again. She took a deep breath and went on her way, pausing only to say a rushed thank you to Iris on her way out. "What was that all about?" Iris asked.

"Needed a plaster," Connie smiled, hoping charm would be enough to stop the questions.

Connie raced back to the village. It was dark now and she had to use the moon to illuminate her way as she raced along hedgerows and across fields, following the quickest route she knew.

But when she got back to the village square – her heart lurched in shock.

The pub was shut for the night. And Henry had gone.

With trepidation, Connie walked nervously towards the vicarage. She couldn't hear any sounds from inside. Worrying that she might open the door to find Vince standing over Henry's broken body, she lifted the latch. Or maybe they'd just be in deep conversation, with Vince telling Henry some unpleasant truths about his new wife. The hallway was quiet, the faces of the disciples staring blankly at her as she silently made her way to the living room.

The sight that greeted her felt like another queasy nightmare.

Henry was sitting, tight-lipped at the table, a cup of tea in front of him and the weight of the world on his shoulders. Vince Halliday was standing by the fire, in front of the mirror, smoking a cigarette. It looked like two friends having tea, discussing the issues of the day. And if it wasn't for the bruise on Henry's cheek, Connie would have been convinced that that was all that it was. Hang on, a bruise on Henry's cheek!

"Henry! Are you all right?" Connie rushed to his side.

"He's fine," Vince growled. "Just needed a little lesson in respect, that's all."

"I told him to leave," Henry stammered. "It's my house. And he was here."

"And I said that wasn't a very Christian thing for a man of the cloth to say," Vince laughed.

Connie knelt by Henry's side and told him how sorry she was. In turn, he told her that he'd waited at the pub as it closed, but got a sudden rush of anger about staying away from his own home. It wasn't right that he couldn't go back. And besides, he worried about what the stranger in their house was doing.

Vince let them talk. He knew that he was in control here. Connie said that she had the things from the hospital. She could sort Vince out now and get him on his way. A paper-thin civility descended on the room as everyone played their role. Connie told Vince that she was ready to stitch his hand.

"I'm sorry I lamped him." Vince flicked his dog end onto the fire. He crossed languidly to the table and pulled out a chair, sitting opposite a Henry who vehemently refused to make eye contact.

"Not me you should be apologising to, is it?" Connie spread the bandages, needles and cotton wool on the table.

Vince lay his thick arm on the table so that Connie could get to work. She smiled winningly, wondering inside how long it would take Vince to realise that she had absolutely no idea about what she was doing. She was guessing it wouldn't take very long.

Connie threaded a needle. Even this activity took her some

time. With each second seeming like a minute in the tense silence around the table, Connie struggled to get it right. She'd never been good at sewing, once darning a sock so that she couldn't get her toes in it.

"Come on, Con. What's going on?"

"The light ain't that good."

Finally, in this still and silent room, her shaking and sweating fingers managed to thread the needle. Hurrah! She took out the iodine tincture and doused it onto the cotton wool. Vince winced slightly as she cleaned his wound. At this point, she saw Henry close his eyes. It was almost as if this act of gentle washing seemed like an act of betrayal. Connie might as well have been tenderly stroking another man's hair. She tried to make it look business-like and without tenderness and finished as quickly as she could. Then decisively, she crossed to the sideboard and returned with a tumbler and a whisky bottle. Vince looked questioningly.

"I ain't got nothing to make it numb. So drink this, take the edge off."

She slugged out a large measure. After a seconds' consideration, he took it and gulped it down. "I could get used to this sort of medical treatment." He nodded that he was ready.

Connie wished she could have a large whisky to blot out what she was about to do. She pushed the needle into the skin around Vince's wound. He grimaced and a little spittle formed on his teeth, but he nodded for her to continue. Henry looked resolutely at the table throughout. It took Connie twenty minutes to stitch the deep wound closed – and it was the most haphazard bit of sewing that she'd ever seen in her life. Even worse than the sock. But finally it was done. She was shaking with exhaustion and breathing heavily as she put a fresh dressing on the wound. Then she fastened a bandage around his hand.

Vince poured himself another tumbler full of whisky and downed it.

"Thanks, Connie. Knew I could rely on you."

Connie offered a tight smile, glancing at Henry out of the corner of her eye. He was avoiding eye contact; unreachable. Vince coughed and got unsteadily to his feet, flexing his injured hand.

"It's dark now. I think I'll stay."

"But you can't," Connie stuttered. Henry let out an audible sigh, something between disappointment and anguish.

"Make me up a bed, Connie. I won't ask a second time." Vince glanced at Henry menacingly by way of emphasis, as he opened his jacket to reveal the handle of the pistol.

Connie's throat went tight and her eyes moistened with fear. Dimly, she was aware of her flattened hands doing a desperate calming motion. She knew that Vince was enjoying the tension. The fear. How could this be happening? How could such a sliver of her dark past be here? After a long moment, Vince fastened his jacket, obscuring the gun. Henry staggered from his chair, any energy and vitality that he'd had earlier had vanished.

"I'll help," he said. "Make up the bed."

Vince looked at the pair of them for a moment. Deciding that he'd broken their spirits enough, he nodded his consent and Henry and Connie went from the room. Vince listened to the sounds of their footsteps as they scampered upstairs. He poured himself another whisky and smiled to himself. A plan was forming. A plan that in his alcohol-hazy head seemed like a good idea.

Connie and Henry went into the spare room. It was a small musty box room with a sloping ceiling, its single window looking out onto Helmstead High Street. The curtains had been shut for weeks and the wallpaper was a sedate pattern of tulip buds. The bed had been stripped since the Bishop had stayed a few months ago and they hadn't had a visitor since. It was quite a leap from a stuffy man of the cloth to a brute with a gun. Connie fetched some clean sheets from the chest of drawers and she and her husband starting to make the bed in strained silence. Connie couldn't stand it. She kept her voice low and asked:

"What did he do to you?"

"Hit me. He hit me," Henry said angrily, embarrassed that he hadn't been able to stop him or stand up to him. Embarrassed by having to admit it to his wife.

"For no reason?"

"What reason do people like him need?" Henry replied, tersely. Then he offered some explanation. "I marched in and I told him in no uncertain terms that he wasn't welcome."

"And?"

"He punched me in the stomach and then in the face. Not even a word. Not even—" Henry was clearly upset by this unexpected violent aggression. He didn't come from a world where this sort of thing happened. Connie saw the anger, frustrated anger, welling up inside of him. "Why does this always happen?" The accusatory words were pinched and strained. His eyes flashing with annoyance and impotence. It hurt Connie to see him like this. She put out a hand to touch his, but he retracted his hand as if he'd touched a hot stove. That hurt her even more.

"I'll get rid of him tomorrow," Connie said, seeing the pain in his eyes. "I promise."

Henry nodded in a non-committal way that made it clear that he didn't believe her promises. Not after last time. Danny Sparks had nearly wrecked their lives. He'd nearly killed Connie and Finch.

"You said this sort of thing – you said it wouldn't happen again."

And with those damning words, Henry Jameson left the room. Connie sunk down onto the freshly made bed and felt her heart breaking.

As they tossed sleeplessly in their own bed that night, Connie tried to get Henry to say more about what he was feeling. She tried to tell him that she was sorry and that this wouldn't be like when Danny came just before they got married. There were differences. Danny had wanted Connie to help him with a robbery. Vince was injured and she assumed he just wanted to put them through the wringer a bit before moving on.

"We've just got to hang in there," she whispered.

"Have we?" A broken voice of weariness.

"What do you mean?" There was no reply. "Henry?"

But Henry didn't want to discuss anything. Like Connie,

he was exhausted from this evening's events and he urged his wife to try to get some sleep too. But as Henry eventually drifted off into a fitful sleep, Connie lay awake looking at the ceiling, wondering about the monster sleeping in the next room.

By the time the hammer on the alarm clock was ready to strike, Connie was still awake and ready to turn it off. Five o'clock in the morning. Now she had another dilemma: go to work and leave Henry alone with Vince or stay at home and get in trouble from Farmer Finch for not clocking in? It didn't feel right leaving. She rolled over in bed and clutched hold of the man beside her. Henry murmured but didn't wake. And he didn't recoil this time, which was a blessing. Her face close to his back, Connie breathed deeply, taking in his reassuring scent. Finally she drifted off. Troubling dreams washed over her; fragments of things that she'd left behind a lifetime ago.

Connie dressed in her best frock walking into the foyer of an upmarket London hotel. Connie offering a flirtatious smile to a businessman. A gold band on his wedding finger. The businessman fumbling for the room key to open the door of his hotel suite. He can't believe his luck. Connie leading the eager man towards the bed. Connie sitting astride him on the bed, his shirt off. His hands everywhere. And then Vince bursting through the door. The explosion of a flash bulb and the man's startled face as his eyes frantically try to adjust; as his mind frantically tries to work out what's going on. The impotent fury as he realises he has been caught in a blackmail scam. Finally Connie saw her and Vince leaving the room, all the man's money and jewellery in their hands. Laughing. Another victory.

But then something unfamiliar in the dream. Something that never happened in real life.

Reverend Henry Jameson was standing halfway up the hotel stairs. As she ran from the hotel room, he looked disapprovingly at Connie, the laugh dying on her lips. Then a sudden and alarming sound:

Bang. Bang.

Connie was confused. What was that?

Bang.

Dully, she realised it was the front door. Real life breaking in. Connie woke with a start, happy to leave her troubling dream behind. She was aware that someone was trying to get their attention.

She peered a groggy eye from the bedroom window and saw a worried Iris Dawson below, looking up at the house.

"Connie?" she shouted. "It's six-thirty."

"Coming." Connie mouthed the word so as not to wake Henry. She pulled her robe tightly around her and ran out of the room, pausing momentarily to listen as she passed the spare room. There was no sound.

Connie ran downstairs and opened the front door. As she did so, she immediately adopted a pained expression and a tremor to her voice. A sick voice. "Sorry. Iris, I don't feel so good."

Iris looked concerned. "What's wrong?"

"I think some dodgy gammon. I'll be right as rain with a bit of rest."

Iris nodded. She gave her sympathies and hoped that Connie felt better soon. "I can tell Farmer Finch."

"Thanks." Connie winced, hoping it added to a convincing picture of someone with food poisoning. She watched as Iris walked away and then closed the front door. Leaning against it, she listened for any sound from upstairs. Nothing. In the cold light of day, were things quite so bad? Somehow Vince didn't seem so scary and their problem didn't seem so suffocating. She remembered how they used to be together. The exhilaration of the scams, the excitement of living a fast and loose life. But crucially she used to be able to control him. It'd be Connie who'd stop Vince getting into hopeless fights in bars. It'd be Connie who would stop him drinking and make him take her out dancing. It'd be Connie who'd draw the line when she didn't feel in the mood for sex. She could control him then. That meant she might be able to control him again. Today she would get rid of him. Yes, he'd be sent packing today.

Connie served up breakfast. Eggs and bacon. And she and Henry watched silently as Vince lumbered downstairs to the table, dressed in a vest, with his braces hanging like dachshund ears around his trousers. On the table were three delicate china cups and saucers, a bread board with a loaf on it and a bread knife. Henry had a small, grey bruise on his cheek.

"What a lovely day, eh?" Vince filled the chair. "Praise be, eh, Reverend?"

Henry's face didn't move. This seemed to amuse Vince even more.

"Leave him," Connie said, pouring the tea.

"That sounded like an order, Miss Carter." Vince pushed his tongue into the side of his cheek, in the manner of a music hall act doing a 'fancy that' face. It was incongruous and unsettling, a weird camp gesture for such a thug of a man. He lent closer to Henry. "Is she telling me what to do?"

Again, Henry didn't reply. It was up to Connie.

"Sometimes you need ordering," she said, as lightly as she could. She was chancing her arm with a sentence designed to test the water. She was banking on it revealing some hint of the rapport they used to have. Would he respond like he used to? If he did, it would mean there was some hope for her controlling him; getting rid of him.

"I need a lot of things, Con," he said, fixing her with a lusty look.

That wasn't quite the response she was hoping for. Now she was flirting with her old boyfriend in front of her husband. That wasn't good. Snapping back to that rapport wasn't something she wanted. The door on that particular cupboard from the past was best closed forever.

Vince hungrily attacked his breakfast. Connie felt deep unease. She'd forgotten exactly what he was like: a large, lugubrious and bear-like man, hedonistic in every way. Even if Henry was eating, which he wasn't, he would pick at his food like a thin bird. But Vince was shovelling in big greasy forkfuls.

Henry was scowling by the time their unwelcome house guest mopped the last of his egg up with a crust of bread. Connie felt strangely adrift. Henry was her rock, and despite their differences and difficulties, she'd hope that he'd help her in some way. But he was sitting, saying nothing. As useful as one of the paintings on the wall.

"So where will you go?" Connie asked, a little too sharply.

Vince shrugged, his cheeks bulging with the final mouthful.

"I don't have anywhere to go, do I?" he said finally, wiping his mouth with his hand. "Need somewhere where I can keep a low profile." Connie tried not to let her face show her concern. "There are lots of empty barns to the north of here," she said hopefully.

Vince let out a sharp laugh, making Henry start in his seat.

"Once upon a time you had nowhere to go, Con. Remember that? I found you, though, put you on your way. 'A Nightingale Sang in Berkeley Square'. Remember?"

Henry's brow wrinkled. He'd heard the story from Connie last night, but to have it referenced by their unwanted lodger rammed home their shared past. They'd done things that Henry would never know about; shared times and laughter, despite Connie's insistence that they were dark times. And then there was the sex. He couldn't think about the sex.

Connie noticed Henry shut his eyes. She knew he wanted this nightmare to end. The bread knife glistened on the table. For a split second, Connie wanted to grab it and just press it hard against Vince's throat. She could force him to leave. Chuck him out like she'd throw a rat out of their home. But she worried that it would lead to more violence.

"I helped you then, didn't I?" Vince said.

"Yeah. And I am helping you here, ain't I?" Connie protested, a look of fire in her eyes.

Vince looked malevolently at her and was about to reply, but Henry suddenly spoke. It surprised both of them.

"Then my people will live in a peaceful habitation, And in secure dwellings and in undisturbed resting places."

"What's that?" Vince spat.

"Isaiah 32-18," Henry replied. "You should leave us in peace. Connie had repaid the debt to you by taking you in last night, dressing your wound and feeding you."

"Is that so?" Vince said. "And that's the extent of the Christianity on offer, is it?"

Vince stood up and yanked his braces up onto his thick shoulders. Again, Henry flinched, silently cursing himself for his body betraying his fear of this violent man.

"Here's the thing. You go about your business." Vince looked at Connie and Henry. "You do your digging or whatever you have to do. You ride around tending to your flock. And then, tonight, when it's dark, I'll go and have a butcher's out of the village, see where I can go next. That seems a Christian thing to do, don't it?"

Connie glanced at Henry for his reaction, but after his outburst he had withdrawn again, looking at the table cloth and avoiding eye contact. Connie considered what Vince had said. It sounded the best offer they had on the table.

"All right."

"No one knows I'm here. And no one must know. Got it?" Vince said. "If you betray me, I'll shoot the first person who comes through that door stone-cold dead. Including either of you."

Connie nodded. Henry said nothing.

Despite the threat of violence, she was more worried about whether her marriage could survive this dreadful ordeal than who might die.

As Vince went to the bathroom to shave, using Henry's razor, Connie urged Henry to leave the house. It was best for him to be out of the way. If he and Vince were both cooped up all day, like in a pressure cooker, then Vince might become antagonised by Henry. Or that Henry might not be able to restrain himself from saying something that would make Vince explode into violence.

"So I have to leave again?" Henry hissed, resentment spilling out.

"It's safer."

"Maybe I should just get the Home Guard."

"You heard what he said. He'll kill the first person who comes through that door. We have to play it his way. But I ain't going to let him walk all over us." Connie hoped her words would rally Henry, but he slouched into his coat and made for the door. She couldn't let him go like this.

"Say you don't hate me," she whispered.

He looked at her with a studious expression for what seemed like an eternity. "I don't hate you, Connie. But I don't know you, do I?"

Before Connie could respond, Vince lumbered down into the hallway. He had to move to one side for Henry to pass. He looked threateningly at the bookish vicar. This close Henry could smell stale cologne and sweat.

"Don't do anything stupid. If you play hero and get the Home Guard or the police, Connie will be dead."

Henry couldn't stop himself from gulping in distress. He left. Vince waited for the front door to close before he looked at Connie.

"I never want to have to do that."

"Glad to hear it," Connie said as chirpily as she could manage.

Vince poured himself another cup of tea from the pot and urged Connie to sit with him.

She sensed that Vince was in the mood to talk. Maybe that could shed some light on the situation she was in. Every bit of information might be useful. And sure enough, Vince started to tell her about what had happened in London. He told her about the deal on Barnes Common, about the misdirection with the boxes; about how it had all gone wrong. He told her a little about Gloria Wayland.

"The girl – she's young, keen. Not a patch on you."

"Where did you find her?" Connie found herself asking. She didn't quite know why she wanted to know.

"She wasn't singing like you was, that's a fact." He breathed deeply, lost in thought. But he wanted to talk about them rather than the gangly teenager. "We had some times, didn't we? And I don't want to mess things up for you."

Connie felt herself relax slightly. The words sounded hopeful, like a promise. Maybe she could just talk to him, keep him calm and then he might go.

"Remember that time it was your birthday?"

"And you got me a red dress."

Roland Moore

"Paid for it too. It weren't nicked."

"Bought with stolen money, though, wasn't it?"

Vince chuckled. That was true enough. "Still got it?"

Connie pulled an expression that said she was struggling to remember. But she knew full well what had happened to it. She'd burnt it on a fire when she first came to Helmstead. After clearing some scrub land, Finch had entrusted her to burn some felled brambles and she'd sneaked to her room, brought down her suitcase and burnt a whole load of clothes from her past. The dresses she'd used for the scams, the shoes. She didn't have many frocks left after that night.

"I think I might have it somewhere," she lied. But Vince was already thinking about something else.

"We'd do all those posh hotels, make a lot of money and then we'd walk over Chelsea Bridge with a bag of chips."

Connie laughed at the memory. "Why did we do that?"

"Maybe we thought if we spent a lot of money it'd draw attention. Who knows?" He drained his tea. Then he turned to her, his eyes softening. "I missed you when you went."

Connie felt the hairs on the back of her neck stand up. This wasn't right. She shouldn't be talking like this, listening to this sort of stuff. This was her married home. It was like a sudden alarm call, shocking her back to her senses. This man had hit her husband, taken over their house. She had to get rid of him. Connie knew she had to steer him onto more current thoughts, rather than their shared past.

"What happened on Barnes Common? With Gloria?"

"Oh, she messed up. Nearly got me killed."

Messed up? Suddenly, there were so many questions buzzing

120

for attention in Connie's head. But she knew it was like treading on eggshells. Pick the wrong one and Vince would explode, clam up, or just lie. Connie had one big burning question and she needed an answer. What had happened to the girl?

"She told me to go, save myself. So I did." The coldness returned to Vince's eyes. "No point us both ending up brown bread. Sad. But you know."

Sometimes Connie knew when Vince was lying. And this was one of those occasions. From Vince's coldness, she guessed it had been the other way around and that Vince had left the girl to die to save himself. But she knew better than to push things and ask.

"And how did you hurt the hand?" Connie asked.

"The boss had a knife. As I was fighting my way out, he lunged at me. So I put my hand up to stop him."

Vince flexed his bandaged hand. It was wet from the shave, the white bandage stained darker from the water.

"Who were you scamming?" Connie asked.

Vince shook his head and snorted. "Another time," he said, closing down her questioning. "I'm going up for a kip." The audience was over.

He lumbered out of the room. Connie listened to his heavy feet on the stairs. She wanted to know more about what had happened. Who was the poor girl who'd died? And perhaps, more worryingly, who was the man who'd stabbed Vince? Was that man still alive?

The bicycle wheels clattered along the stony, unmade path. Henry felt the wind cooling his hot face and freshening his hair as he cycled to see the elderly Dr Beauchamp. He was on the lane bordering Pasture Farm and Swallow Farm – and in the distance he could see the tiny figures of the Land Girls, in their head scarves, toiling in the fields. If any of them waved at him, he didn't notice. His mind was racing with the troubling events at home and the dark, malignant force that had invaded their lives. It was causing him many conflicting feelings. Henry had been praying silently and continuously since he left the vicarage that his wife would be all right. He felt guilty at leaving, and had even turned back at one point. But he was also angry that she had brought this on herself; on them both. Once again, she had blighted their futures with her past. Could they ever be free of it? And were those suitable thoughts for a Christian to have? Shouldn't he be doing everything he could to help his wife? Maybe he would, if it wasn't for the fact that she had never mentioned Vince before. "Oh by the way, there's this psychopath I used to be with". After the Danny Sparks business, Henry assumed that their troubles from the past would be over. He felt both small-minded and petty for not helping; and justi-fied that he had been somehow betrayed by her actions.

As he rounded a corner, ducking under an overhanging branch, Henry saw a figure coming the other way. A large man in a battered hat and a heavy woollen cardigan was swaying an unsteady path. It was Frederick Finch.

He put up a heavy hand and motioned for Henry to slow down. The vicar skidded to a shaky halt of his own.

"Padre." Finch said, with the sureness of a man who might have had an early lunchtime drink or three whilst delivering the eggs.

"Hello, Mr Finch," Henry replied.

"I heard about your missus. Hope it's all sorting itself out," Finch said.

Henry's mind raced. How could Finch know? Had he somehow seen Vince coming to their house the night before? Finch was incalculably nosey, but there was no one who knew about Vince Halliday, surely?

"Hopefully," Henry said, offering a cover-all-bases reply. Was it enough?

"I remember the last time. It dragged on a bit then," Finch said.

What was he talking about now? Danny Sparks? Was he referring to when Danny turned up before the wedding?

"We're hoping it'll all be better soon," Henry said, unsure about how long he could keep this up. It was like one of the Crazy Gang's crosstalk routines. Only with more serious consequences and no one in the mood for laughing.

"Well, I'll be on my way. See if Esther can be persuaded to put the old kettle on, eh?" And Finch started back on his uncertain journey. "Hope Connie feels better for tomorrow!" he shouted over his shoulder.

Finch didn't know about Vince! It was the food-poisoning story that Connie had invented. Henry had felt uneasy about her lying, but he breathed a sigh of relief as he dug his heels into the pedals and set off again.

The hammer missed the nail and made another small dent in the wooden baton. Connie muttered a curse and lined it up for another shot. Coming outside into the garden to fix the hen run had meant that she could escape the feeling of brooding claustrophobia in the small vicarage. Or, more accurately, the man causing that feeling of brooding claustrophobia. The chickens, Esther and Gladys, were flapping back and forth, agitated by the activity in their coop. Connie consoled them with softly spoken words. But all the while she was thinking about the girl who Vince had mentioned. Mixed feelings tumbled around her head. Sadness that the girl had died; queasy relief that she hadn't stayed with Vince and met a similar fate, and, most infuriatingly, a fleeting illogical hint of jealousy. Was it because she felt she'd been replaced? What sort of relationship did Gloria have with Vince? Did it matter? No, of course it didn't matter. Or it shouldn't matter. Connie shrugged it off, thinking she'd had a lucky escape. If she hadn't left she wouldn't have found her new friends in the Women's Land Army, she wouldn't have married Henry Jameson. Who knows what would have happened otherwise?

Left on Barnes Common to die.

Connie batted the taunting thought from her mind.

Realising she couldn't stay out here forever, and that she had to face their unwanted guest sooner or later, she picked up the hammer and the remaining nails and sloped dejectedly towards the house.

Nothing could have prepared her for the sight that greeted her inside.

Vince was sitting in Henry's chair reading the Bible.

"You won't find the racing results in there," Connie said.

Vince grinned, lowering the book. "You always made me laugh, Con." His smile faded when he noticed the hammer.

At that same instant, she realised that she was still holding it.

Connie quickly put it on the table. Neutral. Non-threatening. "I've just been repairing the coop, ain't I?"

"Thought for a minute you were going to be stupid," Vince said, his tone flat, his eyes icy cold; perhaps a little hurt.

"Don't be daft," Connie stammered. She looked at the rusted, heavy hammer as it lay on the table mat. She hadn't viewed it as a weapon until the last few seconds. Perhaps she should have done. Could she have done it, though? An uneasy silence ensued.

"Do you believe in this nonsense now?" Vince tapped the Bible with a heavy finger.

"I've always believed in it."

"Yeah, right," Vince snorted.

"I never said out loud. But I always prayed."

"Even when we was together working the scams?" Vince mocked. "Don't play me, Connie."

"I'm being honest, Vince. I always prayed. Not for really Christian things, but I prayed we wouldn't get caught. Prayed you wouldn't get hurt. Prayed I wouldn't neither."

Left to die on Barnes Common.

But it was true, she'd always talked to God even during her days in the children's home. She had no idea if she was doing it right, but she guessed there was no right or wrong way.

"Learning something new about you, now." Vince was amused by this development. "And there was me thinking it was all for the Reverend."

This stung Connie. "What you saying? That I'm scamming him?"

"Nice set-up here. It wouldn't be the first time, would it?"

"I love Henry."

Vince took this in, his face unconvinced. "He sees you as a charity case."

These words stung even more. At this moment, she hated him more than she'd ever done; with his roughness and his uncultured views and his scant regard for anything nice and decent. Yes, she'd scammed men, playing on her attractiveness, but she'd never scam Henry. She'd never deceive him. She wasn't lying about praying. It wasn't part of some elaborate scheme.

"Even prayed when I was a kid. I always prayed me mum was going to come back." She looked saddened by this memory. The nights in the noisy children's home. She remembered herself lying in one of the lower bunks, in the semi-darkness, mouthing prayers until she fell asleep. And always with the hope that the next day she'd open her eyes to see her mother staring down at her, smiling. A kind young woman, ready to take her home. That day never happened, though.

Connie thought that her words were hitting home. The smile had disappeared from Vince's lips, replaced by a troubled wince. But then she realised it wasn't their conversation. She noticed that Vince was flexing his injured hand as if it was playing him up.

"Giving you gip?" she asked.

"A bit," Vince replied. "Maybe it's just the stitches binding up or something."

Connie went to the kitchen and put the kettle on the stove. She looked at a painting of Jesus looking down at his disciples and under her breath she offered a new prayer. It only had two words.

"Save me." Connie sighed.

After a long hour in Dr Beauchamp's quaint but cramped thatched cottage on the edge of Gorley Woods, Henry was relieved that he could leave and return to Connie. For better or worse, hadn't they been the vows? Maybe they were getting all the worse parts out of the way and the rest of their marriage would be an idyllic time. He waved a hasty, but he hoped not indecently hasty, goodbye to the wheezing Frenchman at the front door, pushed down on his pedals and started on his way. Twenty minutes later, Henry was surprised to again run into Frederick Finch. This time, Finch was sitting on his tractor on the other side of the hedge, munching on some pickled eggs.

"Afternoon, Reverend!" Finch chirped.

It looked as if he'd totally recovered from his intoxicating morning, robust and rosy as he pulled his battered hat down to stop him squinting in the early-afternoon sun. "When we going rabbiting again then, eh?" Finch called.

"I don't know if I've got time."

"Come on. We can go later, if you like."

"No, I really don't think I—"

"You can use the shotgun then, how about that?" Finch smiled.

Henry stopped in his tracks. Shotgun. He remembered

Finch's heavy double-barrelled shotgun. That was a weapon that commanded respect. For a moment, he imagined marching into the vicarage with it, demanding that Vince left immediately. Vince would back away, hands in the air. Connie would relieve Vince of his pistol – and they would demand that the vile man never came back. Maybe Connie would respect him if he used his brawn.

Finch could see Henry's mind wandering off.

"Tempting, isn't it, eh?" Finch said.

"Yes it is," replied Henry.

But it was probably not a good idea. Henry cycled off along the rocky path. Finch saluted him with a tip of his hat and then returned to his pickled eggs.

When Henry got home, he parked his bicycle against the vicarage wall. When he got inside, he wanted to hug Connie, but something stopped him. He was still angry with her. None of this would have happened if it wasn't for her. And yet, he'd known what she was like, hadn't he?

"I'm pleased you're all right," he said.

Connie felt relieved to hear those simple words. But right now she was taking any sliver of hope that Henry didn't hate her.

"Where is he?" Henry whispered.

"Went for a kip a couple of hours ago."

Connie had just served up some scrambled eggs. She placed them on the table in the dining room and listened for sounds of movement from the spare room. Nothing. She told Henry that she'd called Vince to the table a few minutes ago and got no reply. Now, starting to wonder whether he'd already left the house, Connie edged her way up the stairs. She reached the closed door to the bedroom and knocked a couple of times, hoping that there would be no reply. Henry was behind her on the stairs, praying that Vince might have miraculously disappeared. Connie was praying that Vince wasn't about to spring a nasty surprise on them. She knocked again. "I'm sure he's in there."

"Why isn't he answering?" Henry said.

But she heard a breathless, exhausted plea come from within: "Connie." The voice was weak, drained of energy.

Connie and Henry shared a momentary look of foreboding. Then Connie quickly opened the door and went in.

Chapter 8

The room was warm, thick with dead, stuffy air. On the bed, a fully clothed Vince Halliday was staring with glassy eyes. A beached whale gasping for breath. His face was flushed and his brow was covered in sweat. Beads of perspiration hanging like bunting over his top lip. His lips were parched and cracked. He struggled to focus watery eyes on her. Connie knew immediately that this was no ruse, no trap.

"What's happening? What's happening to me?"

Connie felt his brow. Cold and clammy. She didn't notice Henry wince at the sight of her concern, her speed of action.

She had seen this thing before in the hospital at Hoxley Manor. When she'd stitched Vince's wound it had seemed angry and inflamed – but she'd hoped that the iodine would sterilise it. But it looked as if it had blossomed into a full-blown infection coursing through his body. "You're burning up," Connie said. "You need a doctor."

"No doctors. Nobody must know I'm here," Vince rasped.

"But I don't know what to do," Connie protested.

"Find out, then." Vince narrowed his eyes and with immense effort, he propped himself up into a sitting position. Sweat had pooled around the neck of his vest. His pistol was on the bedside table, incongruous amid the decorations of Christian devotion above the bed and the Bible next to it. Vince had meant his movement to be a warning, but it had just served to draw their attention to the weapon. Emboldened, Henry's eyes darted to the pistol. Could he pick it up? Could he force a sick man to leave their house at gun point? He felt ridiculous for even thinking such thoughts, but Connie had seen the gun too. But it seemed she was troubled by something other than a moral dilemma. Something else had drained the colour from her face.

On the ivory plate of the pistol handle were two letters. A monogram of the owner's initials. AA. Connie felt as if someone had slapped her. She forced herself to clear her head. "Amos Ackley," she said. Henry looked confused. "You've got his gun." Henry felt stung as Connie spoke. Here was another shared reference point. A man who he'd never heard of, someone, something that connected his wife with Vince Halliday.

But Connie just wanted to uncover the truth. Her tone was insistent and urgent. "Was he the one what stabbed you?"

Vince was finding it hard to focus. The effort of sitting up had left his head swimming, the blood pulsing fast in his temples, a rushing sound filling his ears.

"Just get me some medicine or something!" Vince half screamed, half cried. Connie rested her hand on his brow, concern trumping her worry about upsetting Henry. Surely as a vicar he'd understand such compassion and not read anything into it? "You'll be all right, Vince. You always are," she said, with something approaching warmth in her voice.

"You say that sort of thing when someone's going to die." He winced. But suddenly they were back in the psychological place where they'd been before. Two misfits against the world telling each other that it would all work out.

"I'll sort it." Connie took her hand away, and glancing back a final time, left the room. Henry stayed a moment longer and looked coldly at the man on his bed. He left the room.

When they were alone in the dining room, Henry asked what was going on. "Who is that Amos man?"

"Amos Ackley works most of South London. He's a really dangerous man. You remember I told you at the pub about him?"

"He sounds like a variety act." Henry pondered, not making the connection with what Connie had told him before.

"Yeah, but the only turn he'd do is a bad one. To anyone who crosses him."

"But he must be dead?" Henry reasoned, trying to process the scant facts. "If Vince has the man's gun, surely he's shot or killed this Ackley chap?"

Connie wasn't sure. Vince had said there were some bad people after him. She always liked to think the worst where Vince was concerned. "I think Amos must still be alive."

"Well maybe if he turns up, it'll be a good thing," Henry said, rubbing the bridge of his nose. A thumping headache was beginning to embrace his temples like an unwelcome aunt hugging a small child. He was out of his depth here, more used to offering comforting advice based on the scriptures than predicting what one gangster might do to another.

132

"Maybe he'll take Vince away?" An uncharitable part of his brain silently added "Or kill him".

Connie had to remind Henry. Perhaps she hadn't spelt it out clearly enough in the pub, when they were woozy with drink and struggling to take in the upheaval of Vince's arrival.

"Thing is, Amos Ackley is the man I tried to scam," Connie admitted. "He'd be quite keen to find me too."

Henry's face fell. And his headache suddenly got much worse. It wasn't just Danny or Vince he had to worry about. Connie seemed to have ties to the whole seedy underworld. It felt as if he didn't know his wife at all.

Sitting around the dining table, Henry and Connie struggled to work out what the best course of action might be. Connie wanted to ask him how he felt, but she guessed he was too angry to talk to her about anything other than the practicalities of their situation.

"This adds a spanner to the works," Connie said, attempting some levity. But Henry just shook his head; a disapproving school teacher refusing to be drawn into a child's joke.

A hand-drawn poster for a cake sale sat on the table between them. Henry had been busy drawing it. It was in aid of Lady Hoxley's latest Spitfire Fund. On the poster was something that Connie thought looked like a squashed bag. Henry informed her proudly that he'd drawn a fairy cake with a candle in it. Connie gave an encouraging smile. Of course it was.

Toying with the poster between his thumb and forefinger, Henry pondered the Vince problem.

133

"Could you ask Dr Channing for advice?" Henry asked. "About his illness?"

Connie rejected the idea. Channing would want to know what was going on. He was a smart man who'd have too many questions.

The other option was to ask Dr Wally Morgan for advice – but the feckless drunk probably didn't know what day of the week it was. But of the two doctors, one who would report them and one who would probably forget he'd seen them, Wally looked the most likely candidate.

But she remembered Vince's warning. He would shoot the first person who came through the door.

"What if he kills him?" she asked.

"Surely he'd realise the man was here to help." Henry sniffed in sudden derision. "Of course, we're not dealing with a normal man, are we?"

"We've got to take care of it ourselves."

Henry studied her. Her dark eyes. The things they'd seen. Who knew what other secrets they held?

Connie knew there was only one thing they could do. At Hoxley Manor, she could steal some medicine. Just like she had taken the iodine and the bandages. She knew they had stocks of Tyrothricin, an antibiotic that had been introduced at the start of the war for treating wounds and ulcers. The hospital even had small amounts of a new medicine called Penicillin that seemed miraculous in its power to heal. But Connie knew that these drugs were carefully monitored. The stocks had to be eked out to treat a large number of injured servicemen. It would be dangerous to steal any of the tablets.

"He's got you stealing for him now," Henry snapped. Finally, he couldn't contain it.

"This is how we get rid of him," Connie argued. "We have to do this. I have to do this. I thought you'd help me, though."

The comment hung in the air. Henry was troubled and tired, and wrestling with more conflicting emotions than he knew how to deal with, but finally he knew he had to help her. "I will."

Connie looked as pleased as she had when he'd proposed. It was ridiculous. Another wave of resentment coursed through Henry. She scurried off upstairs to tell Vince the plan.

Vince was lying on his bed, rubbing his head and moaning. He had tried to sleep but the pain in his hand was too bad, throbbing as if it had been resting in a hot grate. Connie told him that they planned to get some drugs for him. But both of them needed to go to Hoxley Manor to stand a chance of getting them.

Vince protested and said that one of them had to stay.

"But it's the only way," Connie said.

"One of you stays," he gasped.

"I can't do this alone."

"All right." Vince relented. "But you bring the police or anyone back, and I'll—"

Vince trailed off, the effort of talking exhausting him. But he fumbled for his pistol and with great effort returned to his position on the bed, the gun resting on his sweat-soaked chest, ready to grab if he was betrayed.

"I know." Connie left the bedroom.

When they arrived at the Manor, Lady Ellen Hoxley was emerging from the front of the house, frowning at some American servicemen who were smoking and stubbing out butts on her drive. She was a slender and classically beautiful woman whose every motion was one of elegance. She didn't notice Connie at first, but when she did, a pleasant and businesslike smile crossed her face. It had been eight months since Ellen's husband Lawrence had died. She felt mixed feelings being free from that awkward and sometimes difficult marriage, but the circumstances of his death – and his betrayal with one of the Land Girls – still caused Ellen anxiety and sleepless nights. It was true that, in the intervening months, she had rekindled an old friendship with Dr Richard Channing, a man who had predated Lawrence in her affections, but she wasn't ready to totally commit herself to that relationship yet. She consoled herself with a steady approach to life, a need to always do things properly and in a way that befit a lady of her standing in the community. Haste was unseemly.

Lady Hoxley's smile broadened when she realised Connie was with Henry. At first, the marriage had amused Ellen Hoxley – never believing it would last. The mouthy alley cat and the reserved vicar. But here they were, one month on, seemingly in love and talking in hushed tones to each other. Ellen assumed the pair were sharing sweet nothings and had no idea they were discussing how to engineer a theft of medicine from the hospital.

"Oh, how lovely to see you, Reverend. Mrs Jameson," Lady Hoxley said.

"Afternoon," Connie said, wondering whether a curtsy was in order, but wisely decided against it.

"What brings you here?"

"I had a spare hour, Lady Hoxley, so I thought I'd see if any of the patients were in need of spiritual guidance," Henry said, his lie impressing his wife. She never knew he was capable! He flashed Connie a look that showed his own contempt for how far he'd been forced to fall.

"Of course." Lady Hoxley turned with a questioning look to Connie, and Henry answered quickly.

"We thought the servicemen might appreciate a song." He smiled winningly.

"Yeah, that," Connie said.

Ellen Hoxley thought it sounded like a fabulous idea. She knew that Connie and Henry had met when Farmer Finch had tried to organise some concerts, having recognised Connie's extraordinary singing voice. Henry was drafted in as a last-minute piano player to accompany her. And the unlikely duo hit it off. Lady Hoxley bid them good day and went on out into the driveway to admonish the cigarette-tossing Americans.

"Excuse me, it seems you have mistaken my gravel for a gigantic ashtray."

Connie and Henry used this distraction to dart inside the house. Henry whispered that he was unhappy about having to lie and deeply unhappy about stealing.

"How many commandments do you want me to break?"

"I'm the one doing the stealing."

Connie motioned for them to head to the East Wing. Two

nurses were sorting bedding into piles in the corridor. A doctor moved quickly past in the other direction. Connie saw the medicine room. It was a small room no larger than ten feet square. Lord Hoxley had used it for storing his guns but now, in a twist of irony, it was used for life-saving medicines.

As Henry scanned the corridor and tried to block people's view, Connie turned the handle.

But it was locked.

"This day gets better and better," Connie muttered.

"Who has the key?" Henry whispered, desperate to get this ordeal over with.

At that moment, Dr Richard Channing appeared around the corner, jingling a key fob in his hands. He threw them a querying look and then opened the door to the stock room and went inside.

"There's your answer," Connie replied under her breath.

Dr Channing was in his early forties and his charm and easy manner had made him a hit with everyone at Hoxley Manor. Especially Lady Hoxley. But, like Iris, Connie was wary of him. But it wasn't because he made her feel dim. Perhaps it was her instinct for trouble or just the fact that some people just don't get on, but Connie felt a deep unease around him. She'd heard how he had been a hero. He'd actually saved Lady Hoxley's life when a collaborator had caught her in the stables and was about to stab her. Channing had shot the man dead – and there was much chatter among the Land Girls about how fortuitous his intervention had been. Lady Hoxley was eternally grateful for this, although she kept her joy in check, and as befitted a woman of social standing, she simply allowed Channing to move from the cramped servants' quarters downstairs to one of the larger bedrooms upstairs. But later, Connie had wondered how he'd known that Lady Hoxley was in trouble. Why was he even in the stables with a gun?

Connie couldn't worry about that now. She had a key to obtain. And a violent ex-boyfriend to oust.

Dr Channing came out from the stockroom with a bottle of pills. As he locked the door, he nodded hellos to Henry and Connie. "Aircraft Gunner Arthur Tallow is in bed fourteen. He wants to make his peace with God," Channing said.

"Of course." Henry nodded, taking the invitation. With a quick look to Connie, he moved off down the corridor, bracing himself to witness another man's dying moments.

Dr Channing considered Connie for a moment, who was looking somewhat forlornly at her disappearing husband.

"You're not on shift today, are you, Mrs Jameson?"

"No. I was feeling ill earlier but I'm all right now."

"Good. All right enough to empty some bed pans?"

"Lovely." Connie grimaced.

Dr Channing smiled charismatically, pocketed the keys in his white coat and marched off back to his duties.

Connie glanced momentarily at the locked door. And then she followed him. How was she going to get those keys?

Sometime later, Connie was washing some metal bed pans in hot water in the auxiliary kitchen – a large, unmodernised room, which was only usually used when a large number of guests had to be catered for at Hoxley Manor. Its days of such parties had faded into memory as the war and rationing had taken hold. And then, until the secondment of the Manor as a military hospital, it had fallen into disuse. Like a lot of Hoxley Manor.

Connie finished her work. Joyce Fisher entered, dressed in her Land Army uniform.

"You feeling brighter?"

"Yeah. Thought I'd do my bit."

"You missed an exciting day." Joyce smiled, removing her boots.

"Really?"

"Yes, some brilliant manure today." Joyce laughed. Connie stood by and idly chatted while Joyce stripped from her muddy uniform and put on a nurse's uniform. Connie was still wracking her brain as to how to get the keys from Dr Channing. Could she pick-pocket him? She'd only pick-pocketed two people before, both in the hustle and bustle of Oxford Street when she was about fifteen. One of the victims – a large middle-aged woman in a big fur coat – had been an easy target, her cavernous coat pockets easily accommodating a lithe girl's hand. But the second victim, a bean-pole-thin businessman, hadn't given up his assets so easily. He'd felt Connie's hand in his pocket and nearly managed to grab her wrist. Connie had been forced to run for it as the man called for the police and gave chase. Luckily, she'd lost him at Oxford Circus, and empty-handed had pledged never to try pick-pocketing again.

But could she get away with it one final time?

Connie felt her heart lurching. It wasn't from nervousness,

but from a sick feeling that she was going back to her old ways. A virtuous and lovely man had trusted her and loved her enough to marry her. And now she hadn't just dragged him through the wringer once, but twice. And the ordeal wasn't over yet. Would she be as lucky as she was with Danny in getting rid of Vince? And even if Vince went tomorrow, what damage had been done to her marriage? Did she even deserve his love now? Connie forced herself to put the thoughts out of her head. She had a more immediate problem.

The pockets on a white coat were large and baggy. It should be easy: one quick and well-timed delve and she could have the keys in her hand. There were no hustle and bustle distractions of Oxford Street. What had Vince termed it? Misdirection. Connie knew it would be even easier if Henry was around to cause a distraction. However, with Henry tied up, Connie realised she'd have to do it alone.

"Right. That's me ready," Joyce said, smoothing down her uniform. "First job, make Dr Channing a cup of tea."

Connie's ears pricked up at this, a plan forming quickly in her head. "Oh, I can do that."

"But, no disrespect, your tea isn't all that good, is it?" Joyce said as tactfully as she could manage. But the wincing, lemon-sucking expression she pulled was anything but subtle.

"Finch likes it."

"Finch likes everything."

"All right. You make it and I'll deliver it. Yeah?" Connie said.

"Why?"

Connie thought fast. Her old skills of thinking on her feet

and lying were, somewhat worryingly, coming back to her all too easily. Like a cat knowing to land on its feet the right way up.

"I'm in his bad books for being off ill. Tea will smooth it over."

Joyce shrugged okay and Connie waited for her to make a pot of tea. While it was brewing, Joyce joked that she was sure Connie could handle it from here and she went off to find some chores to do.

Alone in the kitchen, Connie poured some of the tea into a cup. She added a splash of milk and then filled up the rest of the cup with cold water from the tap. She wondered if she could get away with what she was planning.

She took the cup and saucer and marched down the corridor to find the doctor. He was standing by a desk in the small ward consulting some notes. He nodded thanks to Connie and told her to leave the tea on his desk.

This was the moment. Do or die.

Connie got close to him as she moved the cup and saucer towards the desk. At the last moment, she upended it down his front. Channing threw his arms up in alarm.

"Oh, so sorry!" Connie screamed.

"You stupid little—" Channing stopped himself, trying to regain his composure as he tried to brush himself down. His shirt and tie were soaked, but also the left panel of his white coat.

"I'm really sorry. Let me help you."

"Please just – leave it." Channing fumed, throwing off his white coat like an angry snake shedding its skin. "I'll have to change." He thundered off down the corridor.

Connie breathed a sigh of relief. Leaving the coat had been an unexpected bonus. Checking no one was watching, she picked it up. Surreptitiously, she removed the fob of keys from the pocket as she folded it up. Once she would have felt elated at this victory, adrenaline coursing through her veins. But now she just felt a resigned sense of relief.

Part one of the mission had been accomplished.

As she moved off down the corridor, she stopped when she caught a glimpse of Henry. He was standing by a bedside in a private room. The occupant of the bed had a badly burnt face and was motionless as Henry talked to him.

"God will be waiting to welcome you," Henry said softly. "All this pain and the suffering will be gone."

"My wife's there," the man murmured.

"Yes, you'll see her again."

Connie felt close to tears. How could Henry do this job? His warmth and compassion for others took her breath away. It only made her feel more wretched and worthless. She didn't deserve him.

Connie soon reached the locked room. Checking no one was around, she put the key in the lock and entered the room. Closing it behind her, she scanned the boxes and bottles on the shelves, her eyes glazing in panic as she tried to quickly find what she was looking for. All the names of the medicines looked like impenetrable hieroglyphics. This was the most dangerous part of her plan. If she was caught now, it would be very difficult to think up a good enough lie to avoid suspicion. Connie glanced at a shelf just above her shoulders. Tyrothricin! Three bottles side by side. She pocketed one and turned to leave the room. Turning the handle slowly, Connie opened the door. No one was in the corridor. She hastily emerged, closed the door and locked it. She ran back to the small ward and reached it at the same time as Dr Richard Channing returned with a new white coat.

"Where have you been?" he asked, a hint of suspicion in his voice.

"Put your whites in the wash," Connie said with a smile. She handed back the fob of keys. "Found these in the pocket."

Channing took them, nodding his thanks. He pulled the new white coat over his arms and returned to his notes.

"I'll be off, then," Connie said. But Channing didn't look up.

Seamless.

Vince's cracked lips opened and he sucked in a pill. Connie told him that he should take four of them a day and that they should fight off the infection.

"I feel bloody dreadful," Vince croaked.

"You've got to rest."

"You always knew what was best for me, Con." He smiled, closing his eyes.

Connie glanced at the gun on the bedside table with its monogrammed handle. She wanted to ask about Amos Ackley and whether they were in danger now. But she knew that Vince wasn't in any condition to talk. She guessed that she could probably grab the gun and force Vince out of the house, but she needed to know what danger she and Henry faced first. Would Amos be on his way? She couldn't risk not knowing the answer. So, with some regret, she put thoughts of grabbing the gun out of her head.

She pulled his curtains shut and encouraged Vince to change into pyjamas. Bringing a fresh pair of Henry's night clothes, she turned her back as Vince stumbled and fumbled his way into them. He was straining with the effort of coordinating his limbs. The buttons didn't fasten as his chest was bigger than Henry's; the trousers looked like sausage skins that might burst at the seams at any moment, but finally he was back in bed, the exertion having worn him out. Connie tucked him up and left some water and the Tyrothricin on the side.

She wondered again about the girl. The one on Barnes Common.

Forcing the thoughts from her head, Connie left the room.

Chapter 9

During the next few days things took on a queasy normality in the vicarage as the occupants settled into some kind of routine with one another. Vince remained in his room, the ill patient sleeping most of the day. Connie would leave a stack of sandwiches for him as she left for work early in the morning. Henry would busy himself with as much parish business as he could to stay out of the house for as long as possible each day. With Vince laid up, it was certainly easier for Connie to believe he wasn't as much of an intrusion into their lives. And at night, Connie would persist in trying to break the wall of silence that surrounded Henry. But it seemed as if he'd withdrawn deep into himself, with only the occasional flicker of resentment coming through from time to time. She didn't know how to reach him; she didn't know the words that might magically unlock his anguish. She didn't know what he was thinking; an unreachable island. So Connie busied herself with something tangible, something that she could focus on and perhaps change. Getting Vince out of her house.

But that was the problem. Vince didn't seem to be getting any better. He would lie in bed, sallow-faced and beaded with sweat, red-eyed, tossing and turning in small bouts of snatched sleep. When Henry was out, Connie would go to his room. She felt as though she was betraying her husband in some way, but on the other hand it felt that he had already emotionally left their marriage. She was so confused, with no idea how to make things right. But she knew it would help if Vince was gone. So she'd sit with him and talk, in the hope that the memories would help him recover in some way.

"You remember that steak we had in Southend?" Connie waited for a reply that didn't come. "You got so angry that it was red all on the inside, didn't you? Practically raw, you said, eh?"

Vince might offer a grunt in recognition to these memories. Sometimes a strained smile.

Connie wasn't sure if it was doing any good, but she knew he seemed to like it. When she had tried to leave after a few minutes one day, he'd grabbed her hand and indicated for her to stay. He wanted some more stories; tales from the good old days. Connie found herself looking at his hand on hers. His grip was clammy, but it was a soft gesture for once. Maybe he didn't have the strength to be more forceful. And she realised that she didn't want him to move his hand away. She sat carefully, so as not to dislodge its fragile grip on hers. Why was she doing that? Was it for his benefit to make him feel better? Suddenly, seeing the picture of Jesus on the wall, she felt a rush of guilt and moved her hand away as if his was a hot coal. His arm slumped like a streamer down the side of the bed, but he didn't seem to register the rejection.

But that wasn't the only time Connie found herself behaving

oddly around him. Once when Connie was sure he was asleep, she found herself talking like she hadn't before. A chance to have an audience. A confessional, perhaps.

"Do you think he hates me?" she whispered, not wanting or expecting an answer. "He hasn't spoken to me since you got here, not really, not properly. He'll ask if I want a cup of tea. Or what time I'm going to the farm. But we never talk about nothing that matters." She sighed sadly. "We used to talk before. I'm sure we did."

Vince had murmured, a waking beast. So Connie clammed up. Back to business, she put a new flannel on his forehead and left the room, regretting her candour. What if he'd heard? Oh, what did it matter? The whole thing was a mess. Her life was falling apart and she had no idea how to put it together again.

With Vince seemingly getting worse, finally, Connie realised that she would have to ask for professional help. Henry taciturnly urged her not to mention it to Vince. Connie set off to get some advice from Dr Wally Morgan, the town doctor. His consulting room was in the top room above the town hall, and a winding set of narrow wooden stairs snaked to a dingy waiting room at the top. When Connie got there, she realised that Dr Morgan was already with a patient, so she sat down next to a large unhealthy-looking pot plant that was starved of both water and light and flipped through a copy of *Picturegoer* magazine while she waited. It was an old copy with Dorothy Lamour on the cover, but it gave Connie a few moments distraction. She wondered how many people had thumbed through the magazine. People she knew. Esther might have taken note of the fashions, wondering if she was too old for some of the racier dresses. Iris might have excitedly looked at the showbiz glamour and wished it was her life. Mrs Gulliver probably wouldn't even have picked it up: unwilling to see pictures of the harlots inside. Connie closed the magazine just as an elderly woman emerged from the consulting room. She, like a lot of elderly woman in Helmstead, gave Connie a little scowl of disapproval and went on her way.

Dr Wally Morgan appeared in the consulting-room doorway. He was a small Welsh man in his late fifties with rheumy eyes and a complexion that spoke loudly of his drinking habits, complete with a large red nose and rosy cheeks. He always looked as though he'd been poured into his clothes, usually a scruffy tweed suit and a tie at half mast. There were rumours in the village that, once upon a time, Wally Morgan had been a doctor with a prestigious practice in Cardiff. But if that was true, those days were long forgotten now.

With effort, he focused his eyes on the newcomer.

"Mrs Fisher?" he asked.

"Mrs Jameson," Connie corrected.

Morgan nodded, looking none too convinced that Connie was right on the matter. He showed her through to his room, a room which was nearly as small as the medicine room at Hoxley Manor, although Morgan had somehow managed to fit a large mahogany desk, two chairs, a filing cabinet and a medical screen in. He edged himself carefully between the filing cabinet and the edge of the desk to reach his seat and waited for Connie to speak.

"I ain't got an appointment. But I wondered about some advice."

"Is it sexual?" Dr Morgan asked, a slight eagerness in his voice, which made Connie's skin crawl.

"No it ain't," she snapped, keen to put that notion right out of his head. The man was incorrigible. None of the women in Helmstead liked seeing him for anything that involved taking off clothes. On the plus side, he didn't have wandering hands like some doctors she'd heard about, but he certainly liked a good gawp.

At the vehemence of her response, Morgan recoiled in his chair. Trying to adopt a more business-like manner, he nodded for her to continue.

"I need to know something. How long do antibiotics take to treat an infection?" she asked.

"It's a good question." He pondered. "Well, it depends. If they are given intravenously – into the blood – they will work more quickly than if given in tablet form."

"Right, so with tablets: how long would they take to kick in, then?" Connie asked.

"Maybe three days, a week even?" Morgan replied. "It takes time to build up the levels of the medicine in the body."

"I see," Connie said, rising. "Thanks for your time, Doctor."

Dr Morgan squeezed around his desk and opened the door for Connie. And as she was leaving, he asked:

"Why do you ask about this?"

"I was wondering about a patient at Hoxley Manor," Connie smiled, again finding a lie springing easily to her lips.

It wasn't until she'd gone and was making her way down the narrow stairs to the outside that Dr Morgan asked himself a question. He knew she worked at the hospital some evenings, so why hadn't Connie asked a doctor at the manor house?

Back at the vicarage, Connie found Henry eating a sandwich at the dining-room table. He was about to leave on an errand, but waited to listen to Connie's news. When he'd heard what Morgan had said, he looked worried.

"He should be getting better by now, then," Henry said.

"I know. So maybe the medicine ain't working, I dunno."

"Or maybe—" Henry stopped himself from finishing the sentence. He shook his head, dismissing the thought and nodded his agreement to Connie.

"No, maybe what?" Connie pushed.

Henry fixed her with a hard stare; the logical pragmatist at the end of his tether. "Maybe he's having us on."

Could it be that Vince was better but somehow faking his illness? Was he buying more time? Connie thought it was unlikely, but Henry snapped that Vince was on to a good thing here: free bed and board, a place to lie low until he was sure it was safe to leave. Maybe he'd just used this to his advantage and decided to stay a while longer.

Connie wasn't so sure. "He could just tell us he's staying. He's got a gun. Nothing we could do. So why play-act?"

"Maybe." Henry mulled it over. He shook his head, weary of the whole thing. He didn't hope to understand what was going on in Vince's mind. Connie wondered to herself if he could be right. Maybe Vince was play-acting? Could he be wetting his brow with water when he heard her on the stairs? Putting on the whole delirious thing? She wanted to say that subterfuge wasn't really his style, but feared that Henry would blanch from any reminder of the familiarity between Connie and Vince. She steered clear of saying anything, scared of stepping on land mines.

Suddenly they heard a thump from the ceiling. The patient wanted them.

Connie went to see what he wanted. Vince looked pale and was clammy with cold sweat. He blinked and struggled to focus on Connie as she perched on the edge of the bed to feel his brow. If it was play-acting, then Vince Halliday deserved one of them award things, Connie thought. But then a big meaty hand shot out with surprising speed and grabbed her wrist. He pulled her closer, nearer to his cracked lips. He started to mumble and Connie had to strain to hear the words.

"You've got to."

She was thrown, it didn't make any sense. "What have I got to?" Connie asked, struggling to hear as his mouth tried to make sound.

"Get it. The key."

"What key? What are you talking about?"

Vince grimaced and gasped for breath and collapsed into a fitful slumber almost immediately. Connie realised Henry was standing in the doorway.

"He's not faking it," Connie said. Henry nodded, weighing up the implications in his head.

The two of them went downstairs. For a while they debated their options. Vince was weak and delirious. He may even be dying. Should they go against his wishes and just get Dr

Morgan to visit? Or should they just call the Home Guard now? Surely now he wouldn't be in any position to shoot the first person who came to get him?

"Part of me would love to turn him over," Henry said, uncharacteristically coldly. Immediately he shook his head, as if trying to dispel the thought from his head. It wasn't right for a man of the cloth to speak in such a way, but Connie could see how much Vince's presence had stressed Henry. Her husband composed himself, offered a small, apologetic smile and continued: "But for one thing, he grabbed your wrist pretty quickly. I wouldn't trust that his reactions had slowed that much. Certainly I don't want to gamble an innocent man's life on it."

They decided, despite their desperate wishes to be free of him, and the strains that it was putting on their marriage, that the only course of action was to obey the man with the gun.

Bright late-evening sun poured through the French windows at Hoxley Manor, as if making a last fantastic flourish before the oncoming night. Connie pulled the curtains, shutting out the possibilities of a sunset and walked back into the ward. Once it had been a large drawing room, framed by easy chairs and sofas. Now the only remnant of those luxurious and relaxed days were the well-stocked bookshelves obscured on the perimeter of the room by heavy hospital beds and the ill and the dying. Connie found Joyce and Dolores making two empty beds. She started to help them. Joyce was quizzing Dolores about music. What singers did she enjoy? What was her favourite song? As usual, she was getting nowhere, with Dolores refusing to reveal anything personal about her tastes. Connie wasn't in the mood to join in. She worked silently, a troubled look on her face.

Joyce's low-key and fruitless interrogation was interrupted as Dr Channing breezed in. He needed one of the girls to help him move a patient. Dolores was happy to volunteer and get out of the spotlight.

"I'm never going to find out anything about her, am I?" Joyce huffed.

Connie shook her head, too full of darker and deeper thoughts to get involved. Joyce looked at her friend, wondering what was wrong.

"Penny for them?"

"It's nothing," Connie said, shutting the question down.

Joyce and Connie finished the beds in silence, with Connie lost in her own thoughts. Possible futures. She saw glimpses of what might happen if she'd got the Home Guard. About what Henry had said about Vince still having fast-enough reactions. She saw the three elderly soldiers, in their mismatched uniforms, their makeshift weapons, moving towards the vicarage with their uneven gaits. Enjoying themselves with the heady rush of a proper mission that reminded them of their younger years and the missions of real danger overseas. But while their minds may have been energised, you couldn't disguise the fact that they moved like old men: too stiff to properly crouch over when running for cover; too slow to get out of the line of fire. Connie imagined a massacre in her spare room. Vince could unload his gun into the three old men before they even got near the bed. No, it wasn't an option. She couldn't risk it.

Other images fought for space in her head. Other options.

She saw herself snatching the gun from the bedside table, maybe quicker than Vince could stop her. He was smiling, hands in the air. But Connie shot him anyway. She saw his big, dumb, incredulous look as he realised he had a spreading patch of red on his chest. Could she do that?

As she plumped a pillow on an empty bed, Connie imagined Vince lying there. She pushed the pillow down on his face, using all her weight to keep it there as he thrashed about.

"What are you thinking about?" Joyce wasn't going to accept nothing for an answer.

"You don't want to know," Connie replied, smoothing the pillow over.

Joyce shrugged. Suit yourself.

It alarmed Connie that most of her options for getting Vince out of her life involving killing him. Wasn't that an over reaction? An immature response to an adult problem? Perhaps it was born out of futile desperation to save her marriage. But what was the alternative? Would Vince just leave when his hand got better? Connie couldn't imagine the sunlight dappling the vicarage hallway as Vince said his peaceful goodbyes to her and Henry. "Thanks for having me." No, she couldn't see that happening. Would he want to take her with him? Relive their glory days in some damp hovel. It was a possibility.

Joyce offered a friendly smile. It was a look that said, you don't have to tell me what's on your mind, but I'm here if you need me. Ironically it made Connie want to open up to her.

155

"Do you ever have bad thoughts?" Connie broached the subject.

"All the time." Joyce considered. "Sometimes I'll think about how bad someone looks in a dress, or how old someone's looking. All uncharitable stuff that I'm ashamed to admit really."

"No, really bad thoughts."

"What do you mean?"

"Do you think about that Ulrich bloke?" Connie didn't mean the question to sound as bald as it came out, but that was the danger when you'd been thinking for a while before voicing your thoughts. Questions became the tip of an iceberg of thought, presented with no context to back them up. Joyce raised her eyebrows. An unexpectedly deep and unwelcome question while she was making beds.

Ulrich had been a German airman who had bailed out from his plane in the countryside around Helmstead. While hiding out, he found Joyce on her own as she was riding through with a pony and trap. He forced her to conceal him on the cart and drive him cross country. He had a gun and made it clear that he wasn't afraid to shoot her if she betrayed him or disobeyed. They had driven in icy silence, the only sound the clip clop of the horse's hooves. Then Ulrich began to pass the time by asking about Joyce. She'd revealed that she'd lost her family in the German bombing of Coventry. And that's when Ulrich made a massive error. But the airman made a big mistake in taunting Joyce about it. He implied, whether it was true or not, that he was part of the bombing team on that fateful night. The night that had killed Joyce's parents and sister. Incensed and upset, Joyce careered the pony and trap into a tree, sending herself and the airman flying. Joyce recovered first and got the man's gun. And in a moment, another life was lost as she shot him dead. Did she think about him?

"Sometimes," she said, pondering.

"Do you mind me asking, you know, what it felt like?" Connie asked, taking care to couch the question a little less bluntly than her opening question.

Joyce saw the flash of fire from the pistol.

The airman collapsing.

She remembered the feeling of watching a life disappear at her feet in the woods.

"I did what I had to do." Joyce bit her lip. Connie knew there was more going on in her friend's head, but now wasn't the place to get there. It was Joyce's turn with the iceberg: presenting only what she wanted to be seen on the surface. "I had to keep telling myself, he'd have killed me otherwise. Never know if he would have done, of course."

Connie mulled over the words. Joyce brought her back to the here and now by saying that one of Connie's corners was loose. Connie fastened the bed sheet, realising that Joyce wouldn't talk any more about Ulrich tonight.

Connie wondered what she was capable of. Could she kill Vince to get rid of him? And then perhaps an even more worrying thought rose to the surface: would she want to?

Someone else wondering what he was capable of was Reverend Henry Jameson. He stood at the end of Vince Halliday's bed, watching the large man sleep fitfully. The revolver sat on the bedside cabinet, its handle turned in towards Vince. Henry felt disappointed in himself for feeling hatred for the man. But since he'd arrived, everything had turned sour. And, sure, he and Connie had their problems before he turned up, but things were untenable now. He knew he should stand by her; they should face adversity together. But something was stopping him. And at this moment, he didn't know what it was. Why wouldn't he unreservedly stand by Connie, his wife, and face this hurdle together?

For her part, Connie was trying to find the normality in this abnormal situation, and Henry knew that. And yet he wouldn't let himself give her support; preferring a taciturn demeanour to her rather than an encouraging smile.

Henry felt a wave of remorse as he remembered the night Connie had tried to make him feel better about the situation by suggesting they make love. Now, in hindsight, Henry realised that it would have been so good for their relationship, for the feeling of being united against the darkness. But, at the time, his resentment got in the way.

With the bedroom door closed, Connie was desperate for Henry to tell her how he was feeling. She knew that he had been taciturn and distant. At the time, Connie hoped that they would only have to tolerate Vince for a short while longer. This was before he became ill. With Vince downstairs, drinking in front of the fire, the couple spoke in their room in whispers, all too aware of how sound could carry around their small cottage. This subterfuge further curdled Henry's mood; any inclination he had anyway. He couldn't voice his feelings to

Connie, scared they might somehow open her eyes to his inadequacies. But he felt weak and powerless. He'd prayed to God to deliver him from this foul man, but the prayers hadn't been answered. And even that action had felt like a shifting of responsibility. The plain fact was, it should have been his responsibility as man of the house to force this intruder out. But he saw it as Connie's problem. Her past. So he felt that she should be the one who got rid of him. If he could have discussed his feelings, even these feelings, to Connie, then things might have got better between them. But instead, Henry clammed up, as he always did, somehow expecting his wife to guess.

"Let's go to bed," Connie said, pulling off her clothes. Showing willing, Henry pushed the bedroom chair against the door handle. He knew that it would be good for them, for their bond, if he could. But he felt at his most vulnerable in bed and the last thing he wanted was the chance of Vince bursting in.

Once under the sheets, Connie nestled into him. She started to kiss his neck. Henry tried to respond, but a noise from downstairs broke the moment for him. He stopped kissing Connie and sighed.

"Come on. It's been a while," Connie whispered.

Henry knew exactly how long it had been since they'd last made love. It coincided exactly with the arrival of the monster downstairs.

"Forgive me if I'm not in the mood." Henry pulled back the bed sheets and rubbed the back of his tense neck.

"He's not here, though, is he?"

"He's near enough, Connie."

Connie urged Henry to forget about him. "He can't take this away from us."

"Don't you see? He already has." And Henry turned away. He didn't want to see the sadness and the shock on his wife's face. And at that moment, Henry Jameson, mild-mannered Reverend of the Parish of Helmstead, felt a deep rage welling inside of him. Vince Halliday had taken away everything he had. His home, his marriage, the intimacy of making love to his wife.

And now, here he was, with potentially the upper hand at last. Vince was sick in bed, and his pistol was within reach. Henry took a step closer. Maybe he could grab it? Maybe he could force Vince to leave? Henry reached out a tentative hand. Edging forward, his fingers were a few inches from the gun when—

BANG BANG.

Henry's heart nearly burst out of his chest. Vince awoke groggily and grabbed the pistol, curious eyes focusing on Henry. What was he doing here?

BANG BANG.

There was someone knocking on the door downstairs.

Vince struggled to place the noise, time and space falling back into place around him.

Before Vince could ask any questions, Henry bolted from the room and took the stairs two at a time, his heart beating like a steam-engine piston in his chest. He'd come so close. Could he have done it? He suspected that he knew the answer. He wasn't man enough, was he?

Henry flung open the front door with a look of annoyance – but it was focused mainly on his own feelings of inadequacy. He couldn't stand up for his wife, morally or physically. He lacked backbone.

A surprised Gladys Gulliver was standing there. Suspicion in a beige coat and pillbox hat.

"Have I interrupted anything, Reverend?" she said, her beady eyes scanning Henry for any clues. The village busybody – Mrs Gulliver was a self-proclaimed upstanding member of the community with an opinion on everyone. She would gossip about anyone and everything – all with the self-justi-fied motivation of it being her Christian duty. For his part, Henry felt pity for the old woman. He knew she had been parted from her beloved husband too soon and he suspected that her life was empty without him. Other people's business had filled the void of loss.

"What can I do for you, Mrs Gulliver?" Henry said, trying to control his fast breathing.

"Is it a good time?"

"I've just run down – yes, it's fine. Just a bit out of puff."

"What have you been doing up there?" Mrs Gulliver enquired, raising an eyebrow. What was this she'd stumbled upon?

Henry thought the real answer would probably prove more shocking than anything the old lady could imagine.

"Just rather busy," Henry stammered, realising it was better to just steam roller over it and get rid of her as quickly as possible.

"I came by to give you this, Reverend." Mrs Gulliver handed

a Henry a small book with embossed gold lettering on the spine. "It's a book about purity," she added caustically.

"Right. Thank you." Henry realised that the infernal woman had somehow managed to move into his hallway during the conversation. Like an insidious gas, she had wafted past him. So now he had to – as politely as possible – usher her out.

Mrs Gulliver was just about to leave, when they both heard the noise

THUD THUD.

She looked at the source of the noise. Had it come from the top of the stairs? One of the bedrooms?

"Is that Mrs Jameson?"

"No."

"Who is it, then?" And she took a step back into the hallway.

"Mice." Managed Henry, adding, "The handyman from the Diocese is upstairs trying to fix some – traps."

Mrs Gulliver looked suspiciously at the Reverend. Would a man of the cloth actually lie? She doubted that Henry Jameson had the gumption to tell an untruth.

But before she could ask any further questions, Henry closed the door. With a sour look of doubt, Mrs Gulliver took her leave. She listened against the wood – paying no heed or feeling no embarrassment to the people passing by – and heard Henry running back up the stairs inside.

What was going on in the vicarage?

Chapter 10

Three days later.

Frederick Finch was excited at the prospect of an evening playing cards in the Bottle and Glass. He sucked the top off his pint and paid the barman. Sitting at a nearby table, Dr Wally Morgan was trying to shuffle the pack with shaking hands. An impatient-looking Frank Tucker sat watching, keen to take the cards and do it himself. But Wally shooed him away. It was all under control. Three cards spun off under the table and Frank started to chew his lip in frustration.

"Heh heh, ready, lads?" Finch said, bringing over another round of drinks.

"By the time he's shuffled, it'll be closing time." Frank winced.

Wally dipped under the table to collect the errant cards, banging his head in the process. Now, Finch winced – in sympathy.

"Here, give 'em to me," Finch said, taking the pack.

His thick fingers started to shuffle the pack with a surprising dexterity when he sensed a figure standing near

163

his right shoulder. He looked up into the sour face of Gladys Gulliver. She was frowning. Mind you, he'd have been more unnerved if she was smiling.

"Heh, the garlic around the entrance must have fallen off!" Finch chuckled.

"Mock all you like, Frederick Finch. I'm here on a serious matter. Do you think I'd set foot in this hellish place if it wasn't important?"

Finch shook his head, sheepishly, feeling suitably reprimanded. The irony – and sadness of the situation was that once, long ago, Finch's wife and Mrs Gulliver had been good friends. Friends enough to warrant their poles-apart husbands to try to make small talk with each other and try to get on while the women laughed and chatted with an enviable ease. But when Finch lost his wife and then Mrs Gulliver lost her husband – they slowly became more distant and antagonistic. Finch thought – when he cared to examine the matter – that things got worse when Mrs Gulliver threw herself into the Church. It supported her in her loneliest hours and gave her comfort. A string of Parish priests – up to and including Henry Jameson – had given their time to her, indulged her, stopped her feeling so alone. And as the Church became everything to Mrs Gulliver, so the heathen lifestyle of Frederick Finch – a man who thought nothing of sleeping in the Bottle and Glass all night so he wouldn't have to walk home – grated more and more. Now, from once sharing drinks together with their partners, the two were polar opposites with daggers drawn.

"What's so important, then?" Finch sighed. He wanted to

get rid of her as quickly as possible so he could relieve Wally and Frank of their money.

"I think Reverend Jameson is –" She couldn't finish the sentence, the words stuck in her throat.

"Is what?" Finch asked. "Isn't very good at football? Isn't a dab hand at catching rabbits? Here, Frank, you should have seen him trying to catch one. He was all fingers and—"

"Mr Finch!" Gladys Gulliver snapped.

"Oh, sorry," Finch replied, cowed.

Frank Tucker threw a "that told you" look to Finch. Wally Morgan's head poked up from under the table, the Jack of Clubs in his hand. His eyes tried to focus on the thin, angry woman in front of him. For her part, Mrs Gulliver became distracted by the doctor's sudden appearance. Where had he been all this time? Finch brought her back to the moment:

"What is Henry doing?"

Mrs Gulliver craned her neck and lowered her voice. "Incredible as it may seem, I think he's having relations with someone else." She lowered her voice even more on the word "relations" so it was barely more than a mouthed shape.

Finch and Tucker took a moment to process this statement and then they erupted with laughter. This angered Mrs Gulliver, whose hopes of a serious and useful discussion about the matter were fading fast.

"No, see, that wife of his was out. I knows she was out because I'd seen her leave-"

"You see everyone leave."

"So he wasn't at home with her. And when I went round, he was all furtive and sweaty."

165

Finch had had enough. The clock above the bar was ticking away his chances of winning other men's money.

"Henry isn't having relations. He's the last person to carry on like that. He loves Connie."

"She's a beautiful woman," Wally Morgan slurred. "Who?"

"The lengths he went to get her-" Finch continued. "He's the last person to be unfaithful."

"Well, I feel wrong suggesting it, of course. He's the Reverend. A close personal friend," Mrs Gulliver said. "But I wondered if you'd heard anything. I'm hoping I'm wrong about it."

"I'm sure you're wrong about it, Mrs Gulliver," Finch said. He threw a look to Frank, indicating for him to deal the cards. Frank obliged and started to deal three hands onto the table. Finch hoped it was the signal that Mrs Gulliver needed.

"I can see you're busy," Mrs Gulliver said, moving towards the door.

Finch glanced at her troubled face. Fifteen years ago, he could have asked if she fancied staying for a port and lemon – and she would have probably said yes. And they could have chatted while he played cards: platonic friends. Lonely people reaching out to one another. He knew she was isolated, but he also knew that her pride wouldn't let her soften in front of him. Too many distancing choices had been made by the pair of them ever to have that easy closeness again. The moment passed, somewhat to Finch's relief. He didn't offer her a drink and Mrs Gulliver left the pub.

"Right, show me your money, gentlemen," Finch said chuckling, turning his attention to the here and now.

The last three days had been a time in limbo for Connie and Henry. They couldn't relax and they couldn't get on with their lives and the wall of silence from Henry was getting more testing for Connie. He barely spoke, choosing to answer questions as quickly as possible. He spent most of his time out of the house. Connie was waiting to see what would happen with Vince.

Connie pulled the curtains in Vince's room. The colour in his face was returning and he didn't have the deathly pale sheen on his skin any more. The alternating intense heat and clamminess on his forehead were also lessening. Connie went to pick up the empty water glass by his bed, when his eyes slowly opened. He focused on her, eyes clearing. Brighter than before.

"Feeling better?" Connie asked.

"A little, yeah." Vince licked his parched lips.

"Take another."

She opened the bottle and tapped a tablet into the palm of her hand. Vince's ungainly fingers plucked it from her grasp and popped it between his lips. As he did this, he pulled her hand up to his mouth. Connie was shocked, too shocked to resist, as Vince kissed her fingers. He let go of her hand and she pulled it away, scalded.

"Thanks, Con," Vince said, a genuine-looking smile filling his large face.

"It's nothing," Connie replied, eager to get away. She felt uneasy about what he'd done and was annoyed that her face had flushed.

"You saved my life," he said, taking her in.

"I just want you well enough to leave. That's all," Connie said, finding her steely resolve once more. His puppy-dog expression unnerved her. She'd seen some of the injured servicemen falling for their nurses. It was a known syndrome, or something. The last thing she wanted was Vince falling for her. No, she just wanted him to get well so he could leave. So she could patch things up with Henry before it was too late.

She left the room. But rather than getting angry at her words, Vince smiled to himself. A look of silent satisfaction. He'd seen how her cheeks had flushed when he kissed her fingers. She couldn't hide that reaction or cover it up. Vince thought he might still have a connection with Connie, some-thing primal, linked to their shared past of highs and lows. Here with Henry – what sort of man was he? A stuffed shirt. He wasn't a man, was he? Scared of his own shadow and lost in books about a make-believe God. Pah! With Henry there was no excitement. He'd not heard them make love – despite their room being next to his – since he'd arrived. Maybe they didn't sleep together? Vince didn't know for sure. Even if they did, would such a bookworm be able to satisfy his Connie? But he'd bet every penny he had that Connie's life didn't have any excitement or danger in it now.

And who knows, maybe she missed that. Yeah, maybe she needed some excitement again.

Michael Sawyer sat in front of the fire in his little cottage cleaning a piston. It had come from his garden pump, an ancient device that had seen better days. Michael hoped it might last one more summer. But parts were hard to come by, what with the war, so he had to make do and mend. Vera Sawyer sat nearby, knitting a jumper for him, her eyes growing heavy from the heat of the fire. Margaret was in her room. The sobbing had stopped about thirty minutes ago and Vera thought the child had gone into a fitful sleep. Michael couldn't understand why the child was always crying. She didn't seem to respond to the simplest discipline and she invited a lot of the trouble herself with her argumentative attitude. They had sent her to bed with no supper after she argued about taking part in an event at school. The teacher had wanted the pupils to bring something from home which meant something to them – with the view to discussing the items and learning about one another. Margaret had asked if she could take in something of Michael or Vera's. For her part, Margaret thought she was being nice, embracing them as the surrogate parents they had become. Showing thanks for them taking her in after her mother died. But Michael had flatly refused. "I don't want them nosing into our business!"

Margaret was genuinely surprised by this attitude as she thought he would welcome her gesture.

"Your father's right," Vera admonished. Whether she agreed or not, it was important to back him up, as she always did.

"But everyone is bringing something. Even the evacuee kids that haven't got things," Margaret protested. She had seen some of those children making up things to feel better about their lives. At least Margaret never did that.

"Will you stop answering me back!" Michael roared, his voice tremulous with rage. For the second time in a few seconds, Margaret was surprised by the over reaction. She cowered away, apologising and feeling hot tears welling in her eyes. She scurried to the stairs. To the place. But the penalty this time would be worse than the cupboard.

"Go to bed! No supper! Get out!" Michael screamed. Vera calmed her husband and encouraged him to sit down. She gave him a cup of tea, but his hands were shaking so much it tidal-waved into the saucer.

Margaret went slowly to her room. She didn't realise that things were soon to get much worse.

As Michael finished mending the piston, his wife watched him, pleased that he had calmed down. He had some oil on his hands from the components, so Vera offered to get some newspaper to wrap the parts for him. She handed him a copy of *The Daily Mail* and he opened it out on the floor, placing the oily piston in the centre of the spread. He couldn't believe it. There, in black and white was a photograph of Margaret with Connie Carter.

Michael couldn't comprehend what he was seeing at first.

Vera was equally confused. How could this be? She knew a reporter had asked the girl some questions. Vera was being treated for cuts and bruises at the time and didn't see whether a photograph was taken.

"It's got her name," Michael stammered. "It says where she lives. Oh God."

He was breathing heavily now, anger building.

"It'll be all right," Vera said. "It's dated – last week. And nobody's come for you, have they?"

"You don't know that. They might have wheels in motion, I don't know."

"They haven't come," Vera stated firmly, as if calming a child.

But she couldn't calm him. "Get her now," Michael shouted, his brow suddenly beaded with sweat, his eyes wide and scared.

From upstairs, Margaret was listening against her open bedroom door. Her blood had run cold. It was catastrophic that they knew about the story. From their tone, Margaret knew that this would be the darkest night of her life if she didn't escape as quickly as she could. She had to act fast. She closed her door, firmly but quietly, and slipped the bolt across it. Then she went to her bed and removed the small suitcase from underneath it, filling it with anything that meant anything to her – her diary, the cutting of her and Connie, her favourite dress (the one she had arrived in).

BANG BANG BANG!

Furious knocking at the door, the wood shaking on its hinges.

"Open this door right now!" Michael screamed in a voice almost as high-pitched as Vera's.

Margaret was terrified. What could she do? She'd hoped to have been able to take her case and run for it, but there was no way she'd get past them now.

"It wasn't my fault. I didn't say nothing," Margaret said.

A softer voice – seemingly calm, but somehow more terrifying. "It's all right. We just want to talk." It was Vera. Margaret could almost sense her looking at her husband with a pleading look of "Let me try".

Margaret looked around. The only way out was the small

window. She pulled open the curtains and unlatched the window. The cool night breeze nearly took her breath away. She couldn't see a thing below the window, but she knew there were box bushes there in the front garden. She hoped they might break her fall.

"Come on, love." Vera again.

She never called her love. That was doubly chilling.

"I told you we should never have taken her in." Michael's voice. Almost a sobbing cry of regret.

He banged on the door again.

So with one final look behind her at the strange prison she'd known for three years, Margaret Sawyer jumped out of the window with her suitcase. Her foot caught the drainpipe and spun her into a head-first dive. Crashing into the box hedge below, she felt the scratches of the foliage as it tore at her face, her chest winded from the impact. She struggled not to make a sound as she picked up her case and started to run, dreading looking behind her in case they were at the window. Or worse still, coming out of the front door.

Her heart pumping in her chest, Margaret bounded over the small picket fence that surrounded the front garden and ran off into the night. Some distance behind, she could hear the front door opening and Michael howling into the night:

"Come back here! Or I'll kill you!"

It was incentive enough to keep running and the terrified little girl kept running until her feet were sore and her head was pounding with stress. Where could she go? She had a friend in Branford. Maybe her mother would let her stay for a few days. She slowed down, trying to catch her breath, to control it enough to hear other sounds in the night. Were they still pursuing her? Had they given up? Or were they circling round her? Margaret moved slowly, keeping all her senses alert for danger as she neared a clump of trees. It was so dark that she wasn't quite sure where she was. Certainly it was some way from Jessop's Cottage. And then she found a stone wall in front of her. Climbing over it, she was relieved to see Helmstead Village Square. She ran behind the large ornamental well in the centre of the road and sat behind it, trying to get her head straight.

That night, Connie, feeling the chasm between herself and Henry growing, decided to do something about it. She couldn't get through to him and whenever she tried to open him up it had no effect. He didn't want to talk. Instead he sat brooding, scowling at her as if he hated her. Could he hate her? That possibility chilled Connie. This was the love of her life and she thought that she was the love of his life too – despite their differences. Differences that seemed of little importance now.

They hadn't spoken properly since Vince arrived. The conversations would be functional and free of the easy chemistry that they'd naturally had when they'd been courting. Connie had tried to get Henry to talk, but he wouldn't, instead snapping – as much as Henry ever snapped – that he was fine and to leave it. She resigned herself to the fact that he wouldn't talk in the same carefree way until Vince had gone. She knew they wouldn't make love again until he had gone either. Connie worried that Henry might leave her or kick her out when this was all over. She resolved to do all she could to stop that happening. But she needed to feel close to him, needed to make him realise that they would get through this awful time.

Connie had a plan. Perhaps a last-ditch attempt to cement things back together.

So she waited in their bedroom for Henry to come home from his visit to the ailing Dr Beauchamp. She had laid sandwiches and a bottle of cider on the bedspread, an impromptu "bed picnic". As she waited, she listened to the sounds from the guest bedroom, hoping and praying that Vince would be asleep soon. At gone ten o'clock, she heard the latch on the front door lift and recognised Henry's soft footsteps as he wiped his brogues on the door mat. She guessed that he was trying not to wake Vince either.

Darting to the top of the landing, Connie attracted his attention before he went into the dining room.

"Psst!"

"Connie?"

"Keep your voice down and come here."

Soon she had a confused Henry inside the bedroom and was hastily closing the door behind him. She helped him remove his coat and hat while fielding his questions.

"What's happened?"

"Nothing's happened. Didn't want you waking him, that's all."

"What are you doing here?" Henry noticed the food and drink on the bed. Two tumblers had been placed either side of the cider bottle, and Connie had picked a handful of field flowers to decorate the bedside cabinet.

"What's all this?" Henry asked.

"We haven't had a supper to ourselves for ages, have we?"

He took this in, considering. Since Vince arrived, Henry didn't act spontaneously any more. Instead he evaluated everything before giving his response. And this was no different.

"That's a lovely idea, Connie," he mumbled, without smiling. But inside he recognised the effort she was making; the effort against adversity.

But even his taciturn compliment was enough to buoy Connie. Maybe it was worth it. Maybe she could reach him after all. Excitedly, she motioned for him to sit on the floor. She sat beside him and lit a candle between them.

"We're not going to sacrifice anything, don't worry," Connie said.

"You need an altar for pagan services. And I don't think the dressing table would cut it," Henry said. A small smile broke through, turning the corners of his mouth up, if not illuminating his eyes.

Connie felt her eyes welling with happy tears. For the first time, she hoped that they were strong enough to get through this. They could do it. She leaned in for a kiss. Henry seemed nervous, withdrawn.

"What's the matter?"

"What do you think?"

"But even if he weren't here. Would you want to, then?" Connie's big brown eyes looked vulnerable. The question had come out without her usual brashness; instead a fractured, fragile thing loaded with hope.

But before Henry could answer, there was a thumping at the front door.

BANG. BANG. BANG.

Henry looked confused. "Amos!" Connie said, terrified. "Who else could it be at this time of night?"

She ran out of the room, a dazed Henry following. "What are you going to do?"

Connie burst into Vince's room, where he was already pulling his large frame out of the bed and trying to stand on fever-drained legs. As he looped his braces over his shoulders, Connie could see the butt of the pistol sticking out from his pocket.

"We just need to talk to him," Henry stammered. "If it's Amos."

"Yeah, give him a sermon, Rev, that'll work," Vince snapped. He took a step forward, the blood rushing to his head and making his legs buckle like a day-old foal. Connie steadied him.

"But how could he even know you're here?" Henry asked.

"Just be quiet. I need to think," Vince growled.

"What shall we do?" Connie asked him.

Vince rubbed the bridge of his nose, desperately trying to clear his head, to think straight.

And despite the agitation he was feeling, Henry felt further irked by this turn of events. At the first sign of danger, Connie had run to Vince not to him. And now she was asking him what they should do. It was as if they had slipped effortlessly back into their old ways. The first sign of danger and it seemed they were reunited. Partners in crime. The old adage about being as thick as thieves seemed horribly true. Henry felt sick.

Connie ran down the stairs, eyeing the normally cosy image of her front door as a new danger.

176

"Open it," Vince said, from half-way up the stairs, the gun in his hand.

"You're not going to shoot him in the vicarage," Henry protested. "Let me past and I'll talk to him."

Connie flashed a look back. "Might be worth a try."

"Just open it and I'll blow his brains out. End of story," Vince said, levelling the gun with an unsteady hand in the vague direction of the front door.

"Please. I implore you not to use violence—"

"Get out the way."

Having a semi-delirious man waving a gun in his general direction was enough to make Henry Jameson see the good sense of getting out of the way. Reluctantly, and with resentment, he pushed himself to one side of the stairs, allowing Vince to lumber down. Now the thug stood in his hallway behind Connie, his gun raised, ready. Connie moved her hand to open the front door.

Henry's blood was pumping through his ears, pushed by a rapidly beating heart. He imagined that Connie and Vince were equally fired up and on edge. Connie opened the door and flung it open. Vince levelled the gun –

But it wasn't Amos Ackerly.

It was a terrified nine-year-old girl.

Chapter 11

Margaret Sawyer drank nervously from the mug. Henry had given her some hot milk and she was cupping it with both hands, desperate for both its warmth and comfort. Connie knelt on the floor at her eye level and was trying to work out how long she had been outside in the cold. Why had she even come here this late at night? But the main priority since her arrival wasn't asking questions. It had been to calm her down, to get her to relax after being greeted by the sight of a sweating, bullish man waving a gun in her face. That wasn't the sight you expected to see when you knocked on the door of a vicarage in a sleepy town.

"Feeling better?" Connie smiled.

"Yes," Margaret squeaked, in the sort of voice that didn't really convince either way.

Vince, despite Connie's hope that he'd go upstairs to make it easier to calm the visitor, was sitting at the dining table, staring balefully at the little girl. Connie assumed that his mind was whirring with questions too. Mostly concerning what he should do about this situation. Now someone else knew he was here. It wasn't just Connie and Henry. Connie knew that this was when Vince could be at his most dangerous. He'd never been good at keeping his temper when things got out of hand, out of his control. She remembered the nights when she'd stroke his forehead as he sat in the flat, trying to calm him; trying to talk him out of doing something rash or dangerous.

Yeah, she'd been good at that. Much better than she'd been as a vicar's wife.

Connie shut the thought out of her head. She focused back on the situation in hand. Vince's eyes had narrowed and he was staring intently at the little girl. Something clicked into place in his head.

"I recognise you," Vince said. Margaret looked up, brushing her blonde fringe out of her eyes. "You was the girl in the newspaper photograph."

Margaret looked shocked at being spoken to by this man. With the nervousness she was feeling, she doubted her own name, let alone whether she had been in any photograph.

"Which explains how he found us," Henry added in an aside to his wife.

"Don't matter how he found us, does it?" Connie replied. "He's here now."

"As if I could forget it," Henry said, shooting a sour look at her. Connie felt instantly apologetic. She hadn't meant her reply to be so dismissive; just meaning that the history wasn't the most important thing right now. But maybe she'd somehow felt it was innate criticism. If she hadn't been in that photograph, none of this would be happening. It was her fault. Just like it was her fault that she couldn't make a decent cup of tea. Or entertain the bishop without giving him a sing song.

Now it was Connie's turn to bridle. She was a good person. She knew she was. And she'd done the right thing saving those people on that train. Who did Henry think he was?

Henry looked confused. Why was she glowering at him?

Connie realised that she'd let her mind run away with her. All from one little comment. She put it out of her mind.

"Please may I use the toilet?" Margaret said, suddenly nervous at the attention. It was a relief for Connie to have an excuse to leave the room. Connie guided her to the stairs, and pointed out the room to her. "Door on the left."

Margaret went upstairs. As she rose up, Connie noticed that one of her legs was badly scratched, a long, jagged red line as though a demented stocking seam running up her calf. It was like she'd been scratched by a thorn bush or a hedge or something. Connie returned to the dining room.

"Make me a cuppa," Vince growled.

"Make it yourself," Connie snapped.

"Not you. Him," Vince said. "Your tea is diabolical."

"You was quite happy to drink it."

"It was still diabolical." They caught each other's eyes. A strange moment of warmth and shared memory amid the tension. Connie heard a small laugh coming from her mouth. It was the stress of the last few minutes bubbling up and over into laughter. But laughing between two ex-lovers wasn't what Henry wanted to hear. He went to make the tea.

Letting him go, Connie pulled a chair out and sat at the

table, nearer to where Margaret had been. She glanced as Vince stared at the embers in the hearth. He started to unwind the bandage on his hand, staring morosely as each layer of fabric spun away. Picking off the pad over the wound revealed a cut that was pink instead of the angry red it had been previously. The untidy stitching had held. Connie felt relief. It might mean that Vince would go soon. Hope upon hope.

"You done a good job."

"I did me best." Connie decided that she might as well be nice. It might be easier.

"You can do the holes in my socks if you like."

"There's an offer, innit?"

In the kitchen, Henry found himself enraged. He didn't understand how Connie could joke with him. It seemed that she could easily fall back into their old ways. When they had been together. The thoughts hurt Henry, welling bolts of hot tears into his eyes. He didn't want to lose her. But he didn't understand her and felt miles apart from her sometimes; unlike Vince who seemed to tap into her psyche with his rugged charm. If you could call it charm. Was it made worse because he was a man who was everything Henry wasn't? A threatening and dangerous man without a concern for manners, etiquette or people's feelings. Henry knew how to deal with people who were like him. But Vince was unpredictable, a continent of experience so distant from his own that he wouldn't even know how to sail there.

Before, this place had been a calm house: an oasis in the turbulence of war, a sanctuary for those who came here. Troubled souls would sit at the table, sipping tea, calmed by the reassuring tick of the mantelpiece clock and they would feel restored; perhaps feeling their troubles slightly eased, concerns lifted. But now there was something evil here. A malevolent presence that had stomped over the niceties of polite conversation and the gentle tinkle of china cups on saucers. And now the evil was spreading, affecting the young girl, who had come here for help. Would they be able to help her? Would they be allowed to help her? Margaret had sought sanctuary but what was here might be even worse than whatever she was running from. Henry knew he had to do something.

But what?

Meanwhile, Connie used the opportunity of being alone with Vince to ask the big question that was on her mind. The thing that had been gnawing away at her, placing a venomous ball of unease in her stomach since she had first seen the monogram on the handle of the pistol.

"So what did you do to Amos Ackley?" Connie asked, as lightly as she could manage. She had to know the situation. "Am I in danger? I mean, are we in danger?"

Vince gave a little snort and smiled at her, amused by her slip. She was thinking of herself first, not Henry and herself. Maybe she'd already mentally shut off from the marriage, leaving its wreckage to concentrate on personal survival. Vince hoped so. That was his Connie.

Henry brought in an empty cup and saucer, annoyed at how his hand was shaking. The crockery was rattling, betraying any stern facade he was trying to muster.

"It's brewing. My wife – We just need to know what danger we're in," Henry stammered.

Vince's eyes became like granite.

"You're in plenty of danger, Reverend," Vince said coldly. "From me. You see, she and I go way back. But you're just an inconvenience to me. A random fella in the way of things. I've got to work out what to do about you. And the kid, for that matter."

Henry swallowed hard, trying to find some saliva in his mouth to speak. But he couldn't find the words.

"We're in this together," Connie said, rising and standing by Henry's side. She knew she was over-compensating for her slip. But she had to stand by her man. Henry felt both comforted and oddly undermined by her support. The old-fashioned part of him knew that he should be the one making the stand, not his wife. He should have made a stand back in the hallway when Vince was pointing a gun at the door. And he should be making a stand now. But making a stand was hard when you couldn't even find the words to speak and your legs felt like jelly.

"He's my husband," Connie added, defiantly.

"Indeed he is." Vince raised his eyebrows in mock surprise.

"What's that supposed to mean?" Henry stuttered.

"You two is hardly fish and chips, are you?"

"What are you talking about?" Connie looked confused.

"Things that go together naturally. Fish and chips. Tea and milk. Sausage and ma—"

"I get the idea," Connie snapped. "We go together just fine, don't we?"

Henry nodded feebly. And Connie hated him for that moment. Why couldn't he bluff? Why did he have to be so damn honest the whole time? Where was his backbone?

Before Connie had time to say anything, Margaret's footfalls on the stairs made her change tack. She turned her attention from Henry to Vince.

"Vince here would like to apologise for waving a gun in your face. Wouldn't you?"

"Thought you might be someone else," Vince said, uncomfortable about having to apologise. He offered what he thought was a reassuring smile which, ironically, made everyone feel even more uneasy. "Don't like people coming here."

"That's okay. Michael always gets uptight if anyone comes to the cottage as well," Margaret said.

"Is Michael your dad?" Connie asked.

Margaret pulled a face, her mouth contorting in the way that children do when they're pondering how to answer a big question. The young girl was about to reply, but she stopped herself and looked at her feet. Connie tried a different approach.

"Why did you come here, Margaret?"

"I should go back," the girl said, suddenly worried. What had she done?

"It's too late to be trekking back over those fields," Connie said. "We've had crashed German airmen wandering about and all sorts."

"You should stay here tonight," Henry said, kindly.

Margaret nodded reluctantly.

Vince arched an eyebrow, as if he should have perhaps have

been consulted on this matter. Again, Henry enjoyed the small, empty, victory of apparently being master in his own house. A charade, of course, but it was all he had. Vince stretched. Both men knew that Henry was only the master on the surface. There was a different man in charge now.

"I'll take you back tomorrow on me way to work. We'll make you up a bed down here," Connie said, pleased to be taking action. This was one situation amid the madness that she could manage. The vicarage was a haven once more.

Vince looked uncomfortable. Connie told Margaret to come with her to collect a blanket and a pillow and they disappeared upstairs. Henry set about putting some more kindling on the fire to keep the room warm enough for their new visitor.

"Who is she?" Vince hissed.

"The girl from the photograph," Henry replied. "Beyond that, I don't know."

Vince looked towards the door, perhaps mulling things over, perhaps planning what to do.

Henry felt a sick fear rising in his throat. Could this man contemplate killing the child? With deep unease, Henry realised that he had no idea what Vince was capable of.

But he knew one thing, categorically and without question. He knew he had to do everything in his power to rid them of this monster.

After an uneasy night's sleep, during which Connie had checked on their young guest a couple of times, she and Henry made breakfast for Margaret. Vince slept in upstairs. The young girl fell on the scrambled eggs and toast as if suddenly remembering how hungry she had been from her run the night before, colour returning to her cheeks. It was five-thirty in the morning and just as dark as it had been when she'd arrived. Connie put on her Land Army sweater and pushed her hat on her head.

"You're really beautiful," Margaret said.

"Ha. No one's beautiful in a Land Army get-up," Connie laughed. "I think the whole thing's designed to make you as unappealing to the GIs as possible. Look at this chunky old sweater, makes me look the size of a house!"

"But Connie isn't trying to attract any GIs." And shooting a look at his wife, Henry added pointedly, "Is she?"

"No, 'Course not," Connie said, pulling a comical face for Margaret's amusement.

She realised that the young girl didn't have a coat. She must have left in a hurry the night before. Connie opened her little suitcase, but it didn't contain any rational packing: a collection of soft toys, the piece from the newspaper, a skirt and a dress, a single sock. Everything had been grabbed and thrown into the case in a hurry.

"Look, you don't have to go back," Connie said quietly.

"I have to," Margaret said. The truth was, she hoped that Michael and Vera might have calmed down by now. Although she had a friend in Brinford, she couldn't rely on staying with her family for more than a day or so. The truth was that she had nowhere to go other than back to Jessop's Cottage. So her only hope would be that things wouldn't be too bad on her return and that she'd only have to spend a couple of nights under the stairs.

"Well, I'll come back with you, then. Check everything is all right," Connie said, moving towards the door.

She glanced at her husband. Usually he would make a move towards her, to kiss her goodbye. But today he stood with his back to her and Margaret as he fussed with the breakfast things. Connie made no effort to kiss him first. She went into the hallway, not seeing Henry turn and look forlornly at his departing wife. He watched as Margaret and Connie walked down the path and into the high street.

They walked through the overgrown fields to the south of Helmstead, their legs swish-swishing through the dewy long grass. Early-morning crows looking for breakfast were disturbed by these unexpected arrivals and they flew to the skies until it was safe to return. Connie wondered what was going on. She remembered back to the train crash when Margaret had blurted out that the woman she was with wasn't her mother. And now it seemed – from last night – that this Michael might not be her father either. So who were they? Relatives who had taken the young girl in? Perhaps an aunt and an uncle? And why did Michael get as jittery as Vince at any visitors coming to the door?

Connie suspected that she might find out some of the answers very soon, as the small cottage that Margaret called home came into view. Amid a small patchwork of neatly tended vegetable fields, the compact building looked dark and empty. It was only just gone six in the morning and Connie asked if Vera and Michael might still be asleep.

"Michael will be up. He goes to work on his fields early," Margaret said.

"He seems to spend a lot of time tending them," Connie noted, taking in the immaculate rows of vegetables. "He should be a Land Girl."

Margaret laughed. Connie felt a little joy at seeing such a reaction in the young girl. She should be laughing all the time, not looking scared and cowed as if some great weight was on her shoulders. There should be a light in her eyes.

Before they got any closer to the house, Connie stopped Margaret. Although she didn't want to pry, she had to know what she was walking into and, more importantly, what Margaret wanted her to do and say once they were inside.

"Do you want to tell me what's going on?"

"Funny, never told anyone," Margaret said, glancing with foreboding at the cottage.

"Only tell me if you feel you want to," Connie encouraged. "But a problem shared and all that ..."

"They're not my parents. Don't get me wrong, they're not bad people—"

"But they don't treat you exactly right, do they?" Connie interjected.

"But they took me in. They were good like that." And Margaret told Connie about what had happened three years ago. "I was six years old and living with Mum in the East End. She was called Ginny. One day, like on lots of days, there had been a bombing raid. A lot of buildings had been flattened by the German planes."

Tears welled in the young girl's eyes and she batted them away with the back of her hand.

"Only tell me if you want to."

"I'm all right." Margaret caught her breath. "The first I knew something was wrong was when Mum didn't come to school to pick me up. It got later and later – and I ended up waiting in a classroom with one of my teachers. We were both watching the clock."

"And what happened?"

"After a long time, Vera turned up and told the teachers that she was here to collect me. She told me the news. My mum had died," Margaret said.

"So sorry," Connie replied.

"She worked lunchtimes in the Grey Horse on Talbot Street. Did you know it?"

"I didn't know every place in the East End," Connie answered, softly.

"My mum would fetch glasses and pour pints. But the pub had been flattened by a German bomb."

The little girl found the words choking in her throat. "So you see –" She struggled on. "I owe Vera and Michael. And if they want me to pretend then that's what I've got to do, isn't it?"

Connie found this phrase odd. "Pretend? Pretend what?"

"That they are my mum and dad."

"Why do they do that? They're not your mum and dad."

Margaret explained that they hadn't adopted her properly, and said that if she mentioned anything to outsiders then it might mean she would be taken away to a children's home. "Michael said I'd have to go if people found out."

This sounded reasonable to Connie. She knew all about the children's homes in the East End. And she could understand Margaret's reluctance to rock the boat with her current guardians for fear of ending up in a crowded, noisy dormitory, where belongings didn't belong and washing water was never hot. But still something didn't feel right about this whole set up, the whole story that Margaret had told. Half-formed questions were swirling around Connie's mind – but the early hour meant that her brain wasn't firing on all cylinders, connections weren't being made. There was one specific thing that was bugging her about Margaret's story, but Connie couldn't quite catch hold of it; like chasing a sprite through a dark forest.

As she searched for the source of her unease, she suddenly realised that two figures were coming into view, walking tentatively towards them, as if Connie and Margaret might scatter like rabbits if they rushed forward.

Connie recognised the woman from the day on the train. Vera Sawyer. And she didn't need it spelling out that the tall, grim-faced man next to her was probably her husband, Michael Sawyer. Margaret's 'parents'.

The rain lashed down as the bicycle tottered along the dirt track. Henry Jameson realised that he'd been gnawing at his bottom lip since he'd left the vicarage and throughout the entire cycle journey to Pasture Farm. It was red and sore by the time he stopped and parked his bicycle near the old milking sheds. Henry had been working himself up, his mind continually spinning with the casual betrayal he still felt. Connie had gone to Vince – a real man – when there was the knock at the door. Vince would protect her. Did she feel Henry wasn't capable of being a real man? And yet, just before they got married, Henry had knocked Danny Sparks out to save Connie. That was a heroic act. One punch which had surprised everyone. Why didn't Connie remember that in her primal reaction to danger?

Henry liked to think of man as a higher animal, but reading all the books in the world didn't count when it came to facing danger. And that's why Connie had, perhaps without conscious thought, turned to the strongest man in the room.

He marched with determination into the kitchen of Pasture Farm, where a surprised Finch was eating a big plate of fried eggs and swilling it down with a large mug of tea. Esther was at the sink cutting some bread and he could hear Joyce singing elsewhere in the house.

"'Enry?" Finch said, mid-egg. "You're looking anxious. Not come to give us the last rites, have you?"

"Last wrongs in your case," Esther chuckled.

"What does that even mean?" Finch asked, a little irked. He loved a joke as much as the next man, but only if he could understand it.

"I'm here for – business," Henry stated, awkwardly adding emphasis on the last word, hoping that Finch would know what he meant.

Finch looked confused. But Esther knew that it would be easier if she wasn't there. "I'll call the girls. Give you a moment for your – business." Esther wiped her hands on her apron and made herself scarce. "Men," she mumbled as she disappeared.

Finch waited for the coast to be clear and turned to Henry with a conspiratorial air.

"You want some of my playing cards, eh?" Finch said.

"No," said a thrown Henry. "What playing cards?"

"Mucky ones." Finch giggled. "They've got normal hearts and clubs and stuff on one side. But on the other, they've got nude—"

"No. I'm not here for that."

Finch was already doing an unseemly mime of a woman with big breasts. He stopped abruptly.

"I wanted to go hunting again." Henry said. "I think I can do it this time."

"Well, I can't spare the time this morning, Reverend," Finch said, scooping up some egg white on his fork. "Not being off. Just we've got the grain truck coming and it'll be all hands on deck."

"Yes, Connie mentioned that," Henry replied, pondering the problem as if it was a Sherlock Holmes mystery. He had hoped that all his lip-gnawing on the journey had resulted in a fool-proof plan. Now, confronted with the lazy and unpredictable Frederick Finch, he wasn't so sure that things would be as easy to manipulate as he'd hoped.

"You could always go on your own?" Finch offered.

Bingo, thought Henry, but tried not to let his face betray him.

"Yes, yes. I could, couldn't I?"

"And see how many bunnies you can catch without the master to guide you, heh heh."

"Well, if I get one, I'll feel blessed."

"Yeah, take what you need, Henry," Finch said, downing his tea.

And now the big one. Henry had thought about this question. About how to phrase it so it sounded as casual as possible, and not the big flashing red light he dreaded it would be.

"Could I borrow the gun?" Henry asked, putting on his clueless face.

Finch laughed. "I told you, you'll have nothing left to eat if you use that."

"It's just I didn't really get on with the traps."

"Your trouble was a lack of patience, Reverend. That and a clod-hopping clumsiness. And the fact that you'd chatter on all the time."

"Yes, well. Reasons enough to see that I need a faster method of dispatch," Henry said, near to closing the deal.

"All right," Finch said, rubbing his mouth clean with the back of his sleeve. "But don't come running to me if you break your teeth on buck shot. Or blow your foot off. Heh, you wouldn't be running anywhere then, would you, eh? And keep it as long as you need. I've got a spare."

Henry's clueless act had worked. He tried not to let his face betray him, and bit his lip again. This time to stop himself from smiling.

Finch told him that the gun was in the milking shed, so Henry left the kitchen and crossed the yard to get it.

A stray chicken was pecking around the empty milk churns in the shed. It fluttered out of the way as Henry passed. Early-morning sun was pushing through the gaps in the slats like golden searchlights as Henry found the old Purdey. It was open and Henry could see that both barrels were empty. Henry picked up a small bag containing three or four shells. He placed them in his pocket. Then he felt the coolness of the metal barrels, the worn walnut woodwork. How could something so beautiful be so deadly? Henry started to get second thoughts. Could he do this? He even wondered what he intended to do with it. Surely he wasn't going to actually shoot Vince Halliday?

"You there!" the man whom Connie assumed was Michael Sawyer barked. "What are you doing on my land?"

"She's got our Margaret with her," Vera added, as if Michael could have failed to notice.

As they got closer, Connie stood her ground. She was surprised when Margaret took a step behind her, so that although the girl wasn't exactly hiding, she was partially shielded by Connie.

"I ain't got your Margaret," Connie said, sticking up for herself. "She ran off 'cos she was scared and I've brought her back. That's all."

Vera gave Connie a disdainful look before bending towards the little girl. "It's the woman from the train crash. She saved us," Vera said to Michael. His scowl grew in intensity as he stared at Connie. "They shouldn't have been on that flaming train."

"No need to thank me," Connie said, under her breath.

"Why did you run to this whore?" Michael asked Margaret.

"Here! That's a bit strong!" Connie snapped back. "I saved their bacon back at the train, and this is the thanks I get. Blooming marvellous."

Margaret was cowering, her sad eyes hoping that the adults in her life would stop shouting at one another. Vera glanced at Michael, who said nothing, his face unreadable. He was standing a few feet back from the action, ever the onlooker, partially there.

"You going to let him talk to me like that?" Connie snapped at Vera.

"We'll take her now," Vera said, firmly.

"I'll see her indoors, if you don't mind," Connie said, moving towards the cottage – uninvited – carrying Margaret's small case. She wanted to check everything would be all right for the young girl. Check it was safe to leave her here. There was something still nagging at Connie's mind. Some question struggling to form fully. Margaret's mother had worked as a bar maid at the Grey Horse in Talbot Street. Like a lot of the East-End, it was an area full of back-to-back housing and rooms to rent crammed in more tightly than one of Finch's chicken runs. Thoughts tried to reach clarity. The pub. Talbot Street. Vera went to the school to break the news. Margaret waiting in the classroom. But –

Annoyingly out of reach, Connie put it out of her head and tried to focus as she neared the front of the cottage. She was aware that Margaret was some yards behind her and that Vera and Michael were bringing up the rear.

"Go inside then," Vera shouted from behind. Connie pushed open the front door of Jessop's Cottage and stepped cautiously over the threshold. Margaret followed her inside. The decor was old-fashioned – in keeping with the Edwardian look of the furniture inside: heavy mahogany table with chairs padded with discreet floral patterns; a dark wood upright piano with heavy brass candle holders; lace doilies on the sideboard. The place had a feeling of late middle age – the presence of a young child hadn't had any effect on the strange entropy of this dwelling. There were no children's drawings on the walls, no toys or books scattered around the place. It was as if Margaret hadn't been allowed to flourish here. Or that she had been contained in some way. No roots of childhood had spread here.

"Thank you for bringing her home," Vera said, with as much civility as she could manage. She was clearly saying that it was time to go now. There would be no tea offered here. In fact, Vera seemed nervous now that she was inside the house, a woman unused to this sort of interaction. Visitors obviously never came here. She was aware that Michael had moved to the far window of the room, furthest from the rest of them. He was looking out to the fields. Connie wondered why he kept himself apart. Was he hiding something?

She felt a dark cloud of awkwardness and unease spreading invisibly over the furniture, filling the space as Vera's comment hung in the air. Connie knew she had to say something. Say something decisive. Something that would make a difference.

What came out of her mouth surprised everyone. Not least of all Connie Carter herself.

"Well, all right. But I want you to know I'm watching you."

Watching? What was she thinking? Where did that come from?

But the words had an instant effect. Michael looked at Connie and then to his wife. A flash of concern. It seemed the last thing he wanted was anyone watching. He smiled at Connie – his face looking confused, perhaps fearful. The glisten of nervous perspiration filled his top lip.

"There's no need for anyone to overreact," he said, as calmly as he could manage.

"I need to know she's going to be fine," Connie said, gesturing toward the small girl. Connie knew that Margaret had been so terrified that she had run away, through the dark forests nearby, in a desperate bid to escape. She needed to know that this place would be safe.

"You don't need to tell us how to raise our own—" Vera snapped, before Michael cut her off.

"We assure you that she will be fine." He smiled. "Go to your room please, Margaret."

Connie's mind was racing, looking for the missing piece of the jigsaw.

Margaret threw one last look at Connie, picked up her small suitcase of belongings and trotted obediently upstairs.

"It was a shock seeing the story – the picture of Margaret and you – in the newspaper. That's all," Michael said evenly. "It rather threw me, I must say. But I'm calmer about the whole matter now."

"And you going to apologise for calling me a whore?"

Michael looked confused, as if he'd never said it. Vera gave a small nod of encouragement. It would end this encounter more quickly if he apologised. "I'm sorry for calling you that."

Connie felt uneasy about the brittle calmness of his tone.

But as she watched Margaret disappear, Connie suddenly realised what was bugging her. The one thing about Margaret's story that didn't sit right. The story of how she lost her mother in the destruction of the Grey Horse on Talbot Street. The nagging question finally formed clearly in her mind for the first time, like a lighthouse shining through a sea fog. It came through with red flashing lights and a siren honking its presence.

How had Vera Sawyer known who Margaret's mother was?

For her to go to the school to break the awful news of her death, Vera Sawyer must have known both Margaret and Ginny. But how? Were they family friends? Did they know each other from Sunday school or something? Neighbours? Connie needed to find out. It was bugging her.

"Margaret told me what happened back in the East End," Connie said.

Vera and Michael shared a look of concern and then, Connie, after letting it hang in the air for maximum effect, continued, "She told me how you went to the school. How you broke the news about her mother dying."

"The poor woman," Michael added. Vera was looking anxious, wondering where this was going. Why couldn't this infernal woman in the Land Army uniform just disappear? "My wife and I took her in. We've done everything we could for that girl to avoid her living in an orphanage. We moved to the country, sent her to school —"

The lighthouse shining brightly now.

"But how did you know her?" Connie asked, cutting him off.

Michael heard the question but screwed up his eyes as if he hadn't.

198

"How did you know Margaret's mother?"

Vera looked towards her husband for guidance. But this time he was staring at the Land Girl – intense, troubled, his mind calculating how to end this situation as quickly as possible. He'd tried being angry, being calm. Nothing was making her leave. He wanted to return to tending his vegetables. The endless hours of relaxation in the garden, bird song, fingernails clogged with simple, honest graft.

"We knew her," Michael started, hesitantly. "Everyone knew her."

"She was a woman of – certain values," Vera clarified, adding to her husband's foundations.

Connie felt saddened. It was tragic that a woman was known by these euphemisms. "A woman of certain values": the polite way of saying a woman was fast, someone who slept around without a ring on her finger. Some people had slung that one at her over the years, with some justification. Suddenly Connie felt small, unsure of herself. But she was about to take this – somewhat hazy – explanation at face value and accept it, when she saw the little smile between Vera and Michael. And something told her they were winging this, making it up on the spot. Vera's smile, fleeting as it was, was seeking approval. It said "did I do well?"

"I don't believe you," Connie said, breaking their bubble of relief. The atmosphere immediately got frostier. From polite – if strained – conversation to overstepping the boundaries of acceptable, genteel behaviour. She was calling them liars to their faces. In their own homes. She hoped it might earn her an explanation. The truth.

But instead, it earned her the end of the audience.

"I'd like you to leave," Michael said, firmly.

He took Connie roughly by the arm and forced her out through the door. Despite being a slight, tall man, his grip was strong.

"Here, get off me!" Connie shouted. "Who do you think you are?"

Vera protested at his strong reaction, but he ignored her, incensed by this nosey girl, who'd dare to call them liars. Even Margaret went against instructions and ran downstairs to see what was happening. The Sawyers stood at the doorway as Connie moved away from the house, risking one final look behind her as she went down the path. Margaret was looking blankly ahead at her, the hope dying in her eyes.

Connie knew she had to go back. But not now. Not today. Somehow she had to find out what was happening in this small cottage. Somehow she had to discover the Sawyers' secrets.

Luckily, she had an idea how to do it.

It was nearly nine o'clock in the morning, and Connie was already over two hours late for work. But she knew she had to do this before she went to Pasture Farm. She sat on the wall outside the small glass-fronted shop that had been converted to the offices of *The Helmstead Herald*. 'Office' was too grand a word for a single desk at which Roger Curran would sit drafting his stories while the editor sat behind the shop counter, laying out hot metal on a series of plates.

Since she'd been waiting, Connie had watched the village

wake up. Mrs Gulliver was doing what looked like door-to-door enquiries – stopping at each house in a terrace and engaging the old women washing their steps in gossip and chit chat. Three members of the Home Guard were practising their marching in the village square. They had one Lee Enfield rifle between them. One man held a broom handle while the other – an ancient figure covered in liver spots – held a particularly evil-looking machete, probably gained during some earlier campaign when the man was young.

Connie smiled in encouragement at their efforts. She knew that Home Guard patrols had been stepped up since the train crash. The members were out most nights, checking barns and outhouses for signs of rough sleepers who might have been involved in the explosion.

From the wall, she could just about see the vicarage at the top of the street. It's true that she could have gone home to wait there. And perhaps had a nice hot cup of tea. But Henry wasn't there and she didn't want to see Vince. Besides, it was nice to just be idle in the fresh air sometimes. She had so little time these days to just look and take in things – working on the land or at the hospital or cooking and cleaning at the vicarage took all her waking hours. Yes, that was all it was. A break in the air. It had nothing to do with her discomfort at the thought of sitting with Vince as he talked about the good old days. No, of course it didn't.

Sitting on the wall, waiting for an office to open might have bored most people senseless, but for Connie Carter it was almost a holiday. A break from her troubles.

At last, the clock in the village square chimed nine o'clock and Connie spied the portly figure of Roger Curran ambling across the village square. Seeing Connie, he offered a small nod of his head, followed by a frown that said he wondered what she wanted.

"Mrs Jameson? What do I owe the pleasure of this visit?" he wheezed.

"I thought you could show me how to make a decent cup of tea, for starters." Connie smiled.

Oddly flattered, Roger Curran agreed. He fumbled for his keys and opened the office door, ushering her in. Inside, the walls were filled with framed yellowing pages from the news-paper – a seemingly random hodge podge of its history, wilfully ignoring most of the important moments of Helmstead history in favour of a captivating headline or a good photo-graph. Roger Curran filled the kettle and put it on the stove out at the back of the shop. A few minutes later, he and Connie were sipping tea from mismatched cups. Connie knew she couldn't hang around – she had to get this finished quickly so she could get to work. "It's about the girl I saved from the train."

"A heroic act, Mrs Jameson. And it's well deserved that my story was picked up by *The Daily Mail*."

"Yeah well, that gave me no end of trouble," Connie said under her breath, thinking how it had led Vince to her door.

"Anyway, what about that girl?" Roger asked, blowing over the top of his tea.

"There's something odd going on."

"Odd how?" Roger said. He pulled out a jotter from his

desk drawer and licked the end of a pencil. Almost an involuntary response to intrigue.

"I'm not sure it's a story. But they took her in – the Sawyers took her in – when Margaret's mum was killed in a bombing raid in London."

Roger scrawled notes, which looked like some sort of Egyptian hieroglyphics. Connie guessed it was shorthand of some sort.

"Benevolent of them. Were they family friends?" he asked.

"I dunno. They say they knew her. The mum."

"But – what – you're not so sure?"

Connie took a deep breath. It was time to put her concerns into words – to crystallise the thoughts that had been troubling her. But the truth was that she didn't quite know what it was. The Sawyers' story didn't seem convincing. How had they known Margaret's mother well? Had they known her at all, in fact? But what was the alternative? Why would they have taken Margaret in if they hadn't known the family? It was – as Roger Curran had just said – a benevolent act. An act of kindness taking in a suddenly orphaned child. Connie decided that one thing was troubling her more than anything else. Michael.

"There's something not right about the man who says he's her dad," Connie said at last. "He's very secretive. She said he doesn't like strangers coming to the house."

Roger didn't think this was much to go on. "A lot of people don't like strangers. I don't like strangers."

"There's something wrong," Connie insisted. "He's covering

up something. Call it a woman's intuition or whatnot, but I know something is wrong."

Roger shrugged. "What's his name, then?"

"Michael Sawyer. I don't know if he's got a middle name."

"I didn't get any answer to my enquiries when I'd traipsed up Jessop's Cottage. I'd been up there twice since the derailment in the hope of talking to one of the parents. The first time I went, I was sure the house was empty, but the second time, I wondered if I'd seen an upstairs curtain twitch, a man's face staring briefly out. Might be wrong though."

"I just think he's got something to hide. Something which may explain how him and his wife knew Margaret's real mum," Connie summed up.

"I'll look into it." Roger fixed her with an intent look. "You feel protective of this girl, don't you? Almost – maternal." For a moment, she caught a brief glimpse of a talented journalist inside, a burning flame that had been all but extinguished by having to cover endless church fetes and tractor competitions.

The word hit Connie. She had never known her own mother and she had made a silent vow to always show deep love and devotion to any children she might have in the future. And although Margaret wasn't her daughter, perhaps Connie recognised a fragile soul who needed help and protection. Or perhaps it was just borne of the fact that she had saved the girl's life and now felt some invisible but strong bond towards her? She wasn't sure.

Connie got up to leave.

"Well, rest assured, Mrs Jameson, I shall look into Michael Sawyer – and let you know what I find."

Connie bid him good day and went on her way. As the shop door shut behind her, Roger Curran looked at the cup she'd had. It was still full. So much for making a decent cup of tea, he thought with a smile.

Henry got back to the vicarage. He couldn't hear Vince – and assumed he might be asleep upstairs. The journey back on the bicycle had been harder than usual – as Henry tried to balance the shotgun across his legs and peddle at the same time. The sight must have been a strange one for any passer-by to witness: a man of God carrying a weapon. Old Mrs Clements had been the only one who saw him. A skeletally thin woman who appeared to be held together by a voluminous coat and hat. She had looked twice at the young vicar, assuming her rheumy eyes were deceiving her. Surely that's a fishing rod he's got there?

Henry quietly entered the vicarage and walked straight through the dining room. Vince had left a newspaper sprawled out across the table. He passed through the kitchen with its collection of unwashed crockery and went out into the back garden. He scurried over to the chicken coop – offering a silent prayer that Esther and Gladys wouldn't make too much noise. Henry pushed the shotgun into the back of the chicken run, covering it over with straw. His heart was pumping so fast, he feared it would rip straight out of his chest. He would leave the gun here and then tonight, when Connie was doing a late shift at Hoxley Manor, Henry would take the gun and he would force Vince Halliday to leave. Yes, that's what he would do. He crept back into the

205

house and went silently upstairs, assuming that Vince would be sleeping.

But as he peeked into the spare room, he was shocked and wrong-footed.

Because Vince Halliday had gone.

Chapter 12

"There was more in the paper about it," Joyce said, leaning on her spade as she batted a wasp away from her headscarf. The women were in the fields: their satisfying lunch of bread and cheese in the farmhouse seemed many hours behind them. Joyce was discussing the latest theories regarding the train crash. The authorities were certain it was a bomb – and although German components were found in the wrecked shrapnel of the device, there was something else among the debris: home-manufactured components. That had suggested that someone had made the bomb with assistance from the Germans. It suggested that a collaborator was involved. And the latest article in *The Helmstead Herald*, a think-piece by a local historian, suggested that such a collaborator could be right under the noses of decent, patriotic folk.

Folk like Joyce Fisher, who, although not usually prone to gossip, was currently flinging mud in all directions. Connie assumed it stemmed from Joyce being on the train, and having a lucky escape. She was angry about what she'd been through, viewing the event as a stark reminder of what the bombs had done to her family in Coventry. As such, she was keen to find the culprit.

"They said we should report anyone suspicious. Turn them over to the police." Joyce lowered her voice. "The collaborator could be living on this farm."

"Really?" Iris said. "Is that possible, Connie?"

"Yeah, Freddie Finch is really Herr Von Bismarck," Connie said dully. Her mind was on other, more personal, matters.

"I'm telling you, before you and Connie came, there was a girl called Nancy Morrell. We started the same day. She was full of airs and graces. Real la-di-da. And the Home Guard pulled her in for questioning because she was caught writing letters home in Italian."

"So she was a spy?" Iris asked, scanning the faces of the other girls for some clarification. But it didn't come. All of them were fairly new arrivals, and besides, the transient nature of being a Land Girl meant that they often moved to different farms. She knew that Joyce had been here the longest. No one else was able to confirm or deny Joyce's story.

"Well, no, she wasn't a spy. Not in the end," Joyce said. "But the point was – she could have been. And the Home Guard suspected her enough to think she might be. So anyone could be a spy. Anyone could have helped those men lay that bomb on the tracks."

Iris thought it was true enough. But in her heart, she always imagined German spies to be angle-cheeked, dark-eyed men in trench coats. Like in the posters.

But Joyce had a very specific suspect in her thoughts. She felt she knew who it was. Keen not to be overheard, she moved across the furrows of mud to where Connie was standing and indicated that they should move to the trailer that was parked about fifty yards away. When they reached it, Joyce put her spade with the other tools and hoisted herself up onto the platform. She sat facing Connie, a troubled look on her face.

"I'm not one for gossip."

"I know. You see the good in everyone. It's maddening," Connie said.

Joyce returned a tight, if somewhat appreciative smile. "But I think there's someone here we should be watching." And she leaned in close, to make certain her words wouldn't have any chance of being carried by the soft wind to the other girls over the other side of the field.

"Dolores O'Malley," Joyce said.

"Come off it."

"Think about it. We know nothing about her."

"She's not a spy."

"How do you know?" Joyce insisted. She picked at some mud on the mound of her thumb, ignoring Connie's eyes. She knew that on one level her speculation seemed absurd. But it was bugging her. "She's more closed up than Mrs Garvey's old wool shop. We've found out nothing about her."

They watched Iris Dawson walking quickly off the field.

"Yeah, but that don't mean Dolores is a spy."

"I'm not saying she definitely is. Just that if anyone here needs watching – it's her."

And with that, Joyce pushed herself off the trailer and trudged back to the other girls. It was true enough. Connie had seen first hand how difficult, nay impossible, it was to try to get Dolores to say anything about herself. She was a closed book, uninterested in getting close to anyone. But surely that made her stand out? By being the black sheep, Dolores was going to get more attention than someone who fitted in. Someone who laughed with the other girls; shared drunken nights with them. Dolores never went to the dances at Hoxley Manor. She never went to the cinema or out to meet a friend for tea and cake. When she wasn't working, she sat in her room, watching the sun set through her lace net curtains, reading or writing letters home. Connie wasn't sure what to think as she picked up a hessian bag of sprouting onions and walked to the edge of the field. She was going to take the bulbs to the other girls for planting. And that other group included Dolores O'Malley. As she trusted Joyce and respected her judgement, Connie resolved to watch her more closely from now on. It might take her mind off everything that was happening at home.

Connie moved through the stable yard, where Finch's old carthorse – Nellie – was standing idly in the spring sunshine, languidly batting flies with her tail. She reached Iris Dawson and Dolores O'Malley, who were sorting through onion bulbs – separating the rotten ones from those that might burst forth a new plant, given the right conditions. They looked up, necks stiff from bending over their sieves.

"Brought you some more," Connie said, placing the sack down on the stone.

"Oh thanks! Dolores was down to the last dozen. Thought we had the end in sight," Iris moaned.

"The end is never in sight with farming. You should know

that," Connie said with a smile, sitting down and taking some of the bulbs out of the sack for sorting. She looked at Dolores, who had her head down, examining a sprouting onion. "Alright, Dor?"

"Yes, thank you, I am," Dolores said, looking up briefly.

"What you been doing, then?" Connie asked.

Iris shook her head in a now-isn't-the-time kind of way. She didn't have the energy for Connie to engage in another game of finding out about Dolores. As it turned out, Dolores didn't have the energy either.

"What do you think I've been doing?" Dolores snapped.

"All right. Keep your barnet on," Connie replied.

"We need another sieve if you're going to sit there," Dolores said.

Connie took the hint and sauntered over to the tool shed. The sieves were hanging on nails on the back wall of the shed. In front of them were rows of hand tools – spades and forks, mainly – and a pile of scythes. A rusted anvil, hammers, sharpeners, sanders and the spent embers of a small fire were nearby: a repair station for the number of tools that needed new heads or sharpening. Finch found it was a constant job to keep up with the wear and tear wrought by the hard-working girls on his farm.

Connie flicked through the sieves, looking for a serviceable one. Several had gaping holes in the centre: more use as picture frames. She found a reasonable one and plucked it from its nail.

But a meaty hand grabbed her wrist.

Connie was so shocked she found the air trapped in her

throat, making it impossible to scream or make a sound. But for good measure, the man placed his right hand over her mouth. His hand was roughly bandaged and before he spun her around, Connie knew who it was.

Vince Halliday looked at her with steely intensity, his eyes wild with nervous energy. He waited until he was sure she wouldn't shout out and then he slowly released her mouth. Connie touched her lips, sore from the rough treatment.

"What you doing here, Vince?" she hissed.

"I couldn't stay caged up all day," Vince hissed back at her. "Besides, we needed to talk."

"Great. Yeah, come and see me at work. It's always quiet enough for a good old chin-wag here."

"If this two-bit village had a Lyons' Corner House, I'd take you there. How about that?"

"That would have been nice," Connie said softening.

"Eclairs."

"What?"

"They were your favourites, weren't they?" He smiled. "I bet you'd have had an eclair."

"Blimey. I haven't had one of them in years," she mused. "We had four in that Corner House off Earl's Court, didn't we?"

Vince smiled, the happy memory cracking his features and filling his eyes with longing for lost days. Connie glanced back towards the door, suspecting that Dolores and Iris would be wondering why she was taking so long. "Anyway, as nice as this little catch-up is ..."

"Yeah, sorry." Vince composed himself and looked her

straight in the eye. "I don't have a lot of time. I need you to do something. There's something I need."

"There's something I need first," Connie said. "I want to know what the deal is with Amos Ackley. Is he alive? Is coming to get us?"

Vince weighed this up. He nodded slowly.

Connie sighed. At least she knew where she stood now. There was a very dangerous man – even more unpredictable and ruthless than the one standing in front of her – who was out there looking for Vince. A very dangerous man, who Connie had conned back in the day.

"I need you to tell me everything," she said. "But wait here."

Connie sauntered outside. Vince could hear her talking to her colleagues, telling them that she was going to tidy up the tool shed. She'd be about ten minutes. Connie came back inside, closing the door behind her. "Well? What happened on Barnes Common?"

And then Vince told Connie about what had happened during the last moments of the scam on Barnes Common. About what happened to Gloria Wayland. Connie listened with new interest.

She knew she could easily have been Gloria.

"I called her Glory," Vince said. "I took her under my wing shortly after you disappeared. She weren't keen on being involved in all my schemes at first. But when she saw that she was making money, some of her reluctance disappeared.

"She weren't as worldly as you. Barely more than a kid. She always wore this cloche hat and looked a bit like a string bean. So I couldn't use her in blackmail scams as easy as you done 'em."

Connie felt saddened. She had always felt that – at whatever age – she could look after herself, by and large. But this Glory sounded naive and vulnerable. Connie didn't like the thought of how Vince had used her.

"What happened to her, then?"

"There was a man holding Glory. She was trying to pull away, but he had her gripped round the neck."

"What did you do?"

"Told Amos to let her go." Vince was burdened with sorrow. "But Amos just shook his head. None of us were going anywhere. Glory looked scared. The thug was gripping her arm above the elbow. The poor cow looked at me for guidance."

"That's terrible."

"It gets worse."

Connie took a deep breath. She had to know what happened. She braced herself and nodded for Vince to continue.

"I wish I could have done something. I was watching Amos like a hawk, waiting for him to make a move. Waiting for it all to start. He was trying to break my nerve. I was trying to break his. But it was like one of those things in a chess game."

"A stalemate." Connie helped him find the words, feeling empty inside. "And what happened?"

For the first time, Vince Halliday winced as he wrestled with troubling, unsettling memories. He spoke slowly and deliberately – as if taking time to unravel the exact sequence of events in his mind. Events that must have happened in a matter of seconds. With Glory at the mercy of a man with a knife and Vince facing Amos and two other heavies, Vince had had to think fast and act even faster.

"I saw the handle of his gun poking out of his lapel. He had a shoulder holster. It was my one hope."

What happened next took five seconds. But each moment had been pored over endlessly by Vince since they happened. His own private, hellish movie.

"I lunged for Amos, pushing him backwards, pulling the gun free at the same time. One of the thugs tried to grab me, but I used my momentum to spin round, firing the gun. Didn't have time to aim or nothing. It was a desperate shot, but the bullet smacked into the man's arm, sending him flying backwards onto the ground. One of the other men came forward, but I whacked him in the face with the gun." Vince looked at Connie for a reaction. But she was still ashen-faced and waiting for the end of Glory's story.

"Behind me, Amos had recovered his balance and came lumbering forward. So I tried to spin around to face him, but I suddenly felt this sharp pain in my hand. Amos had stabbed me." Vince raised his bandaged hand, as if Connie might need reminding of it. "I lashed out, batting Amos away with the gun. Then I took a step forward, over the grass, towards where Glory was being held. The thug seemed to be holding her arched backwards over his knee, as if they was two ballet dancers. His knife was moving towards her throat." Vince slumped down in the tool shed.

"Did you save her?"

"Before I could get there, a bullet whizzed past my ear. It was so close it stopped me hearing for a while. And that's when I made a big decision. 'Cos I knew I had to make a choice. Run or save her."

"So you ran?" Connie said, sadly.

Vince gave an imperceptible nod, full of shame and remorse. "We'd both have died."

Connie nodded. In a strange way, she could understand. She placed a consoling hand on his big shoulder and he brought up his hand to touch hers.

"And she died, did she? This Gloria?"

The late-afternoon sun was sending him into shadow, so Connie couldn't see his face clearly. He looked away, embarrassed perhaps. "I don't know."

Connie moved her hand away. She knew that she'd have to go back soon – Dolores and Iris would be wondering why she had taken so long to tidy up. They'd think she was shirking. Keen to escape the claustrophobic tool shed, Connie moved towards the entrance.

"Wait." Vince's gravelly voice made her stop in her tracks. "I haven't told you what I want you to do."

Connie felt disgust. It was as if Glory Wayland's death meant nothing. Here he was asking for favours, probably expecting Connie to risk her neck for something.

"She wasn't like you," he said.

"So, what, she deserved to be left on that Common?" Connie spat.

"I've made loads of mistakes. Things I wish I could put right," Vince admitted. Connie couldn't tell whether this was genuine or an act for her benefit. "Most of all, I wish we could still be together."

Connie felt a wave of emotion come over her. She couldn't cope with this. She'd spent so long trying to fit together with a man who was so different to her, she knew it would be so easy, so comfortable to go back to being with someone like Vince. A waspish voice in her head crowed: "That's your station in life. That's where you belong." She knew how a relationship worked with someone like Vince or with Danny. Unstable, volatile and with so many ups and downs. But that was the world she knew.

Wouldn't it be so easy to give in? The voice in her head goaded.

"I'm married," Connie found herself saying. "I'm married and I love Henry. Now, I want you to go."

Vince weighed this up. I love Henry. The words taunting him like a late-evening mosquito. He thought about how Connie had reacted when he'd arrived. She had nursed him back to health, stolen him medicine when he'd needed it. She'd saved his life. And he remembered too about when they were in London together – no more than two years ago, her dressed to the nines and smiling with all her teeth as they pulled off another successful scam and ran off to celebrate at some gin joint into the early hours. He assumed life here was transitory, hitching her wagon to Henry through happenstance and a need for a calming and anchoring figure in her life.

"I'm serious, Connie," he said softly.

"So am I," she said, but her eyes looked haunted, uncertain. "Now what is it you need?"

217

Vince turned his attention to what he needed. "The key to my future."

"What's that when it's at home?"

"I mean it. There's a key. And if I can get it, then I'm sorted for the future. I can go away from here. Escape Amos Ackley. And if I'm not here, he won't find you."

Suddenly Connie was listening. The first indication that he would go. Then she'd have a chance to see what she could salvage with Henry.

Vince told her that there was a key in his bedsit – kept in an old metal tin under the floorboards. The key would open a safety deposit box in which Vince knew there would be a fortune.

"Why haven't you used it before, then? Could have saved you a lot of grief," Connie asked.

"'Cos I don't know which deposit box it opens. It's one at Hatton Gardens." He admitted he'd stolen the key off someone a few months back, when Glory had managed to distract a jeweller at a Lyons' Corner House. As the man tried to dance with the gangly girl in the cloche hat, Vince was rifling the man's coat pocket and, hey presto, he found the key.

"How are you going to find out which box it opens?" Connie asked.

Vince got to his feet and fixed her with a frown, tired of her questions. "That's for me to worry about. I'll try them all if I have to. But the main thing is – I need that key from under the floorboards. And I can't go back to London, can I?"

"But Amos would recognise me too," she protested.

"Put a headscarf on. I dunno, disguise yourself." He smiled softly, holding her shoulders. "Please."

Connie took the sieve. She was already shaking her head – unwilling to be party to such a stupid and dangerous idea. But she had forgotten one thing: Vince was a dangerous man. A dangerous and desperate man.

"I'm not asking you, Connie. I'm telling you."

"A moment ago you were asking me to come away with you? And now you're giving me orders?"

"If you're not with me, you're against me. Aren't you?" Vince's logic was simple and terrifying.

"I'm not against you. But I'm saying no." She extracted herself from his grip and made for the door.

Vince smiled an unnerving smile. "Think it over. Carefully." Connie knew a threat when she heard one. And she also worried that it wouldn't be her who suffered but her Henry.

A cloche hat was on the bedside table. It was one of the few personal items recovered from the patient when she was brought in to Fernley East Hospital in South London. The patient was lying on the corner bed of a six-bed ward in the large Edwardian building as a doctor examined her.

The doctor – a young man of Indian descent – had a gap in his teeth that was only visible when he smiled. He was smiling at the moment because he was pleased with the progress that his patient had made. The young woman had recovered well since her operation. The surgeons had success-fully stemmed the bleeding from her wounds and even managed to remove a bullet from her neck. It had been touch and go as to whether she would survive. And yet here, she was on the road to recovery lying on her bed in Fernley East hospital as the dappled late-evening sunlight flickered through the leaves on the trees into the French windows at the end of the room. The details had been sketchy when she had been brought in, and the doctor knew better than to worry about the whys and wherefores. His main concern was to treat the patients and get them out of the hospital.

"How are you feeling?" he asked.

The girl turned to him and smiled awkwardly, as if it hurt her to move her face. She touched the bandage around her thin neck. She hadn't spoken since she had regained consciousness, and tonight looked like being no exception. The medics wondered if she would ever be able to talk again. But at least she had some colour to her cheeks and her dull eyes were beginning to sparkle with a little life once more.

"Al —" she croaked, attempting to reply.

"All right?" the doctor said, helpfully. "Don't try to speak."

The woman nodded. The doctor smiled and said that he would check on her again tomorrow. But by all accounts, the nurses had reported that she was doing well and that her strength was returning. One factor still concerned him, though, and it was always better to confront such concerns head on.

"We're wondering if you'll talk again," he said.

The girl looked worried. Her large eyes suddenly doleful.

"The trouble is that the bullet may have damaged your larynx. The vocal chords. And that means you might not regain the ability. But we'll see what happens over the next couple of days. But whatever happens, we think you may be strong enough to leave hospital soon." He smiled as encouragingly as he could manage. He knew that she was probably a homeless young woman with no place to go. How had she obtained her injuries – a bullet through the neck and bruises all over her body? She was found on Barnes Common by a man walking his dog. She had been lying in the cold night air for some hours, probably left to die. And even since she'd been brought to Fernley East, she'd just shaken her head at the police officer who had come to her bedside to ask her about it. But whatever reason had brought her here, and wherever she had to go, the doctor knew that she couldn't stay in the hospital indefinitely. He just had to make her well enough to leave.

As he consulted the notes at the end of the bed, the girl looked at her feet.

All Glory Wayland had known since meeting Vince Halliday was the life of a scam artist – and that involved being able to talk and charm your way into situations. How could she do that if she couldn't even speak? She wondered if she had any future outside these four walls – where at least she could get three square meals a day and a bed to sleep in at night. She had no family, no friends. What would she do? How could Vince have left her like this? It was such a mess. Maybe Vince would come back for her.

Glory Wayland felt her shoulders shaking as she was taken over by silent and desperate sobbing. The fact she couldn't make a noise while she cried disturbed her even more, adding a further sense of stinging indignity and injustice.

The doctor touched her shoulder, offered a small conciliatory smile and walked away.

Connie walked over the bridge into Helmstead. A headache had meant that Dr Channing had allowed her to go home early from her shift at the military hospital at Hoxley Manor. She hadn't argued, more than happy to head home. Maybe she could see Henry. But a small figure caught her eye. Margaret was sitting on a wall in the village square, wearing her school uniform and looking at her feet as she scuffed her shoes over the gravel. As Connie got closer, Margaret looked up. A dark bruise ran the length of her right cheek bone. Connie was shocked.

"Oh my God, who did that?" she asked.

"No one," Margaret said, getting up and moving away. Suddenly it seemed she was keen to get home.

"Did Michael do that?" Connie shouted. But she got no reply. Margaret was running over the bridge. Connie felt dreadful. Had she caused Michael to go over the edge by riling him at the cottage? Her mind racing, she knew that she had to do something. She had to stop the awful things that were happening to that young girl.

Henry had spent the late afternoon pacing the dining room, waiting for Vince to return from wherever he had gone. He pored over the options about what might have happened. Maybe Vince had finally just got up and left. No, that would be too good to be true. Maybe this Amos man had turned up and taken Vince away. And yet there was no sign of a disturbance. Or maybe Vince had just gone out and got lost.

He thought about the shotgun. Henry also busied himself praying, mumbled, anxious prayers. He asked forgiveness for what he planned to do. As a follower of God, Henry felt uneasy about brandishing a weapon that could kill a man, so he consoled himself by knowing that he only planned to scare Vince – to threaten him enough so that he would leave. The biggest debate that he wrestled with was whether to load the shotgun or not. If it was loaded, he might accidentally hurt or kill Vince, and that would be something that would devastate Henry. However, if it was unloaded and then Henry had to defend himself, then it would be he who would be in deep trouble.

Why had Connie brought this upon them? He let out an annoyed grunt.

Henry glanced at the clock. It was nearly seven o'clock in the evening. Connie would be back from her evening shift at Hoxley Manor just after eight. He hoped that Vince would come back before then so he could get this over with.

He walked into the kitchen and checked, for the umpteenth time, the shotgun leaning at the side of the stove.

Then he heard the front door latch. Henry moved quickly to the front of the house, leaving the shotgun where it was for now. Vince stumbled into the hallway, knocking one of the framed pictures with his shoulder. He was swaying and slightly red faced, the bandage on his hand dirty and frayed. He'd been drinking. He scowled at Henry and pushed past him, plonking himself down in the armchair nearest the fire. Something was uncomfortably digging into his thigh, so Vince pulled out the pistol that was tucked into his waist band.

He placed the gun on his lap, and ushered forth a deep sigh before fixing Henry in his blinking sights.

"Bet you wonder where I've been, eh?" he sneered, before rambling on in a drink-fuelled stream of consciousness. "Well, I've been celebrating that I might be on my way soon. That's good news, isn't it? But before you get too pleased – cock-a-hoop – about it, I should say that Connie is probably coming with me."

Henry felt the colour drain from his cheeks. "What?"

"She don't belong here, does she? All this fine china and doilies. She's a kid from the streets, like me."

Henry couldn't disagree. Maybe it would be better if she did go. Maybe that would be easier than trying to find some common ground; rubbing each other up the wrong way. No, he loved her. Despite everything, he loved her. Didn't he?

"Has-has she said she's going?" Henry stammered.

"I made the offer. She's thinking about it." Vince closed his eyes and exhaled, feeling slightly nauseous from too much drink and too little food.

With Vince's eyes temporarily shut, Henry reached out a hand, slowly and silently. His fingers were a few inches from the pistol. Nearer and nearer, until his forefinger could feel the monogrammed handle. But then Vince placed a large meaty hand over the barrel. Henry pulled back and silently cursed his hesitation. He should have just snatched it up. Vince started to stir. Henry moved backwards, as quickly and fluidly as he could – towards the kitchen.

Vince licked his lips and blinked open his eyes.

He was shocked to find himself staring down the barrels of a shotgun.

Quickly, instinctively, he went to pick up the pistol from his lap, but Henry used one hand to bat the gun away onto the floor, all the while keeping the shotgun trained on Vince's face with the other hand. Henry steadied himself and got both hands back on the shotgun. It was five inches from Vince's face. The big man glanced to his left, to the salvation of the pistol lying by the skirting board. But it was nearly three feet away and he was stuck in an armchair.

"You won't get there in time," Henry said.

"Just calm down, Reverend," Vince replied as softly as he could manage.

"I'm calm," Henry lied. "I'm calm. Now I want you to leave."

"Don't want to kill me, then?"

"Not unless I have to."

"Even if I take your Connie with me?"

"Don't test me," spat Henry.

"We were talking about the old days earlier. The times we'd dance through London."

"I'm warning you."

"And I'm so scared," Vince said, fixing Henry with a cold, ruthless stare. Henry's left eyelid started to twitch, the pressure of the confrontation getting to him. Vince could see the fear on the man's face, the desperate doubt in his eyes. He wasn't a killer. He knew the last thing Henry wanted to do was to shoot him. But he also knew that the gun might go off by accident, if he made a sudden movement. That was a bigger risk for Vince, facing someone who didn't know how to handle a shotgun. So Vince kept his voice soft, calm and as hypnotic as he could manage.

"Sorry. There you go. I'm sorry. Now put the gun down. We can talk about this."

Henry shook his head and kept the shotgun level, both hands holding it mere inches from Vince's face. "Now, get up, slowly." Henry moved back a couple of steps to allow him out of the chair. Vince hauled himself up, keeping every move as slow as he could, not wanting to spook Henry into firing the shotgun. Henry waved the gun barrel to indicate for Vince to move to the hallway. Henry had seen James Cagney do this in the movies.

"Just be calm," Vince said.

"I am. Get out." And then a moment of insecurity. "Did you really talk to Connie about the old days?"

Vince nodded slowly, keen not to rile the reverend. "But we're bound to talk about the past, aren't we?"

"And you want her to go with you?"

"She don't really belong here, does she?"

Henry pushed the twin barrels against Vince's arms, an admonishment for his comment.

"The worm's turned, ain't it?" Vince said as he moved slowly forwards. "You're the big man now, aren't you?"

"I wouldn't antagonise me at this precise moment in time."

But unfortunately, also at that precise moment in time, Connie Carter was walking up the path. She had spent a few minutes in the square, wondering about whether to follow Margaret. But she'd drawn a blank. Maybe Henry would know.

She opened the front door, surprised to find Vince standing

in the hallway with his meaty hands raised in surrender as Henry moved him at gun point. Connie couldn't help but react with shock at this incongruous sight. "Henry?!"

She would regret doing this.

The Reverend Henry Jameson momentarily took his eyes off Vince. In a flash, Vince used that distraction to his advantage, pushing the gun barrels down to the floor and towards him with all his might. The shotgun flew out of Henry's hands, and Vince twisted it round, in a fluid motion, pinning Henry against his chest and holding the shotgun as a baton tight against the Reverend's neck. He felt the air leaving Henry's lungs as the man choked.

"You dare point this thing at me. You vermin!"

"Leave him, Vince, please!" Connie pleaded. But Vince was enraged, fired up and coursing with adrenaline from his near-death experience. From the humiliation he felt.

"You dare do that!" Vince pulled harder on the barrel, pulling Henry backwards up off his feet, until Henry started to cough and gasp for air, his hands clawing at the barrel to get it away from his neck. His eyes were bulging. "You dare do that!" Vince spat angrily, pulling Henry around like a rag doll.

Connie had to make him stop.

"I'll do it!" Connie shouted. "The key! I'll get it."

Vince stopped the pressure. He released one hand from the gun barrel, letting Henry slump to the floor, like a sack of potatoes. The vicar was gasping and coughing and clawing at his throat.

"I'll go to London to get the key," Connie said.

"And then you'll come away with me?"

"I'll get the key," Connie said.

Connie bent down to her husband's side and helped him slowly up to his feet. Like a newborn lamb, his legs scrambled for a purchase on the carpet as he got up. Connie held him under the arms and led him to the armchair and sat him down. A dark red line was visible on Henry's neck. Connie asked if he was all right. Did he need a doctor? Henry couldn't find his voice, but nodded he was okay, still gasping for air as he started to recover.

Vince took the shotgun and stomped up the stairs to his room.

With Vince out of earshot, Connie bent to Henry's side.

"I'm so sorry," she said.

"Make him go," Henry gasped, starting to cough.

"I'll go to London. Get his key. And then he'll go and we'll be together again, yeah?"

Henry, nursing his bruised windpipe, looked at Connie; his eyes etched with sadness. He was sniffing, on the edge of tears; snot and heartache were pouring out of him. "I don't know if we can do this."

"Course we can. We're strong," Connie pleaded.

"It's twice now."

Connie strained to catch his words. What had he said? She looked questioningly at him.

"It's twice you've brought someone –"

"I never brought no one –"

"He came. Danny came before him." And now Henry was angry, even though his voice was barely more than a gasp.

That made it worse somehow, the sounds of a pained animal. Before they had struggled with their differences as they tried to find a shared path in marital life. Then the biggest question was could Connie fit in? Could she shrug off the self-doubt that stopped her embracing her life ahead? Oh for those easy problems. She stared numbly at her husband. Here he was rasping his words while he sat on the floor, a broken man. "Even if we get rid of him. Who else will come?"

"No one, I promise."

"That's what you said last – time." Henry coughed and winced.

Connie put out her hand to help him up. She was grateful that he took it and she helped him to his feet. But as soon as he was up, he let go as if he'd been burnt. His face was filled with remorse. "I'm sorry, Connie. I really am."

"Well, don't make a decision then." Connie could hear the desperation in her own voice. She didn't know how to save this; how to stop the inevitability of what she knew was coming. She hoped against hope that he wouldn't say the words she feared most. But instead, he spoke about what was really troubling him.

"It's not about Vince. Or Danny. Or whoever else might come." He sighed, finding this hard. "It's about the fact that I don't know you, do I?" Henry kissed her on the forehead. Connie felt bereft. She couldn't find any words, aware that she was making laboured little snorts of disbelief. Was her marriage ending? Was it ending just like that?

"I'll get rid of him," she said, a desperate offer. But Henry was already leaving the room.

A wave of self-hatred washed over Connie. The little voices jabbered away. Mrs Gulliver and the other harpies who had said she wasn't good enough. Who did she think she was marrying their lovely vicar? Connie didn't have the strength to think any positive thoughts. At that moment she felt that her whole happy ending had suddenly turned to dust.

Chapter 13

The next day, as a sullen woman named Connie Carter made the convoluted, lengthy and episodic journey to London, the blue and white-walled corridors of Fernley East Hospital echoed with the sound of coughing. Moved to a small room away from the rest of the ward, Glory Wayland sat on her bed. She finished pulling her blouse over her head. Her body still showed the faded bruising from Amos Ackley's thugs; a yellowing road map of best-forgotten pain. As her blouse had been blood-stained from the bullet wound, one of the nurses had taken it home and washed it as best as she could. Now the white blouse bore some dark, indelible marks but nothing more. But Glory had no other clothing so she had to put up with it. She felt the padded bandage on her neck, secured with lengths of medical tape. It was still sore and sensitive to the touch.

The nurse who had washed the blouse entered the room. Although she was smiling, it wasn't hard to see in her eyes that she was sad to see Glory leaving.

"All set, then?" the nurse said, trying to be as jolly as possible.

Glory nodded, putting on her jacket, a small rip across one shoulder from the fight on Barnes Common.

They both knew the desperate truth: the seventeen-year-old girl had nowhere to go. She'd be sleeping on the streets tonight, begging for coins and taking her chances from now on. The nurse handed her something. Glory saw it was a small notebook and a pencil. "Just until you find your voice," the nurse said. Glory wrote thank you on a page and handed it over. It seemed a fitting first message to write.

As the nurse checked that Glory had everything, they were both surprised when the doctor ran up in the corridor.

"Thank heavens I've caught you," he said, somewhat breathless. "Someone has come to pick you up."

The nurse looked pleased at this news. How wonderful that someone had come to look after the young girl.

But Glory just looked confused.

"He said he was your uncle?" the doctor continued, wondering why she was looking baffled. Such news didn't usually earn a furrowed brow. But he didn't have time to worry about it. "Anyway, he's waiting in the foyer downstairs for you. Good luck for the future, young lady."

And after shaking her hand, the doctor set off towards the ward. The nurse said her goodbyes and followed. Suddenly Glory Wayland was alone. She wondered, with mounting apprehension, about the man waiting in the foyer. She had no uncle – not that she knew about, anyway, and certainly none that might know she was in this hospital. So whoever had said they were her uncle was lying. But what if it was some member of her family? What if it was a real uncle who had found her – somehow – and now wanted to reunite and – no, stop it! Deep down, Glory knew who was waiting for her: and that man wouldn't lead to any violin-and-roses family reunion. She snapped out of her inactivity, clutched her handbag tightly and looked around for some other way out of the hospital. Nearby there were some metal stairs with a sign at the top stating "Maintenance Exit".

The resourceful Glory Wayland clattered down the stairs, her mouth dry with panic. As she neared the last flight, she took a deep breath. She opened the door at the bottom, her hand slippery on the brass handle, half expecting Amos to be on the other side. Her breathing was fast and shallow as she peered through the crack.

He wasn't there.

The relief caused Glory Wayland to feel giddy. She took a second to compose herself and then she scanned the corridor beyond. One way led to the foyer: a place she desperately wanted to avoid, while the other led to the rear of the hospital.

Glory walked quietly and purposefully towards the back exit, scarcely daring to look behind her. With each step, she expected a hand to grab her shoulder and pull her back or a man's voice to yell out for her to stop. But nothing happened.

Daylight was streaming in from outside as Glory approached the glass exit doors. Salvation. A man coughed, making Glory startle. But it was only an orderly leaning against the wall, smoking a cigarette. Glory put her hand towards the glass doors. It was now or never. But would anyone be waiting on the other side?

Glory pushed them with all her might and ran out into

the back alley, aiming to disorientate anyone waiting. But again, there was no one there. She slowed and composed herself. Then, as calmly and inconspicuously as she could manage, she made her way down the alley. Thoughts turned to where she would go. She knew she couldn't go back to Vince's room, not yet at least, as Amos Ackley would probably be watching the place.

Lost in thought, Glory was only dimly aware of the maroon-and-black liveried car parked ahead in the alley. A man in a trilby hat was fiddling with the oil cap, his back to her. Glory went to walk past when the rear door of the car flew open in front of her, blocking her way. She turned to find herself looking at the face of Amos Ackley, sitting on the back seat. All of a sudden, the man in the trilby hat seemed to forget about his oil problems and he pushed Glory into the back of the car. She tried to scream. No sound came out. Forcing her inside, Trilby Man slammed the door behind her. Then, checking that no one had seen, he casually walked around to the driver's side and got in.

In the back of the car, Glory sat face to face with the one man she hoped she'd never see again. He was nursing a blackened cheek bone. "Usually I'd worry about people screaming for help." Amos smirked. "But your doctor says that you're not making much noise these days."

Glory flashed angry eyes at him. But this just seemed to make him more amused.

"Save your voice," he said. "I'll do the talking. It's a simple question. Where is that maggot of a boyfriend of yours?"

Glory shook her head. But Ackley continued regardless.

"See, I can't let Vince get away. He's cost me – not just money, but face. Do you understand what I mean by that? He swans around and gets one over on me and suddenly every other cockroach south of the river thinks they can be smart with me. So I need to know where he's gone. Make him pay."

Glory shrugged. Hastily she wrote in her pad that she didn't have a clue where Vince would have gone.

Amos processed this information, scanning the girl's face for any sign of a lie. Then he prodded a signet-ring-clad finger at her pad. "Think harder. Otherwise you're no use to me."

Amos smiled at his driver. Trilby Man nodded back in the rear-view mirror.

Glory looked at the blank page. What could she write that would convince him?

"Now, my own theory, Bernard –" Amos announced to his driver, "– is that he's gone to ground in the country. Or he's managed to find that wretch Connie Carter and they've gone off to the moon together!"

Glory's eyes glanced up from the paper at the mention of Connie. It always irked her when the name was mentioned – not least because Vince was always berating her about how much better Connie was at the various scams. To Glory, it always seemed that Vince had feelings for Connie. Feelings that would always get in the way of anything happening between the two of them.

She finished writing in the pad and tore off the page, holding it face down.

Amos smiled at her. He took it from her and turned it over. Inside were the scrawled words:

"Get lost and leave me alone!"

As he spun to react, Glory pushed him as hard as she could in the ribs with her elbow. Then she popped open the door and ran hell for leather up the alleyway, her shoes falling away as she went. Trilby Hat was quick to follow, but Amos called him back. A smile played on Ackley's face as he watched the spirited Glory running gazelle-like on her long legs off into the distance.

"Get in the car. Let's see where she goes," he muttered.

Back in Helmstead, Henry and Vince were like uneasy bedfellows as they tried to exist without the balancing force of Connie being present. For his part, Henry was keeping a low profile – talking if he was spoken to, cooking meals for Vince but otherwise not interacting at all if he could possibly help it. Henry was still angry. But he felt bad for having spoken to Connie the way he had. He'd been hurt and upset from having a gun barrel rammed across his throat. Surely she wouldn't believe everything he'd said? It was such a mess.

And Henry felt emasculated that he hadn't been able to make the thug leave – and yet he felt oddly relieved that he had at least tried. Even the failed attempt had boosted his confidence. It was a case of knowing that at least he had attempted to face him down, confronting his own fear of such situations as much as the actual fear of bodily harm. He had crossed the line, even if crossing it had ended in failure.

Vince mopped up the gravy on his plate with a slice of

bread. Henry had made a dumpling stew with gravy. Vince was licking the tips of his fingers in approval. Henry grunted that he was going to see Dr Beauchamp near Gorley Woods. Vince nodded, hauled himself away from the dining table and slumped heavily down in the fireside chair. It looked like a nap was very much on the cards. As Henry put on his coat and affixed his bicycle clips, he supposed that Vince would still be slumped, dozing in that armchair when he returned from his mission of mercy.

Henry took a deep breath and nudged Vince roughly on the arm. The thug wasn't expecting this.

"I've given you your last supper," Henry said, full of steel, with only his eyes betraying his nerves. "I want you to know that I disagree wholeheartedly with you sending Connie to London."

"You do, do you?"

"And when she gives you the key. When she gets back. I want you to leave us immediately."

"Is that what she wants?"

"She doesn't know I'm saying this to you." Henry expected Vince to leap up from his chair and grab his throat, but to his surprise the big man stayed in his seat, transfixed by the flames in the grate as if they were dancers at a burlesque show.

"Got to admire you, bookworm." Vince smiled. "First you try the old violence on me and now you're just using words. But it's obvious you don't want me here."

"That's right. We've done quite enough for you." How much taunting would Vince take before he snapped?

"Well, I planned to go anyway. When I got the key."

"That's as maybe. But you planned to take my wife with you, didn't you?"

Vince rubbed a big paw over his mouth, the sound of stubble being brushed. And then he showed his teeth in a broad grin. "You're smarter than I thought. That's what reading books gives you, eh?"

"Knowledge is power," Henry said tightly.

"A gun in the ribs is power," Vince replied. Henry took a step backwards, ready for an attack. "Relax. I'm not going to hurt you. This is about you and Con, ain't it? Maybe we should give her the choice. See where she wants to go."

"No." There was no debate to be had. "You think sending her to London will make her miss everything you did there?"

"Maybe." Vince considered. "It's her home. Those streets. Those people."

"I love her," Henry said.

Vince couldn't say the same.

"So I want you gone." Henry went out the front door. It was raining. He pulled his bike away from the wall and got on, pushing away down the high street. His legs were shaking and he found it hard to get a purchase on the pedals. But he'd done it. He'd said his piece to Vince Halliday, and he'd found using words far easier than using a weapon. Henry felt both elated and fearful. But, above all, he finally felt brave.

He didn't see Vince Halliday emerge from the vicarage, intent on following him. It was raining hard, so Vince turned up his collar to shut out some of the cold. He couldn't keep up with a bicycle, but he knew the name of the forest where Henry was headed. He knew about Gorley Woods.

Henry Jameson didn't see the man chasing after him.

But someone did. A stick-thin old woman, struggling against the wind whistling down the high street. Mrs Gladys Gulliver.

Glory stopped running three streets away. She couldn't see any sign of Trilby Hat or Amos. She was nursing her sore feet and deciding what to do, when any plans were undone by the wail of air-raid sirens. Dutifully, she made her way – along with hundreds of others – down into the nearest tube station. Packed in like sardines by the platform, Glory waited for the bombing raid to stop and for the all-clear to be given. When it eventually came, it was nearly eight o'clock and night had fallen. Glory Wayland kept to the shadows and made her way to the only place she knew. Vince's bedsit.

Someone else heading there was Connie Carter. She'd alighted from the train at Euston and made her way to the East End. The furious and devastating bombing raids of the Blitz had stopped for the time being, and although vast areas of buildings were still rubble shrines to the houses that had once stood there, the area was slowly getting back on its feet. Lord Latham, leader of the London County Council, had devised his "Plans for London" and Londoners were reassured that their city was going to rise from the ashes of the Luftwaffe bombings. And when the bombing raids did happen, the retreat of people to the haven of the underground stations had become a feature of London life – something as common as going to the markets and popping into the pub for a drink. The normalising of the abnormal had shown, once again, the true resilience of people under pressure.

Connie walked along the rain-soaked pavements, nearing, by each footfall, the old familiar roads of her East End. It felt like home; some comfort after she'd lost everything in Helmstead. The train journey from Helmstead had been a nerve-wracking experience for Connie – not only because she was contravening War Office policy by being a civilian making "an unnecessary journey" but it was the first journey that she'd undertaken since the derailment of the train from Brinford. She'd found herself scrunching her nails nervously into her palms each time the carriages clattered over a join in the tracks. But she was also worried about leaving Henry with Vince in the vicarage, praying that nothing would spark any further arguments and violence between them. Maybe, if nothing else happened, there would be a way for her to get back with Henry.

After the incident with the shotgun, Henry hadn't said much more. When they were in their bedroom, Connie had made a desperate attempt to get him to talk.

"If I go to London tomorrow, I want us to talk when I get back."

"If you get back." He pulled the sheets up to his neck, scrunching up into a foetal position. "Maybe you should stay there for a while."

"No. I want us to work this thing out."

"I'm too tired, Connie. Can't you see?" And he turned out the bedside light. Neither of them slept.

Connie had needed time off work to go to London. There was no way she could just ask for a holiday – there was a war on! You couldn't just slope off when you felt like it. So she did the only thing she could: lying about being ill and then praying that no one would spot her sneaking to Helmstead station. She was lucky. Even the hawk eyes of Gladys Gulliver hadn't spotted her in her best maroon hat and coat running to catch the train to Birmingham. And a reluctant Henry had kept up the pretence, informing Farmer Finch that Connie was in bed with influenza.

It was getting dark and the streets were deserted when Connie got to the building where Vince had lived – a tall brown-bricked Victorian building that had been converted into a warren of tiny rooms, each rented out to the working class of East London. During the walk along the streets, Connie had been sensitive to anyone else she spotted. Were they watching her? Did they work for Amos Ackley? But – to her relief – she had got here unscathed and, as far as she knew, without being followed. Connie checked the address on the piece of paper that Vince had given her and made her way into the building. It smelt of old tobacco smoke. A thread-bare red carpet hugged a twisting staircase around a mesh-gated lift displaying an "out of order" sign. She had no option but to take the stairs. Reaching the third floor, Connie found flat 14. She produced the front-door key, which Vince had given her and let herself in, shutting the door quickly behind herself before turning on the light. It was a tiny room, dominated by a single unmade bed in the centre of the room. A basin on the wall by the window sported a shaving brush and a discarded coating of black bristles around the plug hole. The shaving mirror had a large crack across its surface that gave anyone looking into it a long scar on their right cheek. A pile of old newspapers sat in front of a wardrobe. Connie pulled the single curtain over the single window and moved the newspapers. She opened the wardrobe. There was a blue shirt and a grey suit inside, plus some balled-up pairs of socks that looked like fluffy hand grenades. A pair of brown brogues sat at the bottom, but as Connie glanced at them she noticed something else underneath. A small wicker basket with a wicker lid. Connie took it out and placed it on the unmade bed. Opening the lid, she found some documents: Vince's ration book, his identification documents – including a forged paper that had Vince's photograph with the name Douglas Manning. Connie shuddered to wonder what scam that was intended for. At the bottom of the basket was something else. Something that caused her to stop in her tracks.

It was a small photograph – scuffed and dog-eared – of Connie Carter.

He'd kept it.

Connie smiled, despite herself. It was the first time she'd smiled since yesterday. Maybe Vince had cared for her after all. She composed herself and scooped all the documents – with the exception of the photograph of herself – into her handbag. Vince might need them. Then she hastily pushed the basket back under the tan shoes in the wardrobe. She opened her handbag, keen to finish what she came for. Producing a long metal nail file, Connie went to the single window of the flat. She counted the floorboards from the window – just as Vince had instructed her. One, two, three. And then she pushed her nail file into the gap by the third floor board. The end of the plank was prised up and Connie was able to get a purchase on it with her finger nails. Lifting it up, she caught a glimpse of a grey metal box hidden in the recess. She hoped it would have the key that Vince needed inside. She was about to lift the floorboard higher so she could grab the box, when the door to Vince's bedsit opened. Connie spun round to face whoever it was, the nail file held like a small dagger in her hand.

A thin woman with a cloche hat stared at her.

Chapter 14

The woman in the cloche hat entered the room, closing the door behind her.

For a few seconds the two women weighed each other up. Connie clocked the bandage around the girl's neck, her large eyes dulled by sadness and regret. Despite being in her teens, this was a woman whose worries had aged her. She'd experienced things that she shouldn't have had to. Connie had a good idea who she was, but she wasn't sure how that could be possible, given what she'd been told.

"I was told to come 'ere. By Vince," Connie said defensively, wondering if the woman thought she was trespassing or burgling the place. Who was she? Did she live here, since Vince had left? Or perhaps she lived here with Vince.

The thin woman scowled, taking this in, but saying nothing as she scanned the room. Connie wondered why she wasn't saying anything. The tension of having a long silence niggled her.

"Ain't you going to say nothing?"

Glory pointed to the bandage on her neck.

A rush of confusing thoughts hit her. So was this really

Glory Wayland, the girl on Barnes Common? Didn't Vince say she was dead? What was she doing here?

Connie managed a feeble, "He told me about you." As if she was just some friend of a friend she was meeting at a tea dance. But this one sentence ignited a light in the girl's eyes. She took out a notepad and started to write furiously. Connie wondered what she was doing. Then she realised that Glory couldn't talk. The girl tapped the page she had just filled. It said: "You've seen him?"

Connie nodded. "More's the pity. He's caused a whole heap of trouble. I'm Connie, by the way."

Glory rolled her eyes. A wince of begrudging acknowledgement. She'd guessed as much.

She let her eyes soak up the image of Connie Carter, really examining her, as if she was some mythical creature whom she had only heard tales about. This was the siren who could lure any man. With her dark-red lipstick and up-to-date waved hairstyle, maroon coat, matching hat, plus a long black skirt, Connie looked like a stylish actress out of *Picturegoer* Magazine. Glory always supposed she would be jealous of Connie Carter; a woman whose name had been indelibly rubbed in her face by Vince since the moment they'd met. Connie always did this better. Connie would have got more money out of that guy. Connie knew how to speak to a man to get him interested. Glory was always made to feel in the shadow of this glorious creature.

But what Vince thought didn't matter any more. So Glory found she felt no jealousy or resentment, just a curious interest. Meeting Connie was now a box to be ticked, nothing more.

She scrawled on her notepad: "Nice to meet you. Where is Vince?"

"He's living with my husband."

Glory looked confused.

"It's a long story."

She decided not to pursue it. Connie patted the end of the bed, encouraging Glory to sit down.

"London's not changed. Rubble and rain." Connie smiled, attempting to break the ice.

Glory smiled. It seemed to do the trick.

After this, the two women seemed to bond – although Connie, due to Glory's vocal disability, did most of the talking. But then Connie was happy to talk. And when she wasn't talking, she would try to save Glory from writing in her pad by preempting answers or filling in the rest of a sentence verbally after Glory had written a prompting word or two. They sat on the bed and chatted – time running away with them. Connie had been worried to hear about how Vince had left Gloria at the mercy of Amos Ackerly and his men. Glory wanted to hear about what it was like to be a Land Girl.

Finally, Connie told her more about how Vince had turned up in Helmstead – the place she was stationed as a Land Girl. She told her the whole sorry tale, ending with how she had been sent to get the key from under the floorboards and bring it back to Vince. Then he would, she hoped, disappear out of their lives. Glory shrugged, as if she didn't entirely believe that Vince would keep his word either. Connie smiled, despite herself. They both knew what Vince was like and what he was capable of. And then the warm camaraderie was punctured as Connie remembered something. "Oh my God. The time!" she said in a panic.

It had gone ten o'clock in the evening. Connie had missed the last train back to Birmingham.

There was no way of getting home now. She'd have to wait until tomorrow. Feeling churned up about having to spend a night in London, Connie slumped on the bed, depressed. Glory scribbled on her pad: "Wait." And then she tried to rally Connie's mood by finding a half-full bottle of whisky in the drawer by the bed. She found a tumbler and a mug; as mismatched bedfellows as the women drinking from them. The vessels would have to do. She poured liberal measures for the two of them. The two damaged women in Vince Halliday's life clinked glasses and talked some more.

"This is a bit like his other flat," Connie commented. "Except the other one had more mould."

Glory smiled. She winced at the taste of the alcohol, but gulped it down anyway.

"Odd thing is, I feel more at home here than I do at the vicarage." Glory looked confused at this, so Connie continued, "I live in the vicarage. Married to a vicar. Don't know for how much longer, though. He deserves someone better than me." Now it was Connie's turn to take a gulp of whisky. "We were having problems before Vince turned up. But funny thing was, I thought they'd all fix themselves." She considered this and then became more emphatic. "They would have done. It was just that I was so different to him. He was so different to me. But we could have fixed all that and found some common ground, you know?"

Glory nodded. She didn't really know, but thought a nod was the best form of support for her new-found friend.

It didn't take too much alcohol to make Gloria Wayland quite sleepy. She'd had an exhausting day since coming out of hospital. Gloria fell fast asleep on one side of the bed. Connie wrapped the sheet around her, touched the hair on her head and picked up her notebook to put it on the side. She idly flicked through it. There were a handful of pages that had been used; the odd phrase and question. Please, thank you, no, yes, Gloria. Useful things that could probably be reused time and time again. But one page caught Connie's attention. Glory had drawn a horse, an intricate and fairly accurate portrait. Another page had a cottage drawn on it, picture-book style, with a single puff of smoke coming from the chimney; the windows rounded slightly to give the unintentional appearance of smiling eyes. A happy home. The girl could be an artist, Connie thought, but in her world of late-night dives and sleazy men, and with the breaks she'd been given, it was unlikely that she'd ever fulfil that potential. It was a sad state of affairs.

Connie slipped the notebook and pencil into Glory's small handbag. As she placed it inside, something caught her eye in the dark folds: a glint of metal reflecting light from the lamp in the room. Connie looked closer and realised it was a scalpel. The type a surgeon might use: a heavy and ridged metal handle with a sharp blade on top. She looked at the mute girl and wondered what it was doing in her handbag. Had she stolen it from the hospital? Was it for protection?

It made Connie feel uneasy. She fastened the handbag and

put it down by Glory's side of the bed. Connie contemplated sleeping beside her, and put her head down for a bit. But sleep didn't come easily. Woozy thoughts of Henry, the rationale of clear thought blurred by a large tumbler of whisky. Connie found her stomach rumbling from lack of food, so she decided to go out and see if she could find something to eat. And maybe she could find a telephone to call Henry. She fastened her jacket, straightened her hat and left the sleeping Glory.

Connie found the streets outside the building dark and cold. There didn't seem to be a soul around and all the street lights were turned off, making it hard to find her way. Using the light of the partial moon to see, Connie walked along the widest road she could find – figuring that there might be some late-night corner house open. But the further she walked, the less hopeful she became. Still not seeing another living person, she started to wonder whether there was any point continuing. Her heels clip-clopped along the streets as a fine drizzle started to fall, and her feet were getting sore. Connie turned up her collar and carried on. Starting to feel a little lost, she slowed her pace. Perhaps she should go back? Suddenly she noticed a man in the distance. He was wearing some sort of waterproof coat, glistening darkly in the drizzle, and he seemed to have a helmet of some sort on. He waved his hand at her.

"Oi!" he shouted at Connie, coming over, urgency in his gait.

Connie instinctively backed away, ready to run. Was it one of Ackerly's men?

But as soon as the man came into the light of the moon, everything made sense and Connie felt a bit foolish. On the man's helmet were the initials A.R.P. He was an Air-Raid Precaution Warden. In his forties and with a glossy well-fed face, he berated Connie Carter for being out at night. Didn't she know there was a curfew? It all came flooding back to Connie now. She apologised profusely for her stupidity. She hadn't been back to London for a while. And she was hungry, that's all, and had gone out to find somewhere to eat.

"Well, you won't have much luck at this time of night, young lady."

Twenty minutes later, Connie found herself in the somewhat surreal situation of sitting in an Anderson Shelter with the warden, a man named George Butler, sharing his paste sandwiches with him. They were made by George's wife and, at that moment in time, they tasted like the best food in the world to the hungry Connie. As she ate, he was telling her how the East End had changed. And between mouthfuls, Connie was telling him about where her orphanage had been.

"That street's gone now, I think," George mulled. "Not by the Germans, it was all pulled down before."

"Good riddance," Connie said. She thought of all the pink-cheeked children there, the older ones getting ready to go to foster homes and first jobs; the younger ones still hopeful that each knock at the main door might be a new family to take them away.

George Butler had a large number of sandwiches, which perhaps accounted for his well-fed and glowing appearance. He offered Connie another round, but she refused, thanking him anyway. After they had finished, George offered to escort Connie back to her lodgings.

"I don't want to put you to any trouble."

"It's no trouble. Besides, it's my job to patrol the streets. It just makes sense if I patrol your way."

"You're a gentleman, George. But I think I came a long way."

"I'll make you a deal, then. I'll walk halfway with you, check you're on the right course, and then direct you the rest of the way. How's that?"

"Have I told you, you're a gentleman?"

George put his sandwiches back in his holdall and strapped it closed. He put his helmet on and they set off. As they walked, Connie noticed that George was whistling nervously.

"What's up? Not going to make a pass at me, are you?"

"What? God no." George's cheeks flushed. "I'm happily married. Most of the time."

They walked in silence for a bit. Then the whistling started again.

"What?" Connie asked.

"It's silly. I'm supposed to be playing cards at the end of my shift. I always get a bit jumpy about it."

"I used to love playing cards. Rummy, pontoon, old maid, you name it," Connie cackled, not fully registering how troubled George was about it.

"Well, this is poker. And I need a turn of luck, if I'm honest," George said, seeming to want to unburden himself. Suddenly this rosy-faced man had a weight of worries on his shoulders. Connie guessed that George's ARP patrol often ended in a poker game. A game where he usually lost.

"You play every night?" Connie asked.

"More than my wife knows," George admitted. His patrols were supposed to last eight hours, but because of his rheumatism, he would often stop for a late-night drink in a pub before setting off again. The time spent in the pub grew, minutes bleeding into hours. And then he got involved in a poker game. It was just a bit of fun; a half-hour interlude in a cold, rain-soaked night of checking that the lights were out. But it soon became a habit. And now, he confessed, he was in a bit of trouble.

"I'm twenty pounds down," George said. "I've been shifting money around so my missus doesn't find out."

"Tonight might turn things around for you," suggested Connie, instantly regretting saying something so glib.

"Not unless I get a miracle. But thanks," George said as they reached a crossroads. "That's your way, then, Miss. You're about ten minutes from home I'd say. It's been nice to meet you."

And he started to walk away. Connie stood in the rain for a moment. She watched the shuffling figure retreating, the energy of the man seemed to have been sapped by his impending appointment. Connie guessed it was no longer fun for him. She weighed things up. She was ten minutes from Vince's flat. Gloria would probably still be asleep and wouldn't miss her for a bit longer. George had been very kind to share his supper with her when she was famished. And the pub might have a telephone.

The least she could do was help him.

"Hold up," Connie called. George turned, surprised. "Where is this pub?"

"About five minutes. This way." George indicated, his brow furrowed in confusion.

"Will they let women play?" Connie said with a confident grin.

A few minutes later, George Butler ushered Connie into a small East End boozer. Full of dark furniture, wood-panelled walls and yellowing, nicotine-stained wallpaper, it was like most of the other pubs Connie had been in. Small joyless places filled with smoke, flat beer and broken dreams. Two labourers were nursing pints by the bar, their work boots resting on the brass foot rail by their stools. They did comical double-takes at the glamorous woman in the red lipstick who had entered their little yellow world. Was she some alcohol-induced hallucination? An elderly couple sitting at a table stared through Connie and George, seemingly unfazed by the newcomers. For his part, George Butler had swelled with pride at having Connie as his guest. He ushered her towards a small round table near the back of the pub, around which were seated three men. They looked questioningly at George. What was he playing at? Who was this?

"Your wife's looking well, George." A man with thick grey hair laughed. His companions, a wiry man with round glasses and the demeanour of an accountant, and a bull of a man with red hair looked more wary.

"I met her wandering the streets," George offered. "Thought I'd bring her in for a warming whisky before she goes on her way."

Connie clocked the cards on the table and the small pile of money in the centre.

"What you playing?" she asked.

"Poker," the wiry man said, his eyes boring into her, trying to work out what she wanted. "It's a card game."

"I know what poker is." Connie gave it back with equal contempt. Then she softened, knowing that she needed to draw these men in and not alienate them. "Not sure I know all the rules, but I've seen people play it."

"You can watch some more, then." The wiry man shuffled the pack.

"Can I play while I warm up?" Connie asked, pulling out a chair and not waiting to be asked. As the men threw looks to one another, Connie sealed the deal by opening her handbag and producing her purse. She placed a crumpled white five-pound note in the middle.

"Is that enough?" she said, offering a mock exasperated look. The demeanour of the three men changed. Suddenly they leaned forward, more attentive. This was interesting. What had George found here? A gullible woman with money.

"It's too much money, Miss," George said, standing behind her.

In truth it was too much. Way too much. It was also all the money Connie had left. If she lost it, then she wouldn't be able to get the train home or buy any food before she returned to Helmstead. But she knew she wanted to repay George for his kindness.

"Well, if it's too much, gentlemen, that's fine," Connie said, putting out a hand to collect the note. This would be the moment of truth. Had she pushed things too far?

The grey-haired man shook his head. "No, we can play if you want. Do you know how to play poker?"

"As I said, I've watched people. It's not the one where you have to get twenty-one, is it? No, don't tell me. I know, yes. Pairs and two pairs and all that? Got it." Connie grinned, wondering if they would rumble her. Would they realise she was taking them for a ride? Would they realise she was faking her inexperience? She felt it could go either way, but then the red-headed man snorted, the wiry man laughed. It seemed they took it at face value, not realising they were being hustled. Connie realised that these weren't experienced gamblers, just men who probably came here as George did: for something to do in the twilight hours. The reason they'd taken George's money was just because their run of luck had been better. Connie hoped hers would hold for George.

A small tumbler of whisky was placed beside her. George had bought her a drink. Her head had only just cleared from the ones she'd had with Glory, but she sipped it for the sake of politeness. George pulled up a chair.

When the grey-haired man offered to deal him in, George waved it away and declined. He would let his new friend play a few hands. "I'll take over when she's had enough."

"We'll try not to take her money too quickly," the wiry man said, as the red-headed man gave Connie a pile of change for her note. The cards were dealt and Connie didn't get a decent hand. The second hand was dealt and again Connie had nothing. But this time, she tried to bluff. As she held an ace high, she saw Frederick Finch in her mind's eye with his advice about the art of bluffing. He thought it was all about conviction, totally believing that you could win with a bad hand. But Connie's bluff came unstuck when the wiry man

255

pushed her to reveal her hand. He took the money. Suddenly within two hands, Connie had lost two pounds.

"'Ere I thought there was supposed to be beginner's luck," she said, carefully making it sound like she was confused by the proceedings so far. George threw a worried glance in her direction. Connie ignored it. There was still time to turn this around. And sure enough, the next hand looked more promising. Connie had three fours. It was a pretty decent hand. Carefully maintaining the hesitancy and uncertainty she had shown during the previous hands, Connie added a bet to the pot. Now was her reward for betting on rubbish hands previously, because the men assumed she must have another woeful one. All three matched the pound she had put in. Soon another round of betting occurred. George offered a nervous warning to his friends.

"Come on lads, she don't know what she's doing."

"This will give me a chance to learn, won't it?" Connie said breezily, masking the worry underneath.

With the last of her money thrown into the pot, Connie revealed her three of a kind. To her joy, the other three men folded their hands, their cards obviously weaker than hers. The rules of poker meant that they had no obligation to show them, unless the other player placed a bet and asked them to. The pile of money sat in the middle of the table. Connie played dumb, assuming one of the others had won, before the grey-haired man urged her to take the pot. Suddenly Connie had twelve pounds.

The next few hands went in Connie's favour and soon she was sitting with over thirty pounds in front of her. She felt the same adrenaline buzz that she used to get with Vince Halliday, when they were on a scam together. And she berated herself for feeling that. But it felt familiar and easy, though, unlike sorting hymn books for the Sunday sermon. Maybe this was where she belonged. Her thoughts were broken by another round of folded hands and the wiry man tutting his disgust at her latest successful bluff.

"Now, that's beginner's luck." She laughed and scooped her winnings towards her. George congratulated her. "I'd better be on my way now." She wanted to ask the landlady if she had a telephone so she could call Henry and tell him she wouldn't be home tonight. She needed to hear his voice, needed him to say that he missed her, perhaps.

But the three men weren't smiling now. The wiry man looked with suspicion at her, his eyes glowing with anger.

"You can't just walk away, Miss."

"I thought you didn't have any more money," Connie replied, halfway out of her seat.

"You thought wrong," the man said, producing a small, folded collection of five-pound notes. "One last hand before you go. Double or nothing."

Connie felt her face blanch. Where did this man get that kind of money? Why was he carrying that around? Suddenly she worried that he might be a professional card player after all. Maybe he had seen through her hustle act, but just chose to let her have her fun before launching his counter-hustle. This could all end in tears. This was getting out of control.

"Sit down for one last hand," the grey-haired man said with a seemingly warm smile. It sounded as if she had a choice, but she doubted that was the reality. Reluctantly, Connie sat down again. She downed the rest of her whisky as George leaned over to her. "You don't have to do this," he whispered. "I'm sorry if I've got you into trouble."

She shook her head. One last hand and then she'd be on her way. She whispered to George, "Promise me something?"

"Of course," he whispered back.

"Whatever happens, I don't want you picking up these cards again."

George nodded. He looked at the table to see that the red-headed man had dealt cards to Connie and the wiry man. Everyone else was staying out of it; the stakes too rich for their blood. The wiry man pushed his notes into the middle of the table. Connie did the same. There would be no additional betting. Now they would just turn over their hands and reveal the winner. Sudden death. The wiry man turned his first card and Connie did the same.

Nearly an hour later, Connie emerged from the pub. The rain had broken for a moment and the air was cold and fresh on their warm faces. George shuffled out behind her and closed the door. She stopped in her tracks; her head feeling heavy and tired. Was it the cold reality of what she had done hitting her? The adrenaline come-down after the game? Thoughts of how easily she had snapped back into the world of hustling?

This is where your home is, a small nagging voice chirruped in her head.

And then she banished it from her mind, as more pressing events took over her attention.

For his part, George shook his head in disbelief at what had just happened. But as he tried to talk to Connie about it, she was staring at the street, brow furrowed. Her mouth was opening, but she couldn't quite find the words to speak. Maybe she was troubled by something else entirely.

George thought he knew what it was.

The landlady hadn't had a telephone for Connie to use to call her husband.

George felt sympathy. He'd hate not to see his wife every day or at least speak to her.

"You'll be home soon enough," he said, trying to perk up her spirits. "It'll be all right. I'm sure he'll realise you've missed the last train."

Connie gave a half-smile that implied George couldn't possibly understand what she was going through. But then she seemed to snap out of it, ever the trouper making the best out of a bad situation.

"We did good, didn't we? You must be over the moon, George Butler." She grinned, still feeling as though she'd been slapped.

George couldn't help but beam. This strange woman had come into his life and turned it around.

"Where did you learn to play like that?" he asked.

"I ain't always been a vicar's wife."

George watched her go, half expecting her to just vanish into thin air.

And soon the rain started again, and the only sound Connie could hear was the click-clack of her heels on the wet pavements as she crossed the road.

But this night would come back to haunt her. This night would change everything.

The cottage was cluttered and dark; a picture-book image ravaged by the forces of neglect and time. Inside, wallpaper patterns faded into sepia and window frames were rotting and dirty. Stacks of newspapers lined the walls in the sitting room, only making way for a large brown-leather armchair and a side table in the middle of the room. The side table was long-stemmed and elegant, with space for a single cup or small plate on the top of its lacquered surface. Dr Beauchamp had told Henry that he had liberated it from the café near his apartment in central Paris. He'd had many happy hours playing cards or drinking coffee during his reckless years as a young man in the city – and now a small part of that past was with him during his final years. Henry placed a cup and saucer on the long-stemmed side table and sat on a pile of newspapers – while Dr Beauchamp sat in the armchair and caught his breath.

The old man had emphysema, a slow degeneration of the lungs, which was reaching its final stages.

As he usually did during his visits, Henry would read calming passages from the Bible and try to stir the old man's memory about his time in France. If there was a letter from his family – especially from his son – Henry would be pressed into service to read it aloud, perhaps several times. Dr Beauchamp's craggy face would crack into a smile, as if he could hear his son's voice reaching out to him. And just for a moment, the old man's rheumy eyes would glint with the fire of life once more. This always lifted Henry's heart. The rest of the time during Henry's visits, he would occupy himself with more mundane matters – tending to the washing up, perhaps preparing a simple snack, putting out the washing (Dr Beauchamp had a volunteer from the town, one of Mrs Gulliver's coterie, who kindly came to make him a proper meal once a day). And although it was his Christian duty to minister to his flock by visiting those who required it, Henry also enjoyed the freedom it gave him. For an hour, Henry could forget about the dark shadow of Vince Halliday in his own life; the tatters of his marriage. Instead he could provide support and real help to someone who needed it. Henry supposed that the visits made him feel useful – in a way that he didn't feel in his own home.

As Henry finished washing up the cups and saucers, something caught his eye in the overgrown garden. Had he seen a figure out there? He dried his hands and moved to the back door, sliding the bolt back.

"What's that?" Dr Beauchamp called from the other room, hearing the door opening.

"Just going outside," Henry replied – but his words were drowned out by a coughing fit from next door.

Henry went into the garden. It was a patch no more than twenty foot by twenty foot, bordered by rampaging rose bushes and fruit trees. The grass went up to Henry's knees. He looked into the distance. One of the lower branches of an apple tree was swaying slightly. There didn't seem to be anyone there now. Had he imagined it?

Henry felt uneasy. On the way here on his bicycle, he had

seen the clouds bruising purple and black – a cold wind in the spring air – as if the weather itself had an atmosphere of foreboding about it. And when he had made the pot of tea for Dr Beauchamp, Henry had felt like someone was watching him. He had no proof, just the vague unsettled feeling of something not being quite right; a feeling of a face through the window. The cottage was isolated, on the edge of Gorley Woods, land outside of the vast Hoxley estate; a place where only poachers came. Perhaps a poacher had wandered close to the cottage?

Henry looked around the sides of the house and found nothing, save for an old bicycle which had no front wheel; possibly another piece of Dr Beauchamp's youth consigned to the status of memento. He let himself back into the house, locked the door and finished the washing up. Half an hour later, Henry said his goodbyes to Dr Beauchamp, promising to return in two days' time. Outside the cottage, Henry fastened his bicycle clips and got on the saddle, pushing off along the stone path that led around Gorley Woods and back to Helmstead. The moonlight left a wall of dark silhouetted trees by the side of the path as Henry rode. The only sounds were of the pedals moving the chain round and the infrequent call of an owl somewhere in the woods.

As he rode, and each pedal push took him further away from the isolated cottage, Henry began to forget about half-glimpsed imaginary figures in Dr Beauchamp's garden.

Instead, thoughts of Connie filled his head. He wondered how she was getting on in London, hoping that she was safe. He consoled himself that it was her old environment. She knew the streets of the East End and how to look after herself. She would be fine. In fact, she would probably be on her way back on some clattering steam train right—

WHACK!

Suddenly Henry was wrenched backwards off his saddle, the air smashed from his lungs, seemingly by an invisible force that had slammed against his chest. He landed hard on the stony road as the bicycle flew, spinning upwards into the air, looping over itself and crashing on top of him. He winced in pain and struggled for breath, winded by the impact of whatever it was. Was it a tree? A branch? In his dazed state, Henry didn't see the length of wire that had been stretched across the road between two trees. It was at chest height and had been very effective at dismounting him. A figure moved stealthily between the two trees, unhooking the wire; its job done. As Henry fought for his breath, stars were twinkling in his vision. As a wave of blackness settled over him, he was dimly aware that he recognised the man looming over him. A large dark shape in a dirty suit. He knew it was Vince Halliday.

Henry Jameson just had time to notice that Vince was smiling – as he slipped away into unconsciousness.

Chapter 15

Amid the morning rush at Euston station, Connie Carter and Glory Wayland made their way to the ticket office. Glory had decided to come back with Connie to Helmstead. By writing in her pad, she had explained to Connie what she wanted to do when she saw Vince again: "I want to confront him. Ask him why he left me."

Connie felt uneasy, remembering the razor-sharp scalpel in her handbag. The young woman seemed angry about what Vince had done. Quite rightly. He had abandoned her to die. She said she wanted answers. But Connie also knew that she had the key in her possession that could send Vince Halliday scurrying out of her life. She didn't want to jeopardise that arrangement by returning with a furious, and possibly murderous, young woman. Connie felt so close to getting rid of Vince, she didn't want anything to go wrong.

Despite her sympathies for the girl, Connie knew that she had to leave Glory in London.

As Glory crossed the concourse to the ticket office and started the somewhat lengthy process of writing what she needed on her pad, Connie sloped away. She dived into a throng of soldiers who were moving towards the platforms. Her train was up ahead. The guard was checking his watch. Connie asked him when the Birmingham train was due to leave. By force of habit, he unnecessarily checked his watch again and told her that it would go in four minutes. She let the tide of bodies sweep her along the platform, keeping a weather eye on the ticket office in the distance. There was no sign of Glory. Connie's getaway was slowed by a soldier hauling a heavy backpack onto the train. She willed him to move more quickly, but watching him reminded her of an ant trying to move a raisin. Adjacent doors were equally blocked. At last, Connie stepped up onto the running board of the carriage, feeling a twinge of guilt. She had felt empathy with Glory Wayland, both kindred spirits in a way that had been used and abused by Vince Halliday. But Connie couldn't risk her future for the younger woman. As selfish as it seemed, Connie had to put Henry first and any chance she had of mending their marriage. She had to get their life back: Sunday sermons, afternoon teas, late-night suppers around the fire, tending to the two chickens in the garden.

On board, Connie squeezed past the backpacked soldier and darted down the carriage. Finding an empty compartment, she sat nearest the far-side window. She scanned the stream of people walking along the platform, getting on at various points along the train. Faces, young, old. But there was no sign of Glory Wayland. And then finally, Connie heard the reassuring, insistent sound of the guard blowing the whistle. She realised she had been holding her breath, and now she let out a satisfying sigh of relief, as the train began to chug slowly out of the station. Feeling safe, Connie slumped back in her seat.

A headache was pounding in her temples, formed by the unhappy marriage of stress and too much alcohol the night before. She rubbed the bridge of her nose, closed her eyes and concentrated on the calming rhythm of the train. She wondered how Vince would find the lock that fitted the key, before deciding it wasn't her problem. Maybe he had a system or some information. It didn't matter. She'd done her part of the deal.

Connie heard the carriage door slide open, and waited for the sound of someone sitting down. But she became aware of the feeling of being watched. And then she heard the heavy breathing of a young woman out of breath. She opened her eyes to see a red-faced Glory Wayland staring accusingly down at her.

"I looked for you. We must have got separated." Connie smiled in embarrassment. Glory must have got on the train and spent the intervening minutes searching compartments for her.

Glory wrote something in her pad. Connie could tell she was angry because the pencil was pressed hard against her fingers, draining them white. She held up the page in Connie's face.

"Why were you leaving me?"

"I told you. We got separated, all right?" Connie said, trying to brave-face the situation with a lie.

But this wasn't good enough for Glory. Again she pushed the page into Connie's face, the same message.

"Why were you leaving me?"

"Because you've got a bleedin' knife in your bag!" Connie found the words tumbling out before she could stop them.

This stopped the silent interrogation. Glory's brow furrowed. She wrote something: "How do you know?"

"I saw it, didn't I?" Connie said, lowering her voice. "And I can't have you attacking Vince. Not when I'm so close to getting him out of my hair. Understand?" Now it was her turn to be steely and determined. She'd had enough of people riding roughshod over her. She was a fighter and she was going to finish this.

Glory Wayland seemed contrite. She put her pad on her lap and started to write. This time, the pencil wasn't being rammed into the page, her finger wasn't blanched white by its pressure. She had calmed down.

"I won't attack him." Glory showed Connie the page. "It's protection."

Connie nodded. "I know what it's like, though. I'd like to attack him myself."

Glory looked warmly at her for the first time since she'd got on the train.

"But let me see him first, yeah?" Connie added.

Glory nodded her agreement and then wrote something else. She held up the page and Connie read it.

"Where will I go?" it said.

"Don't worry. I know a place you can stay while I end things with Vince."

"But I don't know the first thing about her," Esther Reeves blustered. She explained to Connie that she'd had a difficult morning, having to deal with the fall-out of a Land Girl on Vernon's farm who had become pregnant. There had been a lot of tears and Esther had needed to make reassurances to the girl. But she also had to explain that paragraph eleven of the Women's Land Army Rules states that any girl found to be pregnant must be demobbed immediately and sent home, with no opportunity to re-enlist.

And after that stressful morning, the last thing she needed now was Connie Carter asking if a strange – mute – girl from London could stay a few days. She wasn't part of the Women's Land Army, she hadn't enlisted through the normal channels; and she would be taking up a valuable bed and food and resources that could be used by a Land Girl. Someone helping the war effort.

Glory Wayland looked sullenly at the floor of Finch's farmhouse kitchen.

"Couldn't we make an exception?" Connie asked. "It's only for a few days."

Esther considered this and then a question came into her head. She turned to Connie with a suspicious look.

"Why can't she stay at the vicarage?" Esther replied. It was a blindingly obvious question. Esther knew that there was a spare, apparently empty, room there at the moment. There was no bishop staying there. The room was empty.

The question threw Connie. How could she explain why there wasn't a spare bed? Connie shook her head slowly, buying herself valuable thinking time. A technique she'd used since an older girl had taught it to her in the children's home. But as she prevaricated, Connie realised that not only was Esther looking at her, but Glory was too. The answer had better be good on both counts.

"She's my friend and I don't want to trouble Henry," Connie said, knowing that the reply was about as convincing as the George Formby impression that Finch did when drunk.

"Then it's out of the question," Esther stormed.

"But please, Esther."

"It's bad enough you skive off and say you're ill. I don't know what you're up to these days," Esther said. The matter was closed and as if to emphasise the point, Esther produced a large saucepan from a cupboard and started to fill it with water. Dinner had to be prepared for all the hungry girls in the fields. The ones who turned up for work. It was business as usual and there was no place for favours for Connie and her mute friend.

Esther bent to get the sack of potatoes and realised a note pad was being proffered in front of her face.

"I can cook," it said.

Now it was Esther's turn to be thrown. Her anger started to subside. She looked at Connie's pleading face and at the wide-eyed innocent face of the girl with the cloche hat. And she felt her own hardness melting away. Yes, there was a war on, but they had to stick together and help each other, didn't they? Always a sucker for puppy-dog eyes, Esther found herself saying she could stay.

"But only for a few days, mind!" Esther said, reasserting some semblance of authority in the situation. She plonked the potatoes in a colander for Glory to start peeling. "And she'd better be good at cooking or she'll be out on her ear faster than you can say Neville Chamberlain!"

Connie thanked Esther. She was about to go home to change into her uniform, when Esther told her to get changed upstairs. With a girl down from Storey's farm, they couldn't afford for Connie to swan off home. She'd have to see Henry later, after her shift. A reluctant Connie did as she was told, getting changed in Joyce's room. She knew she couldn't rock the boat – especially as Esther had been so good about taking Glory in. Once in her Land Army uniform, she put her smart handbag away with her suit, taking the precious key from inside and slipping it into her trouser pocket. It was literally her key out of the mess with Vince and she wanted to keep it on her at all times.

After her shift was over and as the sky began to darken into night, Connie said goodbye to Glory, leaving her with a warning to behave herself. It was a relief that everyone had liked her cooking, and Esther had glowed at the praise the girls were giving, as if she had found some talented prodigy. Joyce wanted to know why Glory couldn't speak and Connie was glad that she was sitting around the table when the question was asked so she could invent a quick lie to close it down. Glory had been injured in a bomb blast in London. End of story. Joyce and the others seemed to buy this. Dolores wasn't happy, though.

"Why do I have to share a room with her?"

"It's the charitable thing to do," Esther reminded her.

Joyce whispered to Iris and Connie that maybe Glory could actually find out something about the mysterious Dolores.

As Connie crossed the small bridge back into Helmstead, a portly figure made her jump, as he called out from across the road. It was Roger Curran. He scuttled over with a sombre look on his face. And when he spoke, it was with a hushed, urgent whisper which made Connie think there was something worrying going on. And there was.

"Have you got a moment, Mrs Jameson?" he said. "I looked into your mystery."

"My what?" Connie said, confused. "What mystery?"

"About Michael Sawyer."

Her head was so full of train journeys, Gloria Wayland and dealing with Vince that she'd forgotten that she'd asked Roger to investigate Michael Sawyer for her. It all seemed less pressing than her current, personal concerns.

"You said Sawyer hated people coming to the house? Was never seen in Helmstead since he moved here? You said that there was something he was covering up?"

"It was probably nothing."

"That's where you're wrong. It turns out he is covering something up." Roger emphasised the "is" with dramatic relish, his face beaming with the delight of a man whose journalistic talents had finally been allowed to shine. He'd obviously found this whole investigation a rewarding exercise, poring over parish records, telephoning the War Office for military records, talking to anyone who could shed light.

And like a great magician, he revealed the trick: "He served in the Great War."

"That's hardly news. Most men in their forties and fifties did."

"And I assumed he was a soldier. When I went to the cottage – the garden was so ordered. Regimented."

Connie wasn't in the mood for hearing about planting schemes, and willed Roger to get to the point.

"So what are you saying?"

"Anyway it was the Fourteenth Service Battalion of the Royal Warwickshire Regiment. Michael Sawyer joined it in October 1915. And in November 1915 it went to the Western Front." Roger was eager to impress with his skills.

Connie nodded, still waiting for the punchline.

"Or rather, the battalion went but Michael Sawyer didn't. He was reported as being injured during training. And when he'd recovered, his NCO came to collect him, only to find he'd absconded. He was reported for absenteeism for four occasions and then reported as being AWOL."

There it was.

"So he's a deserter?" Connie's hunch had been right. Sawyer did have a secret. A pretty major one, at that. It explained his hatred of anyone coming to the house and the reason perhaps why he never left the house. He didn't want to be seen. As a deserter, Michael Sawyer would be a wanted man; tarred by the stigma of being a coward.

But as Connie fitted it all into place, Roger threw a little cold water on the revelation. He wasn't sure that, in the current situation, whether anyone in authority would worry about finding him. "They've got more important things to worry about now, of course."

But that brought him to his second point. Something was worrying him about this case.

"Thing is, he must know he's unlikely to be hauled in for

questioning any time soon," Roger said. "So why is he so – isolated?"

"Maybe he's just got into the habit of hiding all these years?" Connie suggested.

"Or –" Roger said, with the great flourish of Hercule Poirot solving a case. "He's got something else to hide!"

Connie's mind was reeling. "What else could it be?" She pondered if Michael was reclusive because of Margaret. Maybe that was the other thing that Michael Sawyer was hiding: a fear of being exposed for not having adopted her properly. Connie was in two minds about whether to tell Roger about this. What if she was wrong? It would seem as if she was victimising an innocent – if slightly odd – couple who were trying to do their best for an orphaned girl. Connie decided to keep this to herself for the time being. Besides, Roger Curran had his own ideas.

"We should go to the cottage tomorrow and confront him with this," he said. "See what else falls from the tree."

"Is that a good idea?"

"It could be a great story, Mrs Jameson."

The story, yes. Connie had lit a touch paper there. Well done, Connie.

She wondered what they could accomplish. "Michael isn't likely to admit to being a deserter and then open up about anything else he's hiding, is he?"

Roger conceded that she might be right. "You can either come with me or stay out of it."

Reluctantly Connie agreed to come with the journalist

tomorrow. But it would have to be after work. Roger Curran agreed and said he'd meet her outside *The Helmstead Herald* offices tomorrow night. He went off with a whistle while Connie walked quickly up the path of the vicarage.

She opened the door, hung up her Women's Land Army jumper and went through to the living room, where a roaring fire was burning in the hearth. On the table were two plates of sandwiches. Connie's heart soared at how welcoming Henry had made things for her return. Maybe things would be all right and—

But she was surprised when it was Vince Halliday, not Henry, who came through from the kitchen with a pot of tea and a warm smile.

"Where's Henry?" Connie asked.

Vince shrugged. His manner wasn't as brusque as before. "I thought he'd be with you," he said, softly. "How did you get on in London? You weren't followed?"

Connie shook her head. "I got your flaming key."

"I can be on me way soon, then," he said.

She felt like asking him to repeat those words. She doubted her own hearing. That had been easy.

Vince pulled out a chair for her. "Unless you want to wait." And he gestured to the two sandwiches. "One for you. One for him. A little thank you from me."

Connie wasn't really hungry after eating dinner at the farm, but she sat down and picked at a sandwich. She wondered if Henry had gone to see Dr Beauchamp tonight. Vince didn't know. He knew Henry went the night before, but he hadn't seen much of him today. As it darkened and the clock edged

274

towards eleven o'clock, the village square went silent as people went home to bed. Connie started to become troubled. Where was he?

Vince's pleasant demeanour also worried her. Maybe knowing the key was back had made him relax. He didn't have to fling his weight around any more. Wealth awaited in Hatton Gardens in one of a thousand safety-deposit boxes.

He sat in the comfortable chair by the fire, nursing a brandy, staring into the flames, lost in his own thoughts.

Connie fished in her pocket. To her alarm, she couldn't find the key. Panic spread over her face. But then she found it in the other pocket of her trousers. She plonked it on the table by Vince's armchair.

"Brilliant. You done good," he said, leaving it there and taking a sip of brandy.

The mantelpiece clock showed ten past eleven. Vince noticed Connie's worried expression.

"Sure he'll be back soon."

"Maybe he's not coming back." Connie looked at her shoes. "I've been—"

She stopped herself, unwilling to share.

"It's all right. You don't have to tell me." Vince took a slug of brandy. "Do you want me to stay up and wait for him?"

"Why are you being so nice?"

"You got me the key." Vince smiled. "My ticket out of here, away from this dreary little village. No offence."

Connie studied his face, as the skin flickered red and orange, shadowy from the flames in the fire. He looked more relaxed than at any time since he had been here; no longer on edge, no longer fearful of attack. Vince downed the last of his drink and went to the door.

"You sure?"

"I'll wait up," Connie said.

"Night, then."

Connie listened as his heavy frame clomped up the narrow staircase.

Twenty past eleven.

As the upstairs sounds faded, Connie looked at the second, untouched plate of sandwiches and wondered where her husband was. She stood in the doorway to the back of the house, as if hoping Henry might be doing some late-night gardening. Two chairs stood at the end of the garden. No Henry.

She paced and waited; sat down by the fire; boiled a kettle and then decided against making tea. She opened the front door and looked impotently up and down the high street. Was he with Dr Beauchamp? Maybe the Frenchman was about to pass away. Yes, that would make Henry stay a long time.

By one o'clock in the morning, Connie found herself slumped over the dining table, asleep. She thought she'd check the front of the house one last time. The road outside was quiet. There were no lights on apart from at the vicarage and a solitary light in the upstairs room of the pub. Connie shivered and went inside.

She went to bed, sleeping in her clothes, and by three in the morning a fitful sleep claimed her. She dreamt of the time she'd first met Henry Jameson, the nervous young pianist who Finch had coerced into accompanying Connie. They'd played well together and flirted in an awkward way and Finch had bought Henry more pints of beer than he could manage. It had been the start of a strange courtship for the pair of them. Other dreams floated into focus; other memories. Connie was in one of the barns with Henry. He was nervous about them becoming an official couple and she misconstrued his signals as meaning he wanted to have sex. She'd got her blouse off before she realised her mistake. Hurriedly she put it back on – just in time – before he turned round.

The next morning, Connie forced open bleary eyes, half-hoping Henry would be there to fill them. She wanted things to be as carefree as they had been during their courtship. She wanted that Henry back. And he probably wanted that Connie back. He'd tell her about the late night he'd had with a parishioner or something. But it wasn't to be. And the cold, stomach-churning reality made Connie feel sick. She got off the bed, brushed down her crumpled clothes. It was half-five in the morning and she'd barely had three hours' sleep. Running on empty, she dragged herself downstairs, wrote a quick note for Henry – for whenever he came in – and went off to Pasture Farm.

The morning air cooled her tired face as she trudged to work. At the farm, Esther and Glory were in the kitchen, making bacon and eggs for the girls. Glory threw Connie a concerned look. Connie guessed what she wanted to know. How was Vince? Connie made sure that she couldn't be overheard and told her that Vince seemed happy. Really happy. He had mentioned that he would be on his way now that he had the key. She thanked Glory for staying out of things. But Glory scribbled something on her pad:

"But I need to see him."

"You will. I just need a bit more time."

Yeah, I need to find my husband.

Subdued, Connie slumped at the big table in the kitchen and ate breakfast. Joyce was full of chatter about what her John was planning to do, now he was safely out of the RAF. Connie missed the details. Dolores was fielding any questions about her own life with her usual taciturn skill. Glory was amused as Dolores stonewalled any attempts by Iris and Joyce to find out her opinion on anything. Connie had decided that she wouldn't mention that Henry hadn't come home. She didn't need the questions, the judgements. And she hoped that it would all be fine by tonight. He'd be back at the vicarage. Maybe tonight they would be waving off Vince together, Connie thought with a smile.

As Dolores left the kitchen, Joyce voiced her opinion that she didn't trust her. Glory listened keenly to the conversation, while pretending to clean the counter. Esther was disappointed that Joyce felt the need to gossip. It wasn't usually her way. But Joyce protested that it wasn't gossip. Even the newspapers were warning about spies in our midst.

"You think she's a spy? Come off it." Esther chuckled.

"Remember Nancy?" Joyce retorted.

"Nancy wasn't a spy."

"No, but the Home Guard thought she was." Joyce looked at the faces of her friends. "That's my point. She looked innocent, but they thought she could have been a spy. And with

Dolores, I don't trust the fact that no one knows much about her."

Esther shook her head. She wasn't going to have this suspicion – especially not after Nancy's ordeal. Nancy Morrell had been dragged in for questioning and was very nearly shot dead by Sergeant Tucker of the Home Guard. But the bullet had found a different victim – when Tucker accidentally shot Lord Lawrence Hoxley. Esther had seen too many people suffer from false accusations.

"Stop it and get on with your work," Esther said, her cheeks flushing a little.

A reprimanded Joyce slunk off to the fields. And soon the rest of the Land Girls were following, their stomachs full of bacon and eggs.

After Glory had helped Esther wash up the dishes, she went upstairs to the room she shared with Dolores and sat on the bed for a while. She didn't have any other chores until it was time to prepare lunch. Idly, she looked around. A large dressing table took up one side of the room beneath a small window that looked out onto the courtyard. A chair was propped against another wall with a suitcase on it, and two beds filled the rest of the small space.

Glory sat in front of the mirror and touched the bandage on her neck. The fabric had become tattered and yellow, and Glory wondered when she would be able to take it off. The doctor hadn't told her what to do. She looked at her thin face, which seemed to her older than its tender years. Putting on her cloche hat, she decided that she would help the girls in the fields. It would occupy her. But then another thought came to her.

Could she find out if Dolores was a spy?

She opened the drawers of the dressing table. There was a Bible and a hair brush in one drawer. In another, she found some knitting – a red scarf in the early stages, cradled by two thick needles. Feeling foolish, but also quite bored, she decided to look in the suitcase. Maybe having a nose around would help her fit in, make the other girls like her.

Inside, among the clothes that Dolores hadn't put on hangers yet, was a small metal box: ornate with Japanese-style etchings on the lid. It was locked, but that wasn't a barrier to Gloria Wayland. Deftly she plucked a hair grip from her head and went to work on the mechanism. Within moments, she had managed to unlock it. Checking that no one was coming, she opened the tin.

Now she didn't feel foolish. She felt guilty and ashamed. Was being part of the gang worth all this?

Dolores was no spy. Instead, the contents were devastating, searing images on Glory's retinas that she would never forget, a wave of emotion rising in her throat and threatening to choke her. The box revealed a heartache that explained why Dolores never opened up, why she never told anyone anything, why she wanted to keep her head down until this war was finished.

There were some cards, a newspaper cutting and a tiny stuffed bear. The cards were yellowed condolences for the loss of a child. The browned newspaper cutting reported a tragic accident on a boat, where a small boy drowned. And Glory guessed that the bear belonged to that little boy. Dolores's son. Carefully, she put the contents back as close to how she had found them as she could and shut the lid. It was a great deal harder to try to lock the tin with the hair grip than it had been to open it. Glory spent about twenty minutes trying to do it. She would have continued trying but then a voice made her jump.

"Gloria?" It was Esther calling up the stairs for her.

Glory put the tin back in the suitcase – and hoped, against hope, that Dolores wouldn't register that it was unlocked. She raced downstairs, a feeling of sadness and unease washing over her. She felt ashamed for looking and anguished that she couldn't comfort Dolores in any way. But when no one knew Dolores' secret, how could she?

After work, Connie Carter walked back across the fields with Roger Curran. She had to go slowly as he wasn't the fittest of men, huffing and puffing to keep up. Eventually, as the evening sun set, they reached the brow of the hill that overlooked Jessop's Cottage. The home of the reclusive Michael Sawyer.

Connie now had grave misgivings about what they were about to do.

"Won't we just make him angry?"

"I don't know. We'll find out."

"But he might take his anger out on Margaret." Curran looked blank. "The little girl."

Connie didn't want to make things worse for Margaret. Roger reassured her that they were just going to ask some questions. That was all. It was Roger's duty as a journalist

– albeit one on a backwater newspaper. Connie suspected that he felt buoyed, not only by his exciting foray into real investigative journalism, but also because his story about Connie's heroism had been picked up by a national newspaper. Roger Curran was on a roll. Connie feared his gung-ho attitude would lead to an explosive situation with the reclusive Michael.

Roger guessed she was having more doubts. "Stay here if you want."

"I'll come." Connie owed it to Margaret to be present. She reassured herself that she was doing the right thing.

Connie and Roger reached the edge of the neat cottage garden when the front door slowly opened. Michael Sawyer stood there, glaring at them. He'd seen them coming up the path, had been ready for them.

"Didn't you say enough last time?" he hissed at Connie.

"I saw Margaret's face," Connie said. Roger threw her a curious look. What was this about? He didn't like that he didn't know about this aspect of the story. "She had been hit," Connie added for his benefit. "There was a bruise."

Roger announced that he was a reporter for *The Helmstead Herald*.

Michael suddenly looked haunted, unsure of what to do. It was one thing having a nosey Land Girl pestering him, but a journalist was a different matter. He wanted to close things down. "Well, we just live here minding our own business, trying to do the best we can for Margaret. There's no story here, mister."

"We know you're a deserter," Connie said.

It was as if he'd been shot. Michael's face drained of colour, panic in his eyes.

"I want you to go," he stammered.

"Although the authorities haven't been actively looking for deserters since 1933, I'm sure that the story would be of interest to our readers," Roger said, detailing the exact nature of his interest.

"Just leave, will you?" Michael shouted.

"What are you hiding?" Connie chanced her arm.

"Why are you here?" Michael screamed. Without warning, he launched himself towards Connie, knocking her back onto the path. As she struggled to get on her feet, he pushed one forearm over her windpipe and raised a fist. The violence was so unexpected that Connie found it impossible to make a sound or even to really register what was happening. Roger Curran was rooted to the spot, shocked. She knew she was on her own. Michael's pulled back his fist, lining up a shot. Connie had one chance. She brought up one of her wellington boots, kicking Michael as hard as she could between the legs. It was a good shot. He grimaced in pain, his eyes bulging and his face red, as he collapsed in a heap by the path. Connie dragged herself to her feet and brushed herself down, ready to kick him again if he needed it.

"You sure you don't want to tell me nothin'?" Connie shouted. "Why do you hit that girl? What's going on here? Where is she?" Her questions came fast and furious, with no real focus. Each one was an attempt to unlock the vault and get Michael to suddenly admit something.

Roger put a hand on her arm and indicated that they should

go. Michael was gasping for air and in no condition to talk. Reluctantly, Connie allowed herself to be led away. But she couldn't resist a parting shot: "You hit that girl again and you'll have me to answer to!"

Michael groaned and slowly sat up, clutching his groin.

As they walked back to the brow of the hill, Roger admonished Connie for trying to get information under duress. They could never run a story in those circumstances in a family newspaper.

"I wasn't torturing him," Connie protested. "I was saving my bacon. By the way, thanks for all your help there."

"I'm not really a fighter."

"And I am?" Connie tutted.

They walked in silence most of the way back to Helmstead. Connie guessed that she might have made things worse for Margaret. But she also hoped that Michael would behave, knowing the press were sniffing around.

As they reached the bridge into Helmstead, Connie couldn't resist asking Roger if he'd seen Henry. The journalist pondered for a moment and then said he'd seen him the day before last, cycling over the fields on some errand or other. But he hadn't seen him since. Why?

Connie found another lie popping out of her lips. "I just wanted to make sure that Henry wasn't spending too much time with his flock, that's all."

"Such a caring wife," Roger replied.

"Yeah, that's me," she said.

At the vicarage, Connie found things as she'd left them. Her note to Henry sat on the table, untouched. He hadn't come back. Thinking of something, Connie ran upstairs and flung open the wardrobe doors. If there were a row of skeletal hangers in there, she'd know that he'd left her. But all of his shirts were lined up, his trousers folded. Maybe he hadn't left her. But then she remembered stories of men just disappearing from home one morning and starting new lives from scratch. Maybe he'd done that.

She slouched downstairs and crumpled into the armchair and began to sob. Where was he?

Chapter 16

Henry had been missing for two days.

And the morning after seeing Roger Curran, Connie set off to Dr Beauchamp's cottage before work. As she'd left the vicarage, Vince had surprised her by padding out from his bedroom and asking if Henry was back. She'd shaken her head.

"I'm sorry to hear that." He looked genuinely concerned. "I wish I could do more to help you."

"No one can help. But thanks."

Connie found it oddly comforting that he had stayed since getting his key. It meant there was some companionship when she got home, someone to talk to who understood her loss. And Vince was the only one she could talk to, really, without telling the rest of the village that her husband was missing.

As she crossed a stile, Connie berated herself for not going to see Dr Beauchamp sooner.

Getting nearer, her breath condensing in the cold morning air, each footfall left her feeling worried that she might find Henry injured along the side of the dirt path to the old man's house. He might not have left her, he might have been hurt in some way. What if he'd been hit by a lorry or something?

She reached the run-down cottage by six in the morning, knowing it was too early to wake the elderly Frenchman. But she'd come prepared and posted a letter through his letterbox enquiring about when he'd seen Henry. She hoped that his eyes would be good enough to read it and that he didn't give it to his part-time carer from the village to read. She was a friend of Mrs Gulliver's and such an action would mean all the cats would be out of the bag. After posting it, Connie took a shortcut across Gorley Woods to walk the few miles to Pasture Farm. She was deeply worried now. Two days was a long time. She hadn't seen much of Vince – the result of working such long hours – but he seemed concerned and supportive in his own gruff way. She also found some comfort that someone was there in case Henry came back while she was out.

During the day's work in the fields, Connie managed to catch up with Finch. He was sitting on a hay trailer, excavating his fingernails with a pen knife. "You haven't seen Henry, have you?" she asked as casually as she could.

"What, today?" Finch shrugged, answering his own question.

"What about yesterday?"

"Don't think so. Why, has he said he saw me, then?"

"No. I just wondered."

She knew Finch's memory was never that sharp, fogged by idleness and drink, but he thought it had been a few days ago when Henry borrowed the shot gun. But then Finch seemed to remember something. A sudden twinkle appeared in his eye. "I suppose the secret is out now, eh? About what he was up to."

Connie looked confused, until he elaborated: "He was trying to prove he could bring home his own supper. Wanted the gun to catch a rabbit."

She nodded, pretending she knew about this.

"Did he manage to shoot anything in the end?"

"Unfortunately not," Connie said bleakly.

Dejectedly, she went back to work. Finch winced as he cut his finger with the pen-knife.

The rest of the day – like the day before – was spent with Connie wishing the hours away so she could leave the farm and resume her lone search for Henry. At one point, she managed to find Glory Wayland alone in the kitchen. She found herself telling her that Henry was missing. She hadn't intended to, but she felt slightly unburdened. Talking to Glory was like a confessional, a patient listener hearing your sins.

"We had a sort of argument before I left for London," Connie said. "I felt –" It was hard to admit this out loud. "I felt he was going to leave me."

Glory scratched something onto her pad. A single accusatory word: "Vince?"

It took Connie a moment to process this question and what it meant. Could Vince be responsible for Henry's disappearance? She didn't think so. She couldn't be a hundred per cent certain, but she didn't think so.

"He's got what he wants because I brought him that key back. He's got no reason to do that."

Glory scribbled again. "Does he need a reason?"

Connie shrugged. Vince was a loose cannon, but in her experience, he usually did things for a reason, not out of spite. "Just keep your eyes open for anyone who mentions Henry. Any clue could be useful, yeah? But keep it to yourself as I don't want everyone asking me loads of questions."

Connie didn't want everyone else to know he was missing. Plus it might shed too much light on what had been happening at the vicarage. And the last thing she wanted was to jeopardise the fact that Vince Halliday might be about to sling his hook soon. Yes, that's what she wanted. Wasn't it?

Roger Curran was typing up a piece on apple trees when Connie poked her head around his office door. He looked dismayed to see her. What wild-goose chase was she here for now?

"I've come to say sorry. Maybe we shouldn't have stirred up that Michael Sawyer business. But I hope we did some good." She felt that she had given Michael Sawyer a solid warning about how he treated Margaret in future. That, perhaps, validated their interference.

"Apology accepted," Roger Curran said, returning to his work. But Connie wasn't finished.

"And there was something else," she said.

Roger's look of dismay had returned.

"My husband has gone missing. And I need your help to find him."

The journalist raised an eyebrow of concern. He reached for his notebook.

But she placed a hand over his pad. "I need you to do it off the record."

Apart from the issue of Vince, Connie couldn't stand the thought of the legions of wasp-tongued old women in the town who would delight in saying "I told you so. She was always going to be no good and drive him away." She knew she had to find Henry herself, with Roger's help – even if that meant searching the whole of Warwickshire.

The next few days followed a familiar pattern. Connie would sleep little – preferring to get up even earlier than usual and scour an area before she went to work. Then, after she had finished her stint in the fields, she would spend the evening searching again. This was made easier because Roger Curran had a car, an ancient 1928 Morris Minor that looked as if it had been poured around his ample frame. With Connie squeezed into the passenger seat, they would drive, in some discomfort, all around: from Helmstead to Brinford; from Upper Chalcombe to Midberry. There were limits as to how much further afield they could travel as petrol was rationed and Roger had a strict allowance for his work as a journalist. But Connie felt she was doing all she could. They ticked off a new couple of areas during each drive. But still the emptiness of the vicarage greeted her each night; the cavernous bed without Henry looking at her across the pillows. One night, Roger stopped at a village pub and brought Connie a drink and a sandwich.

"Have you ever had any missing persons cases before?" she asked.

He shrugged as he tried to recall any details. "There was a woman in Midberry who disappeared while walking her dog. Back in '36 or '37."

"Did they find her?"

Roger suddenly realised that his anecdote ended badly, but it would do Connie a disservice not to tell her now. "Found her body in a stream. But I'm sure we'll find Henry Jameson in one piece. Alive and well."

During this time, any suspicions Connie had about Vince started to diminish. One evening, he sat down with Connie and told her that they needed a methodical plan to try to find Henry. For his part, he would sneak out each day to search on foot. He was always careful not to be seen leaving or entering the vicarage, and there was a limit to how far he could go. But he was doing his bit. Then later, the two of them would sit at the dining table and cross off areas on the local map. This small, but significant, effort, along with Connie's own searches meant that a lot of the map of the area had black lines through it, as village after village was ticked off.

But despite these efforts, after five days, Connie was getting frantic. Vince urged her to be calm. They were being as methodical as they could be.

But as Connie was struggling to hold things together, she realised something dreadful. A can of worms was about to open and she had no way of stopping it.

"What is it?" Vince asked.

"Tomorrow is Sunday service."

Tomorrow the church would be packed with the congregation – religious stalwarts and those turning up to do their weekly duty. Everyone would expect to see the familiar sight of Henry delivering the sermon. Connie knew that the time for secrecy was running out.

On Sunday morning, Connie lay awake as the first birds started to chorus outside her window. She had been awake for a while, staring numbly at the ceiling, counting the hairline cracks in the plaster. Today was the sixth day that Henry had been missing. She had no idea where he was. She hoped and prayed that he was all right. But the fact that he had seemingly vanished off the face of the earth was gnawing away at her. She couldn't fathom how someone could disappear without a trace. She couldn't work out how the search with Roger Curran hadn't revealed a single lead. No one had seen him. No one knew anything. She dragged herself out of bed. She ate a silent breakfast with Vince around the dining table, a breakfast which he had prepared for her. As she finished, he smiled – with a look approaching softness.

"I hope it goes all right," he said gruffly. "The service."

Connie nodded in agreement. She hoped so too. "There's no way out of it." She had been dreading this moment. Wearing her best suit, she left the vicarage and emerged into the chilly morning sun, the sound of church bells filling the air. Old ladies filed into the church and Connie greeted them with a pleasant hello. Then Connie entered the church, the bells still pealing, and strode past the mostly empty pews to the front. Moving into the vestry, she caught her breath, trying to compose herself for the task ahead. Peeking out, she could see the pews filling. Mrs Gulliver, stony faced and sitting in her usual place at the front, the closest thing to a reserved seat in the whole place. Esther Reeves and the Land Girls – Iris Dawson, Dolores O'Malley and Joyce Fisher. Beside them was a thin, young woman in a battered cloche hat; a borrowed scarf concealing the bandage on her neck. Frederick Finch was at the back of the church, silhouetted in the doorway, as he spoke to one of the ancient officers of the Home Guard. Lady Ellen Hoxley entered, in a fine pale-blue suit and hat – followed at a socially acceptable distance by Dr Richard Channing. Connie was relieved to see the friendly face of Roger Curran scurrying to the front of the church. He sat near a disapproving Mrs Gulliver. She didn't like sharing her pew – and she didn't like Roger Curran. A man who made his living dealing in tittle-tattle. Mrs Gulliver didn't see the irony of this judgement.

Finally, the bells stopped ringing and everyone sat expectantly. There was the odd cough of discomfort as they waited.

Connie couldn't delay things any more. She stepped slowly out and took the short walk to the pulpit, her high heels clipping on the stone floor of the church. It was the longest walk of her life. Mrs Gulliver's brow furrowed. What was going on here? Roger Curran offered a small smile of support to Connie.

Connie surveyed the room and swallowed hard.

"I wanna make an announcement."

"Oh dear Lord, she's pregnant!" Mrs Gulliver hissed, clutching her chest dramatically.

"No. It's not that," Connie replied, somewhat thrown by

hearing her words echoed around the stone walls of the church. It was all so loud. But she pressed on: "Thing is, Henry – your vicar, my husband – has—"

She trailed off, finding the words overwhelming.

"What is it, Connie, love?" Esther said. Joyce and Iris looked concerned too. Finch was whispering to Gloria Wayland – did she know anything? The thin girl was shaking her head. Lady Hoxley and Dr Channing were conferring.

Connie found her voice. "He's gone missing. This is the sixth day that he's been gone."

There were gasps from around the congregation.

"I'd hoped he'd just – come back, you know? That's why I kept the search to myself and didn't say anything. But now I can't keep it a secret no longer." Tears were filling her eyes and her voice was wavering as she struggled to finish. "I've lost my husband. And I know some of you will think that I wasn't good enough for him, but I love him and he's gone," she announced, crumbling, the sound of her sobs echoing alone for a moment around the stone walls.

But then people, friends, neighbours, swelled forward to comfort her. Mrs Gulliver scowled at the unseemly behaviour of everyone going to the pulpit, but then accepted it with unusual good grace. She'd seen her own husband put in the ground and she didn't wish the end of a marriage on anyone. She placed an awkward, bony hand of comfort on one of Connie's heaving shoulders. Finch, Esther, Iris and Joyce were around her. Esther hugged her and stroked her back in a maternal way. "We'll find him, lovey. You'll see," she promised.

Connie rubbed her eyes, buoyed by this support. It really

was true – a problem shared was a problem halved. And if you shared it with a dozen people it was even better. Now they all knew. And that had got to be a good thing.

Esther was true to her word, stepping immediately up to the challenge of finding Henry Jameson. She and Finch organised the entire congregation to spread the word about Henry's disappearance. In the space of ten minutes, the church had transformed from a place of worship to an impromptu command centre. They encouraged each person present in the church to tell all their friends and families, in case anyone had seen Henry in the last six days. Iris Dawson ran to get PC Thorpe – the only policeman in the area, a man who served the larger town of Brinford. She would make the search a police matter – an official missing persons case. Although Connie knew that during war time, so many people were displaced by bombing raids or by evacuation that it was practically impossible to find missing people.

The four elderly members of the Home Guard shuffled out, intending to start a search of the north hills. Connie had told them that she and Roger Curran hadn't searched that area yet as it hadn't lent itself easily to a search by car. Finch got a description of Henry's bicycle, which wasn't at the vicarage, and circulated it to the parishioners. Esther asked Connie to check Henry's belongings in more detail and note down anything at all that was missing. She knew that such detail might mean the difference between someone who had gone missing intentionally or someone who had gone missing accidentally.

Soon the whole town was mobilised in the search for their beloved reverend, Connie's husband.

As everyone went on their way, combing every area of the town and beyond, an exhausted Connie left the church. Glory ran up to her. She gave Connie a smile of support, but then thrust her notebook under her face. It was the same page from before. The same question. "Vince?"

Connie shook her head. "I don't think he's got anything to do with—"

But Glory hastily added to the paper. "And me?"

Realising what she meant, Connie replied, "It's not the right time. Please just – bide your time."

Glory looked torn. She knew she was very close to the vicarage. It was next door. And it was where Vince Halliday was holed up. She was so close to confronting the man who had left her for dead. Part of her knew she should get revenge. And yet, she respected Connie. Maybe there was a way to end this without bloodshed if she did what Connie wanted. That's what she would do, yes. For now, anyway.

Glory ran outside. And while the Land Girls were huddled around Finch, deciding on how best to organise themselves, Glory debated about whether to join her new friends or not. But then she ran over the bridge, back to the farm. Connie walked back to the vicarage. Vince was looking out of the window.

"Wish I could help more, Con."

He followed her around the house as she checked Henry's belongings, as Esther had suggested.

"You really don't know anything?" Connie said, emboldened by the support she'd been shown, giddy by a weight lifted.

"'Course not. I hurt him when he pointed that shotgun at me. I got even then, didn't I?"

"Before, though – you said that he was an annoyance or something. You said you didn't have to tolerate him."

"I don't remember," Vince said, shaking his head. "I probably said a lot of stuff when my hand was gammy. Come on, Connie, you know me. My way is to have it out with someone there and then. Not play games."

"Suppose."

"It's natural you'd think that. It's been difficult for you, me being here, I know. And you wouldn't be human if you didn't think of every possibility to explain what's happened to him."

He seemed so reasonable. A rock of support. Connie took this in, her brain befuddled by the morning. She was exhausted from her announcement in the church – and yet she felt strangely enlivened and relieved. This wasn't just her burden now. Others were sharing it, as they searched the town, the lanes and the hills. Someone would find him. And everything might be all right.

"I suppose if I could blame you, I don't have to blame myself," she said sadly.

"I guess." Vince gave an awkward smile.

Vince brought her a cup of tea and said it was the least he could do. He told Connie that he'd stay out of her way – and then he'd go out after dark to search for Henry, when there was no chance of him being seen. Connie thanked him.

That afternoon, Roger Curran knocked at the door of the vicarage. Connie convinced Vince that it would be all right. It was only the man who was helping her search. She went out and he took Connie over to the village hall, where the Home Guard had organised a central base for the search operation. A map of the Helmstead and Brinford areas was pinned to the walls and one of the officers was allocating search areas to an enthusiastic group of old residents. Mrs Gulliver was looking a little lost. Connie came up to her and thanked her for helping. Mrs Gulliver grimaced – as if something was troubling her.

"Oh what? You think I've driven him away, is that it?" Connie stormed, fed up with the old battle axe's judgemental ways. Even though it was what Connie feared had happened herself. It was one thing admitting it to yourself, quite another to take it from a sneering self-appointed moral guardian.

"No. I don't actually," Mrs Gulliver snapped back. "But I think I know something you don't."

"Go on, then," Connie said.

"You mustn't shoot the messenger," Mrs Gulliver said.

"What do you mean?"

"I know we don't see eye to eye, Mrs Jameson. But I'm only saying what I saw." She pulled Connie to one side and lowered her voice. "Thing is, I went to the vicarage one night when you were working at Hoxley Manor. And Reverend Jameson answered the door to me."

"Right," Connie said. Where was this going?

"But he wasn't alone in there. And yet, he covered up that someone was in there with him." Mrs Gulliver gave a look of genuine sorrow as she said: "As hard as it is to believe, I think he might be carrying on with another woman."

Connie surprised everyone in the hall by letting out an inappropriate raucous laugh. Although she knew the truth, the ridiculous idea acted as a release for all the emotions that were bottled up. As Connie got herself under control, Mrs Gulliver looked aggrieved that she hadn't been taken seriously and darted out of the village hall. Esther entered with a tray of cakes she had made, followed by Finch with an urn. Connie had no idea where he'd found the urn. It was probably best never to ask. But the stout farmer started to fill it with water and to prepare industrial quantities of tea to power the search. Connie left the hall feeling buoyed by the support; a glimmer of hope that Henry might be found.

Someone was waiting in the village square for her. At first glance, Connie thought it was just another woman ready to search the fields. But then she realised it was Vera Sawyer.

"Come with me," she said solemnly.

"I can't just go off. I'm busy." Connie couldn't just leave. She had a search party to organise. Vera closed her eyes as if it pained her to even say the words she'd come to say.

"You've destroyed everything."

"What?" Connie reeled from this statement and didn't register the questions coming from Finch and Esther about the search. She was focused solely on Vera. What did she mean? Connie knew she had to find out. She told Esther where she was going and set off, following Vera, who had already marched on ahead. What had Connie destroyed?

Connie and Vera reached the cottage. Vera had walked ahead in silence, refusing to answer any of Connie's questions until they got there. Sensing Connie's reticence about entering the cottage, Vera said, "It's all right. He's not there. They've both gone. She left and then –" She struggled not to break down. "Then Michael went. He took his gun. He's gone. You've cost me everything."

"What happened?"

"You fighting my husband is what happened. Coming here with a journalist and upsetting—"

"Where's Margaret?" Connie wondered. "Is she with Michael?"

Sitting on the dark, heavy furniture, Vera composed herself. She wrung her hands as she recounted the story.

"After you came to the cottage, Margaret ran away again – probably worried that Michael was going to blame her. Sometimes she used to like to go and stay with a friend – a school friend – in Brinford. That's probably where she is now, until she outstays her welcome and has to trudge back with her tail between her legs."

"And where's Michael?"

"He didn't seem to care that Margaret had run off. He didn't notice. His mind was burdened with something else." Vera didn't know exactly what was troubling him, but his demeanour worried her.

"Did you know he was a deserter?" Connie asked.

Vera Sawyer nodded slowly. "I said I'd stay with him. I understood why he – fled. That war was different. But after he told me, it meant we were looking over our shoulders forever afterwards. That ground him down. He became edgy; obsessed about everything. Any knock at the door. Any person coming up to him. He was a shadow of himself. We lived in the East End, but there were too many people. Too many faces to worry about. So we moved away. First to Brinford – but even there there were too many outsiders poking their noses in our business. And then to here. No one ever came here. We were happy here."

"Where's he gone?" Connie asked. Vera shook her head.

"He took his service revolver. He's probably not –" Vera found it hard to finish, "Coming back."

The words chimed with Connie. Was she in a similar situation with her husband? Connie didn't have any idea what to say about Michael. But with Margaret she felt on safer ground.

"You should go and find Margaret. Tell her he's gone."

Vera caught the implication. Connie thought that Michael was the bad seed in their home life, the one whom Margaret feared. With him gone, surely she'd come back? Vera snapped the notion out of Connie's mind.

"She doesn't like me any more than she liked him. I tried to love her like our own. When we took her in." Vera didn't care any more. She was ready to unburden herself – as Connie had been at Sunday Service. Connie listened as she talked about her life.

"You can't possibly understand. You're young."

"What can't I understand?"

"I couldn't have children," Vera stated. A blunt statement, but one that had taken the joy from her eyes. "At first, I accepted it. It was my cross to bear. But as time went on, I became down about it. The doctors thought I was deeply affected by my body's failings."

"I'm sorry."

"And I know it was wrong, but I'd look longingly at other babies in the street, and obsess over family babies in a way that made mothers uneasy." Vera gave a guilty, embarrassed smile. "Michael tried to help me through it. He said it didn't matter and that we were better off alone. He was still wondering when a hand would grab his shoulder and he would find himself staring into the face of a military policeman – so he had his own reasons for not wanting to bring a baby into the world. As things stood, we could move quickly if there was a chance Michael might be discovered. If there were three of us, things wouldn't be so easy."

"So you made the best of it."

"Four years ago, Michael made plans to buy Jessop's Cottage. The ideal bolt hole in the middle of nowhere. And while we waited to obtain our new house, we went temporarily back to the East End. But even when we got the house and the keys were in our hands, it needed serious renovation. So he busied himself repairing the place, spending his days there while I stayed in the East End.

"It was the time of the worst bombings. The Blitz," Vera remembered. "I used to work in an office, typing pool. And I'd overlook this school. Margaret's school. And I used to see her – from my window – being collected by her mother. One day, I followed them. I don't know why. Loneliness at being on my own while Michael was away. I don't know. Maybe I just wanted to see where they went."

"But then I'd watch every day – on my way home I'd pass the pub and see this little girl sitting there. And I thought – this is no life for a child. You can't say it was a life for a child, can you?" Vera said, wanting endorsement from Connie. None was forthcoming.

Connie wished she'd had a mother – even one who left her outside a pub while she worked inside it. At least then, at the end of the day, a warm cuddle perhaps awaited. In her eyes, anything was better than nothing.

Vera continued her confession. "When children started to be evacuated to the countryside, the East London school started emptying of pupils. But as the numbers dwindled, Margaret still came, dropped off by her mother and then picked up each day. And at the time, there were reports of people going missing – sometimes presumed dead from a bombing raid. I realised that if you wanted to disappear, then there was no better time than during the confusion with all the mass movements of the evacuation campaign. Many people were moving around the country. Going everywhere. The police had lost most officers with them having signed up to fight for the forces, so there was little chance of people being found if they went missing."

"So you took her?" Connie asked.

"That's when I thought. I could take this girl. I could make up a story and take her. Give her a better life."

"What about the fact she had a mother already?" Connie spat.

"I know what I was planning was wrong, but then I realised it was meant to be."

Connie raised an eyebrow. "How could that be?"

"Don't you see? The Luftwaffe bombed Talbot Street on the day I was going to the school." Vera said the words with an almost energetic zeal, as if it validated her plan. It was fate. By virtue of serendipity, the Nazis had helped the Sawyers steal a child. They had ensured that the Sawyers' cover story was true. "With Talbot Street demolished, I went into the school."

Connie could see that Vera felt almost altruistic in giving a new life to Margaret. She couldn't listen to any more. She went outside for some air. She needed to clear her head.

Suddenly she heard a man whistle at her. Not a cat call, but a whistle of hello.

She spun round to find Roger Curran walking up to the garden gate. "Came to check you were okay."

"I hope you've got your note pad," Connie said. "Margaret's gone missing too."

As Roger Curran spoke to Vera, Connie walked aimlessly around Jessop's Cottage. She took in the array of sheds and outbuildings. So many places where secrets could be hidden. Then a thought struck her. What if Margaret hadn't run to her friend in Brinford but had, instead, holed up in one of the outbuildings? It was worth checking. Or perhaps it was just Connie's desire to do something to take her mind off things. A way to avoid hearing any more self-serving justifications from Vera Sawyer. Connie looked in the sheds and buildings, one by one. Each contained the ordered paraphernalia required to run a self-contained small holding: garden tools, seed trays, bean sticks, lengths of timber. In one larger shed, Connie found a wooden seat at a bench and she imagined that Michael would have come here to read the newspaper. There was a tray of keys nearby and a cup and saucer with the congealed remains of tea. Above it on the wall was a small faded photograph of a group of young soldiers. Their faces weren't clear, but it was probably Michael Sawyer; perhaps on the day when he'd joined up, full of optimism and hope. When Connie reached the last shed on the furthest perimeter of the land of Jessop's Cottage, she found the door locked.

She tapped on it and shouted. "Hello? Margaret?"

No response.

Connie remembered the keys in the other shed and raced back for them. To her relief, after a few tries, one of the keys unlocked the door of the last shed. She entered and scanned the room. A table was in the middle of the room and assorted tools were fastened to the walls. As she walked forward, dust danced in the sunlight from the window. It all looked pretty unremarkable.

But then she noticed that a sheet covered a large lump on the table.

Suddenly fearful as to what it would reveal, Connie braced herself. Then she decided that she might need assistance. She wasn't ready to uncover this on her own.

"Roger!" she shouted out the door. "You better come here."

Within moments, Roger Curran puffed his way into the shed, followed by Vera Sawyer.

"I think there might something here," Connie said fearfully, hoping against hope that they weren't going to find a child's body. She stood back as Roger approached the table and the large shape obscured by a sheet. He urged Connie and Vera to stand by the door. Then he took a deep breath and flung back the sheet.

"What is it?" Connie asked, from the doorway.

"I don't know," came the confused reply.

Connie ran over to the table. To her immense relief, it wasn't Margaret.

But she would never have guessed what she would find instead.

There was a large stack of explosives, reels of cabling and some clocks. Some rolls of industrial tape were also stacked up, along with pliers and a soldering iron. Bomb-making equipment. Like Connie and Roger, Vera also looked genuinely shocked.

It seemed Michael Sawyer had one last big secret after all.

Chapter 17

By the time Connie had finished at Jessop's Cottage, the sky was edging from purple to black. PC Thorne had been called in from Brinford and Connie had to wait while he went to telephone London about the bomb-making equipment they had found. As they mobilised special agents, they had instructed him to collect the evidence and to initiate a manhunt for Michael Sawyer. But as PC Thorne was the sole police officer for the surrounding area, he called in the services of the Home Guard from both Helmstead and Brinford to help him. Connie watched as the old men bagged the evidence and took it away.

Roger Curran was using this commotion to his advantage and was attempting to interview Vera Sawyer. But she was remaining tight-lipped. She broke away from his questioning only once to shout to PC Thorne:

"I think my husband has killed himself! Are you happy about that possibility?"

"Thank you for your insight, Madam. We'll keep all possibilities open, if you don't mind," he replied. "The manhunt will be ongoing until we find a body."

As Connie walked home she realised she still had the set of keys that had opened the last shed. On the ring were keys for – she presumed – the rest of the buildings around Jessop's Cottage. She made a mental note to take them back sometime. But now her thoughts were returning to the vicarage. The Home Guard officers hadn't had any news about Henry when they had come to Jessop's Cottage, so she assumed it was still a fruitless search. Connie tried not to think of PC Thorne's words in relation to her own situation. "The manhunt is ongoing until we find a body." But she hoped that there might be some new developments when she got back; perhaps some news that the men had failed to convey to her. Maybe one of the women in the village might have found something?

Mrs Gulliver was waiting across the bridge. She was chewing her lip, fixing Connie with a thoughtful stare.

"What do you want now?" Connie wasn't in the mood for any more hassle. She felt threadbare, emotionally wrung out, unable to deal with anything else. Some people would never help a situation. And Gladys Gulliver was one of them.

"It's about the Reverend." The old woman started with an edge of timidity that Connie wasn't expecting. Was she worried about being laughed at again? But Connie's thoughts quickly turned from any hint of concern to umbrage. Well, if that was the case, she shouldn't be spreading rumours about Henry carrying on with another woman. That was all Connie needed. All her emotional energy was taken, she didn't have the power to deal with false leads and gossip. Especially such ridiculous nonsense.

"I told you, he wasn't carrying on," Connie snapped.

Mrs Gulliver wafted her hand in a "don't be hasty" gesture. "Hear me out. Thing is, I told you about the night when I thought he was in the vicarage upstairs with someone."

"Get to the point." Connie had crossed her arms and was aware she was drumming her fingers on her elbows.

"But I didn't tell you about the man chasing him."

Connie stopped drumming. Now she was aware that her mouth had opened like a goldfish. Because of her exhaustion, she found it difficult to process this thought, let alone put anything into words to reply. Luckily she was talking to a woman who could leave many donkeys without hind legs. Gladys let the bombshell fall, waiting to see the effect it had, and then she continued talking:

"The last night anyone saw him, raining cats and dogs it was, and I was coming home from Mrs Arbuthnott's house."

"Right?" An air of understandable impatience was in Connie's voice. She wasn't one of Mrs Gulliver's cronies leaning on a garden gate, trying to fill a few hours with tittle tattle. This information mattered. And Connie's fuzzy brain was trying to pick out the wheat from the chaff; filtering the ramblings of a woman who enjoyed rambling.

"And as I battled up the high street against the wind, the Reverend passed me on his bicycle. He waved and I went to wave back. But I didn't manage a wave as I was clutching my coat round my neck with one hand. Still feel bad that I didn't wave back."

"For pity's sake, what happened?" Connie realised she'd make a lousy police officer, but this was like trying to tune in to a bad radio station.

"Yes, of course." Mrs Gulliver's eyes narrowed. Here was the juicy bit. The song amid the static. "Moments after he cycled past, this man ran after him."

"A man?" Connie took this in. "How do you know he was chasing Henry?"

"That's just it. He wasn't chasing him. He was following him. Because as soon as Henry slowed by the bridge, the man slowed too. When Henry picked up speed, the man started running again. He didn't want Henry to know he was behind him."

"You're sure?"

"I was going to tell you in the village hall, but you just went and laughed in my face."

Connie felt bad. She should have listened. Was this a lead? Connie wondered if she should tell PC Thorne. But then an obvious question sailed into view through the fog of Connie's thoughts.

"What did he look like? This man?" she said.

And even as Gladys Gulliver opened her thin lips to speak, Connie knew, with dreadful foreboding what she was going to say. She would describe a burly man in a dark suit, slicked-back hair. She may even have caught a glimpse of his blue eyes and the bandage on his right hand.

As Mrs Gulliver recited the details, Connie felt like a cheap music hall act.

"He had slicked hair."

Connie the mind-reader.

"A big man."

Every word fitted the man Connie was already thinking

of. Ladies and gentleman, this is the man I thought you'd describe!

"There was something wrapped around one of his hands, like a bandage, I dunno."

And Connie had a vision of herself showing a matching drawing of Vince Halliday. The crowd would gasp and go wild.

When the old woman finished, she looked intrigued that Connie didn't seem more surprised.

"Do you know him, then? This man?" she asked.

But Connie was already walking away, unsteady legs carrying her to the nearby vicarage, where a warming light was coming through the windows. She heard herself shouting a shaky "Thank you" to Mrs Gulliver as she went up the pathway to the front door.

Vince had made a meal and was laying out some tea cups. Places set for two. Him and Connie. A fire burned brightly in the hearth. Connie's note for Henry was face down on the dining table. It still hadn't been read, but it was no longer a current concern.

Connie entered, unsure of what to do. She had been searching for Henry, using so much energy dealing with all the hundreds of possibilities and outcomes. And now, in the space of a few minutes, she had discovered some of the truth. Vince did have something to do with his disappearance. Glory had suspected as much, but the way Vince behaved seemed genuine, the way he was playing the situation seemed –

Playing the situation.

That was it. Vince Halliday, the master con man had played her. How could she have been so stupid?

He'd said that he didn't do anything without a reason. Well, what was his reason for following Henry? What was his reason for lying to Connie? She had a horrible suspicion that she was about to find out.

"Any news?" Vince asked, with a warm smile that looked so sincere.

Connie shook her head. She had to tread carefully. Vince wasn't about to just open up to her and tell her what had happened. She had to work out the best way to get it out.

Connie had to play him.

But before she could speak, Vince wrong-footed her.

"I'm sorry," he said.

She looked at him. Sorry for what? Was a confession about to burst out?

It was clear he was holding something back, debating whether to tell her or not. With slow, deliberate tones, he relayed some information that he knew she wouldn't want to hear; the calmness of his tone designed to anaesthetise, or at least downplay, the effect.

"I sneaked out earlier. Heard some old women talking. Thought you'd better know that the Home Guard is talking about dredging Panmere Lake."

In an involuntary motion, Connie put her hand to her mouth. The horror hit her hard. What did this mean? That people weren't viewing Henry's disappearance as a missing person any more? Now they viewed him as a victim. Someone to be found. Vince's face was etched with anguish at her suffering. Connie broke down. She had been so strong through all of this, but now, after so little sleep over the last few days and the exhaustion of the endless unanswered speculation, she felt the tears coursing down her cheeks. She felt Vince pulling her close, hugging her, his fingers on her hair. She didn't want this, even though it felt so comforting. Vince the protector. The man who had taken care of her in London.

She needed time and she needed rest. She was too tired to work out what to do. She had to work out how to play the situation.

But maybe this was the way to play it –

Connie stopped resisting and allowed him to hug her. She needed comfort – God, how she needed it – but the action might also make Vince think that she was trusting him at last.

"I'm here," he mumbled.

Once she would have given anything for this closeness, this reassurance. When she'd left the children's home in the East End, Connie had gravitated to the capable Vince like Mrs Gulliver to gossip. He represented everything to her at that point in her life – saviour, boyfriend, protector. But now she knew she shouldn't be looking for comfort in these arms.

"We will get through this," Vince muttered.

We?

This compounded the feeling of it being wrong. He wasn't comforting her and saying it would be all right. He was treating her as though Henry had already gone forever, that he was already dead. Vince's actions, his words, were those of a mourner expressing sympathy for your loss. We.

Two places set at the dinner table.

All at once, a cavalcade of thoughts tumbled through her mind as Connie pieced the jigsaw together.

Why was he even here now? He should have gone after she returned from London. He'd got his precious key. Yes, he said he'd stay on, but why? Vince never did anything without a reason, he said so himself.

She remembered the violence he had meted out to Henry. The struggle she had to stop him going berserk. But he'd let it go. He'd let things go. That wasn't like Vince. Vince liked revenge. Vince did everything for a reason.

Henry attacked Vince and Vince hurt him. But that wouldn't have been enough for Vince. Lessons would have be learnt, people would have to pay to make sure they never did it again.

Vince liked revenge.

Icy fingernails danced down Connie's spine as she realised a possible truth. After Henry made his stand, Vince had sent her to London to get the key. He'd made sure she was out of the way. And she'd gone, like a fool, because she desperately wanted to end his hold over them. Connie had asked how Vince hoped to find the safety deposit box for the key. He'd said that he could do it, that it wasn't her problem. But how could he do it? It was impossible, wasn't it?

And Connie realised a second, horrifying possible truth. The key probably wasn't for a safety deposit box. It was just a random key, a reason to get her out of the way. A white elephant. Connie had played into Vince's hands – into his plan – and trotted obediently off to London to get it, thinking that it would be enough to make him go.

But that left Vince with enough time to—

Connie found tears welling in her eyes. Vince hugged her tighter, thinking that she was letting it all out. Connie felt his belt buckle digging into her. She glanced down as she moved away slightly.

And she realised he didn't have his gun. For once, he didn't have the gun.

She put her hands up to wipe her eyes, knowing it would make it harder for Vince to maintain the embrace. She edged her way out of it as slowly and carefully as she could, feeling like a mouse moving away from a cobra.

She needed to get upstairs.

"I'm going for a lay down," she said, her words barely more than a whisper. "Hope that's all right."

"Yeah. It's your house."

She had to get away, while her legs would still carry her.

She went to the hallway. He was watching, perplexed, trying to guess whether something had changed in her demeanour.

"Don't you want no supper first?"

"Maybe later, eh?" Connie said, as levelly as she could manage.

He fixed his icy-blue eyes on her. She was willing him not to notice anything odd about her behaviour; any little tic of her face that would give her away. This was like all those times when she ensnared some wealthy businessman in a gin bar – hoping they wouldn't clock the deception behind her smiles. The only difference was that this was a life-or-death situation. After what seemed like an eternity, he shrugged. All right, then.

"I'll make a pot of tea when you come down."

"Yes, that'll be nice." She smiled pleasantly.

Too much.

She couldn't make this seem too normal – too much like happy families. She tried to tinge it with slight anguish. But Vince had clocked the expression. A genuine smile. A smile that showed contentment. It was not what he was expecting from a woman who'd lost her husband.

Too much.

That was the danger when two people were playing one another. It was like a deadly game of chess.

Connie walked, slowly and purposefully, upstairs. She had to commit to what she was doing and not give into doubt or stay for any sort of interrogation. She had to hope that Vince would let the odd smile go, discount it as an involuntary reaction. Inside her heart was racing as she took the steps one by one. Another long walk. She reached the top and allowed herself a small sigh of relief.

Downstairs, Vince Halliday struggled to work out why he was suddenly feeling uneasy. What was it about Connie's behaviour that didn't seem right? Then he remembered that his gun was by his bed and his own jigsaw of the situation fell into place.

He sped out into the hallway, up the stairs, taking them two, three at a time. He burst into the spare room to find Connie turning quickly. She was pointing Amos Ackerly's pistol at him.

"Where is Henry?" she said, her voice flat and drained.

"I don't know what you're talking—"

"Tell me," Connie said, cocking the safety catch off the gun. Her brown eyes were staring intently at Vince. And for the first time, he regretted that she knew him so well; every little expression on his face; every little tell-tale sign of emotion. She knew how his mind worked. And he knew that she was, at this moment, looking at his face for any betrayal of emotion. Any clue. He could hear his breathing getting louder. This was a real threat. Unlike when Henry had brandished a shotgun at him with no intention of firing it, Vince knew that Connie could go either way. As far as she was concerned, she'd lost her husband. She thought he was responsible. And that meant she could, potentially, do anything.

Vince licked his lips.

"You were acting like he was dead. Like you knew he was dead. And Mrs Gulliver saw you following Henry." Connie watched for any flicker in his expression. "So tell me where my husband is."

Vince hesitated. "You're being ridiculous—"

Connie's finger felt the smooth curve of the trigger. Momentarily she thought of Joyce, seeing her in her mind's eye confronting the German airman. Connie gritted her teeth and she fired the gun.

At Pasture Farm, everyone piled into the kitchen, exhausted and hungry after their search for Henry. Joyce took off her satchel which had contained sandwiches for the girls during the day, and sniffed the air. The kitchen was alive with the smell of lamb stew. With hungry, eager eyes on her, Esther scolded Iris to wait, when the young girl tried to persuade Glory to give her a spoonful to taste.

"I've got to test it out. Make sure it's all right." Iris laughed.

"I'll give you testing!" Esther, hot from cooking, warned. At that moment, Frederick Finch came through the door behind her and dipped a spoon into the stew. He smacked his lips at the taste. Esther spun round to catch him, but it was too late. He scurried away, slipping the spoon into his trouser pocket. Esther shook her head in disbelief. "He's got his own spoon. Whatever next?"

"Get away from that. All of you," she snapped, taking charge. "If you want to make yourselves useful, you can lay the table and get water for everyone."

Glory smiled. She loved being part of this family. The girls like protective sisters, Esther like a surrogate mother.

Knowing that the quicker they did this, the quicker they would get to eat, Joyce and Iris leapt into action and started to put out knives and forks. Dolores said she would just put her bag in her room and then be down to help. Glory started drying some serving bowls and Esther stirred the stew. The well-oiled machine of the kitchen, borne out of countless meals. Esther knew that hungry people always made the keenest helpers.

Slopping generous portions into each bowl, Esther placed them on the table. As Finch prepared to wolf down a spectacularly large forkful, Esther stopped him mid-way.

"What about grace?"

"Is she the new girl?" Finch raised a knowing eyebrow to Glory. She looked happily back, pleased to be included in the joke. He was a bit like a kindly uncle, she thought.

After a nudge from Esther, Finch dutifully recited a hurried grace. And then everyone dived into their food.

"Did you get anywhere looking for Henry?" Esther asked, making a small attempt to stop dinner becoming just a succession of eating noises. Otherwise it would just make her think of the pigs.

Joyce shook her head, mid-mouthful. Iris took up the mantle: "We walked over from the south side of Helmstead, all the way to Briarly Woods and the old Macintosh farm."

"There's no sign of him. It's just like he's vanished," Joyce said, swallowing.

"But the Home Guard aren't giving up hope. Some man asked them if they were going to dredge Panmere Lake, but they said no, not yet. So that's something," Iris added.

"The worry is that he might have had an accident. Be in a ditch somewhere." Finch said.

"Fred!" Esther admonished. "That poor Connie must be sick with worry. It's been six days, ain't it?"

"They haven't found his bicycle, so that's something, I suppose," Joyce offered.

Everyone murmured, lost in their own thoughts about how they'd feel if their loved ones suddenly disappeared. Joyce had more experience than most of them. When John had been shot down over occupied France, Joyce had faced agonising weeks of uncertainty, not knowing if he was dead or alive. "It's the not knowing," Joyce said. "That's the worst. 'Cos you can cope with anything once you know what you're coping with, can't you?"

Esther nodded. She had seen how Joyce had maintained

her patriotic stoicism after her mother, father and sister had died in the bombing of Coventry. It didn't bear thinking about how Joyce had coped with that, and how she'd then wanted to play her part in the war with a renewed fervour as a result. Now Joyce was Mrs Patriotic, a woman driven by her desire to help her country. Esther knew that Joyce would never get over that tragedy, but it was some minuscule comfort that she knew what had happened to them.

Would Connie get that comfort?

"Go and check on Dolores," Esther said to Gloria. "Her dinner's getting cold."

"That Dolores got out of laying the table, didn't she?" Iris said, admiring the woman's cheek.

Gloria did as she was told, scraping her chair legs back on the red-brick floor tiles as she left the room. She trotted upstairs, the chatter of the kitchen getting softer and more distant. She was already thinking about returning to her comforting stew, to the warmth of the table. To her surprise, Glory found the door shut on her shared bedroom, so she knocked gingerly. There was no response. Glory thought that was strange as she was sure Dolores said she was just putting her bag upstairs. Glory pushed open the door. Dolores was rocking on the end of her bed, tears streaming down her face. She glared accusingly.

"You did it, didn't you?" she said angrily.

Glory looked startled. She shook her head, an automatic response as for a second she didn't know what she was being accused of. But then she saw Dolores's carved box open on the bed. Glory remembered that she hadn't locked it. She'd tried but she couldn't do it with her hair grip. Guilt played

320

on her face for a moment and Dolores spotted it. It was all the validation she needed.

"You're a no-good thief, going through my things," Dolores spat, lunging off the bed at Glory Wayland, pinning her to the rough timbered floor. Glory wriggled free and scampered to the door. But Dolores was fast. She pushed Glory into the door frame, a flare of pain exploding in the girl's cheek bone as she hit the wood. Dolores spun her round and slapped Glory across the face.

Glory Wayland couldn't scream. She couldn't even shout for Dolores to stop. All the bottled-up rage and frustration that Dolores had been carrying around was unleashed. She pulled Glory closer by her collar and prepared to punch her. Glory tried to bring her knee up to push Dolores off her, but she couldn't get a purchase on the floor. But even though Glory couldn't raise the alarm, the noise of the argument and fight had led to racing footsteps on the stairs. Glory frantically tried to get Dolores off her.

Joyce and Esther burst into the room. Instantly, Dolores let go of Glory's collar, letting her fall back onto the floorboard. The girl put her hand to her neck and shuffled away on her bottom into a corner, eyes full of fear.

"Someone mind telling me what the hell's going on?" Esther said.

To everyone's surprise, Dolores turned her attention to Joyce. She thrust the ornately carved box into Joyce's hands as she launched into a tearful tirade.

"You've been cribbing on at me. Trying to find out why I never say anything –"

"What's this got to do with –?"

"Well, the reason I don't say anything. The reason I don't want to make friends with you all. The reason – is this. Look at it!" She gave a curt nod of her head, indicating for Joyce to open the box. Suddenly Joyce didn't want to know anything about Dolores, but the woman was glaring at her. Hesitantly, Joyce put her fingers on the box and prised the lid open. She saw the newspaper article, the photograph, the condolence card. And Joyce realised that far from being a secret collaborator, Dolores O'Malley had much more private and harrowing reasons for keeping herself to herself.

"I'm really sorry," Joyce said, mortified for her own lack of compassion and her slanted judgement. But Dolores wasn't listening.

"Seems she," Dolores said, pointing at Glory, "decided to find out for herself."

Esther turned to the wide-eyed girl. "Is this true?"

All eyes were on Glory Wayland. She'd wanted to be part of the gang, part of the family. But she had no choice but to nod. Yes, it was true. She couldn't speak to tell that she was doing it to fit in, to help them accept her. To make them love her.

Esther's mood changed instantly, hardening and cooling, a look of flint in her previously soft, maternal eyes. Calmly, she asked Joyce and Dolores to go downstairs. When they had gone, and their footfalls diminished on the stairs, Esther looked with profound disappointment at Glory.

"I took you in against my better judgement. Connie vouched for you. But maybe she didn't know what you were like. What you'd do."

Glory shook her head, trying to protest. Her long fingers reached for her small notebook and she hastily opened it, about to write.

"It's too late. I don't want any more lies or excuses," Esther said, putting her hands over the book. "I can't have people going through other people's things. Especially not private things like this. Poor woman."

Gloria Wayland knew what was coming.

"You leave here first thing in the morning. Do I make myself clear?"

Glory nodded, her heart breaking.

The gun shot had echoed around the vicarage.

Connie was shaking. Smoke wisped out of the end of the barrel. She kept her hand on the weapon and kept it aimed at Vince. She had shot it into the wall. A warning.

Vince was shaken, but still he refused to say a word. "I had nothing to do with it."

"Why are you still here?"

"I don't know. I thought you needed some help, that's all."

Connie refused to stop pointing the pistol at him. She indicated that he should go downstairs. She forced him first down the narrow staircase, slowly, one step at a time.

"Go slow. If you run for it, I'll blow a hole in your back."

Doing this slow, careful dance, they reached the dining room.

"Tell me the truth."

"Whatever I say, how do I know you won't just shoot me?"

"You don't."

Vince shook his head, refusing to speak about Henry, perhaps knowing that the wrong answer might cost him his life.

Connie knew he had something to do with her husband's disappearance. "If you had any compassion, you'd tell me what happened. You'd tell me whether Henry was alive. If I ever meant anything to you, you'd tell me."

She'd lain awake so many nights in that empty bed, staring at Henry's neatly folded pyjamas hung over the back of the bedroom chair. Doing this felt like decisive action. Doing this felt the right thing, even though Connie was terrified.

"I don't know what you want me to say." Vince was worried about giving the wrong answer.

"You were wearing me down, weren't you?" Connie said. "All the meals for two, the supportive smiles and concern and all that. You were waiting for me to fall into your arms."

Vince pondered how to respond. What answer would allow him to keep his head on his shoulders?

"You can't blame a man for trying. We were great together. The excitement, eh? Remember the excitement?"

"I have plenty of that now."

"What, with the 'Reverend'?" Vince risked a little snort of contempt.

Connie's arm had begun to lower slightly, but she brought it back up – the gun level with his face.

"All right, don't be hasty." Vince offered reassuring, slow words. "I want you back. And when Henry disappeared, I thought it was my chance to be here for you. I wanted to show I cared for you. I wanted to help you through it. That's all. I was making the best of it, for myself."

Connie squinted, trying to take this in. She was still desperately tired, but the adrenaline rushing around her body was keeping her going.

"I won't pretend that him going missing wasn't good for me," Vince said, softly. "But I didn't have anything to do with it."

"Liar," Connie spat. "Mrs Gulliver saw you following Henry."

"He'd forgotten his Bible."

"What?"

"I was chasing after him. But it was 'cos he'd forgotten his Bible."

Could this be true? Connie tried to remember exactly what Mrs Gulliver had said. Did it fit with what Vince was trying to make her believe? Connie took a step forward, forcing him to fall into the armchair. The heat of the blazing fire was burning the back of Connie's legs, but she didn't feel it.

The gun handle was wet with perspiration, so much so that it was becoming difficult to hold without slipping. She steadied it with her other hand, but Vince clocked the nervous look on her face.

"Gets heavy, don't it?" He smiled.

"Be lighter without another one of the bullets," Connie hissed.

Vince nodded his approval at her threat. Then he glanced at his jacket, which was slumped over a dining chair, a dark oil slick. "Look, I've got my key. Thank you for that. So I'm just going to leave. I've got what I need to start again. If you don't need me here." He spoke slowly, as if trying to mesmerise

Connie with his reasonable tone. "Question is – am I going alone?"

There it was. Whether Vince had anything to do with Henry disappearing or not, there was the reason he'd stayed after getting his key. He'd wanted to win her back, and what better way than to be the shoulder for her to cry on? His blue eyes bored into her, a strand of his thick black hair had fallen over his face. He offered hidden promises of excitement and danger, a chance to feel alive.

Am I going alone?

A crossroads reached with an exhausted mind, unable to think straight. A sweat-soaked gun in the hand. One direction led back to London, to a life of late nights and petty crime and excitement. The other direction led to sedate Sundays, dusty books and gentleness. The choice wasn't balanced, though. If Connie stayed in Helmstead, and if she could find Henry again, she'd have to see if she could repair her marriage. A lot of uncertainty. Vince's way was more straightforward. They could be on their way back to London –

Connie heard a piano playing in her mind. A jaunty tune. Henry finding the keys as he turned his boyish smile in her direction. She loved Henry. And as hard as it was to fit together some aspects of their personalities in their marriage, this was where she wanted to be.

"The only question is – where's my husband?" Connie said.

"Come with me, Connie," he said, his eyes still intent on hers. "What if he's never coming back? You going to mope around here all your days like those sad old spinsters out there?"

This unlocked something. Against her will, and unable to control it, Connie felt her body heaving, her shoulders rising as the choking wave of tears overwhelmed her. Stinging tears rolled down her cheeks, her vision blurring. She wiped her eyes with the back of her hand, the gun still held as tightly as she could manage.

"Thing is, Vince. Even if he never comes back, our time is over."

"We were great together," Vince pleaded. "Come on."

"I'm not coming with you." Connie indicated the hallway and that Vince should go.

Vince was surprised at this turn of events. She was letting him go? Alive? He wasn't about to look a gift horse in the mouth. He slid out from the armchair, Connie taking a step back to allow him up. Carefully he retrieved his jacket from the dining chair and put it on. There was a strange, expectant silence. Connie broke it as Vince reached the door to the hallway.

"You can go if you want. But I want you to know one little thing."

Vince turned back to Connie, to find himself staring down the barrel of the gun. Connie looked composed, steely. The tears had stopped, replaced with a look of cold detachment.

"If you leave here without telling me, I will shoot you."

"Told you, I don't know."

Vince took a step towards the door.

BOOM!

Connie blew one of the paintings off the wall, inches from Vince's shoulder. The frame of a picture of an autumn meadow shattered into splinters as the bullet hit it; the painting itself fluttering free like a canvas butterfly.

Vince couldn't hear, the gunshot temporarily deafening him. "Blimey!" A mix of surprise and fear tinged with a little anger.

"Tell me," Connie reiterated, levelling the gun. This time it wasn't pointing at the wall, but at Vince's head. "I've got nothing here without Henry. Nothing to lose. I will shoot you."

There was a long moment. It reminded Vince of the stand off on Barnes Common that had led him here. How could he get out of this one?

"All right. But then you let me go?"

"Tell me."

"I'll take you to him."

Connie's heart suddenly lurched into her mouth. Vince had known what had happened to Henry. And now he was going to lead her to him. Her Henry. Henry was going to be back home, tucked into bed next to her, sharing dinners in front of the fire with her. She could make everything all right again. She could mend their marriage.

But as Vince walked out of the door of the vicarage, he looked solemnly at her and uttered some words that broke her heart all over again. "Don't expect him to be alive."

Chapter 18

Full of nervous trepidation, Connie walked with Vince. They made their way through the village square and over the bridge past Roger Curran's newspaper office. Soon they were trudging across the wet fields of long grass towards Gorley Woods, the moon the only illumination for their journey. Connie kept the gun at her side as Vince walked ahead. Neither of them spoke. But it was a certainty that they were both thinking the same thing. Would Henry be alive? And while Connie was desperate to know the answer for her future happiness, Vince's interest was based purely on self-preservation. If Henry was dead, then the chances were he would be too.

Finally Connie spoke. She needed some information. Something to go on.

"Tell me what you did with him?"

Vince seemed reluctant to speak, in case it hastened his demise.

"I need to know."

"All right. One of those nights you were working at the hospital. Henry mentioned that the farm next to the French man's cottage wasn't occupied. That it hadn't been for years.

Henry was worried or something about the old guy having no neighbours if he needed help. So I got thinking it might be a good place to get Henry out the way for a while."

"So you could work on me?"

"Lengths I'd go to, eh?"

But Connie was in no mood for his rough-hued charms. She asked him curtly, "So what did you do to him?"

"I knocked him off his bicycle. And then I locked him in an out house."

"Was he hurt?" Connie said.

"Don't think so."

"Was he hurt?" She realised she was gripping the pistol handle more tightly than ever; her knuckles almost popping with the strain.

"No." Vince wanted the questioning to stop. Truth was that he had no idea if Henry had been hurt by what he did, and no idea if he'd still be alive. He knew that he had to be ready for the moment, if it came, when Connie would try to shoot him.

Vince rubbed his temple with his bandaged hand, stopped briefly to work out which way to go and continued to lead. Connie felt the loathing in her body for this man increase ten-fold. She had to stop her finger skating over the trigger.

As they reached the edge of the field, and the clouds hung like purple cotton wool in the darkening sky, Vince stepped onto the stony path that led to Gorley Woods. Connie could see the fields of Pasture Farm to the right of her, the distant cosy lights of the farmhouse where the girls might be sitting round the kitchen table having a late-night drink and a laugh together. She felt so alone. Oh what she'd have given for the girls from the farm to come to rally to her aid; all of them marching to Gorley Woods together, their reassuring smiles and support. But she was on her own, in the fading light, with a dangerous man, about to find out if her husband was dead or alive.

Vince trudged on, his city shoes crunching on the stone path. Suddenly Connie spotted someone. It was a lone figure walking from Pasture Farm, directly over the field, heading straight for her. At first, she wondered if her wish had come true. Connie stared, trying to focus on the figure. Was it just a scarecrow? No, it was definitely moving. Moving towards them. It was impossible to see much detail in the dying light. But finally, squinting, Connie made out one detail in the moonlight. The figure was wearing a cloche hat. The figure was Glory Wayland.

Vince was up ahead of Connie and hadn't seen what she was looking at. But now he turned round. Seeing that she was staring at the field, he looked too. Bemused, he noticed the figure moving across the fields towards them.

"Who's that?"

And then, as the glimmer of recognition hit his brain, he looked worried.

"Glory?" he almost mouthed. "No, that's not possible."

It must be a mirage. A trick of the light. There was no way that Glory Wayland could be here. No way on earth. Vince started to back away, suddenly fearful. "It can't be. It can't be." His feet scraped the verge on the other side of the path, and Vince had to steady himself to stop himself from falling over.

The thin, gangly woman was getting nearer to the fence that bordered Pasture Farm. Nearer to the stile that meant she could climb over.

"This can't be happening!" Vince Halliday was spooked. Ghosts didn't exist, and yet here was the proof in front of his own eyes. A woman who was dead, moving across a field, in a place where she would never be, coming to get him.

It was too much. He didn't care that Connie had a gun any more.

He stumbled backwards and started to run. Connie was surprised by the reaction. Vince scrambled back over the fence into the field with the long grass and he bolted for it, falling several times in his haste. Connie contemplated stopping him, but she decided that it would be easier with him gone. She knew where to go now. So Connie looked back towards Pasture Farm, where Glory Wayland had also started to run. The thin girl leaped over the stile and landed hard, but still upright, on the stone path. Connie grabbed her arm, stopping her.

"Wait a minute. What are you doing?"

Glory stared Connie in the eyes. She pointed back towards Pasture Farm and then shook her head, trying to communicate that things didn't work out there. Connie realised that Glory was holding the scalpel, the metal blade glinting in the fading light.

"Why aren't you at the farm?"

Glory turned her head, and Connie could see the glitter of tears welling in her eyes.

"You can't go after Vince now," Connie said, looking into the distance. Connie couldn't see any sign of him. "Once he gets his wits back, he'll realise that you're no ghost, and he'll wait to jump you or something. Do you want to take that risk?"

Glory was torn.

"Besides, I want you to come with me." Connie's words were vulnerable and heartfelt. "Oh, why aren't you in the farm?"

Glory pushed the scalpel into her pocket and took out her battered notebook. She wrote quickly and with small, neat lettering. Then she turned the page to Connie, who angled it to the moon to read it. "Dolores didn't want me to stay."

Connie handed the pad back to Gloria. "Come with me. I'll make sure you're all right. Yeah?"

Glory took one final look at the field into which Vince had disappeared. And then she followed Connie Carter along the dirt track, past the foreboding black shadows of Gorley Woods and into the night.

Connie found the edge of the farm that bordered Dr Beauchamp's cottage. And then she found a single building on its perimeter. The outbuilding was sunken into the corner of a field of brambles, the large sandstone blocks of its walls capped with a flat stone roof. Tiny slots in the walls acted as windows, making it resemble a dilapidated pill box rather than a storage area. It looked as though it had been abandoned for years. Connie forgot the name of the farm, but she knew that Finch had spoken about it once or twice. He used to bring his son, Billy, to the deserted land so they could practise using a shotgun. The decaying keep-out signs and the wrecked barbed wire on the gates offered no deterrent to Frederick Finch as he trained his young lad in the art of blowing holes in trees.

Connie walked fast along the hedgerow to where part of the fence had collapsed. She put the pistol into her belt and hopped over into the long, damp grass of the ghost farm. Glory silently followed. And although Connie could hear herself panting, she registered, in an oddly surreal moment, that Glory made no such noise.

The women reached the outbuilding.

"It must be this one." Connie's voice faltered. She fought to clear her throat, trying to find some volume. "Henry?" she shouted, her voice shrill, scared in the cold night air. Glory listened. They were deathly silent as they waited for a response. But there was no reply.

"Henry? It's me, Connie." Again, nothing.

The door of the outbuilding was sealed with a sturdy bolt but no padlock. With trepidation, Connie slid the rusting bolt back, her shaking fingers finding it hard to push against the peaks of rust in the carriage. She pulled the door towards her; its metal creaking in protest after decades of inactivity. With it open, frantically her eyes fought to see in the gloom. There were sacks of ancient oats, overgrown with weeds. Plant pots were stacked up in one corner. An old rake without a handle was near the door. To her surprise, the moon managed to illuminate some of the inside of the outbuilding thanks to a small hole in the roof. It was from this light source that Connie saw something that made her heart lurch in her chest.

Henry's hand, the wedding ring on his finger.

His still, unmoving hand.

He was lying on the floor, sprawled out, lifeless.

Connie scurried to his side and tried to rouse him. "Henry. It's me, Connie. Henry! Henry!" But he didn't move. His body was cold to the touch. Turning him over, she saw that his lips were dry and cracked, canyons of dehydration radiating from his bleached mouth. She bent her ear next to him to feel for breath. Nothing. Connie started to shudder, her body moving with a rhythmic rocking motion as she took in the dreadful realisation that Henry was dead.

"No, this can't be happening. No!"

Connie felt Glory's hand on her shoulder. Comforting. The girl bent down beside her and although Connie was turned away, she gave her an awkward hug. There was a wailing sound and Connie was dimly aware that she was the one making the noise, as she howled into the night. Glory held her tight, turning her slowly away from the body, shielding her pain. And as Glory rocked her amid the wailing, Connie noticed something about Henry's pullover.

It had moved.

Slightly, but it had moved. Or was it just her own movement disturbing it?

"Henry?" Connie peered more closely. No, it was true, the fabric on Henry's chest was moving, with the faintest tremor, up and down. A glimmer of life. It was a fragile but significant sign. When she was sure of what she was seeing, Connie seized on this and rested her head gently against her husband. She could feel the faintest heartbeat.

335

Henry Jameson was alive!

"Henry!" Now her cry was full of desperate hope.

But Connie knew from her work at Hoxley Manor hospital that he didn't have long left. His breathing was shallow and weak; he was too cold to survive much longer. He needed medical attention urgently. Connie's brain tried to work out what to do. She could tell Glory where to go, how to get to Hoxley Manor. But the girl couldn't speak and no one knew her there. That would just delay things.

At another crossroads, Connie made a decision.

"Stay with him, yeah? I'll go to get a doctor."

Glory nodded.

And then Connie bent close to her husband's ear and whispered, "I love you."

Then Connie Carter rushed off into the night, in a headlong dash towards the dirt track. But as she reached the perimeter of the abandoned farm, she tripped over some tangled metal, hitting the ground with a thump. Connie pulled herself to her feet, feeling a twinge of pain in her ankle.

That's all she needed. She rubbed her ankle, quickly realising that, thankfully, it wasn't broken.

But then she realised that it wasn't just a heap of metal that had tripped her. It was a bicycle. Henry's bicycle.

Connie pulled the bicycle up out of the grass and mounted it, wondering whether it was quicker to ride to Hoxley Manor for a doctor or go to Helmstead to get Wally Morgan. She struck Wally off her list of medical hopefuls. He would probably be drunk at this time of night. But Hoxley Manor was about twenty minutes away. It might be nearly an hour before she could get Channing or someone here. That might be too long. More crossroads.

Still, that seemed her only option.

But then Connie happened to glance the other way, behind her. And in the distance, against the dark barrier of Gorley Woods, was Dr Beauchamp's cottage. A doctor. Two minutes away. And true, he might not be awake or capable of helping, but it was a risk she had to take. Connie cycled at full speed. When she reached the cottage, she dumped the bicycle in his garden and hammered on his front door.

"Please don't let him be a doctor of literature or nothing." Connie realised that she had no idea if he was a medical doctor. She prayed as she heard shuffling from the other side of the door. Dr Beauchamp opened the door, small and gnarled like a hedgehog that had been woken from hibernation. Pushing his half-moon spectacles nearer his eyes, he tried to focus on the anxious young woman in front of him, no idea who she was.

"I'm Henry Jameson's wife," Connie started. "And I need your help."

Dr Beauchamp blinked. "I've not seen him. The blighter hasn't shown up for days."

"That's because he's in your neighbour's outbuilding. He's dying. Please." Connie was already heading back up the path. Dr Beauchamp frowned as he tried to process this information. "Dying?" Then, he pulled his cardigan tightly around his wheezing chest and set off in slow and lumbering pursuit. His breathing didn't allow him to move very fast at all, and Connie had to keep turning back and waiting for him to catch up. It was deeply frustrating but she knew that he couldn't go any faster. And it was still quicker than going to Hoxley Manor.

"Are you a medical doctor?"

"A what?"

"A medical doctor?"

"Not now, dear."

"But you were once?"

"What?"

Connie shook her head. She didn't have time for this. Dimly she realised that the old man was still wearing his slippers, as his feet crunched on the stony path. She helped him over the dip in the hedge and then stood aside to let him enter the outbuilding. Glory looked up from beside Henry's prone body, as the old man stood in the doorway. The glint of Dr Beauchamp's spectacles in the moonlight made him look slightly menacing, but Glory knew he was here to help. She stood aside as Connie and the old man moved to Henry, the Frenchman bending slowly on popping arthritic knees to get closer. He placed a gnarled, leathery hand on Henry's neck, feeling for a pulse. Then he craned his ear close to Henry's mouth to listen for the sound his lungs were making. He looked back to the women, his face anxious.

"He is alive. But it is not good," Dr Beauchamp wheezed. The exertion was more than he was used to and his head felt woozy with the effort. He forced himself to focus, closing his eyes to concentrate on what he needed to say. "You," he said, pointing to Glory. "Rip open those grain sacks. Cover his body in the hessian. It will keep him warm." Then he turned to

Connie. "You need to telephone for help. There is a telephone in my cottage."

The women went to work, Glory ripping open the sacks, Connie running off to the cottage. Dr Beauchamp continued to monitor Henry, stopping only to give a brief, curious look as he noticed that Glory was using a surgical scalpel to rip open the hessian bags.

"Are you a nurse, dear?" he wheezed.

Glory didn't answer, consumed by her work with the sound of ripping bags filling her ears.

Dr Beauchamp noticed a dried line of blood on Henry's upper right arm, below the shoulder blade. Something had sliced through his shirt, cutting him. It wasn't a deep cut, more of a blunt trauma. The doctor wasn't to know that this was from where Henry had hit the trip wire that ran taut between the trees. The vicar's skin was grey, no longer sporting the rosy tint from lazy summer bicycle rides.

Glory brought over two grain sacks. Something small scurried out of one of them into a dark recess in the building. She helped Dr Beauchamp to cover Henry in the hessian. The disturbed dust caused the doctor to start coughing. It took over his body, and the elderly Frenchman couldn't stop the coughing fit as he struggled to kneel back to admire his handiwork. Glory looked concerned. Was he going to die too?

Finally the coughing subsided. Dr Beauchamp patted the edge of his mouth with a handkerchief as he regained his breath. And then with a look of utter sadness he turned to Gloria Wayland and said something. At first, she had no idea what he meant.

"This is why they made me hang on a bit longer," the doctor said, in a moment of tragic clarity. "One last mission of mercy, eh?" And then his leathery face cracked into an accepting smile. "One last good turn." He sat in the building, moonlight filtering through the hole in the roof, watching as Glory finished tucking Henry up. And then the two of them waited for help to come.

By the time seven in the morning came, and the sun was rising in the sky, Connie had been awake all night, her eyes sore with tiredness and her skin taut with stress. For the last few hours, she had been sitting by Henry's bedside in a private room in Hoxley Manor. Connie guessed that the room might have been a small study before its acquisition as temporary hospital space, noticing a row of hard-bound books that traversed the length of the sill of the single window. Connie had memorised all the titles as she sat there, during those interminable hours; her hand on Henry's unmoving hand, her arm lying across the crisp white sheet.

He was still cold to the touch.

Shortly after he was brought in, the doctors went to work to save his life. She watched through the window of the closed door as they gave Henry air and tried to elevate his temperature. Long moments stretched out. She attempted to read the doctors' body language, the little looks they gave one another. Were they hopeful? Were they giving up? As she watched this awful silent mime act, an image popped into her head. She had to struggle to get it to go away. It wasn't the right time. Go away.

She saw herself in the vicarage, pointing the gun at Vince. The man who had done this. She pointed the gun and pulled the trigger. Vince flew backwards into the armchair, dead before he even sat down.

Connie shook the thoughts away. Not the time.

The doctors busied themselves. Did one just smile at the other? Was that a smile of good news or a smile of condolence? Then, at last, she realised that Henry had stabilised.

Since then, nothing else had happened. But Henry didn't show any signs of waking up. He hadn't responded to anything and Connie was starting to become unnerved. From working in the hospital, she recognised the worried looks exchanged between doctors and nurses, and she knew the dangers of patients who had very weak vital signs. In the last hour, Connie had been informed that Dr Channing had arrived to take over from the night team and monitor Henry. Connie knew that he would be straight with her. He'd tell her what's what. From what she had gleaned so far, Henry was suffering from exhaustion and malnutrition. The nurses had attached a drip-feed down his nose to give him much-needed water and nourishment while he was unable to feed himself. They had also wrapped him in thick sheets to try to increase his core temperature. But his heart beat was weak and his breathing shallow.

Could he even feel Connie's hand in his?

Dr Channing came into the room and Connie looked up expectantly.

"It may be a while before there's an improvement." He scanned her face, perhaps working out how much she could cope with knowing.

"But that means there will be an improvement?" Connie said, latching onto any shred of hope.

"I can't promise," Channing said, perusing the notes on Henry. "We must presume that he's been without food or drink for several days."

"How is that even possible?" Connie was confused. She knew that you could survive for quite a while without food, as long as you kept drinking. But she thought that people couldn't survive without water. "Perhaps he managed to drink. Somehow." Channing pondered. "Did he have access to water?"

Connie remembered the small hole in the roof of the outbuilding. Maybe her resourceful and clever Henry had found some way to collect the rain water over the last few days. Then she remembered something else. The plant pots in the outbuilding. Maybe Henry had put one of those up to the rain and filled it up, struggling to block the holes in the underside as he waited for enough to drink. And perhaps he'd eaten some of the rotting oats from the sacks. It was guess-work, but Connie thought about what she would have done in that situation. Henry must have done something similar to stay alive. Rain water and rotting oats.

"I suggest you go to my office and try to sleep for an hour or so," Channing said.

"I don't think I could." Connie resisted.

The doctor put his hands on her shoulders and gave her an imploring look. "You've got to be well for when he comes round, haven't you?"

Connie looked torn. Channing smiled. "I'll let you know if there's any change."

"You're sure?"

"Go and sleep."

She gave Henry's hand a final squeeze and left the room. Glory was in the corridor, sitting with Dr Beauchamp. The old man had a blanket around his shoulders. He looked ashen and ill, his night in the cold and the dust in the outbuilding having done his chest no favours. Connie asked one of the nursing staff to take a look at him. She thanked Glory for her help. Glory smiled encouragingly. She showed her the notebook and it was obvious that she had had time to write a lot of thoughts down.

"Glad you found him. I have to find Vince now."

Connie didn't think it was a wise move.

Glory pointed to the sentence "I have to find Vince now" for emphasis. Then she showed the next page. "I kept my part of the bargain. Helped you."

Connie nodded. That was true enough. And Connie didn't care what happened to Vince now. He had left Henry for dead. He deserved everything that was coming to him. But Connie didn't want to see Glory get hurt by him. She wasn't sure the young woman could take on Vince Halliday and win.

"Why don't we wait for Amos Ackerly to show up?" Connie suggested. "I'm sure he will soon."

To her surprise, Glory shook her head. But she was smiling, knowingly. What was going on? Glory scribbled in her note pad. It wasn't just a few words, but a whole paragraph. Connie waited, trying to glimpse the odd word: a sneak preview. But Glory was writing too fast and too small for her to see it. Finally she turned the page, and, as Connie read it, she understood what was happening. Things came into sharp focus.

Connie thought she'd been lucky in London evading Ackerly and his men. She remembered checking on the train from London, watching out for the gangster. Watching out for people following. She just assumed that she'd managed to elude them. Lucky Connie. But she hadn't been lucky at all.

Glory Wayland took the scalpel from her handbag, her eyes doggedly intense.

The writing started with a short sentence: "I made a bargain."

After Glory had escaped Amos's car and ran off down the alley, Amos had changed his mind. He didn't want to wait for her to turn up at Vince's bedsit. He told Trilby Hat to drive after her. The car thundered down the alleyway, cornering Glory at the end. She thought they were going to kill her and she closed her eyes for the inevitable impact. But the car stopped inches from her, Amos laughing his head off in the back seat. Glory couldn't get out and watched as Amos left the car and walked towards her.

"Got a proposition for you."

And he'd made Glory an offer she couldn't refuse. The terms were simple. She would find Vince and kill him. Then Amos would leave her alone. She would be a free woman. And as a strange sign of his benevolence, he handed something to the young woman. The two shoes she had lost running in the alley.

"You're working for him?" Connie said in disbelief. She remembered that the unlikely assassin had come to the bedsit, which must have been her only lead to finding Vince. And then Connie had led her to him. Talk about making a situation worse. But that's why Connie wasn't in danger in London.

Glory flipped the page back to the first thing she had shown Connie: "I have to find Vince now."

Connie's head was thumping. She didn't know what to do. Would Vince even be in Helmstead now? He had his key, surely he'd be on his way. But then Connie remembered what she thought about the key. It wasn't really for a safety deposit box in Hatton Gardens, was it? It was just a ruse for Vince to get Connie out of the way so he could –

So he could get rid of Henry.

She thought of Henry, lying in bed. The doctors trying to save his life. Vince had very nearly succeeded.

Another glimpse in her mind's eye of her shooting Vince dead in the vicarage.

She couldn't do that, could she? She couldn't be a murderer? Why not? Joyce had done it.

Connie got shakily to her feet. She could feel the weight of the gun in her pocket. She asked Glory to wait for a moment. She needed to talk to the doctor.

In his office, Dr Channing sipped at a cup of tea. Connie wanted to know whether she could nip back to the vicarage for some things. Would that be advisable? "Would Henry be all right?"

"He's pulled through." Channing considered. "He's sedated and we've put him on oxygen. He's stable, and I'll monitor him. But, Mrs Jameson, I want you to prepare yourself for the worst. Go home, but don't be too long."

The words sounded so final.

Connie walked numbly from the room, where Glory was waiting. Henry had nearly died. And Channing was saying that he might actually die. Suddenly she felt something rising up inside her. It wasn't tears or anguish, but a dark and twisted anger. Vince Halliday had done this. He had come here, taken over their lives, driven a bigger wedge between them and then, coldly, attacked Henry and left him imprisoned to die. And even while he thought Henry might be dying, he was trying to insidiously get himself closer to the distraught Connie, to win her away. The shoulder to cry on, hoping that the grieving widow would eventually fall into his arms.

Seething with anger, Connie strode down the corridor. A confused Glory caught up with her. Sensing what was on the girl's mind, Connie offered an answer:

"Maybe you had the right idea," Connie said. "Let's find Vince and finish this."

As Glory struggled to keep up with Connie as she marched through the fields towards Helmstead, she sketched a shakily written question on her notebook, finally managing to put it under Connie's nose.

"What about Henry?"

"I won't be long and I'll be back at his side. We might have missed Vince anyway. He might have scarpered already." Connie's brown eyes looked cold and hard. "But if he hasn't, I can't let him go."

Ten minutes later, the unlikely executioners reached the small bridge leading into Helmstead. Connie looked at the familiar scene: the village square, the Bottle and Glass pub, the vicarage. She marched with purpose towards her home. As she passed the church, she stopped momentarily, something catching her eye on the church notice board.

A handwritten poster for a cake sale with an inept drawing of a fairy cake. Henry's drawing. The cake that looked like a crushed bag.

Glory had spotted something more relevant. In the dawning light, Vince was approaching a car on the other side of the square. Had he been waiting to find a vehicle in which to make his escape? Glory tugged at Connie's arm. Connie was thinking about her gentle husband, a decent man who had only ever once raised a weapon in anger. She knew that Henry was pushed beyond his limits for him to try to use the shotgun to oust Vince. But usually he abhorred violence. And in a moment of clarity, Connie wondered what future they would have together if she killed a man. Could they ever come back from this?

She saw Vince flying back into the armchair, a patch of crimson blooming over his chest.

Would it leave a dark, empty core in her relationship with Henry? The goodness and the laughter always tainted by "the thing Connie had done". They couldn't cope with the problems they had, let alone one of that enormity.

And, never mind the emotional cost, then the cold, hard logistics tumbled into her mind.

Suppose she could actually kill Vince. If Henry survived then she would hang by a noose for a premeditated murder. She couldn't even say it was self-defence. It was revenge, pure and simple. But this man had left Henry for dead. He had tried to tear them apart with callous and psychopathic disregard. He deserved it, didn't he?

Alternatively, if, God forbid, Henry died, would that mean she'd get away with it? Then it would still be revenge, but the judge might take pity on a grieving widow who was pushed over the edge.

The drawing of the fairy cake. Her sweet, innocent husband.

Vince smiling and telling her about misdirection.

Maybe there was a way that would mean no one would die?

Connie's fingers feverishly fumbled the gun in her pocket. She could feel the cold metal of the mechanism, the smoothness of the chamber. Could she do this?

Misdirection.

Henry at death's door.

As these conflicting thoughts tumbled around, fighting for focus in her tired head, she turned in annoyance. Why was Glory tugging on her arm?

And then she saw Vince Halliday, his back turned towards them, forcing the door open on the parked car.

The time for thinking and evaluating was over. Connie found herself striding over the square, her hand holding the gun in her pocket. Glory was beside her, and from her peripheral vision, she could see her unhooking the scalpel from her handbag.

Was she really going to do this?

Revenge.

They got closer to the imposing figure of Vince Halliday.

He was fiddling with the car door, and with a final exertion, he wrenched it open.

"Not so fast," Connie said flatly.

Vince slowly turned. Who had caught him in the act? He was shocked to see Connie. Doubly shocked to see Glory. It seemed the girl wasn't a ghost after all. Her blade glinted in the air.

"Connie?" Vince said, trying to work out the situation. "Glory?"

"I've made up my mind," Connie said.

Slowly she took the pistol from her pocket. Vince looked nervously at her brown eyes. Then at the girl with the knife. The girl he had abandoned. His mouth contorted into a broad smile. So this was how it would end. Vince was no coward. He'd thought about his demise a million times, wondering how it would come. But always he hoped he'd face it with strength, not giving his killers the satisfaction of seeing him crumble. And it would be no exception now that two wronged women were about to end his life in an idyllic rural town.

Connie raised the gun.

Vince exhaled, a final breath of acceptance. He refused to close his eyes. He would face death head on.

Connie smiled as she lined the sights up with Vince's head.

Then she heard a gasp somewhere behind her. An old woman's voice by the church notice board. "She's got a gun!" It was Mrs Gulliver, witnessing the bizarre scene. An execution in the village square. That would give her enough to dine out on for years. But it only distracted Connie for a second. Nothing would stop her now.

Vince and Connie looked deeply into each others' eyes.

"Go on, then," Vince urged, fed up with waiting.

"This is how it ends, Vince."

"Is that right?"

Connie looked along the line of the gun barrel. Vince's head, his eyes staring at her. Daring her. She felt the impatience of Glory next to her. She realised she couldn't delay it any longer.

Connie turned the gun around and, holding it by the end of the barrel, she proffered the handle towards him.

Chapter 19

Glory was open-mouthed in shock, and if she could have spoken, she would have surely screamed "What the hell are you doing?" to Connie. What the hell was she doing? This was madness, perhaps the result of a mind pushed over the edge with exhaustion and worry. Vince was equally confused by the gun that was being held out for him to take. He didn't quite believe it was happening. Maybe he was dead already. But he found his fingers reaching for the handle, as Connie let go of the barrel. What was going on?

Connie put a gentle hand on Glory's arm, encouraging her to put the scalpel away. But the girl in the cloche hat kept it raised in front of her.

"What you up to, Connie?" Vince seemed more scared than when the gun was pointing at him. He could understand violence, but not this.

"I'm coming with you. Realised I'd made a mistake. This isn't my life," Connie said, indicating the village square.

"I knew it!" shouted a triumphant Gladys Gulliver from behind them. "Guns and gangsters! That's where she belongs."

"Shut up for once in your life," Connie snapped, without turning round.

Glory looked betrayed. She stared at Connie, wanting some clarification.

"Henry's not going to make it," Connie said, eyes blazing as adrenaline coursed through her exhausted body. "And I've got nothing here without him. I'm making the best of things. Sorry."

Vince's eyes darted between Glory and Connie. He was finding this hard to cope with. Two minutes ago, he was preparing to be shot dead in the village square. Now, it seemed Connie would be back on the team. They'd be together again. London, the scams, that's what he wanted, wasn't it?

"What about her?" Vince pointed to Glory.

"Oh, she wants to kill you," Connie said simply. "But she wants me to be happy an 'all."

Glory's eyes were blazing with hatred at Vince.

"I don't trust her," he said, pointing the gun at Glory. "Maybe I should just kill her."

Connie shrugged. "You'd hang for it. There are witnesses." She indicated with her head to where she assumed Gladys Gulliver was still standing, watching ringside.

Vince realised this was a good point. "Get her to put away the knife."

Connie indicated for Glory to put away the scalpel. As Connie did so, she managed to momentarily turn away from Vince. And she mouthed two words to Glory Wayland that changed everything: "Trust me."

Glory obediently tucked the knife back in her bag. Whatever was going on, her mission for Amos could wait.

"Come on, then," Vince said, indicating the recently acquired car. "Let's get going."

Connie shook her head. "I've got to go back to the hospital. Say goodbye to Henry. Least I can do. Even you can understand that."

"Well, I can hardly wait here for you, can I? Not with the car and that old bag watching," Vince muttered. "I'll drive you to the hospital."

"Who are you calling an old bag?" Mrs Gulliver shouted. "Who is he?"

"Probably best if you go home!" Connie shouted to Mrs Gulliver. The old woman scurried off to the safety of her house, where her net curtains would still afford a good view of the action.

"No, I don't want driving. Besides, we need you to keep a low profile with that car, don't we?"

Connie's mind was racing. Would this actually work? It was a plan concocted in a moment's panic. A plan made by staring at a badly drawn poster of a fairy cake. A plan that meant she wouldn't have to face the noose for killing Vince Halliday. A plan that meant he'd be out of her life forever. She hadn't had any time to spot any flaws. It was a massive gamble.

But then, whereas Connie Jameson was a new woman, Connie Carter thrived on taking risks.

"There's a cottage a few miles away. There's no one there.

It's called Jessop's Cottage. I'll write down the directions." And Connie nodded to Glory. Confused, the girl took her notebook from her bag and gave it to Connie, who sketched the route to Jessop's Cottage. "You can wait there." She tore off the page and gave Glory her notebook back.

"How do I know there's no one there?" Vince said, taking the piece of paper. "That it's not a trick?"

"It was where that little girl lived. Remember? The one who turned up at the vicarage. But her family's gone away now. She's gone too. There's no one there."

"Where they gone?"

"Does it matter? Come on, we haven't got much time," Connie said. "I'll be there in an hour."

Vince looked impassively at them. He wasn't sure if something wasn't quite right here. What was Glory doing here? Why was Connie coming with him? And yet, she'd given him his gun back? She knew they were great together. Of course she did. Shrugging off his doubts, Vince thought that Connie had at last seen sense. His plan had worked. Don't look a gift-horse in the mouth.

"All right. But if you're not there in an hour, I'm away. And any tricks, remember, I've got this."

"You've got all the cards on your side. Trust me, Vince."

"I want to believe you."

"I've been through so much, Vince. I just want to come home."

Vince weighed the gun in his hands. They watched as he climbed into the car and started it up.

He drove slowly out of the village square. Connie watched

it leave over the bridge. And then she felt a familiar tugging at her sleeve. A furious-looking Glory had written a new note: "What the hell are you doing?"

Connie shook her head and exhaled. "Taking the biggest risk of my life," she said.

But before she could explain further, a red-faced Roger Curran emerged from the office of *The Helmstead Herald*, pointing to the car that was disappearing over the horizon. "Hoy! That's my car! That's my car!" he hollered.

Later, Connie was sitting on the other side of the desk in the cramped office of the Helmstead Herald.

"And you're sure about that?" Roger asked for what seemed like the tenth time.

This was the moment of decision. The moment that would rid her of Vince once and for all. She thought of Joyce's words about the German she had shot: "I did what I had to do. I had to keep telling myself, he'd have killed me." And so it was with Vince. He had crossed the line. He had left Henry to die. And now Connie had no choice but to protect herself. She had to get rid of him. And this was the best way which didn't involve putting a bullet in him herself.

She told Roger that she was certain of what she was saying. "He's one of the bombers, I'm sure of it. He was stealing your car –" She turned to Glory as she said, "– and we tried to stop him. Didn't we?"

Glory nodded, having no real idea what Connie was doing.

"And when he recognised me, he started shouting about

how I'd driven Michael Sawyer away. How I'd blown the whole thing. I don't know what he was on about, but then I thought, maybe he's working with Michael. You know, with the explosive-making and stuff." Connie felt no prick of conscience at spinning this lie. She wanted Vince Halliday to be arrested, and whereas before she had worried about the elderly Home Guard officers or the lone PC Thorne taking him on, she knew that they would send fully-armed professionals from the Secret Service to arrest a bomber. Connie knew that the special agents, with their training and weapons, would be the only ones who could stand a chance of getting Vince Halliday under arrest. He wouldn't be able to explain the real reason why he was in the cottage. And even if he could, they would find him in possession of a gun; a weapon which might further point towards the nefarious activities of one of the collaborators.

Connie was banking on it being enough to get him put behind bars for a long time.

"I'd better call the London boys," Roger said. Connie could see that the light had gone back on in his eyes. A real story. Another one of the bombers caught in the bomb-making cottage. This could really make his name! He dialled the operator on his phone and asked to be put through to the War Office. Connie and Glory could hear the woman on the other end of the line trying to make the connection for him. And then they listened in silence as he related the story to the officer on the line.

Glory put a note under Connie's nose: "But he's not a bomber."

Connie scribbled a reply. "But he's a lot of other things."

Glory snapped shut her note pad, as Roger Curran came off the phone. He smiled reassuringly at the women. "They're sending a squad of agents over from Birmingham. Be here in thirty minutes. They know the way to Jessop's Cottage because the police were there taking away all the explosives and things. Been busy coming back and forth. They brought a van down the other day. Well, we may as well have a cup of tea while we wait." He looked at Connie, remembering her abysmal efforts with a kettle and winced. "I'll make it, shall I?" Roger headed off to the kitchen.

"Yeah, that'll be lovely."

Connie felt a need for fresh air. Her head was swimming with the enormity of what she had just done. She stepped outside while Roger made the tea.

Her hopes of some quiet time to reflect were dashed by a thin figure with a hat and a sour smile who wafted over like a nosey ghost.

"What's going on, then?" Gladys Gulliver usually looked judgemental as she asked that question, but this time she looked angry, as if she'd been personally affronted. "What were you doing in the square?"

"It's too complicated to go into."

"You were waving a gun around."

"Full marks for observation," Connie said, trying to close the conversation down. Glory stepped out of the newspaper office to see what was going on. But this provided more fuel for the fire for Mrs Gulliver.

"And who's she? She had a knife." Gladys glared at Glory,

who stared right back at her. "What's the matter, cat got your tongue, young lady?"

"She can't speak. It's a long story." Connie sighed. "Look, we weren't going to hurt anyone. I just needed to get rid of him, all right?"

Gladys Gulliver was full of questions, but for once, she'd seemed to have soaked up enough gossip to not ask anything further. Guns, knives and showdowns in the village square. This was a step up from gossip about Mrs Bradshaw having dirty nets. Connie supposed that Gladys might be in shock from what she'd seen.

"I'm going to bed. Had quite enough for one day." The old woman started to shuffle away. Connie just had time to smile at Glory before Mrs Gulliver turned back. "Oh, before I go, you know that young girl who was in the photograph with you? Well, she was here half an hour ago, asking if I'd seen you."

"What did you say?" Connie feared the worst.

"I told her to steer clear of you. Don't worry, I didn't tell her why. I didn't think she needed to know all about the guns and things that you get up to. Heaven forbid that a young mind needs that."

An awful thought struck Connie: "Did she say where she was going?"

"Said she was going home. That was the message. Tell Connie Carter that I'm putting on a brave face and going home. You let her go, that's my advice. Guns indeed!" Gladys Gulliver turned and walked away. She didn't see Connie's desperate expression. Margaret was going back to the cottage! But by the time Roger came out of his office to say the tea was ready, Connie and Glory were racing across the bridge, out of Helmstead.

Connie had been awake for so long, running on pure adrenaline, that she no longer knew what time it was. But she knew that every muscle in her body felt tired and the skin on her face was stiff with fatigue. They ran over the fields of rain-soaked grass until they reached the brow of the hill that looked down on the patchwork fields around Jessop's Cottage. She couldn't see any signs of life in or around the cottage. Connie wondered if she'd made a dreadful mistake. Was Margaret there? Or had she been and gone before Vince got there? What would Vince do if he saw her? Maybe Mrs Gulliver had got it wrong?

If she was there, Connie had to get Margaret away from the place before the special agents arrived. But how could she do that? For once, Connie, feeling drained and desperately tired, ran out of ideas.

Glory dropped to the ground and indicated for Connie to do the same. They were behind a small rise on the brow of the hill overlooking the valley. They could see the entire cottage and surrounding grounds from up here. Connie felt uneasy at staying where they were, exposed.

"I can't just stay here and watch. If they come mob-handed to arrest Vince, and Margaret's there with him, he's got a ready-made hostage, ain't he?" Connie couldn't allow that to happen.

She knew that despite the dangers, she had to save Margaret Sawyer for a second time. She didn't have a plan, but she knew she had to do something fast.

In the cottage, Margaret Sawyer was in her bedroom. Her small case lay open on the bed. This time she had packed more sensibly than before, packing a loaf of bread in grease-proof paper along with her dolls, as well as a change of dress. She had been staying with various school friends in Brinford, but now realised she had to go elsewhere. She was pondering whether to try Connie Carter again. Looking at Connie's smiling face in the photograph in the newspaper cutting made Margaret desperate to see her heroine again. Yes, maybe Connie would let her stay this time. That would be nice. She could live with Connie Carter.

Suddenly there was a creak on the floorboards behind her.

Fearing that Michael or Vera had come back, Margaret turned, ready to argue her case. She would tell them she had been staying with one of her friend's mums in Brinford. She wouldn't mention that her friend's mum had told her to go home to face the music.

But to her surprise it wasn't Michael or Vera coming up the stairs. Instead, a bullish man in a dark suit was standing by her bed. One of his hands was wrapped in a dirty bandage. It took Margaret a few moments to recognise him. It was the nasty man from the vicarage. She didn't like him. He had mean eyes and he made Connie Carter unhappy. What was he doing here in her house?

"What do you want?" Margaret said, in what she hoped was a strong and warning voice.

"I'm waiting for Connie," Vince said softly. "Where are your parents?"

Margaret shook her head. She didn't know.

"Why don't you know?"

"I ran away. But I came back."

"Obviously." Vince smiled. He had too many teeth when he smiled. Margaret thought he looked like a pike fish.

"I'm packing my case." She wondered where Michael and Vera were. It was usual for Vera to go out, but never Michael. Maybe he was in one of his sheds. But what was this man doing here? Margaret felt a wave of unease. Something wasn't right. "Is Connie Carter coming here?" Margaret said, focusing her thoughts on happier things.

Vince nodded, staring out of the window, across the fields, seemingly having lost interest in the girl. "Why is she coming here?"

"Got a lot of questions, ain't you?" Vince said. "We're running off together, if you must know. Like grown-ups do."

Margaret pulled a face. "Why would she do that? She said she wanted you gone. That's what she said." And then, when Vince's brow darkened, Margaret Sawyer realised she'd said the wrong thing.

Vince's attention turned from the window to what the girl was saying. From the mouths of babes. He tried to process it. Maybe the girl had got it wrong? "Is that what she said?"

"No."

"You said that's what she said. When did she say that?"

"When she walked me home after I stayed at the vicarage."

Vince tried to process this. Maybe she'd misremembered it? No, she seemed certain. Well, all right then, she might be remembering it correctly, but then Connie had seen sense since then and changed her mind. "She said she wanted you gone." The words echoed in Vince's head. What other options were there? Connie secretly hated him. Connie was coming with him. Or Connie was tricking him in some way.

There was a knock at the door. Vince peered out of Margaret's window. Below, on the front steps, was Connie Carter.

She was coming with him!

"Looks like you can ask her yourself," Vince said. Margaret took a step towards the bedroom door. Vince pulled his revolver out from his pocket and waved it threateningly. "Be good to find out what's going on, though, won't it?" Suddenly, Margaret wished she'd stayed in Brinford. They went down the stairs together and Vince indicated for Margaret to open the front door.

The small girl lifted the latch. Connie's face fell when she saw Vince with his revolver pointing near Margaret.

"What you doing?" Connie barked.

"Insurance," Vince replied. He indicated for Connie to come into the house. It was the last thing she wanted to do. Ideally she wanted to get Margaret and herself away from the cottage. Time was ticking away. The special agents would be here soon.

But she didn't have a choice. Connie went inside. Vince closed the door.

"What's going on, Connie?" Vince's steely blue eyes searched for any hint of a lie or a trick. She had seen him like this before, almost feral in a heightened state of anxiety.

"I came. Like I said I would," Connie said, smiling at Margaret, trying to reassure her.

"Where's your stuff? You didn't bring a case?" Margaret asked.

Connie winced. Why did children have to say things like that? Vince frowned.

"Thought we were starting again, didn't I?" Connie brave faced it. "Now, why don't you let the kid go?"

Vince breathed deeply, considering. "Talking about starting again. There was no safety deposit box, Con. That key you got was just for an old meat locker at Smithfields."

"I thought there wasn't any money," Connie replied. "Just a way of getting me out of Helmstead, wasn't it?"

"You're not mad at me? Even though I've not got any money?"

"We've both made mistakes, haven't we?"

"We'd have to work the scams again. And hope you can still turn a few heads." Vince's attempt at a joke fell on deaf ears. Connie was feeling too edgy to even register he'd made a joke, let alone to laugh at it.

Margaret looked imploringly at Connie. "Why are you going with him?" she asked.

Connie glanced up from the small girl and looked Vince in the eyes.

"I'm not," she said.

She let the sentence hang in the air, seeing Vince struggling to work out what fresh trickery this was, seeing Margaret trying to work out why Connie had said she was. And then Connie finished it. "Not unless he lets you go. Come on, Vince. I think enough people have got hurt. We can go and get in that car and get out of here."

Vince mulled this over. He indicated for Connie to lead the way. She opened the front door. Vince followed, his arm around Margaret's neck. Curran's car stood yards away. But still he felt that this would be a trick. It was strangely quiet. The birds had stopped singing. Vince edged away from the front door, holding Margaret tightly to him. Cabbage-white butterflies danced around the borders. Vince looked around. He glanced back to the house, where Connie was lingering near the doorway. She looked sweetly at him. Those big brown eyes, the long cascading hair framing milky white skin and a smile that could dazzle the heavens. Vince wanted to believe. He wanted to stop fighting and trust someone. He wanted to trust Connie, standing there in front of a picture-book cottage.

It would be easy for them to get in the car and head to a new beginning. Why was he still suspicious? He had the gun. He had the power here. And yet something was unnerving him. And with a slow, sickening jolt, he realised that he'd seen that sweet look on Connie's face before. It was the same look she used on the rich old men as she distracted them while Vince was rifling their overcoats. The look that held their attention, while something else was going on.

Misdirection.

He realised that she was distracting him!

Vince spun round to look up the hill. And he saw what Connie had noticed moments before: four men in grey suits running down the incline towards the house. They all had pistols. Vince squinted. They didn't look like Amos Ackerly's clowns. These guys were more polished, fresh-faces, neat hair, men plucked from Oxford and Cambridge to join the special services. They all had the same type of pistol, obviously standard issue. Government officers from the War Office.

Vince's survival instincts kicked in.

He grabbed Margaret tightly and pointed the gun at her head. Connie moved forward to stop him, but he shook his head angrily. "Don't try it." And then to the men on the hill: "Stay there!"

The men running down the hill stopped. One of them indicated for the others to take it easy. Vince moved Margaret round, the gun tight against her. A human shield to show all his would-be assailants that they'd better not mess with him. The men were still edging down, but they had slowed to a careful, gradual descent. All eyes were fixed on Vince Halliday.

"You tricked me!" Vince spat.

"You left Henry for dead," Connie snapped back. "Give yourself up. It's over!"

Vince shook his head. Margaret's eyes were wide with fear. "You're hurting me!"

"Tell them to stay back or I'll kill her," he snarled.

"Don't hurt her, please," Connie said. "You give up and they'll just lock you up. You hurt her and you'll hang."

"You tricked me!" Rage and loathing bubbled from Vince's mouth.

Connie's eye caught sight of something. Hiding behind Roger Curran's car was Glory Wayland. She was holding her scalpel and sneaking, in small hunched movements, closer and closer. Vince gripped the small girl and spun round, gauging his options, a full three-sixty-degree turn, the gun held against her forehead. Could he escape? Which way could he go? Could he make it to the car and drive his way out?

The men in suits were edging closer. Behind the car, Glory was getting closer.

Then the men stopped. Vince stood upright, trying to sense what was happening. Glory edged around the side of the car, low to the ground. The scalpel was in her outstretched hand. Nobody could see her apart from Connie, as she was shielded from the agents' view by the car. Vince and Margaret could only see her if they looked down.

Connie prayed that they wouldn't look down.

Misdirection.

"I'm sorry it worked out like this, Vince," she said. Vince glanced toward her, momentarily, taking his eyes away from the area where Gloria was edging forward. Then he looked up high, watching the agents on the hill.

Glory kept moving, but then something happened to break the stand off. It all happened in a split second:

The wind caught Glory's cloche hat. As it whipped it off her head, she instinctively reached up a hand to grab it. Her precious cloche hat. In his peripheral vision, Vince caught sight of the movement of her hand. He spun round, bringing the gun to bear on the new target.

But Glory was quick. She plunged the scalpel deep into Vince's shin.

With a reflex action, he kicked out with his other leg,

sending Glory to the ground. She was on her back. Vince howled in pain. His leg was bleeding profusely, the trouser glistening and dark, the handle of the scalpel all that was visible above the stained fabric. In that instant, the agents started to run down the hill towards them. Vince was about to shoot the prone Glory, but now he was forced to turn the gun back on his hostage. He still had his arm around Margaret's throat.

Vince indicated for the agents to stop.

"Stay there! Stay!" he howled.

Connie watched the agents. Although still a distance away, they were pointing their guns at Vince. Ready to shoot him if they had to.

"Drop the gun!" The man in charge shouted, with the calmness of voice that indicated this was a daily part of his job. He might as well have been asking for case files or a coffee to be brought to him.

Vince shook his head. "You drop yours!"

He gripped Margaret Sawyer tightly. She looked terrified. "Please," she squealed.

He pressed the gun to her ear. She could smell the stale sweat on this nasty man, feel the thumping of his heart in his chest. The end of the gun was hurting her head. Glory was on her back on the ground, aware that any movement could get her shot by Vince.

Connie shouted to Vince, and he half-turned to listen, while keeping one eye on the agents.

"You've got a choice."

"Oh yeah, what's that, then?" Vince barked.

"Give up and live. Or don't and die," Connie said.

"What are you talking about?" Vince spat. "Why should I give up when I'm going to escape? I've got her, ain't I?"

"Last chance to let her go. And for you to live," Connie said. "Believe it or not, I don't want you to die."

Vince sneered at her. He shook his head.

"What do you mean, last chance? How are you threatening me? You're not the one with the gun!"

"No," Connie said quietly, her face etched with regret. "But I'm the one with the bullets."

And she slowly held out her hand. In her palm were the four remaining bullets from the gun. Connie had removed them before she had given the gun back to Vince in the village square.

With horror, Vince realised what this meant.

The agents, with their raised guns, saw the bullets and realised that Margaret wasn't in danger. There was nothing to stop them opening fire now.

Vince had one chance. He pushed the girl in the direction of the men, to act as some sort of shield and he ran the other way; each step agony because of the knife embedded in his shin.

Vince Halliday jumped the first row of box hedges.

He could see an outbuilding ahead. Ten feet away. If he could just get to that, he'd have cover—

Three neat cracks of gunfire echoed around the valley.

Vince tumbled into the flower bed. Hydrangeas broke underneath him as he fell, the empty gun flying from his hand. The last thing he registered was the smell of the flowers as the pollen puffed out around him.

Connie went to help Glory, but she shooed Connie away. She was all right. Glory brushed herself down and retrieved her cloche hat, placing it back onto her head. Connie ran to Margaret and reached the little girl just as one of the agents did.

"You her mother?" he asked.

Margaret gave a wistful look. If only.

Connie hugged her close and kissed her head.

Chapter 20

Connie was fighting to stay awake, her eyes glazing over at the small text of the book she had in her hands. It was taken from the shelves in Henry's room as she waited for him to wake up from his nap. Sleep hadn't come easy for her, and she assumed she might actually be too tired to sleep, if that was possible, after everything she had been through. Emotionally and physically, it had all taken its toll and she felt threadbare. Henry had woken properly for the first time this morning and they had shared a few words before he dozed off again.

"Connie?"

"I found you, Henry. I came and got you."

"Thank you." And he'd smiled contentedly as he drifted off to sleep. Connie had felt his hand grip hers tightly for a moment before it let go. She had sighed in relief.

Since then she had stayed, waiting for him to wake again. And when his eyes opened this time, she could see that he had more energy, more awareness of what was happening. Connie filled him in quickly with the practicalities of what had happened: how she'd found him, how she'd got Dr

Beauchamp, how she'd waited for him to wake up.

"And Vince?" Henry asked, with a furrowed brow.

"Vince is dead," Connie said flatly, squeezing his hand. "And I promise you, there are no more skeletons in my closet. No one else is going to turn up. I promise." She scanned his face for a reaction. He was looking towards the end of the bed, taking it in, perhaps considering what he felt.

"But I've put you through so much, Henry. No one deserves what's happened to you on account of you hitching your wagon to me. So I'll understand if you want me to go."

A long moment passed. Henry licked his lips, trying to find the saliva to speak. Connie realised that he was thirsty, so she poured him water from his bedside jug, managing to soak the arm of his pyjamas in the process. "Sorry, Henry, I haven't got any less clumsy." Henry smiled and drank the water, taking so much of his energy that he had to compose himself after-wards, catching his breath.

"So do you want me to go?" Connie asked.

"It's what you want that matters," he whispered.

"I could have gone with Vince. That's what it was all about, him wanting me to go back to London. And I know that world, I know what makes it tick and how to survive in it. But I didn't want to—"

Connie trailed off as she realised that Henry was asleep.

The train was going to London.

The clackety-clack of the train wheels was weirdly hypnotic, and Connie Carter found herself fighting a battle against sleep. She pinched her fingers to force herself to stay awake. It was a hard battle as she was still exhausted from the last few days, both emotionally and physically. After the events at Jessop's Cottage, Connie had told her friends at Pasture Farm what had happened, right from the start. She started with an impromptu conference around the kitchen table, where she told the girls, Esther and Finch. There was no way it would stay a secret, so she thought it best to tell her version of events. A few days later, Roger Curran ran a story in *The Helmstead Herald* about how plucky Connie Carter had foiled a vicious criminal.

Connie hoped that this one wouldn't make the nationals.

She felt a contented yawn coming and stifled it behind the back of her hand. Margaret Sawyer giggled as Connie pulled an unintentionally funny face as a result. Then Connie got out some biscuits that Esther had made for their journey. Margaret took one, but Connie encouraged her to take a spare one for later. Margaret liked Connie Carter. She wished that she could have kept her. She'd be an amazing mum. But Connie couldn't take in the young girl. It would be better if they could find some of her extended family in London instead.

Connie smiled warmly at the third person in the carriage. Henry.

They had survived their darkest hours and had been reunited, and Henry was fighting his way back to full health. He was still tired a lot of the time, but each day he was getting stronger. Connie liked the way the kaleidoscope of sunlight dappled on his face through the passing trees. She had longed for him to be all right and to be back by her side. And now her prayers had been answered. They hadn't managed to discuss what was said at the hospital, and Connie didn't want to push Henry into a conversation before he was ready. It was enough that she was there to support him; they could discuss their future another time.

In the hospital, Henry had come round after two days of intensive oxygen and nutrition therapy. Connie had been the first one to see his eyes open. She'd cried with joy at seeing the first fluttering of his eyelids; the moment when he came back to her. Henry had stayed at the military hospital for ten days, getting stronger and stronger, before being allowed back to the vicarage under Connie's care. She had done her best to feed him back to health, cooking hearty stews and soups.

And she tried to get better at making cups of tea for him. But that hadn't gone well.

Being a popular young reverend, it wasn't only Connie who found herself looking after him. The trio of Mrs Arbuthnott, Mrs Fisk and Mrs Hewson would pop round regularly, often with some hot dish under a tea towel, to enquire how he was getting on. They would all talk at once, asking a thousand questions. On other occasions, Frederick Finch had popped round to see if Henry fancied a game of cards. But no cards were played and instead Finch spent his time drinking the vicarage brandy. It was the thought that counted, though. Esther had kindly taken their washing twice a week, laundering it up at the farm and bringing back freshly ironed linen and shirts.

Connie didn't mind all the visitors, all the intrusions motivated by kindness. But she felt out on a limb, as she had always done. Did she belong here? Could she ever fit into this world?

Henry was dressed in his best suit, and Connie had her maroon jacket and skirt on. Margaret, who was wearing her best dress, felt nervous, unable to settle. She had mixed feelings about returning to London, worried about the visceral reminders of seeing the places she and her mother used to go. Margaret wasn't happy, but she could hardly stay in Jessop's Cottage on her own, with Michael gone and Vera facing prison. Connie hadn't found the right moment to tell Margaret what had happened to Michael. The troubled man had shot himself in the forest. The agents from Birmingham had linked him to the bombing of the train tracks and later found his body. Although they'd initially assumed that Vince Halliday was one of the gang, they knew that one member was still at large. The accomplice who helped Michael Sawyer laid the bomb on the tracks. But they would find him. They always got their man eventually.

Margaret stared, trying to focus on the fast-moving collage of places and lives behind the window pane. She offered a stoic look to Connie, trying to be brave. Perhaps Connie and Henry would change their minds if she showed how grown up she was? Secretly, she knew that they wouldn't change their minds. They couldn't.

Taking her to London to find someone she knew was the best idea and all they could do in the circumstances. Despite her misgivings, she trusted Connie Carter; the marvellous Connie Carter who had saved her life, not once but twice. Connie would make sure it was all right.

Margaret hadn't been to London for three years. As she had only been six at the time when Vera had come to the school to tell her teacher the shocking news about the Grey Horse pub on Talbot Street, her thoughts and memories of the time were hazy now. Where did they used to live? Could she really remember it? Could she recognise any of her aunties or uncles if Connie managed to find them? It worried Margaret that she wouldn't be able to remember the places but also that she would, and she'd feel upset at the fact her mum wasn't around any more. Her stomach knotted. Connie gave her a kind look.

"It'll be alright," she said.

"Yes," Margaret said bravely, not believing it.

"Eat your other biscuit."

Connie's thoughts turned to Gloria Wayland. The damaged young woman in the cloche hat had been promised her freedom by Amos Ackerly if she murdered Vince Halliday. Well, that was one happy ending that Connie was able to make come true. As their train thundered closer to London, Connie imagined Glory scrubbing the front step of Jessop's Cottage. Connie had given her the set of keys she had for the place. Glory had always dreamt of living in a cottage, and now, for a time at least, she could make that dream become a reality.

Connie glanced at the young girl beside her and wished, with all her heart, that she could give her a happy ending as well.

Connie remembered the final hand. All or nothing. George Butler looked more nervous than she did. The grey-haired man sucked his cigarette so hard that Connie feared he'd suck

Roland Moore

it right into his mouth, scorching his cheek. The wiry man smiled when the first playing cards were turned over. He had a king and yet Connie, the flashily dressed young woman who'd tried to hustle them, only turned over a five.

George Butler furrowed his brow. This wasn't a great start.

The red-haired lump next to the wiry man gave a jolly chortle. This would show this interloper!

The rest of their cards awaited. Connie wondered what hers held.

It was time. They turned a second card each. Connie got a seven while the wiry man got another king.

Disaster!

He already had a pair. A winning hand. And she had nothing.

Connie knew she would have to be lucky with her remaining three cards if she was going to beat him and not have to walk back to Helmstead. She breathed out, steadying herself. George gave her a small nod of encouragement and support. It wasn't over yet. Connie was aware that the game was attracting the attention of the rest of the patrons in the pub. The couple had shuffled over to watch, the two labourers were leaning against the wall. Free entertainment. And the landlady was gazing with curiosity as she over-polished a glass behind the bar.

They turned their third cards. Connie got an eight. The wiry man got a ten.

He still had a pair. Connie still had nothing.

Nothing.

"Go on!" The red-haired man cheered.

They had two cards left to turn.

Connie wondered what Finch would do in a losing situation like this. She couldn't help smile. He'd probably get his pig, Chamberlain, to rush in and knock over the table. Game void, sorry lads. Unfortunately, Connie didn't have a large Tamworth pig that could conveniently save the day. No, she had to see this out to the bitter and unpleasant end.

The next cards flipped over. Connie got a nine. The wiry man got another ten.

No! He had two pairs now. That was a pretty strong hand in anyone's book. And Connie still had nothing.

She looked at her four turned cards: a five, a seven, an eight and a nine. It was nearly a straight run of cards. But nearly wasn't good enough. To win, she needed to get a six to make a straight of five, six, seven, eight and nine.

That was one thing. But also, to win, she had to pray that the wiry man didn't turn over either another king or another ten. That would give him a full house – three of a kind and a pair.

If he got that, he'd win.

If Connie didn't get her straight, then he'd win even without turning his last card.

Connie wished she could just disappear.

"Come on!" The red-haired man punched the air. The grey-haired man, smoking his cigarette, studied Connie. He wondered who she was. How had she come to this place? He knew he wouldn't find out. Just as Connie would never know any of their names or their lives. They were all destined to be ships that passed in the night, for one brief moment of contact that would probably be forgotten in a dozen years.

George rubbed his mouth nervously.

Connie felt perspiration on her top lip. Her throat was dry.

The wiry man was enjoying her discomfort. Only one card would save her now. He motioned for her to turn.

Connie's long fingers reached towards the table, towards her last card and she turned it over.

Henry perused the menu. He always loved coming to a Lyons' Corner House, and he knew it would be the ideal thing to distract Margaret from her troubles. The young girl had looked at the cakes on offer, wanting to try everything on the menu. Vera had rarely made cakes. In the end, she whittled her choices down to either a flapjack or a Victoria sponge. Two elderly women, dressed very grandly for afternoon tea in the East End, smiled at Henry. To any outsiders, it looked like a young father out with his daughter. As the waiter came to take their order, Henry asked for a pot of tea and prompted Margaret to make her choice.

"It's so hard," she said, still agonising.

The waiter tutted. A busy Saturday afternoon meant he didn't have time for children who couldn't make up their minds.

Henry wasn't having her treated like that! He took control.

"Well, if you can't make up your mind, there's only one thing for it," he said. "You shall have both!"

Margaret squealed with delight. The waiter nodded obligingly, probably unimpressed with Henry's parenting skills, and went away.

When their order arrived, Henry told Margaret about a

game he liked to play. With strangers in church, he would try to guess their names, making up the most outlandish ones he could for them before he learnt their real names. Margaret thought that game sounded like fun. Henry demonstrated by glancing around the packed Corner House. His gaze fell on the two overdressed women.

"Tabitha Featherstone Harland," he said in a low voice.

Margaret giggled. She had a go at christening the other lady: "Minerva Grape Bottle".

"You're good at this," Henry laughed, conspiratorially. And soon they were working their way around the room, giving everyone a daft moniker. Margaret found this terrific fun and it was only when the tea and cakes arrived that they had to compose themselves and settle down.

"It's fun giving people names, isn't it?" Henry said, stirring his tea.

And then a flash of sadness washed over Margaret.

"Sawyer isn't my real name," she said. "That name was given to me too."

"What is your real name?" Henry asked softly.

"Margaret Hawkins," she said. It was a name she hadn't been called for three years. A name she hadn't said for three years. Michael and Vera had insisted that she take their surname while she was under their roof. "They took me in, so I had to do what they said."

There was a moment's awkward silence, but then Henry would have been surprised if he could have kept the atmosphere light throughout the whole afternoon tea. They both knew that Margaret faced an uncertain future. Neither of them knew where she would be staying tonight, which relative, if any, they could find. But Henry felt burdened with the additional guilt of thinking he should have gone with Connie. It wasn't right that she was out there, in the East End, trying to find somewhere, while he was playing silly games in a Lyons' Corner House and eating cake.

"Friston D Grumpington," Margaret said, pointing to the waiter.

Henry couldn't help but laugh. Then they noticed Connie tapping on the window and beckoning them to come. The game was over. Margaret looked nervous. "Has she found one of my aunts?"

"Let's go and find out." Henry left some money and Margaret grabbed the rest of her flapjack to put in her pocket.

The last cards were waiting. Connie turned hers.

A six! She was overjoyed. She had a straight hand of five, six, seven, eight and nine.

At that moment, she was beating the wiry man's hand of two pairs. But she knew that if he turned a king or a ten, he would get a full house and he'd still win. People exhaled nervously amid the cigarette smoke as the wiry man reached out his leathery fingers to turn his final card. As he turned the card, Connie looked at the queen. He'd turned a queen. He'd failed!

George erupted in an uncharacteristic holler.

"You only gone and done it, girl!" he shouted.

The wiry man shook his head in frustration. How could she have such luck?

As George helped to scoop up Connie's winnings, she turned to take the congratulations from the rest of the patrons. The labourers suggested that she should get a round in. Connie thought why not. Her head woozy from the tension, she stood and took a handful of notes to the bar. This was like the old days.

"What you all having?" she shouted.

Then she turned to the suddenly-happy landlady to give her large order of pints and shorts. As the small woman busied herself behind the bar, pouring drinks, Connie idly glanced at the row of spirit bottles in the optics in front of the mirrored area at the back of the bar. It was a mirrored area, the same as she'd seen in a dozen pubs.

Her reflection stared back at her.

Connie stopped smiling.

Connie led the way, with Henry and Margaret following. Setting quite a pace, it was hard for Margaret to follow. She was finding it hard to eat the rest of her flapjack and keep up, her lungs not giving her enough air for eating and walking. She parked the flapjack back in her pocket, deciding to have it later.

"Where are we going?" Margaret asked.

Connie seemed very tense, troubled, and unwilling to say much.

"I've found someone who can take you in," she said, offering a warm smile. But her voice was cracking. Margaret wondered whether she was finding the prospect of saying goodbye a sad one. Like she was.

"Don't worry. You can come and visit," Margaret said, hoping it would cheer her up.

Connie bent down to her level. Her eyes were filled with tears. "Bless you, you sweet little girl, you."

Henry put a comforting hand on his wife's shoulder. "Let's get it over with, eh?" he said softly. Margaret wondered why they were finding this so difficult. Why was Connie getting so upset?

Margaret caught up with Connie and put her hand in hers. They could have one last walk together, couldn't they? Connie felt the warmth of the small hand in hers and she struggled not to cry. She had to be strong. She had to hope that Margaret would be allright.

They turned the corner onto a small side street and they found themselves staring at a three-storey building bookended by the rubble of shattered houses either side. The three-storey building was still standing. In fact, it was the only place that had survived, in a street that was just mountains of brick debris and buckled girders.

It was a pub. And above the ground-floor windows was its name.

The Grey Horse.

Margaret recognised this place, but was confused. This didn't make sense, upending everything she had known and held onto these last three years. She looked to Connie for an explanation. The Grey Horse. But Connie was staring up at the building, transfixed, as though it was a miracle. Margaret looked back at the building. Her eyes must be deceiving her. She struggled to process what she was seeing: a place that shouldn't exist. A place that was gone for ever. A place where her mum used to work.

Henry glanced at the street sign near the pub to confirm what he already knew. He prompted Margaret to look at the sign too. "It's true," he said, softly.

Talbot Street.

Although the rain had stopped, George Butler was keen to get moving before it started again. Why was Connie holding back, outside the pub? Water glistened on the street sign. Connie couldn't take it in. She looked up at the pub name in disbelief, her mouth opening and closing as if to find the words. George Butler assumed that she was upset because the landlady hadn't had a telephone for her to use to call her husband.

The Grey Horse.

"You'll be home soon enough," he said, trying to perk up her spirits.

Connie gave a half-smile that implied George couldn't possibly understand what she was going through. She couldn't begin to tell him the story about Margaret Sawyer and the train crash.

Instead, she did her best to snap out of it; ever the trouper, making the best out of a bad situation.

"We did good, didn't we? You must be over the moon, George Butler." She grinned.

And half an hour before, on that night, Connie was ordering the drinks from the excitable landlady. Connie stared idly at her reflection in the mirror beneath the optics. Etched across the glass in ornate lettering was the name of the pub. The Grey Horse. That was how Connie had realised she was in a place that shouldn't exist.

Connie found herself gabbling to the landlady: "What street is this?"

"Talbot Street," the landlady said, popping two pints on the bar, before busying herself with more pouring.

"The Grey Horse on Talbot – but wasn't that hit in the Blitz? Demolished?"

"No, love. We survived every raid. And if you'd seen the wreckage all around us at the time, you'd think we had God's hand over us."

Had Vera made up the story about the building being hit in the Blitz just so she could lure Margaret away? It was all a lie. She'd gone to the school and told them that the pub had been hit, that Margaret's mother was dead. And then another question bloomed in Connie's mind, one which made hot tears well in her eyes and a rawness appear in her throat.

"Do you – is there a barmaid here called Ginny?"

"Why do you ask?" The landlady's voice carried a note of suspicion, but her eyes had already registered the name.

But before Connie could say more, George came over, gave her a big hug and whisked her back to the table. The patrons converged on the bar and took their drinks, toasting Connie in the process. By the time they had finished, Connie had thought twice about telling the landlady what she knew about Margaret. The danger was that if Ginny knew her daughter was alive, then she might travel to Helmstead and confront Michael and Vera Sawyer at Jessop's Cottage.

And that could end badly.

Connie planned to tell Margaret when she got back to Helmstead.

But when Henry had vanished, all thoughts of Margaret went out of her head.

And now, outside the pub that shouldn't exist, Connie and Henry turned to Margaret.

"But my mum – when the pub was bombed," Margaret said in bewilderment.

"It was never bombed," Connie said. "Vera lied to the school. She did it so she could take you away. I'm so sorry."

"She lied?"

"But it's going to be all right," Connie said. "Before we came to London, I spoke to Henry about what to do."

"We decided that we should meet Ginny – your mother – first. Just to see how she was before raising your hopes," Henry continued.

"Just in case she'd got married again or had got other children. Perhaps you coming back would be difficult. So we made up the story about trying to find a relative just in case it didn't work out. Didn't want you being upset all over again. Henry was dead against me lying to you. But I just wanted to protect you." Connie could see that Margaret was still struggling to take this in. "But we were hoping with all our hearts we could find your mother."

"I don't understand what's happening," Margaret said.

"I came to the pub to find your mum. And when it was all right, then I came to the tea shop to collect you both."

But Margaret wasn't listening to the explanation.

She had seen a ghost.

Her mother had emerged from the pub. A blonde woman with the same round face as Margaret. The same kind eyes. Eyes that were currently filled with tears. She hadn't been able to settle since Connie Carter came in an hour ago. Connie, the woman full of impossible promises. A woman who told her she knew where her daughter was and promised she would bring her to meet her. Ginny hadn't believed that Connie would return, but Connie had promised that she would.

Just wait here, I'll be back.

Connie had wanted to break the news to Margaret first, on the way over to the pub. But in the end, she couldn't do it, when she realised she wouldn't be able to get the words out. Finding a lost mother was all too raw for Connie Carter. So instead, she got Margaret to Talbot Street as quickly as she could. And throughout the walk, she imagined the glorious surprise that Margaret would have when she saw her mum. Henry had glanced at his wife, wondering when she was going to tell Margaret what was happening. But for Connie, keeping one last secret seemed the best idea in the world. The best surprise present that Margaret could ever have.

Ginny Hawkins put her hands to her mouth, unable to stop the tears welling in her eyes and pouring down her cheeks.

"I thought you were gone forever," Ginny gasped.

Margaret ran to her and they hugged so tightly that the air was forced from their lungs. Ginny had so many questions, so much to say. She wanted to tell Margaret that it was a stupid extra shift at the pub that had meant she'd been late coming to the school that fateful day. She wanted to say how she'd looked for her endlessly afterwards, about how she had got the police involved. She wanted to tell her how the search petered out with the mass evacuation of children and the displacement of hundreds of people from bombed-out homes. Suddenly it was impossible to find anyone. She wanted to say that she never gave up hope.

She wanted to say all these things and more.

But now she couldn't even speak. Instead she let out a primal howl of blissful emotion. Connie hugged them both, smelling the mix of carbolic soap and cigarette smoke in Ginny's hair.

"Mum!" Margaret wailed.

"My darling, oh my darling," Ginny said, finding some words again, holding her tight.

"Why didn't you come for me?" Margaret said, through her sobs.

Ginny stroked the back of her head. "I didn't know where you was. But I never stopped thinking about you, darling. Never stopped hoping."

"I always hoped too. Hoped I'd see you coming up the path."

"You're back now. Oh dear Lord, you're back."

"Oh, Mum!"

They hugged, letting time stand still in a moment that both of them hoped would never end. And as Connie watched mother and daughter, she guessed it was one of the images that would stay with her for the rest of her life. Connie had moved back to allow them their reunion. Their homecoming. Henry placed an arm around her shoulders, his thumb stroking her skin for comfort. Connie was trying not to cry at the scene in front of them.

That evening, Connie and Henry said their goodbyes and left Ginny's modest house. Before Margaret fell asleep in the bed she hadn't used for three years, she unpacked her suitcase. She got out her teddy bear and her few clothes. And she got out the newspaper cutting of her with Connie Carter. She stuck it above her bed. Her mum said they would always keep it. Margaret and Ginny would have their new life together, thanks to the train crash and Connie Carter.

Connie and Henry walked towards the nearest underground station as night began to fall and the ARP wardens started their patrols. They were woozy with both the emotion of the day and the vodka they'd had to celebrate Margaret's return at Ginny's house. Finally, Connie felt the moment had come. It was time. She couldn't wait any longer to know what would happen to her and Henry.

"I can stay here, in London, Henry," she said. "If that's what you want." There, it was out in the open. A brusque and unsentimental ultimatum designed to force a response, to open a conversation about what happened next.

He took a while to reply. "What about our marriage?"

"Like I said, I've put you through more pain and suffering than any husband has a right to put up with."

"We did say 'for better and for worse'," Henry said, with an uncomfortable smile.

"It's all been for worse, though, ain't it?" Connie said. "I love you. You're a sweet, lovely man and I hoped we'd have a long time together, until we were old and toothless. But we're different and I know you wanted me to change, and I wanted you to change. But maybe that's not the way it should be. Maybe I'm not the one who can make you happy. Maybe I was never made for your world."

"So I'll go back to Helmstead? Alone?" He seemed shocked, which Connie found odd. Surely he'd been thinking about this during all those endless silences and his refusals to talk about their future. Or maybe he'd never expected to have to confront it head on in this way; the awkwardness of confrontation.

"Tell Mrs Gulliver and the rest that they were right. Tell them I was no good," Connie answered. She guessed that his lack of argument was answer in itself. Perhaps a man as gentle as Henry Jameson could never bring himself to categorically break something. She would have to do it. She kissed his cheek, looked sadly at his sweet face. This was goodbye. "Goodbye Henry." Connie turned and walked away.

"Wait," Henry called. Connie waited, not daring to turn. Would this be some sort of tirade to say good riddance? "So what if we're different? All this has rather put that into perspective, don't you think? It's all not that important."

Connie turned. This sounded like the end of all the petty squabbles they'd had before Vince had turned up and the problems got much bigger. "I guess it's not. It don't matter if we have our different ways."

But then her heart sank as he continued: "The bigger problem was that this made me realise I didn't know you; that I couldn't trust you after Danny and Vince turned up. How many more would come? That's what I was worried about."

"I told you, there's no more. But I understand. I've put you through too much, Henry."

"But I trust you now." The words froze Connie to the spot.

She looked into Henry's eyes as he continued: "And I may not ever know you, not everything about you, but I know one thing that I didn't before. That I can trust you. You came back for me. You never gave up. You saved me."

"Well, I love you, don't I?"

"And I know you love me above anything else."

"I do, yeah."

He put out his hand. "And I love you. So will you come back with me?"

Connie's face broke into the biggest grin of relief. "I'll have to think about it. I still won't be able to make a decent cup of tea, though."

"It really doesn't—" He never finished the sentence, as impulsively, Connie Carter pushed her husband into a doorway and planted a kiss on his lips. Usually Henry's reserved nature would make him embarrassed by such public displays of affection. But not today. Not after all they had been through together. Today, he responded straight away, with no hesitation, and he pulled her into the doorway with him.

Surprised by his abandon, Connie felt his hands clawing through her long hair.

"Oh Henry!"

They kissed passionately. Somewhere in the distance, an air-raid siren went off.

Acknowledgements

It all started with a photograph – an elderly woman standing on her friend's wheelchair to peer over a garden wall. They had gone back to see the rectory where they had been stationed in the Women's Land Army during the war. They obviously hadn't managed to gain entry to the building but didn't let a detail like that stop them. That image of those indomitable women captured the essence of the TV series I wanted to create. I hoped that *Land Girls* would honour those amazing women – all eighty thousand of them – who toiled in unfamiliar fields to ensure that Britain wouldn't starve during the Second World War. The TV series would also allow me to write intense human stories of courage, love and loss on the Home Front and explore the day-to-day lives of these resourceful, strong women. And now, I'm delighted that I have a chance to continue those stories, for both those who are familiar with the TV series and those who are new to these characters.

I'd like to thank my wonderful family for giving me the time – and tea – to write this novel, and for their unstinting support. Thank you too to Charlotte Ledger and her talented

team at Harper Impulse for believing in me and my ideas. Also, I'd like to thank the *Land Girls* cast and crew, Will Trotter, John Yorke and everyone at the BBC who brought the series to the screen – enabling me to create the lives and loves of Connie, Joyce, Iris, Esther, Nancy, Annie and Bea. I'd also like to thank my brilliant agent, Julia Wyatt, for her help and support. Thanks too to my grandmother, Annie Beatrice, and my mum, Annette, for being big parts of this story – and to Diane, Jill and Ewart. Finally, thank you to all the loyal viewers, for staying with us over three series. I hope you enjoy the book.

Roland Moore